Marguerite w[...]
nudging him. [...]
and flung an a[...]
from a blow. [...]

"Who goes there?" he rasped.

"Your wife," she whispered with alarm.

"So," he hissed. "The wretched succubus returns. See what you have wrought!" He snared her wrist in a crushing grip and bared his teeth wildly, as if ready to attack. She winced and struggled to wrench free.

"Lord Donsky," she pleaded. She knew he did not see her. "It is I, Marguerite."

The white blaze slowly faded from his eyes, and his entire countenance melted into a boyish grin. "Ah, Marguerite," he said lightly. "Have I been neglecting you?"

She shook her head, dazed by pity and fear.

Ravenloft is a netherworld of evil, a place of darkness that can be reached from any world—escape is a different matter entirely. The unlucky who stumble into the Dark Domains find themselves trapped in lands filled with vampires, werebeasts, zombies, and worse.

Each novel in the series is a complete story in itself, revealing the chilling tales of the beleaguered heroes and powerful, evil lords who populate the Dark Domains.

Ravenloft

BOOKS

To Sleep With Evil

Andria Cardarelle

TO SLEEP WITH EVIL

Random House and its affiliate companies have worldwide distribution rights in the book trade for English language products of TSR, Inc.

Distributed to the book and hobby trade in the United Kingdom by TSR Ltd.

Distributed to the toy and hobby trade by regional distributors.

Cover art by Robh Ruppel.

RAVENLOFT and the TSR logo are registered trademarks owned by TSR, Inc.

All TSR characters, character names, and the distinctive likenesses thereof are trademarks owned by TSR, Inc.

First Printing: September 1996
Printed in the United States of America.
Library of Congress Catalog Card Number: 95-62249

9 8 7 6 5 4 3 2 1

8072XXX1501

ISBN: 0-7869-0515-8

TSR, Inc.   TSR Ltd.
201 Sheridan Springs Road   120 Church End, Cherry Hinton
Lake Geneva, WI 53147   Cambridge CB1 3LB
U.S.A.   United Kingdom

For Troy

Acknowledgements

Thanks to the members of TSR's game design *kargat*, especially Bruce Nesmith, for shaping the mysterious mists with their tenuous islands of terror; Bill Connors, for introducing Jacqueline Montarri to the RAVENLOFT® campaign setting; and David Wise, who authored *Van Richten's Guide to the Vistani*. Finally, thanks to Barbara and Peter, "editors in relay," and of course to Brian, for patience, encouragement, and for leaving my fingers intact.

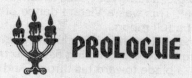 **PROLOGUE**

The gypsy stood in a moonlit circle of blossoms, dancing slowly to the rhythm of the drums. She was naked, concealed only by a curtain of wild black hair that tumbled just past the curve of her waist. On the ground outside the circle crouched the drummers—three withered, silver-haired sisters. Like the dancer, they wore no clothes, only a coating of white clay that had dried and cracked in the folds of their sagging skin.

If the women were aware of their watcher, they showed no sign. Roused from his slumber by the throbbing of Vistani drums, the man had followed the sound into the woods and pressed himself into the shadow of a tree, becoming one with its dark shape— a silent voyeur, held captive by sight of the dancer.

The Vistana moaned with each swirl of her hips, turning slowly in the moonlight. She was luminous. She extended one perfect arm aloft, tracing a serpentine path through the air, fingers unfolding like a fan. The hand dropped slowly, descending past her face and across her torso like a feather drifting to the ground. She began to chant in low, unintelligible tones.

The moon overhead was swollen with power. The dancer threw her head back and stretched both arms toward the silver orb, commanding its strength to flow into her.

The voyeur felt its power too.

He knew it was forbidden to watch—that no man, let alone a *giorgio*, a nongypsy, was meant to witness this sacred ritual. This was a Vistani dance of the *lunaset*: the night of a full moon.

Yet no one noticed him. No clucking females sought to drive him away with shaking fists. No tribal captain brandished a blade toward his throat. And no *rauni*, or tribal queen, threatened him with a curse or the evil eye.

To the voyeur, this proved that he had powers of his own. He squared his shoulders and stood straighter in the shadows. Soon, he mused, he would be nearly as potent as the god the dancer hoped to summon. It could be that he was already. Perhaps that was why the drums had roused him from his slumber, had drawn him into the dark wood; it was he she called, and not some elusive being.

He knew this woman; he had seen her before, in the Vistani camp, her dark eyes and wine-colored lips fascinating every *giorgio* and gypsy male alike. As lord of the manor and leader of his own band of thieves, the voyeur had been invited to stay by the campfire. There she had danced, her bright silks swirling and her round hips rolling, until his longing had grown almost painful. Then, of course, he and the other *giorgios* had been dismissed from the camp. But no one would dismiss him tonight. And tonight, the dancer was even more bewitching.

She snatched something small from the ground beside her feet and held it aloft. It was a clucking black hen. "Ravallah," she intoned. Strangely, the hen fell silent. "Ravallah-niri."

The dancer arched her back and held the bird above her, plucking its feathers until they fell upon her breasts like black snow. Her body glistened with sweat, and the feathers clung to her damp skin.

"Ravallah-niri," she said again, pleading, almost in a whisper.

The voyeur saw that her face was wet with tears.

The dancer plunged her sharp nails into the hen, digging her fingers deep into its living breast, then killed it with a twist of the neck.

The drumbeats quickened.

"Goddess of the moon," said the woman, "send me Ravallah. Let him pass out of the darkness and into me, that he may show us the way through the mists. Show us the way home."

Blood streamed from the hen, and the gypsy clutched the bird to her heart. Her tears ran red.

The drumbeats reached a savage pace. The dancer placed her hands upon her thighs, letting the dead bird fall to the ground. She shifted her weight quickly from one foot to the other, chanting, swaying her hips, painting her smooth skin with the hen's darkening blood. The voyeur was spellbound.

She let her head fall forward, then rolled it from shoulder to shoulder as if the weight were too great to carry.

"Ravallah come to me," she pleaded, amid a strange chorus of sisterly moans and sighs from the trio of withered drummers. "Come and show me the way."

The voyeur did not know Ravallah, did not know who or what he was. It hardly mattered. From the pleading intonations, he gathered that the gypsy's summons had never been answered. These lands were not the kind where prayers were heeded—at least not the prayers of ordinary men.

But certainly he was no ordinary man. The voyeur dug his fingers into his hands, until his nails tore his flesh and dampened his palms with his own blood. He felt drunk with the promise of transformation. On this night he would will himself to be something greater. He would shed his weakness and cast out the pathetic creature he loathed, the one who toadied to other lords. Who were these gypsies who camped on his land as if it were their own? He had feared them once. Now they would fear *him*—fear him and worship him.

"*I* am Ravallah," he called. It was a lie, yet he almost believed it himself.

The drummers stopped. The dancer continued to sway.

"I am Ravallah," he repeated. He entered the clearing. A vein pulsed in his forehead, echoing the rhythm the drummers had let fall silent.

He drew his sword, and the withered sisters stared with watery eyes at his blade. They did not rise. He swung his weapon and sliced through the first crone's neck. The others did not cry out. He whirled, as if performing his own macabre dance—a *lunaset* ritual to celebrate the harvest—and beheaded the second drummer. The third sister bowed her head, then he spun again and struck it off.

The pale sphere rolled across the circle of blossoms toward the dancer. When it came to rest, its milky blind eyes gazed skyward, glowing faintly. Dirt and fragments of leaves clung to the moist stump of its neck.

The gypsy dancer was frozen in place, her face awash with horror.

The voyeur stepped into the circle. He kicked the head aside, then took hold of the dancer's hair, grasping it behind her neck and pulling it backward to lift her face. Her only reaction was a vacant stare. He brushed the dark tears from her cheeks, staining them with the blood from his lacerated palm. He traced a path across her skin with a fingertip, meandering from her neck to her breasts, to the fullness of her right hip. In its wake, his finger left a faint red trail. The tendons on his hand were raised and taut, and the skin was turning black. He did not notice. He was lost in a tempest of his own creation.

"I am Ravallah," he said, now for the third time. His tone was low and measured. "And I am here to show you the way."

 # ONE

Marguerite's head snapped back violently, striking the narrow wooden planks behind it. A single blow vanquished her slumber, and the dreams that came with it retreated into oblivion. Her eyes flew open. The wagon plunged into another muddy rut and, for a second, held fast. The stout gray ponies snorted loudly, jerking their heads in protest. Marguerite's skull struck the wall again. Then the wagon pulled free.

Night had fallen, and the gypsy caravan journeyed through a sea of darkness. The air was cold and wet and pungent with the smell of pines that crowded against the road. Marguerite's head throbbed, and her neck ached. She righted herself on the wagon seat, then pulled the green hooded cloak around her like a cocoon. It did little to ease the chill that had invaded her body.

She stared at the driver beside her. His eyes did not leave the road, though what he could see through the black shroud of night, she could not imagine. He was fully two heads taller than she and nearly twice as broad at the shoulders. Beside him, she looked a child—not nearly the woman of twenty that she was.

A red gem adorned the side of his nose—a mark of vanity, but to Marguerite it resembled a blood blister. A similar bauble pierced his brow, while a trio of small gold hoops dangled from his left ear. His black hair, oiled and slicked close to his head, fell in greasy ringlets to his shoulders.

She sniffled at the cold air and caught his scent: a mixture of damp wool, acrid tobacco, and spicy sweat. His name was Arturi, but she knew little else about him. It didn't matter, she supposed—not as long as he fulfilled his purpose and ferried her to her new life. Fortunately, he would not be in it.

As a young girl, she had viewed the Vistani with awe, drawn by their aura of danger and their dark physical allure. They had passed through her village each year, bringing ponies from the distant land of Nova Vaasa or performing sensual gypsy dances to enhance the harvest. She had watched them in secret (her father would never have approved), reveling in the thrill. In fact her first kiss had been bestowed by a Vistana, a young rake whose lips had suddenly and lightly fulfilled an eleven-year-old's fantasies, leaving her quivering but unscathed. Her childish illusions had faded with time, of course, but Marguerite remained fascinated by the Vistani's wild, mysterious manner. Proximity must quell desire, she thought. Now, sitting next to Arturi's rank body, Marguerite felt no attraction whatsoever. She longed for her journey to be over.

As if reading her thoughts, Arturi drew the wagon to a halt. About ten paces ahead, the road forked into two equally dark branches. Without a word, the Vistana stepped down from the seat and strode to the side of the wagon, where he busied himself with some ropes.

"Why are we stopping?" Marguerite asked, craning around the seat to peer at him. Her head felt heavy and dull, as if it had been embalmed while she slept.

Arturi didn't answer. Marguerite could barely make out the next vardo in line—the graceful upward curve of its roof, the swaying sacks and darkened lanterns suspended from the eaves. The remaining wagons in the caravan, two or perhaps three, were obscured by the night. For a moment, Marguerite wondered if they were still nearby, but then she heard the chickens clucking in their crates secured beneath the vardos. A bear groaned; the beast was tethered at the rear. Inside these rolling chambers, women and children slept. Marguerite, however, had not been invited to join them. She was a passenger—living cargo, nothing more.

Arturi grunted something unintelligible to the driver of the second vardo. The Vistana, an older male, nodded and came forward to help pull at the ropes.

Marguerite's eyes began to penetrate the darkness. The feathered shapes of the pines came into view alongside the road. Tendrils of slow-moving mist swirled around the base of their rough black trunks.

"Why have we stopped?" she asked again. "Are you adjusting the load?"

Arturi chuckled, and, for the first time since their journey began, he spoke. "You might say that. Soon we'll be one woman lighter."

"This can't be the place," Marguerite protested. "Lord Donskoy would not have his bride deposited in the middle of nowhere. And surely not in the dead of night."

Arturi arched his brows, mocking her with his smile. "Wouldn't he?"

She stiffened. Could the tribe have some treachery in mind? Were they breaking their end of the bargain? No, they wouldn't be paid in full for her passage until the journey was done. But what if they didn't care?

Marguerite pulled herself up to her full height, mustering her strength. She said evenly, "Your arrangement with my parents was that you would deliver me to Donskoy's keep. We can scarcely be out of Darkon."

Arturi scowled. "Darkon is only a memory now. This is the place, and we travel no farther. Donskoy's own men will take you the rest of the way."

He and his companion freed Marguerite's bridal chest from beneath the vardo, then set it at the edge of the road. The trunk was not much to look at, a plain brown box decorated with a few simple carvings. Beside it, the two men laid a second crate from beneath the vardo, a black oblong box as long as Marguerite was tall. It was crudely built, with planks that gaped along the side and heavy spikes driven in at the corners.

"That isn't mine," Marguerite said. "I brought only the square chest."

"It belongs to your lord," said Arturi. "For the time being."

"What is it?" Marguerite asked.

Arturi shrugged. "Cargo. And none of your concern, I imagine." He glanced at her intently. "But because you are curious, I can assure you it is nothing of importance. I believe the contents are ultimately destined for Barovia."

Marguerite was intrigued; she had heard of Barovia once but thought it lay an eternity away from Darkon, if it existed at all. She had no time to ponder the exotic name, however. Arturi reached up to guide her from the wagon seat, and if he had been any more forceful, she would have landed face down in the muck.

"How could we possibly have reached Donskoy's lands?" she asked. Her head throbbed as she spoke. "I thought the journey would take several days."

"You have been asleep longer than you know," replied Arturi. "Besides, the trip went quickly— thanks, in part, to your new lord's eagerness."

He leaned uncomfortably close to Marguerite, so that their bodies almost touched and his mouth hovered just above hers. She smelled liquor mingling with his tobacco and sweat.

"Can't you feel your lord's presence?" He dropped his voice to a deep whisper. "No? Can't you feel the heaviness in the air, the way it presses like a weight?"

Marguerite stepped backward, pulling her cloak around her neck defensively. His boldness astonished her.

Arturi pressed forward. "Your lord is not the only one who is eager. So are the others," he whispered. "Can't you feel their old eyes upon you, watching? Watching and waiting?" He licked his lips. "You have entered a sticky web, sweet *giorgia*. Take care not to get eaten."

Marguerite took a half-step back, then jutted out her chin. "If you're trying to frighten me," she said, "you'll have to try harder. I'm not the little fool you imagine." Despite her bravado, she shivered.

Arturi laughed. "What I can imagine and what you actually know are worlds apart, miss, with a bottomless pit between them. But just the same, I'm sure you're nobody's fool, save perhaps your own. Now, I suggest you stand back even farther, unless you fancy being soiled as we pass." He pulled her brusquely toward her belongings at the side of the road. "Sit here and wait. Donskoy's men will come shortly."

Marguerite's head swam, and her stomach seemed about to turn inside out. It was more than fear; she felt queasy and flushed. "Please stay with me," she pleaded, changing her approach. "I don't think I'm well. What if Lord Donskoy's men are delayed?"

Arturi turned his back and walked away.

Marguerite called after him, struggling to sound imperious. "I demand that you wait with me! Are the

Vistani as immoral and untrustworthy as half of all Darkon presumes?" No sooner had the words escaped than she regretted them. "Besides," she added, "you won't get your full payment if you abandon me."

Arturi continued to ignore her. Marguerite squinted into the darkness, following the Vistana through the purple night shadows with her eyes. He passed his vardo and went to the fork in the road, where he withdrew his knife and carved something into the trunk of a tree. Then he stepped into the brush and bent over. When he returned, he was carrying a small sack.

He shook it at Marguerite. A soft jingle came from inside. "You see?" he said, jeering. "The deal is complete." He spat on the ground.

Marguerite opened her mouth to protest, to ask him once again not to abandon her, but she stopped short. It was futile.

Arturi climbed back onto the wagon seat. He smiled grimly at Marguerite. "*Endari vitir*, Miss de Boche." It was the Vistani farewell. "*Endari vitir.*"

Arturi waved to the driver behind, then gathered the reins and slapped them across the ponies' backs. The wagon lurched forward and passed into the dark embrace of the forest, veering left at the fork. The remaining vardos followed solemnly. None of the drivers gave Marguerite so much as a glance. Even the tethered bear paid her no attention as it lumbered past.

Marguerite watched the last vardo vanish into the night, then heard a soft whinny behind her and turned.

Something shone in the darkness—the glint of a silver bridle chain. A sleek black horse took shape, stepping crisply toward her, straining its head sideways against the stiff restraint of the reins. One dark, watery eye rimmed in white met Marguerite's gaze. The beast snorted, spraying gouts of steam from its nostrils.

Upon the horse rode a man dressed in black from head to toe. A heavy cloak grazed the top of his high boots. His head was covered by a black felt hat with a narrow upturned brim and a rounded crown. Marguerite had never seen the Vistana before, yet he must have belonged to Arturi's tribe. He shared the same brown-olive skin; the same strong, straight nose; the same high cheekbones and full, wide mouth. But unlike Arturi's face, his was well balanced, and completely unpitted and unpierced; he wore no jewelry except a single hoop, barely visible upon his right ear. The gypsy's clothing was simpler and darker than Arturi's, and more somber than the Vistani garb worn even among the most austere tribes in Darkon.

Marguerite marveled at the smoothness of the Vistana's skin; it seemed completely unlined, like a boy's, though his expression and demeanor were that of someone at least thirty or more. His dark, wavy hair flowed to his shoulders without pomade or grease to control it. It was shot through with white around his face, creating a kind of halo against which his dark eyes gleamed.

He smiled at her, then tipped his hat. The eyes tilted downward at the corners, and they looked a little sad.

Marguerite forced herself to break the stare. She nodded but said nothing. She did not want to appear meek, nor did she wish to invite the improper company of a stranger. Caution was warranted.

In a deep voice, the Vistana said, "Arturi can be off-putting."

She wondered how he knew.

"Nonetheless, he spoke the truth," continued the man. His voice was oddly soothing. "Wait here as he told you. Donskoy's men will arrive soon. And there is no safety in the cover of these woods."

Again Marguerite wondered at the extent of his

knowledge. He spoke as if they knew one another, as if they had passed the entire journey chatting together in some cozy conveyance. Prudence dictated she remain on guard, but she felt the tension easing from her body.

The Vistana rode to the fork and reined his horse to a stop. The beast pawed impatiently at the ground. Though full morning still lay an hour beneath the horizon, false dawn was approaching; the sky had lightened to pale gray, against which the rider and his horse stood in dark silhouette. The gypsy turned toward Marguerite, tipped his hat again, then guided his horse toward the left fork. A roiling cloud of mist suddenly drifted across the road, engulfing his form. When it passed, the man had vanished.

Marguerite sat on the oblong box Arturi had placed beside her bridal chest, suddenly more alone than before. Waiting seemed her only option. She pulled her cloak near. The worst dangers lay behind in Darkon, she told herself, with the fiends of Lord Azalin's secret police, those inhuman monsters who had ravaged her sheltered and simple life. Ahead lay the promise of sanctuary, perhaps even affection.

She drew her knees up onto the long black box and rested her head upon her arms, her cloak flowing around her like a tent. Her gaze remained fixed upon the road ahead. A trio of little gray-and-white warblers flitted past; they were vista-chiri, the bright-songed followers of gypsy caravans. Except for the birds and the lightening sky, the scene remained unchanged.

Marguerite tried to imagine the men who would come to retrieve her. Perhaps they would steer a carriage in which Donskoy himself rode. She wondered what he would think of her, whether she would please him. So much depended on it. Certainly others had found her desirable. But if Donskoy knew of one suitor in particular, he might be repulsed.

Creaking wood and jangling chains disrupted her thoughts. She started and rose.

A narrow old wagon drawn by a tired gray horse was approaching from the right side of the fork. The cart groaned and clattered, protesting the kettle-holes and jagged rocks beneath its wheels. On the bench huddled two men. The driver was tall, narrow, and rigid, like a wooden pole in a slim dark coat. He looked even taller because of his peculiar fur hat, which resembled a black bee hive built upon his head. Despite the uneven ride, he swayed only slightly.

His companion, in contrast, jiggled like half-jelled lard. He sat barely as high as the tall man's shoulder, yet his haunches eclipsed nearly two-thirds of the bench. With his ridiculous grin, he looked like a squat happy toad swaddled in tattered brown woolens. His elbows bowed outward and bounced with the rest of him, creating the impression that he had just told a joke and was nudging his companion to emphasize the punch line.

The wagon drew to a halt. The tall man tipped his head toward Marguerite. Like his body, his pasty face was long and narrow, with damp gray eyes set beneath a pale silvery brow. A fringe of white hair dangled beneath the rim of his hat.

The driver said, "Marguerite de Boche, I presume?" He lifted one eyebrow to punctuate the question. The rest of his face remained strangely immobile.

Marguerite nodded, but could not find the words to speak.

"Allow me to introduce ourselves. I am Ekhart, and this is Ljubo." Ekhart waved at his oafish companion. "We are humble servants to Lord Donskoy. It is our pleasure to escort you to your new home."

Ekhart's words were practiced and polite, but he

barely moved his jaw as he spoke; his mouth looked like a long incision drawn horizontally across his face. The gash was rimmed by a pair of thin, bumpy lips— grayish pink and slightly raised, like scar tissue. At the corners, they were so dry and scabrous that to smile might cause them to bleed.

Ljubo grinned ridiculously, exposing his broken and stained teeth. "So very nice to meet you." He gave quick little nods as he spoke, a silent and staccato yes-yes-yes to underscore his words. Even after the nodding stopped, his sagging red cheeks continued to jiggle.

"The feeling is mutual," replied Marguerite. "For a time, I was afraid no one would come."

"Yes," said Ekhart. He paused, as if annoyed by the burden of conversation. "It can be lonely out here in the wild."

Ljubo oozed off the seat and plopped his feet onto the road. His legs all but disappeared as they bowed to absorb the shock of his weight.

He waddled toward the cargo. Ekhart watched carefully but made no move to assist.

Marguerite watched too. Ljubo's hands were stubby and round. He wore the tattered remnants of woolen gloves, and his fingertips, left bare, were dirty and rough.

Despite his almost crippled appearance, the squat man readily hoisted Marguerite's bridal chest into the back of the cart. But he struggled with the heavy oblong box, succeeding only in lifting one end until it stood upright like a sarcophagus. Ekhart grunted, then reluctantly climbed off the wagon to help. Beside Ljubo's doughy shape, the tall man looked brittle.

They secured the box, then Ljubo hefted himself into the wagon alongside the cargo, leaving the bench free for Marguerite. He grinned again and gestured toward the seat.

Ekhart extended his hand. "Milady," he said curtly. He helped Marguerite onto the perch, then settled beside her and reclaimed the reins. The horse turned the wagon through the neck of the fork, and they journeyed in the direction from which the men had come.

Morning was full upon them, though no sun was visible. The air was still damp, and the sky glowed faintly with a cold white light. Black spruce and heavily fringed pines towered beside the road as far as the eye could see, leaning toward one another as if ready to fall. Some had already toppled against their neighbors, with tangled roots tilting out of the soil like bodies unearthed from the grave.

"Is it far?" Marguerite asked.

"Half an hour, maybe less," Ekhart replied.

Marguerite nodded and smiled faintly. She was glad the journey was near an end. Though part of her feared the future, she did not regret her decision to leave Darkon. She could not. There had been no choice.

"You're lucky," said Ljubo behind her.

Ekhart frowned and glanced over his shoulder, but Ljubo ignored the look.

"Oh?" said Marguerite. She wondered if Ljubo had somehow been reading her thoughts.

"Often this road can't be traveled at all. The castle gets sealed in for months at a time, what with the ice or mud or fallen timber. Then, when we can travel out again, we've all but forgotten the paths. Some of them—"

"Ljubo," Ekhart interrupted. "Do not prattle on like a fool."

Marguerite turned to smile at the man behind her. "Oh, but I'm interested."

"Of course, milady," Ekhart replied evenly, "but it should be your lord's pleasure to acquaint you with your new home. He would be displeased—rather, quite disappointed—if we stole that opportunity by speaking out of turn."

Ljubo fell silent and stared at his nails, which were caked with reddish brown soil. He began to pick at the frayed dry skin around the nail bed, showering his lap with tiny flakes. He appeared to be disintegrating. Marguerite returned her gaze to the road.

For a moment, she remained silent as well. But her curiosity was piqued. Determined to learn something about her new home, she tried another tack. "Perhaps you wouldn't mind telling me about yourselves, then," she said. "Are you native to these parts?"

"No, miss," Ekhart replied. He offered nothing more.

Marguerite was not daunted. "And how is that you serve Lord Donskoy?"

"We retrieve things," chimed Ljubo, "like—"

"Such as yourself, Mistress de Boche," interrupted Ekhart. "But 'retrieve' is not the best description of our tasks. Ljubo does not choose his words wisely. I am the stable master, and Ljubo is my assistant. Therefore we handle matters of conveyance." He paused. A little muscle in his cheek pulsed. "Truly, it would be best if you reserved your questions for Lord Donskoy."

Marguerite did not wish to vex him, so she remained silent.

The wagon journeyed on. Soon the dense evergreens gave way to a patch of beech and aspen. The forest retreated from the road, leaving marshy ground in its wake. Dead grass and fetid brown pools spread on either side, dotted with brambles and rocky outcroppings. The tangled shrubs had refused to let go of their withered leaves; they shivered as the wagon passed.

Marguerite inhaled deeply. The cool air stung her nostrils, filling them with the nauseating smell of rotting flora. The road turned sharply, and her stomach twisted along with it. Bile rose suddenly in her throat, and she choked it back. The wagon plunged once more into the forest. A black, icy stream flowed along one side. Then the road began to rise, and they passed over a little stone bridge that crossed the stream.

Ljubo nudged Marguerite. "Look there," he said.

Without warning, the keep confronted them. The massive block of gray stone thrust up from a low rise, looming nearly twice as high as its width. A low curtain wall extended before it, crumbled and gaping, with only the skeleton of a gate remaining. A higher wall extended from the left side of the keep, creating a court. To the right, the ground gave way to a steep ravine. Round towers jutted from the corners of the castle and flanked the entrance. Decay had ravaged the entire structure. Dark red-brown lichens now spread their lacy fingers across the stonework and hung from the crenelation like sloughing skin. Tall, narrow windows pierced the upper half of the keep. Where they were barred, the ironwork had rusted and wept, creating long, dark streaks on the facade below.

"Impressive, huh?" said Ljubo.

Marguerite felt a fresh wave of nausea. She held her breath for a moment, then replied quietly, "Indeed." The keep was immense and chilling. Like Ljubo, it appeared to be falling apart. She hoped the lord of the manor was in better repair. Then she chided herself. Besides curiosity, pessimism was her worst trait—and it was one she had intended to leave behind in Darkon.

The wagon drew to a halt before the main entrance. Ekhart helped Marguerite down from her perch.

"I must assist Ljubo briefly in the stable," he said stiffly. "Then I will return to escort you. Please wait here."

"What about my bridal chest?" asked Marguerite

tensely. Suddenly she felt a pang, as if parting with her possessions—the last vestiges of her former life—meant losing more than cloth and a few mementos.

"Ljubo will bring the chest to your chamber," Ekhart replied. Then he climbed back onto the wagon seat and guided the horse toward the doors that breached the wall flanking the castle. The doors opened. Ljubo gave a quick little wave from the back. Then the wagon disappeared through the gap.

Once again, Marguerite stood waiting, deposited like a sack of goods. She shivered. Somewhere just along the edge of her vision, she saw a dark shape moving. She looked toward the wood, but discerned only the swaying of a branch. The shape flickered again, disappearing at the corner of the castle. Was it, she wondered, a man perhaps? Someone observing her arrival?

Marguerite shook her head. "Your imagination," she said aloud. It was a phantom planted in her mind by the unsavory Vistana, who took pleasure in creating unease.

Marguerite gazed at the long stair before her. It seemed to stretch and retract subtly, beckoning. She was cold and weary, and simply standing made her more so. Who was this Ekhart to detain her? Wasn't he, indeed, soon to be at her command? Of course, he might be more than just a servant to Donskoy—his clothes and his manners suggested as much. She decided to climb the stair anyway, but to wait for Ekhart at the top.

The steps were narrow and awkwardly spaced. Each had been worn smooth by the not-so-gentle caress of countless feet. Marguerite tried to picture those who had passed before—loyal soldiers, lords and ladies, a swarm of hunched and hairy monstrosities prepared to batter the door above. For some reason it was easier to imagine a departure; in her mind's eye, men tumbled from the maw above like broken teeth. She grew dizzy with each step she took. She began to count them—thirty, thirty-one—but soon lost track.

When she reached the top, Marguerite felt disoriented and weak. Perspiration had glued fine wisps of reddish-gold hair to her forehead. Ahead lay the door, at the end of the short and gloomy passage embraced by the flanking towers. The door's wooden planks stretched to twice her height and were bound in rusty iron. The surrounding stones had been carved into an ornate relief of twisting vines; clawed, grasping hands; and ghoulish faces with gaping sharp-toothed maws. The faces were pitted and half the fingers had fallen away, as if claimed by leprosy.

Marguerite stepped forward, hesitantly. The doors were parted slightly, with the right side leaning inward. A thin, dark shadow bled between them. Without thinking, Marguerite called out "Hail," then added, "Is anyone there?" The voice did not seem like her own.

The doors parted farther, groaning on their hinges like a wounded warrior stirring on a field of dead. A musty breeze caressed Marguerite's face. Suddenly her head felt even lighter, her footing unsure. She swayed backward.

A stiff hand gripped her elbow. It was Ekhart. She had failed to notice his ascent.

"You were to wait," he said sharply. His fingers bit into her skin, and she turned to look at him in pain.

He eased his grip. Apologetically, he added, "Excuse my impertinence, miss. But it is not for my sake alone that I ask your cooperation—I am carrying out Lord Donskoy's instructions. Please heed what I say. I am to escort you."

"I'm sorry," she replied. "I was growing so cold and tired. I was afraid if I stood still too long I might not be able to move again."

He brushed past her and pulled the door open another foot. "You may come in now," he said evenly, then passed through.

Marguerite did as she was told, slipping between the doors into the cavernous room beyond. It was dark and dank. Marguerite imagined she could hear the sound of running water. She began to step forward.

"Not that way," said Ekhart. "Never that way. You must turn, and rise again."

"What lies that way?" asked Marguerite.

"An impatient fool's demise," Ekhart replied dryly. He was standing in an open doorway to the left. A narrow staircase curved upward behind him. "Just a few yards across from the door, a pit plunges deep into the ground. It is a defensive structure, designed by whoever constructed this keep. Invading hordes were expected to rush straight on and plummet to their deaths. To follow suit would be . . . suicidal. And most unfortunate for one so young."

"Thank you for the warning," said Marguerite quietly.

The wall behind Ekhart was lit by a torch; it guttered in the breeze. When he was sure she was following, he turned and ascended the stair.

The passage led to a large, torch-lit foyer that was almost completely barren. The dark stone floor had been strewn with herbs. Their scent was strange and exotic—a mixture of deep, grassy notes and a sweet, earthy smell that Marguerite could not identify. They crunched beneath her suede boots.

Somewhere to right, Marguerite could hear a man and a woman speaking. The woman laughed. Marguerite paused to listen further.

Ekhart clucked his tongue. "This way, Miss de Boche," he said. "I will show you to your chamber."

"My chamber?" asked Marguerite. "Does Lord Donskoy know I'm here?"

Ekhart stretched the dry skin at the corners of his mouth into something resembling a smile. "Lord Donskoy will receive you this afternoon. In the meantime, I would suggest you take this opportunity to refresh yourself. Surely you would like to make a good impression. Perhaps you should nap. I mean no insult, of course, but the journey has left you looking rather worn and tired."

Reluctantly, she nodded. She was, indeed, exhausted. The sickly sweet smell of the herbs had a dizzying effect. She followed him to the next level, growing wearier with each step. It was as if the whole castle were a soporific drug.

They traveled down a wide, dimly lit hall. In her growing fatigue, Marguerite stumbled, and Ekhart turned to catch her arm.

"You see?" he said. "You are too tired to meet anyone just yet."

They turned, passing several doors, and climbed another three steps. With each one, Marguerite seemed to grow weaker, until she could barely stand. Finally, Ekhart paused before an arched door, inserting a key.

As the door creaked open to reveal the dark chamber beyond, the last of Marguerite's strength drained away. She swooned. Ekhart's bony fingers clutched her arms, and a whirlpool of blackness closed in. His rasping voice swirled past her on an inky wave: "Weak. Like the last little bitch."

Then Marguerite heard, and felt, nothing more.

 **TWO**

When Marguerite awoke, she was nestled in the pit of a large, soft bed enclosed by a cocoon of wine-red draperies. Soaring dark posts and a massive wooden frame held the curtains and the canopy aloft. Beyond the softly wavering walls, she heard the crackling of a fire. A breeze toyed with a breach in the cloth at the foot of the bed, creating a tall, thin line of flickering gold light. A heavy blanket made of gray rabbit pelts lay before the glowing fissure. Upon the pelts lay a lily white robe trimmed in beige lace. Marguerite smiled—the robe was a gift, no doubt, from her husband-to-be. The castle might be crumbling around them, but he still had an eye for finery and a penchant, perhaps, for gestures of affection.

Someone was shuffling across the wood floor in the room beyond. Marguerite crawled forward to probe the narrow gap between the curtains, gentling parting the cloth. A maid, perhaps fifteen or sixteen years old, was placing a kettle before the hearth, where a fire blazed. She looked frail and thin, her body all hard lines and angles; Marguerite could see the girl's skeleton poking against her simple linen tunic and long brown overskirt. Her brownish blond hair was bound in a thin plait that hung down her back like a rat's tail, emerging from beneath a little brown linen cap.

Marguerite reached for the white robe and pulled it around her, covering her nakedness. She imagined Ekhart's cold, stiff fingers undoing her traveling clothes, brushing against her bare skin, but she shook the notion from her head. Certainly this girl or another maid-servant had undressed her. A haunting phrase drifted just beyond the edge of her memory, something Ekhart had said as they entered the room. It hovered, teasingly, then was gone. Marguerite thought perhaps she had dreamed it. She turned her attention to the girl.

"Well met," she said. The words sounded stiff and formal.

The girl turned to her and nodded but said nothing. Her features were delicate, her skin pale. The flesh beneath her light brown eyes was dark with fatigue, two purplish crescents on a sallow field.

Marguerite smiled as warmly as possible. "I'm Marguerite de Boche," she said. "But you must know that already. Thank you for lighting the fire, if that's also your doing."

Still the girl said nothing, though she nodded again and smiled faintly with downcast eyes. A log exploded, showering the hearth with sparks. The girl nervously brushed them aside.

"What's your name?" Marguerite asked.

The girl touched her own lips and shook her head.

"I don't understand," said Marguerite.

The girl repeated the gesture.

"You can't speak, is that it?"

A simple nod came in response.

"Oh, I'm sorry," Marguerite replied. She didn't know what to say beyond that.

The mute girl busied herself around the room, purposely avoiding Marguerite's gaze. She lit a series of fat candles, creating a dozen pools of warm yellow light, islands in a sea of shadows.

Marguerite surveyed her new quarters. Besides the massive bed, the chamber held several ancient-looking pieces of furniture. Two heavy wooden chairs flanked the fire like thrones, worn silk cushions resting upon their seats. A small service table huddled beside each chair, and a matted fur rug lay between them; but for this, the floor was bare, save for the straw and herbs that had been strewn freely about. Marguerite scanned the shadows for vermin but saw none. To the right of the fire, near the windowed stone wall, stood a wash stand and a luxuriantly tall mirror that reflected the warm glow of the candles and the hearth. Against the wall loomed an enormous cabinet. Marguerite's small bridal chest sat beside it.

The mute girl reached for a kettle near the fire, then filled a porcelain basin upon the wash stand. Steam drifted into the air like smoke. The girl stepped toward the bed and pointed to the slop jar just beneath the edge.

Marguerite puzzled for a moment, then said, "No, thank you, it hasn't been used." She was not accustomed to a personal maid.

A muffled knock sounded at the door. Before Marguerite could reply, the door creaked open and an old woman entered. She was small and stooped, dressed completely in black. Her rough, layered skirts swept the floor, and a simple scarf covered her head.

Marguerite assessed the woman, and in turn the woman gazed at her. The visitor's plump face was deeply crinkled, the skin chalky and dry. She had an intense stare, with round dark eyes that sparkled like a possum's. The wrinkled lips parted in a smile.

Marguerite had expected to see gums, but the teeth were unusually white and strong.

The old woman clasped her withered hands before her. "Zo, you are awake." Her voice was low, but it crackled with age, and she spoke with an accent unfamiliar to Marguerite. "That is good. Ekhart informed us that you fainted earlier. Are you feeling better, my child?"

Marguerite nodded.

"Very good. But you must not worry if you feel a little tired for a time. A new home requires adjustment. And you may still be somewhat weak from the potion your escorts gave you."

"The potion?" asked Marguerite.

"I am only assuming, of course," the woman replied. "But it is customary to introduce a sleeping potion on journeys such as yours. A passenger who is asleep is less troublesome for the Vistani, yes?"

Marguerite felt a wave of indignation. This certainly explained her prior nausea and her embarrassing swoon into Ekhart's arms.

The old woman added, "I have even known of one caravan who ferried *giorgios* heaped in a cart like the undertaker's corpses, but of course the passengers yet lived. I trust your own journey was more pleasant?"

Marguerite nodded, stunned. In truth she had no recollection of how she had spent her journey. She had evidently slept the whole time.

"I am Zosia," continued the old woman, "cook and companion to Lord Donskoy. And when the time comes, I shall serve as your midwife; you could ask for no one more skilled or better suited." She pointed at the mute girl. "And this is Yelena. She has no tongue, as you might have guessed."

Yelena stood in the shadows beside the door, head bowed, almost invisible.

"Yes, the tongue is gone," Zosia rattled on, "but her other parts remain functional. She can still be quite useful when my own hands grow tired. Will you need Yelena's assistance to dress, Marguerite?"

Marguerite shook her head.

Zosia shooed the girl away with two sharp, quick waves of her hand. Yelena curtsied, then opened the door and retreated into the dark hall beyond. The heavy door creaked shut of its own accord.

"Do you feel hunger?" asked Zosia.

"Yes," replied Marguerite. Suddenly she realized that she was famished.

"That is convenient. Lord Donskoy awaits you downstairs and expects to dine with you soon. You can find your own way after you have dressed. Go left from this door and follow the hall to the first stair, then climb down to the foyer. The door just opposite is your goal. Carry a candle and guard it well; the passages are drafty."

Marguerite felt as if she had been issued instructions for invading an enemy's camp.

"I have looked in your chest," Zosia added. "Your clothes are not suitable. Lord Donskoy expects his wife to dress in a manner that compliments his stature. The cabinet contains several gowns that he has procured." She stroked her chin thoughtfully, her eyes sliding up and down Marguerite's body as if to measure it. "Put on the purple silk. I'm sure that it will fit to satisfaction."

Marguerite did not know quite how to respond to this barrage, so she nodded and said, "I'm sure it will be fine."

Zosia continued, "Pull the bell rope if you wish Yelena's assistance, after all. Unfortunately, neither she nor the bell can always be relied upon."

The old woman gestured toward a silk cord that

hung beside the door. Then Zosia herself passed into the hall, her exit marked by the dull thud of wood against wood.

Marguerite stood alone. The room seemed strangely silent, though the fire still crackled and the wind howled softly in the flue, a distant ghost. She gazed around the chamber. It seemed almost familiar, as if she had stood here a long time ago or had seen this place in a dream. But then she had often read tales about ladies in their keeps.

Save for the exterior wall, which was stone, the chamber was paneled in carved wood. It had a single shuttered window set deeply into the corner. On either side of the fire hung tapestries—one depicting a fox treed by a pack of hounds, the other portraying a group of noble ladies standing beside a garden fountain.

Marguerite went to the wash stand and cleaned her face. Then she opened the great cabinet and peered inside. A gasp of astonishment escaped her lips. A dozen dresses hung on wooden pegs, with their accoutrements folded and stacked below. She fingered the fine fabrics—smooth silks and plush velvets and soft, supple wools, each a rich, vivid color, including a noble's scarlet and purple. Oddly, the gowns appeared to be of slightly different lengths. A cloth-of-gold skirt caught her eye, and she fingered the fabric until she noticed a rusty stain in the folds. So they are not new, thought Marguerite. She was thrilled nonetheless. Such a collection befit the wealthiest of ladies, representing a high, uncommon stature. She had heard tales of the great, decadent fêtes that Lord Azalin hosted in Darkon, but surely not even the nobles and favored trollops in attendance could boast such finery. Marguerite withdrew the purple silk as Zosia had recommended, noting its wide neckline and tight bodice. The ivory undersleeve was tightly buttoned to the wrist, with the oversleeve wide and sweeping. A matching velvet mantle lay folded below in the cabinet, but this she left inside.

Marguerite removed her robe and replaced it with the purple gown, then inspected herself in the mirror. The dress fit well enough; it was a little loose about the shoulders, perhaps, but it hugged her slender waist and fell from her hips in a graceful cascade. She was more concerned about how Donskoy would find *her*.

Would he be pleased by how her amber hair formed a fine cloud about her face, by how it fell almost to her waist? Perhaps he would find her bowed mouth and upturned nose too girlish? She had dark eyes, not blue like her mother's, and if he looked closely, he would see that they contained little flecks of violet. Her grandmother had liked to tease her that they showed a hint of gypsy blood, as did her skin, which was smooth and the color of milk-tea. Marguerite doubted the claim, but she thought Lord Donskoy would enjoy this hint of the exotic. Her mother had told her that men liked the spice of foreign beauty.

Marguerite lifted her hair to examine the skin of her neck. To her relief, the marks were almost gone— barely noticeable. The memory of the blood-sucking soldier who had left them—the *kargat* officer from the secret police—would take longer to fade. But no good would come of thinking of that now; it had ended when she left Darkon.

Marguerite took a deep breath, gathering her courage, then stepped into the hall. She followed Zosia's instructions and found the designated door in the foyer. There she stopped, hesitating.

She smoothed her skirts, pinched her cheeks, and drew herself up straight. Earlier she had been eager and hopeful for this meeting. Now a dozen questions

flooded her head, borne on a wave of apprehension.
Could she hide her displeasure if he were an old hermit, as leprous as Ljubo? And, ugly as he himself
might be, would Donskoy find some fault in her
appearance or manner and cast her out? Or worse
yet, would he use her to seek a sadist's pleasures?
None of these horrors had been forecast, of course.
The Vistani matchmakers in Darkon had painted a
picture of an average lord of better-than-average
means, thirty years her senior but robust, alone in a
remote land, seeking an heir and a young wife's companionship. The matchmakers had a reliable reputation, and they had claimed the union was ordained by
fate. Yet there was always a chance the gypsies had
lied. More than once in her past, hope had been the
forerunner of despair.

Marguerite dismissed her fears with a deep breath.
She forced her delicate lips into a smile and knocked
gently.

No one answered.

She inhaled sharply, then knocked harder.

This time, a man's deep, muffled voice bade her to
enter.

She pushed the door open and was greeted by a
haze of yellow-brown smoke, caustic yet faintly sweet.
Across the dimly lit room, a slender gentleman sat in
a large, plush chair. His hair was gray, but his posture
was straight and elegant. A long, slender white pipe
protruded from his lips—the source of the smoke. The
ornately carved stem dropped in a languid curve to
the center of his chest before joining a bulbous bowl
cupped in his right hand. He wore a pair of black
gloves. Upon seeing her, he laid the pipe on a side
table and rose from the chair.

Marguerite breathed a sigh of relief. While the man
before her was more than twice her age, he was

neither deformed nor decrepit. He looked about fifty, of average height and slender build. An air of dignity surrounded him. For a moment, he studied her, pushing a gloved hand through his thick silver hair. She curtsied weakly and smiled, not wanting to speak before he addressed her. The man bowed his head and returned her smile, almost mockingly.

Then his grin became genuine and broad. "I am Milos Donskoy," he announced, "and the sight of you, my lovely bride, could warm even a dead man's blood."

He came forward with a bold, exaggerated stride, like a performer making a grand entrance on stage. Marguerite stood still, unsure of her own role, certain only that she should not retreat. When he reached her, he clasped her hands in the softness of his black suede gloves. Beneath the supple leather, his flesh was hard, his grip firm. He lifted one of her hands to his lips and kissed the top of her fingers, dropping his gaze. A peculiar sensation crept up her spine. His lips were cool upon her skin, but his breath was warm.

Marguerite studied the pale face before her. He had heavy eyelids set beneath a strong forehead and wiry brows. His nose was straight but hawklike; below it, a full white mustache overshadowed a bowed mouth that was delicate and almost feminine. The smooth, clean-shaven jaw had relinquished itself to his neck—except for the point of his chin, which was still strong and rounded, with a little cleft she found almost charming.

He lifted his head. His eyes were a startling ice blue, marred only by the web of fine red veins surrounding them. He locked gazes with Marguerite, suddenly serious. The silence was discomforting.

Then his smile returned. "You do speak, do you not?"

"Yes, of course," Marguerite stammered, suddenly

realizing that it was she who had been silent. Long before her journey had begun, she had practiced an introduction. She had memorized an entire roster of witticisms designed to entertain and to impress. But all her clever ideas had retreated to the most inaccessible corners of her mind. Now, like vexing little demons, they refused to be summoned forth. "I'm so sorry, my lord," she continued. "I'm Marguerite de Boche."

"So I gathered," he replied with a wink. "I was expecting no other bride-to-be."

She felt the color rising to her cheeks.

"Furthermore," he added, "you have no cause to be sorry, my dear." He released one of her hands but kept the other. "Have you recovered from the journey?"

"Yes," she answered. "Almost."

"Well, I'm certain a meal and a full night's rest will restore you completely."

He gestured broadly to a sofa at the side of the room. "Let us sit for a moment together." He slipped his hand to her waist. "The dress becomes you," he murmured.

Marguerite stiffened a little, and he removed the hand. She chided herself for her apprehension.

Before the sofa was a low table. A teapot had been set alongside a decanter of brandy. He offered her both; Marguerite chose the tea. Instead of pouring, he looked into the shadows at the edge of the chamber and beckoned.

To Marguerite's astonishment, the mute girl appeared. Apparently, the servant had been lurking in the corner, either cloaked by shadow or behind the cover of one of the voluminous tapestries.

"You have met Yelena, have you not?" Donskoy asked.

Marguerite nodded, marveling at the girl's stealth.

"She's rather quiet but useful," added Donskoy,

"when she remembers her instructions."

Marguerite felt a pang of sympathy for the girl. Zosia had described the servant in much the same way—as if Yelena were some kind of tool, broken yet still functional. Marguerite wanted to ask how Yelena lost her tongue, but she refrained. It was a forward question, much too forward to ask this soon, and perhaps embarrassing or painful in front of Yelena. It was even possible that Donskoy had had something to do with the injury. Marguerite dismissed the thought as soon as it entered her mind. She had no reason to believe such a thing.

The waiflike servant decanted a brandy for Donskoy, keeping her eyes fixed on the floor. Then she poured tea for Marguerite and presented a little cake. Marguerite accepted it gratefully, but it proved dry and stale. She took one more bite and set it aside, focusing on the tea. Yelena retreated to the shadows like a beaten dog.

Donskoy watched Marguerite carefully. "I did not have much prepared, because we will be dining soon."

"This is more than satisfying," Marguerite replied. It was a lie, of course. The cake had left a lingering taste, reminiscent of moldy earth. She tried to wash it away with more tea, but met with limited success. She hoped the meal would be more palatable.

"And is your chamber to your liking?" Donskoy asked.

"Yes, very much so. The bed is immense and soft, and there's no trace of vermin whatsoever. I'm unaccustomed to anything so grand." It was the truth.

He laughed softly. "I would not call my castle grand anymore. No, it has begun to crumble, as you must have noticed. It is my own doing." He sighed. "I was married once. Did the gypsies tell you that?"

She shook her head. They had not.

"My wife died tragically," he continued, fixing his gaze at some point in the shadows. "I do not care to discuss the details. I mention it only so that you understand what your arrival means to me. It is my chance for rebirth. For decades after my first wife's death, I became as lonely and as brooding as the land around us. I did not embrace life, and I entombed myself in despair." He turned to her. "It has been my curse. But you, my dear, will change all that, won't you?"

Marguerite felt a wave of compassion. "Of course," she replied. Without thinking, she extended her hand and placed it on his. Realizing how bold that might seem, she began to withdraw it, then felt his gloved hand firmly seizing her own.

"You," he said, "will help restore this place to glory." His voice was low and even. It was virtually a command. "Will you not?"

Marguerite nodded, wincing at the tightness of his grasp. "I will certainly try."

"No," he replied. "You will do more than try. Together, we must succeed."

Marguerite felt her compassion aroused again, along with her instinct to nurture. Apparently, she and Donskoy had something in common—a desire to build a future that would block out the past.

For a moment, Donskoy seemed lost in thought. Then his tone and his grip relaxed. "But first," he said cheerfully, "we shall share a proper meal."

Marguerite noted how quickly his moods seemed to change, how complex the thoughts behind his well-chosen words appeared. Or perhaps he was simply as nervous as she.

Donskoy led her across the foyer into a hallway, then onward to a modest hall established as a dining room. A fire blazed in the hearth. In the center of the chamber lay a dark rectangular table. It held two place settings with silver goblets, one at each end before a high-backed chair. There was no other seating. Additional furnishings lined the sides of the chamber, but they were draped in sheets, an audience of ghosts.

Donskoy seated Marguerite, then walked to the opposite end of the table. As if by some silent cue, Yelena reappeared, bearing a tray. She decanted red wine into the goblets. Then she lifted the lid from a platter. Four tiny carcasses lay at the center. She presented three to Donskoy, and the last to Marguerite. They were birds, prepared with their shriveled heads still attached, laid to rest in nests of barley. Yelena scuttled out of the room.

"A local delicacy?" Marguerite asked, picking at the fragile, bony mass before her. With each probe, the head jostled on its broken neck.

"Seasonal, I suppose you might say," Donskoy replied. "They're vista-chiri. Migrant birds. I netted them myself for the sport of it. Not much meat, but they make a satisfying appetizer."

Marguerite took a few bites to be polite, but she refrained from any further dissection. It discomforted her to devour the songbirds who trailed the Vistani. Some peasants in Darkon claimed the birds were spies. Her grandmother had once told her they might even be gypsy spirits, for they shared the Vistani's uncanny ability to flit in and out of shadows, slipping so easily into the Unknown.

Donskoy did not appear to notice her hesitation. While he snapped off little wings and raked them through his teeth, she sipped her wine and feigned a smile. She thought it odd that he had not removed his black gloves before handling the moist flesh.

Yelena reappeared, struggling with an even greater

platter. Marguerite took inventory with growing hunger. This fare was much more familiar to her, and the rich aromas resurrected her appetite. Soon her plate was heaped with succulent hare and enormous mushrooms, accompanied by creamy white turnips and blood-red beets. Marguerite was ravenous. She had to force herself to eat slowly, so as not to appear uncultured.

The wine flowed readily with the meal. Donskoy chatted idly about the food and the room, the recent period of misty weather. He raised a toast to her health, their union, and their future sons. Before she realized it, the wine had seeped into every sinew, loosening her finely woven defenses. Her head grew light.

Donskoy speared his last piece of hare and devoured it heartily. "I hadn't much appetite before you came," he said. "I should thank you for returning it."

"I'm glad you're pleased," Marguerite replied. "I was afraid you might actually send me back." The words escaped before she could contain them. She hoped they wouldn't plant a suggestion.

"Not at first sight, certainly," said Donskoy, licking the juice from his lips. He gazed at her with an appreciative little smile.

Marguerite felt like the next course, but she didn't entirely mind.

Donskoy motioned to Yelena to refill their goblets yet again. "You are truly quite lovely," he said, wiping his lips on a cloth. "And more charming than I had allowed myself to hope."

"Thank you," she replied. "You are very kind."

"Some might consider a girl of twenty a little old for marriage, but you remain appealingly fresh."

Marguerite did not know how to answer such a peculiar compliment. Still, she was glad not to have appeared stale.

Donskoy continued, "And do I please you as well?"

"Of course," she answered quickly. "I am very fortunate."

He looked at her for a moment, then smiled. "You are lying just a little," he said. "But that is all right."

"No, I do feel fortunate," she protested. "I—"

He raised his hand to interrupt her. "I have steered the conversation badly, toward topics that will either become treacle or uncomfortable. We understand one another's needs, I believe, and if not, that will certainly come in time." He paused, dabbing his mustache with the cloth again. "Why don't you tell me about yourself and your family?"

Marguerite hesitated. Ironically, these were not comfortable subjects either. She was unsure precisely how much Donskoy knew. She would be truthful, she resolved, but discreet.

"I come from a village in Darkon called Malanuv," she said. "Just south of Nartok on the Vuchar River."

"About a week's ride from Avernus, Lord Azalin's castle, is it not?"

Marguerite was surprised. "You know of Darkon's Avernus?"

"By reputation," he replied. "Geography is one of my interests. I traveled a great deal in my youth. And, of course, Lord Azalin's name is quite familiar to me."

"I have never traveled farther than Nartok before this trip," she said. "So I am not as worldly as you, my lord. I still do not quite understand how the gypsies brought me here. Perhaps it was magic."

Donskoy chuckled.

"No, I mean it sincerely," Marguerite prattled on. "Have you ever heard the assertion that the mists can be magical, perhaps even animate? And that the gypsies can mold fog into mounts and ride them whenever they please?"

"Your description is rather fanciful," Donskoy replied. "I myself find the mists quite nauseating and oppressive. And I can assure you, your journey had more to do with gold than magic. Which is to say, with my payment, as well as your father's contribution. Tell me about your family."

Marguerite winced. "My father is the village master." At least, he would be if he were still there, she thought. She hoped her parents had fled Malanuv. Otherwise they might be dead.

"Yes, that was my understanding," said Donskoy. "That your father was a petty bureaucrat—no insult intended. He had come down a bit in the world, I believe."

"You are well informed. Father was a baron; he ruled a small city in the north before I was born. He claimed he preferred the simpler life of Malanuv, further removed from the politics of Lord Azalin's court." Marguerite began to stumble over her words, fearing that she had painted herself as too common. "I do not mean to say we were poor, of course; we lived very well by local standards. Though, naturally we did not live as well as this."

"Indeed. You must feel proud to be marrying so well. All this is yours to enjoy, with scarcely a dowry." He spoke mockingly, and Marguerite could not tell whether his words were sincere.

Donskoy's eyes lowered briefly, sliding to her bodice, then back to her face. "No holdings, but your other charms are obvious," he said. "How is it that you did not marry sooner? Certainly there must have been suitors."

"One," she said quietly.

"But you did not marry, or . . ."

"Oh, no," she replied. "He died before any formal arrangements were made."

"How very unfortunate," said Donskoy evenly. He watched her closely from across the table. "How did it happen?"

"His neck was broken." Marguerite chose her words with care. "No one saw it happen. Apparently he was thrown from his horse." Though she had meant to be honest, this was only half true. Her beloved's spine had been snapped by the same member of Lord Azalin's *kargat* who had opened her eyes to the secret terrors of Darkon.

She waited uneasily for Donskoy's reply. The wine had diminished her self-control; without warning, she found herself on the verge of tears. She did not wish to offer or remember anything more.

Donskoy broke the silence. "It seems we both have known tragedy. Let us forget the unpleasantries of the past, then, and focus on the future—at least for tonight."

Marguerite nodded at him gratefully, saying nothing until the wave of emotion passed.

He smiled and continued, "Yes, we have happier topics before us. Such as our own marriage. I hope you will be content with a very simple, private ceremony. The subsequent fête will be somewhat grander."

"I will be content with whatever pleases you," she said softly.

"My land is remote and without many inhabitants. As I have become more reclusive through the years, so too has the local population. Occasionally I entertain guests from neighboring lands. Otherwise visitors are rare. But I can muster a priest. And I will leave other arrangements to Zosia. Will the day after tomorrow be too soon for you?"

"No," she replied.

"Good." He rose from the table. "Then I shall see you in your wedding gown, the day after tomorrow.

We shall marry after the sun has passed its peak."

"Won't I see you before then?" she asked.

He walked over to her chair and took her hand, then kissed it lightly. "Would you like to?"

"Yes," she answered truthfully. Courtship was by no means inherent to their arrangement—nor was companionship, for that matter. Still, she had hoped to get to know him better before the wedding. Or, more to the point, before the wedding night. The thought of it sobered her.

Donskoy touched her shoulder gently. "As much as your eagerness pleases me, I regret that I cannot comply. I have other matters to attend to before we wed. Tomorrow, I'm afraid, you must find a means to entertain yourself. Perhaps you could take a walk outside. Ekhart will accompany you to see that you do not become lost or injured. The terrain can be challenging."

The thought of a stroll with Ekhart did not appeal to Marguerite. "Or I could look around inside the castle," she suggested. "I'd like to get to know my new home."

Donskoy paused. "If you wish to explore the keep, I would prefer to accompany you. Or that you ask Yelena to do so. Unfortunately, she will be rather busy making preparations for the wedding."

"Am I not to roam freely?" Marguerite asked, somewhat affronted.

"Of course. Within limits. And when you are familiar with the dangers. Until then, you are free to pass along the corridors you already know. You are hardly a prisoner."

"Ekhart warned me about the pit in the foyer," Marguerite said. "And I will certainly exercise caution."

"The pit is not the only danger. The keep has many twists and turns, and much of it lies in disrepair. The doors in the lower levels are particularly unreliable, and prone to holding fast. You might become disoriented or lost. Or worse." He smiled at her. "And I would not wish to lose you so soon."

"I see," Marguerite replied.

"I have an extensive library that you might enjoy. The room at the crest of the stairs near your chamber houses part of my collection. You can read, I assume?"

Marguerite felt a little sting. "My upbringing was perhaps simpler than some, but not without education. In fact, I used to read stories as a glutton eats sweets. I also read music, and I can play the clavier and lute."

"Really," he answered dryly. "I was unaware of such talents. I am not a great lover of song, but the castle does have a music room of sorts. No one has visited it in years. I will have to show it to you after we wed."

Lord Donskoy gripped her shoulder a little more firmly. Marguerite sensed his annoyance.

"I will look forward to our time together," she said. "And tomorrow, a walk outside and a visit to the library will make for a full day."

He took her hand and kissed it again. "Until the wedding, then. Now Yelena will escort you back to your chamber."

He left her.

Marguerite and Yelena walked quietly through the winding corridors and up the stairs, cutting a glowing path through the darkness with a torch. When they reached the door, Yelena opened it and went to check the fire. It was fully stoked. Apparently, someone had prepared the room earlier.

Yelena turned and slunk from the room, pulling the door shut behind her. A moment later, Marguerite heard a dull metal click. When she went to the door to investigate, she discovered it was locked. No key was in the lock on her side. She knocked softly. "Yelena?" she called. No one answered.

Marguerite sighed. Tomorrow morning, of course, or perhaps even later tonight, Yelena would return to restore the fire. In the meantime, she was to remain alone and in this room. Despite Donskoy's assurances as to her freedom, she felt more like a prisoner than the mistress of the keep.

She walked to the window and drew open the shutters. The glass was covered with a delicate frost. Marguerite blew upon it and watched a dark spot appear. The water melted away in a peculiar pattern, forming three lines running parallel toward the sill. Marguerite shrugged and wiped away the rest of the frost, looking off to the terrain she would explore tomorrow. An amber light pulsed deep in the wood. *A fire*, she thought to herself. Or perhaps a gypsy camp. But then she remembered Arturi's refusal to venture any farther onto Donskoy's land. More likely, it was simply a traveler or a distant farmer's watch.

Shivering against the cold, Marguerite closed the shutters. Then she stripped off her fine gown and crawled onto the soft, feathery bed, pulling its curtains closed behind her.

THREE

Marguerite woke once during the night, roused by a woman's hearty laughter. When she realized it must have been a dream, she sank back into slumber's deep embrace. In Darkon, dreams had often disturbed her sleep, bringing unwelcome visitors. But thankfully, for the rest of this night, no other phantoms made their presence known.

When she woke again, her mouth was dry and cottony, and her head felt leaden. She sat up and drew on her morning coat, vowing to imbibe less wine in the future.

The room was cold. A tiny cloud of breath took shape before her lips, then drifted away and dissolved. Beyond the bed's velvet curtains, the morning light beckoned. She rose, cringing at the touch of the icy floor beneath her feet. One of the shutters on the window had swung open, allowing a sunbeam to penetrate the chamber. She must have failed to latch the shutter the night before.

The castle seemed unnaturally quiet. Embers glowed softly in the hearth, but the flames had died out. Marguerite scurried to the heavy door and tried the handle. It still held fast. Disgruntled, she strode to the hearth and tossed another log onto the grate. The coals stubbornly resisted her offering. She poked and prodded at their charred remains until at last they relented, and the log burst into flame. For a moment, she watched the tongues of flame devouring the wood. Then she went to the nightstand and lifted the water pitcher to her lips, drinking gratefully.

From outside came the muffled echo of wheels grating harshly against stone. Marguerite padded to the window and drew open the remaining shutter, wincing at the sudden brightness. Though a delicate pattern of frost partially obscured the view, on the drive below, she could still make out a black carriage behind a team of dark horses. A slender, feminine form stood beside the coach with a gray-haired man. The woman merged with the black shape of the carriage, disappearing inside. The man patted the door.

Ekhart, perhaps? thought Marguerite. No, this man was not as tall or as rigid. Further, his hands were black. Marguerite remembered Donskoy's gloves. She rubbed the glass hastily. The man stepped out of view and the coach lurched forward. Marguerite noticed a long dark crate secured to the back of the conveyance—the same crate that had accompanied her to the castle. Shortly thereafter, a horse cantered away from the keep. It overtook the carriage and assumed the lead. Apparently Donskoy was providing an escort. The road turned sharply, then both the rider and the coach disappeared into the dark folds of the forest.

Marguerite recalled the laughter that had roused her during the night. It had been a woman's. While the source could have been a servant, it certainly was not the tongueless Yelena, and Marguerite had observed no sign of frivolity in anyone else at the castle—save

Ljubo. The explanation that came to mind did not please her. Donskoy had entertained a visitor, one he did not wish to reveal. A paramour perhaps? It was not out of the question. Yet he had claimed that guests were rare. All that morose banter over not embracing life, she mused. And meanwhile, he was embracing the warm flesh of a woman.

Perhaps. Perhaps not. There were probably countless explanations. The mysterious visitor could have arrived only that morning, for example. And the laughter Marguerite had heard might well have belonged to someone else, if not to her own fertile imagination.

But who was this woman, then? A well-wisher? Family? Marguerite reminded herself that she knew very little about Donskoy's history. The Vistani in Darkon had claimed he lived virtually alone, but that did not preclude a visiting relative or two. This woman might have been Donskoy's cousin, for all she knew, or his sister. Better a sister, of course. Cousins were still competitors.

The door opened behind her. Marguerite turned as Yelena entered, carrying a tray with bread and a pot of tea.

"Good morning, Yelena," Marguerite said evenly. She abandoned her conjecture about the woman in the carriage. It was time to interrogate her jailer.

Yelena nodded shyly.

"I would like to ask you a few questions," said Marguerite.

The tongueless girl looked surprised and pointed meekly to her lips, shaking her head.

"No, of course I don't expect you to answer. Not with words. But you are quite capable of understanding me, and communication is not beyond you."

The servant stared at the floor, and Marguerite's

anger was softened by pity—softened, but not dissolved.

"Did you lock me in this room last night?" she demanded.

Yelena looked up, her eyes wide beneath the ruffled rim of her cap. She shook her head no. Marguerite was almost convinced. Duplicity seemed beyond this poor girl. But appearances, Marguerite knew, could be deceiving. Even the innocent could mask the truth.

"Well, someone did," she continued, "and now you are here. So you must have used a key to enter."

Again, Yelena shook her head no. She walked to the door.

"Do not leave yet," Marguerite commanded.

The mute paused and pulled at the door, with no result. She tugged again and it opened, scraping against the floor. She looked at Marguerite with a questioning expression.

"That proves nothing," said Marguerite harshly. "It was locked before. Now it is not."

Yet even as she said the words she began to doubt her conviction. It *had* been locked the night before. She had heard the key, and had pulled with all her might. But this morning? Perhaps she had not tried as hard. She began to wonder whether it was worth pursuing the matter with Yelena at all. The girl's fearful expression told her it was not. For now, the servant's life seemed difficult enough.

"All right, we'll forget about the door," Marguerite said softly. "But wait here while I dress. I'd like to eat breakfast downstairs in the kitchen."

Yelena shook her head and pointed at the tea pot.

"What now?" asked Marguerite. "Yes, I see what you've brought, but I prefer the kitchen. Surely it isn't filled with some mysterious peril. And you can guide me there, should someone object to my leaving this room without an escort."

Yelena simply nodded. She moved to the fire, looking guilty, then bowed her head and made a gesture from her heart toward Marguerite.

"Apology accepted," Marguerite replied.

The servant mustered a faint smile, tight-lipped as always. She took the kettle from the fire and filled the wash basin, then waited while Marguerite dressed.

Marguerite chose her clothing carefully. If she was to explore the grounds and woods outside the castle, she would have to be prepared. She donned a long, heavy tunic with split sides, cinching it at the waist with a wide belt. Then she pulled on leggings and tall boots. Because she intended to leave directly after breakfast, she took the green woolen cloak as well.

"All right, then," she said. "To the kitchen."

Yelena turned and led the way. They descended the same stair to the foyer, then followed a passage that seemed to skirt the back of the dining hall in a series of jogs. With only an occasional sconce to provide light, the corridor gave no hint of the time of day. Donskoy was right. The castle was a veritable labyrinth.

Yelena opened a door and they descended a short stair, then turned sharply and entered a large room with a blazing hearth. A heavy oak table lay in the center. Bundles of herbs hung from the beams in the ceiling. Baskets and barrels lined the walls.

Zosia stooped by the fire, stirring a kettle. She rose slowly and turned, her expression impassive.

"Good morning," Marguerite said brightly. "I trust you won't mind the intrusion, but I'd like to have breakfast here. I was feeling a bit cooped up in my chambers."

"Then the *wandeln* you have planned for later should provide much satisfaction," said Zosia, in a deep and throaty voice. "The wandering-out-of-doors,

I mean to say. That is why you are dressed so, is it not?"

"You are very observant," Marguerite remarked.

"Only the blind could miss such obvious signs, child," Zosia replied. She cackled. "Yelena, fetch Marguerite some ale and bread. And perhaps some smoked eel to thicken her blood. She looks a bit pale."

Marguerite seated herself upon a rough chair before the table while Yelena scurried in compliance, probing one of the small storerooms adjoining the kitchen.

When a full platter and mug lay before Marguerite, Zosia motioned for the servant to leave. Yelena hesitated for a moment. When Marguerite did not object, the mute girl curtsied, then crept up the stairs and disappeared.

"Zo," said the old woman. "You have already grown weary of your chamber. Does it not suit you?"

"No, it's not that. The room is quite nice," said Marguerite. "But—"

"But you are restless. That is natural. I too was restless once."

"I was about to say," Marguerite added quickly, "that I did not appreciate being locked in my chamber."

Zosia raised an eyebrow in mock surprise. "Locked in? How peculiar. Perhaps the door swelled and became wedged into place." She paused for a moment and winked, then added, "And where is it that you would like to go in the middle of night?"

"Nowhere. That's not the point—"

"Ah—" interrupted Zosia. "Then perhaps while experiencing a walking-dream you locked the door yourself? To keep someone out, not in. Did something disturb your sleep?"

"No," said Marguerite, exasperated. She had the feeling Zosia was not listening—or that she was listening, yet talking to someone else. Then Marguerite recalled that her sleep had been disturbed by a woman's laughter. She decided to switch to a more interesting subject. Yelena could not speak of the visitor, but Zosia could. Marguerite chewed on a piece of bread for a moment, wondering how best to approach the topic. If the strange woman's presence was meant to be kept from her, she would have to be deft.

"I saw a woman here this morning," she announced lightly.

Zosia's dark eyes sparkled. "Did you, child? A woman with raven hair perhaps?"

"I don't know," Marguerite replied. "She was outside the castle with Lord Donskoy this morning."

"Ah," said Zosia simply.

Marguerite paused, expecting more, but the old woman added nothing further. "Yes," said Marguerite. "She must have been a guest here overnight."

Zosia took a small bundle of herbs from the mantel and began grinding them with a mortar and pestle. "And what makes you think that?" asked the old woman, seemingly disinterested.

"I heard her laughing while I slept. She woke me."

"You must be mistaken, my dear. You heard the normal sounds of the castle. Don't let them disturb you. The stones have absorbed much through the centuries; it is only natural that they should let something out."

"I did not hear a stone," retorted Marguerite.

Zosia turned to her and smiled slyly. Her black eyes sparkled. "Why do you not simply ask what you are thinking? You want to know who the woman is."

"I am curious, yes," said Marguerite.

"Curious, naturally," said Zosia, chuckling. "It is one of your little faults."

Affronted, Marguerite started to reply, but Zosia

stopped her with a raised hand. "*Tsk*," the old woman
said. "Allow me to answer your question. The woman
is a close acquaintance of Donskoy. They have known
each other for many years, since Donskoy first
assisted her in a matter of some procurement. She
visits him when the mists are willing. He would not
like you to know of her yet. But she knows of you.
And she is, no doubt, intrigued. Still I think Donskoy
wants to treasure you for a time, so as not to share his
new bride with any others too soon."

"Share me?"

"Simply to display you. This woman might be a
little jealous, you see. But you need not be jealous of
her. You will be Donskoy's bride, not Mistress Jacqueline Montarri. Of course, you must not let it be known
that I have told you these things. You must allow your
husband to think he reveals his own secrets to you,
when he chooses."

Marguerite was stunned. She had not expected a
complete exposé, yet she had done nothing to stop
it. Now she wondered if this might have been a test,
a little game designed to measure her loyalty to
Donskoy.

Zosia sighed. "You are apprehensive now," she said.
"Curiosity can sometimes lead to that state."

"I do not wish to keep secrets from my husband,"
said Marguerite. "Or to show disloyalty before we
even wed."

"Oh, but you do keep secrets, do you not, child?"
Zosia replied. "About yourself." She cackled again.
"And some, you keep so well that even you have
forgotten them."

Marguerite was silent. Clearly, the old woman had
unusual powers of perception—perhaps even a gypsy
rauni's perception. But Marguerite had never heard of
any Vistana who had embraced a sedentary life. The

Vistani were, by nature, nomads. She began to suspect that Zosia was a sorceress. A witch. Or perhaps
she had simply made a well-calculated guess, hoping
to trick Marguerite into revealing some flaw.

Zosia continued, "Yes, of course, I see a great deal.
For as an old woman I have seen so many things, so
many times, that I now recognize them without effort.
Do not fear an old woman, Marguerite."

"I'm not afraid of you." It was true. Compared to
other threats she had faced, Zosia seemed quite
manageable.

"Good. It is all right that we speak together. Soon I
shall seem like a grandmother to you, and you will
come to know me as Donskoy's first wife did."

"His first wife?" Marguerite asked. She had posed
the question without thinking, intrigued by this new
glimpse into Donskoy's life. It was bold and improper
to pry—even unwise, if Zosia intended to report this
indiscreet behavior to the lord of the castle. Still, Marguerite could not resist.

Zosia had turned to busy herself at the kettle, seemingly oblivious to Marguerite's spoken and unspoken
questions. Perhaps her old ears had not heard.

"Donskoy told me his first wife died in a tragedy."

"Did he?" Zosia asked. "That is rare. It is not a subject he enjoys."

"Well, he didn't speak at length."

"I should think not, dear child. Even he would not
dwell on the dead while entertaining his new bride for
the first time. Even later, I doubt your lord will tell you
more. Donskoy prefers that the dead should rest, you
see, though whether he acknowledges them or not
cannot alter their condition."

"How did she die?"

Zosia sighed. "It was very long ago, and an equally
long tale. Some day, perhaps, I will share it with you.

But now, I must return to my work."

Marguerite felt dismissed. It was odd, she thought—
hadn't Zosia herself broached the subject?

The old woman hobbled over to her and patted her
hand. The touch was dry and cool. "We will talk again
tomorrow, before the wedding," she said. "Now why
don't you begin your explorations outside? Shall I
send Yelena to find Ekhart?"

Marguerite hesitated. Another test, perhaps? Donskoy had not quite insisted that she walk with a chap-
eron, yet the desire was clear.

Zosia answered her own question. "No, naturally
you do not wish the company of a stiff old man, so I
will share with you another secret—a way out through
my garden. And then you will enjoy your *wandeln*
alone." She raised a finger at Marguerite. "You must
take care not go very far and become lost. For then I
shall have to send Ekhart with the hounds to search
for you."

"I won't get lost," said Marguerite. "I'm accustomed
to hiking. In Darkon I often ventured into the woods,
and I never lost my way."

"Very good. Remember what I have said to you; do
not venture very far. If the mists rise up, they can be . . .
disorienting." She paused and frowned. "Have you truly
finished eating already? Such a tiny appetite, like the
vista-chiri."

Marguerite had barely touched the oily chunks of
eel on the wooden platter before her.

"For now, yes," she answered, "but I'll take another
piece of bread with me—if that is all right."

"But of course," said Zosia.

The old woman led Marguerite to a small door
across the room, which let out into a winding hall. The
rough stone walls stood barely a shoulder's width
apart; the cavelike ceiling hung so low that Marguerite

stooped beneath it. The corridor ended before another door, which opened onto a small outdoor court, completely surrounded by high walls. Despite the looming enclosure, the court housed a garden. Neat rows of short, withered plants filled one side. The only living flora was a cabbage, brilliant scarlet, glazed with frost. Tiny mounds of earth occupied the other half of the court, resembling miniature graves, freshly dug. Small glass domes flanked a cobbled walk that split the graveyard in two. Set with their mouths to the earth, they reminded Marguerite of cupping jars, the kind healers used to suction and burn human skin while "bringing forth the blood."

Zosia hobbled across the court, her black skirts sweeping the earth. Marguerite spied a dark form crouching at the base of the far wall. A large cat, perhaps? That would complete the strange picture—a sorcerous old woman, a garden of oddities, and a black cat familiar. But when the creature moved, it exhibited none of a cat's grace. Rather, it half shambled and half hopped toward Zosia. The old woman scooped up the animal, stroking and cooing as she turned back toward Marguerite. In her arms lay an inordinately large, lumpy toad. Forget the cat, thought Marguerite. This amphibious wonder was the size of a small dog. Its skin was dry yet gleaming, as if a mass of bubbling and frothing tar had hardened to glass. The creature paddled one fat, clawed leg impatiently through the air, then quieted, fixing its damp, glistening gaze on Marguerite. The eyes appeared to be set more closely together than an ordinary toad's. Marguerite was both fascinated and repulsed.

"This is Griezell," said Zosia, in a voice that resembled a soft growl. She stroked the creature's flat head and clutched it to her breast. "Our restless Griezellbub."

Marguerite recalled an old wives' tale about hags suckling their familiars from mystical teats that oozed blood instead of milk. Like a grandmother to me, indeed, she thought.

Noting Marguerite's gaping expression, Zosia clucked, "My dear, it is only a toad, though most certainly a queenly specimen. Surely you have seen toads in Darkon."

"Of course," Marguerite replied, "but I guess I'm not so well acquainted as you."

"No? Then perhaps you will be soon." One of Griezell's dark eyes closed in a wink. "I have heard claims that a bed full of black toads ensures conception, especially on the wedding night."

Marguerite grimaced. She hoped Donskoy would put no store in such a disgusting superstition. "I have no intention of sleeping with toads," she said firmly, "whatever their powers may be."

Zosia chuckled. "I am only teasing you, child. Oh, yes, it is true that toads can be useful for medicinal purposes, as any good cook and wise woman knows. But Griezellbub is much too unusual to be reduced to pickled liver and powdered bone." She cackled. "As if such a thing were possible."

Still nestling the creature in one arm, Zosia turned to the far wall and probed the stonework. She uttered something Marguerite could not understand, and an opening appeared. A tangled curtain of dead, woody vines hung just beyond.

"My secret escape," said Zosia with a feral, satisfied grin. "Though in reality it is more of a convenience. It's only a secret to my enemies."

Marguerite parted the vines and stepped outside. The magical door shut behind her. She turned and ran her hands over the stones.

"Zosia?" she called.

There was no reply. Part of her felt relief; it was still morning, yet she had experienced enough eccentricity for one day. A mysterious trollop, a grinning toad, a tongueless servant, and a witchy cook—not one of them made the castle cozy, and Marguerite was glad to leave them behind. Clearly she would have to find her own way back into the keep. But for now, she was free.

 **FOUR**

Outside the wall, a clean, moist breeze caressed Marguerite's face. She inhaled deeply, savoring the air's comparative freshness. She had not realized just how dank the castle had been. Even the atmosphere of Zosia's courtyard had been permeated by a musty, earthy smell. Marguerite felt revived.

She stood upon a narrow, mossy path that hugged the sloping base of the castle wall. Vines covered the masonry, yet they seemed to shy from the path, leaving it untouched. The ground fell away steeply on the other side, sinking into a wooded ravine—a deep, forbidding tangle of gray scrub and leafless trees. The towers protruding from the wall ahead and behind looked identical. Marguerite took a moment to orient herself. The walled court surrounding the stables lay on the opposite side of the keep. Ahead lay the road.

Using the vines for support, she followed the slim path toward the front of the castle. About halfway there, the ravine turned sharply away, plunging into the evergreen forest. A swath of gray, leafless trees marked its path, pointing toward the horizon like death's bony finger. The green-black forest blanketed the terrain all around it, sinking low, then rising again in waves toward a rim of sable mountains that pushed against the gray, misty sky.

The previous night, Marguerite had seen a campfire burning deep in the wood. She tried to recall its location. If it were visible from her window, it had to lie somewhere ahead and to the left. As she gazed into the dense primeval wood, she wondered how it had been possible to spot the fire. Surely the trees would have blocked the light.

She padded along the path until she reached the corner of the castle. To go any farther, she would have to enter the clearing and risk being seen. Even now, she imagined Ekhart's stern, reproachful gaze upon her, his scabrous lips bent in a condemning frown. Just ahead, another path appeared to dip into the evergreens. She scampered to the cover, then ducked into the trees. Panting, she turned and looked back toward the clearing. No one had seen her. Marguerite's spine prickled. At least, it appeared no one had followed.

The pines pressed in around her. She stroked their soft, feathered branches and drank in their scent, reveling in their heady embrace. She headed deeper into the wood. The path soon ended, splintering into myriad fingers of soft ground that wrapped themselves around the trunks of trees, then disappearing completely beneath the carpet of needles. Marguerite broke a branch to mark her passage, in case she should lose her direction on the return.

Somewhere in the distance, she could hear a soft rushing—a small waterfall perhaps, or a stream surging over a course of rocks. She followed the sound. In time, her path merged with a deer trail skimming the edge of a shallow cliff. Below, she could see a ribbon of black, glistening water.

She walked on until she came upon a broad, open expanse of rock sparsely covered with gray-green lichens. It overlooked a small waterfall below. She sat near the jagged edge, gazing across the chasm at a wavering wall of branches. The drop to the water measured at least fifteen feet, but the stream was narrow; with a running start, she could probably gain the other side. Years ago, when she had shared the follies of reckless children, she might have attempted it. Now she contented herself with the thought.

She sat for a moment, enjoying the solitude as she finished the bread she had carried with her. Of course, she was not completely alone. She had the company of the creatures into whose realm she had intruded. She scanned the trees for signs of them. From the flat crown of a black spruce, an enormous raven took wing, circling once overhead, then veering out of sight. Upon the towering skeleton of a lightning-struck hemlock, Marguerite spotted a great owl, sitting motionless, watching her with bright yellow eyes. It had twisted its head almost backward on its gray-brown body.

How patient it must be, she mused. Come nightfall, when moonlight touched this clearing, the owl would still be watching—waiting to glimpse some small furry shape as it scurried across the open space. Then the majestic bird would swoop down silently, gliding in for the kill. What must this quiet predator be thinking of her now? That she was in the way, no doubt.

She called out a greeting: "*Whooo . . .*" The owl blinked, looking bored, and turned away.

Marguerite smiled. She leaned back until she lay spread-eagle on the rock, her cloak spread beneath her like a pair of great green wings. A swath of gray sky hung low overhead. In summer, the sun would pierce the opening in the bower and strike the rock, warming it and everything upon it. She would lie here and offer herself to its heat. This would be her private spot—her sanctuary. Here, she could read or sketch, pursuing the pleasant occupations of noble ladies. Or perhaps she would simply gaze at the clouds drifting overhead, losing herself in daydreams. Some summer day. Not now.

Feeling a sense of achievement, she rose, brushing herself off. It was time to head back to the castle. She did not want Ekhart to discover she was missing and then come looking for her—especially not if he were to be towed by some beastly pack, as Zosia had suggested. Marguerite could almost hear the hounds now, whining and baying, eager with anticipation.

But it was not baying that she heard.

It was someone, or something, screaming.

The high-pitched sound was distant and muffled at first, filling the trees all around her.

Then it came again, sharp and chilling. It cut into her suddenly like a barb, tugging and tearing at her nerves. She gasped and held her hands to her ears. The sound echoed in her skull as if she had trapped it there.

Marguerite dropped her hands and forced herself to listen. Someone might be hurt, after all, and need assistance. The third cry struck her like a black wall—strange and spectral, unnatural and cold. She had never heard or felt such a thing before.

She began to run.

Whether she stumbled toward the sound or away from it, she could not tell. She simply felt compelled to run, to keep moving, and that compulsion led her ever deeper into the forest.

When at last she stopped, she had no idea where she stood. She was hopelessly lost. She scolded herself. She had allowed her imagination to run away

with her—literally. In all likelihood the sound had
issued from an animal. Death was common in a forest and usually as unpleasant as it was natural.
When seized by a hawk, a rabbit could scream like a
frantic child. The hapless victim she had heard was
something larger, perhaps, but probably an animal
nonetheless.

She listened carefully to the sounds around her. No
scream came. If only she could hear the sound of the
falls, she might find her way back. But the breeze had
picked up; all she heard now was the wind sighing
through the canopy overhead, and the occasional
creak of protest from a winter-chilled branch.

She stood, turning all around. The trees pressed in,
blocking the horizon. She crouched and studied the
ground. It seemed that she had run downhill, rather
than up, but the terrain had rolled, so she could not be
sure. Marguerite took her best guess and started walking, scanning her path for landmarks.

In time she entered a part of the forest where a few
naked beech and oak trees intermingled with the
pines. Occasionally she saw a dark form flitting
between the trees alongside her—a raven perhaps,
but too large. She kept on.

The forest floor grew tangled. Her pace slowed as
she struggled to keep the brambles and scrub from
tearing at her hands and face. She had stopped to
wrestle her cloak free of a thornbush when she spotted a dark gray shape about twenty paces away—an
abandoned hunting shack, she wondered? Or a dove-
cote?

She neared the structure.

To her amazement, it was an old, rotting vardo—a
gypsy wagon—cloaked by a web of leafless vines. In
its prime, it must have been elegant. Pale, weath-
ered streaks of gilding were still visible upon the

swirling patterns that had been carved in the paneled base. Ornately turned braces still adorned the eaves of the barrel-shaped roof, though half had fallen away. An octagonal window was fitted in the rear door; remarkably, its wine-colored glass remained intact. It was etched and hand cut; a single wild rose sprouted within.

The vardo reminded Marguerite of a skeleton she had discovered long ago in the woods of Darkon. A stag had caught its leg in a mass of brambles and had died. Undisturbed by predators, the deer had remained on the bed of thorns until its flesh had dissolved and the brambles had woven a tangled grave over its bones. Like the stag, the sight of the vardo touched Marguerite with sadness; her chest and throat tightened in sympathy. A thing of grace and motion had been rudely stilled. The vardo should have been burned rather than abandoned. In this passive, undignified state, it appeared unnatural.

How long had this wagon been here? she wondered. Certainly more than a decade. She could see no sign of a road or a rut that would have carried it to this spot.

Something rustled softly in the trees. Marguerite paused, scanning the area around her. She had the strangest sensation that she was being watched. She smiled. She was imagining things. One always feels a surge of paranoia upon discovering a treasure, a mystery.

She moved in closer, pulling the vines from the rear of the vardo. She stooped down and looked beneath the wagon. The wheels had well-turned spokes, and these too had once been finely gilded. A shallow, painted black box with tiny holes was still strapped to the bottom. Though the paint had faded, Marguerite could still make out the design of a great, coiled serpent with golden scales.

A man's deep voice spoke behind her. "It's a snake charmer's vardo."

Marguerite scrambled to her feet and turned, and found herself facing a tall, slender figure in black—the gypsy who had passed her on the road, just before Ljubo and Ekhart had come.

He smiled, fixing his dark, luminous gaze upon her. Marguerite sighed with relief. Then she recalled the screams, and a horrifying image leapt into her mind. Perhaps the victim was human after all. She started to run—or tried.

The Vistana's arm caught her wrist and tugged her back with tremendous strength. He pulled her against him, clamping an arm firmly around her shoulders. One hand covered her mouth.

"Promise me you won't cry out," he said softly. "and I'll release you."

Marguerite nodded. She intended to break the promise just as soon as the hand left her mouth—but then she realized it might only serve to anger the gypsy. After all, who would hear her but him?

He loosened his grip and turned her to face him, one hand on each arm, pressing them to her sides. "Don't be afraid."

"I'm not," she lied, whispering hoarsely. She stiffened her jaw in a semblance of dignity and defiance, but her legs trembled beneath her. She hoped it wasn't obvious.

He studied her. When he spoke, his tone was condescending. "Let me relieve you of your fear. I have no intention of spoiling Donskoy's bride before the wedding night. If such games interested me, I would have seized you yesterday on the road."

Marguerite was silent. What he said was true. "Then why have you seized me now?" she blurted.

He released her arms. "To prevent you from bolting like a fool again. As I said on the road, these woods are not safe."

"As you are living proof!" she replied. His answer had surprised her, for it meant he had not simply come upon the vardo and discovered her. "How long have you been watching me?"

"Since you invaded my solitude by crashing past," he replied smoothly. "In fact, it is I who should be affronted by this meeting."

"This is *my* land," she retorted. "I'll do as I please here."

He smirked. "Your land?"

"Donskoy's land," she corrected herself. "What are you doing on it?"

The Vistana shrugged, then replied lightly, "I wish only to help you."

"Your help I can do without."

"Are you certain? Perhaps you should think on the matter."

"I am certain," she said emphatically. "And you still haven't answered my question." She looked around, then softened her tone. "Did you lose your horse?"

"No," he replied.

She waited for an explanation, but he offered nothing more.

"Then where is it?" she asked.

"Do you intend to question me like some backwater constable? Yes, I can see that you do. To ease your mind, I will be patient. My horse is roaming freely. It will return when I have need of it."

"How convenient for you," she said tersely. "So, if you didn't lose your mount, why didn't you continue with the rest of your tribe?"

"They are not my tribe," he answered smoothly.

"But you traveled with them—"

"As did you, but you are not one of them."

"And you look like them. A little bit anyway."

He exhaled sharply, as if in disgust. "To the crude eye of *giorgios*, most Vistani look alike."

"Arturi and his caravan refused to come so near to the keep. Why did you?"

"We have already established that I am not of his caravan. They do as they are paid to do. I do as I am compelled."

"That's an odd choice of words. From your behavior, I imagine you do as you please."

"I admit that I do not shun pleasure. Nor, I imagine, would you, if you were not shackled to a *giorgio*'s notion of etiquette. Nonetheless, we all must face unpleasantries from time to time. As Donskoy's bride-to-be, you are doubtlessly acquainted with that concept."

She scoffed. "It's highly improper to insult my lord while trespassing on his land."

"I am not the best judge of propriety. What seems to you an insult is to me a statement of fact. Now, if you do not wish my help, I shall leave you."

"We have already established that I do not need your assistance," she said sarcastically.

"No?" he answered. "I thought certain you were lost and wished for someone to guide you back to the castle. Apparently, I was mistaken." He turned and began walking away. The air was heavy with mist; tiny droplets of water coated the fine, wooly hairs of his dark jacket, forming a glistening skin.

Was this a trick? she thought, or some manipulation? If she asked for his assistance, he would gain the advantage. Reluctantly, she had to admit that he already had the upper hand. Without his help, she had little chance of getting back to the keep before nightfall. She was lost, and to make matters worst, the glowering sky threatened rain. While there was no guarantee this man actually knew the way, he represented her best option.

"Wait," she called.

He stopped and turned, offering her a thin, self-satisfied smile. "Yes, Marguerite?"

She exhaled sharply, struggling to abandon her pride. Then it struck her that he had used her name, though she had never offered it. "You seem to know a great deal about me."

"Arturi and his caravan described you freely," he replied.

"No doubt they misinformed you, though my name is indeed Marguerite. What is your own name, then?" she asked. "I do not enjoy the disadvantage."

"Ramus," he answered. He tipped his hat.

"Well, then, Ramus, I would indeed be grateful if you would simply point me in the right direction."

"That will not be sufficient," he replied. "Follow me, and I will escort you back to your well-cut walls."

She began to protest, but he had already turned. If she did not follow, she would lose him.

The Vistana carved a meandering path through the underbrush. It was difficult to converse as they walked, but Ramus seemed uninterested in speaking further. She remained a few steps behind, studying him. He walked gracefully yet with strength, penetrating the undergrowth with ease. He seemed to know instinctively when to wend left or right around each obstacle, never leading her toward a snag that would force their retreat. She halted briefly to adjust her cape, and realized that nearly all the snapping and thrashing had been caused by her comparatively clumsy gait. Ramus seemed to her like a great cat, a panther. Suddenly she felt awkward and ridiculous by comparison.

As a girl she had fancied herself skilled in the
woods. It was a private pride, of course—ladies did
not "go a-loping," as her father said. "The only
women who wander are gypsies, whores, and sell-
swords. Stray too far from home, and you'll meet with
danger or disgrace." How ironic that in the end, he
had been forced to send her away in the hands of the
gypsies he privately insulted, into the arms of a man
no one knew.

At last she could see the dull glow of a clearing
ahead. A light rain was falling, but the trees protected
them from its full force. Ramus turned to her. "We are
nearing our goal," he said. He let her pass him just
near the edge, then reached out and held her arm,
pulling her back into the obscurity of the woods. "Marguerite," he whispered.

She steeled herself, thinking that some advance on
his part might follow. Instead Ramus pointed into the
clearing, where Ljubo was walking. A livid and bloody
shape hung over the plump man's shoulder. The Vistana pulled her gently to the ground, so that they
crouched together, watching as Ljubo made his own
way across the field. Through the heavy veil of
branches, Marguerite struggled to see what he was
carrying. Was it a sack stained with blood? Or a torso
of some kind? She shuddered.

"Perhaps it is your damsel in distress," Ramus said
quietly, answering her unspoken query. He leaned in
closer, speaking in her ear. "Perhaps it's the tender
meat you imagined suffering beneath my lecherous,
murderous hands." He laughed softly and gently
kneaded her arm with his fingers. "Yes, she proved to
be a bore, so I took my revenge on her."

Marguerite flinched, then saw that Ljubo was
hauling the carcass of a large swine. Oddly, the rear
legs of the pig had been severed, and they now

swung from Ljubo's belt. "A boar," she said dryly. "Very funny."

"The pig might disagree," the gypsy replied. "Isn't it remarkable how fear of the blade binds men and animals together? Horses, pigs, *giorgios*—when they stand at the brink of death, nostrils brimming with their own blood and fear, the screams sound very much alike."

They rose together, and she turned to him in amazement. "What a vulgar description," she whispered hoarsely. "And I notice you did not include Vistani in the equation."

"Vistani fear one thing more than the blade," he said.

"Oh, do tell," she replied. "What might that be?"

"Confinement. When the alternative is being trapped or held captive, a swift death is sometimes merciful."

Marguerite recalled the series of screams. "I don't think the pig's death was so swift," she said quietly.

"No," Ramus answered, "maybe not. But no doubt you will soon be tasting its succulent flesh, and thinking only of your own belly's pleasure. The kill portends a celebration. When is your wedding to occur?"

"Tomorrow."

The Vistana sniffed. "He is wasting no time," he said. "But that was expected."

Before Marguerite could reply, Ramus gently covered her mouth to silence her, pointing toward the clearing again. Marguerite gasped. Ekhart was striding across the clearing after Ljubo, behind three hellish black hounds. Had Zosia betrayed her? The animals had hulking, muscular bodies with massive chests and low-set haunches. Froth and drool dangled from their lips as they strained at their tethers. Ekhart halted them in the center of the field, then turned toward the woods where the refugees hid.

The gypsy's lips brushed her ear. "Not a word," he whispered, in a voice like a breeze. "*Yekori-akiri*. Let me shield you."

Marguerite felt a strange surge in the air around her as Ramus's other arm slipped around her shoulders and drew her back into the shadows of the trees. She stared at the hounds as they sniffed the air. The dogs remained silent.

But Ekhart had not paused to scent the couple in the wood. A third figure entered the scene. Marguerite's heart sank; it was Donskoy, riding toward the castle. What was he doing here? Hadn't he planned to be away until tomorrow? Evidently, plans had changed.

Donskoy reined in his mount before the tall, thin man. Distance muffled their conversation, but Donskoy's annoyance was obvious. He circled his horse around Ekhart, growling at him, berating him with some unintelligible tirade. The horse's hooves loosened muddy bits of turf, flinging them about. Donskoy raised his crop, swinging it through the air about Ekhart's head. The old man never flinched, but the great hounds sank to the ground, cowering. The sky grew darker, lowering, as if to reflect Lord Donskoy's wrath.

Ramus stood behind Marguerite as she gaped at the scene. He whispered into her ear. "When you face Lord Donskoy, I would not tell him about our meeting or reveal how far you wandered into the woods. It would not be wise."

"I have no interest in your advice," she hissed, not turning to meet his gaze. Anxiety lent a steel edge to her voice. "You take me for something I am not. A virtuous woman does not keep secrets from her husband—certainly not to protect the interests of another man."

"Another burst of propriety?" Ramus mused. "You slip so easily into the role. I pray you are as good an actress with him. It's true that a noble wife does not converse with strangers about personal matters. Of course, a good *giorgio* wife also does not meet with unfamiliar men under circumstances such as these."

"This is hardly my fault."

"Isn't it? Who dragged you into the wild? Protecting my interests is the least of your concerns. And you are not Donskoy's wife—not yet."

She felt Ramus's eyes burning upon the back of her neck. She had no reply. Surely Donskoy would not be angry with her about the situation, she thought, attempting to conjure hope. The day's events were such a small matter, a trivial transgression. What had she done but go for a stroll? Perhaps he was upset about something else. Then she remembered his capricious changes in mood, his firm attempts to control her movement. A simple fact remained: she had ignored his wishes. She knew in her heart it would not go unnoticed. As to Donskoy's response—and as to whether he would refuse her hand because of this transgression—she had no idea.

Marguerite stood silently, watching the two men as they headed through the drizzling rain toward the castle and disappeared through the gate to the stables. Ramus was right. She had put herself in a compromising position. She had not let Ekhart accompany her, and she had wandered too far. Time had galloped on; night appeared to be approaching. Certainly Zosia had encouraged her lark, but she alone was responsible. She had risked everything. And it was too late to change it.

When she turned to say goodbye, Ramus was already departing. His black shape slipped silently between two trees; then he was gone.

Marguerite bolted across the clearing toward the main entrance to the keep. The wind whipped through the air above the turf, creating clouds of fine, stinging spray. She made a plan as she raced. She would go directly to her chambers. If Donskoy confronted her about her wandering, she would not lay the blame on Zosia—it was a feeble excuse anyway, and it might only serve to bring the old woman's wrath upon her. She might say she left by the front door, meaning only to walk the clearing, then foolishly succumbed to the lure of the forest. Contrite and apologetic, she would admit to having lost her way; that much would be obvious from the circumstances. But as to Ramus, she would not mention him.

She hurried up the long flight of stone steps, twice slipping on their wet surface and falling to her hands and knees. She prayed the doors would not be locked, sparing her the humiliation of battering on them till someone—probably Ekhart—appeared from within. By the time she reached the summit, she was soaked to the skin.

To her astonishment, Yelena stood at the entrance, holding the great door ajar. The tongueless waif motioned frantically for Marguerite to hurry, emitting gravelly little squeaks from her cavernous mouth. Marguerite did not need the encouragement.

They flew up the stairs. Marguerite slowed their progress twice—first to seize a torch to light their way, next to stop at the library near her chamber. Indiscriminately, she grabbed three books from a shelf while Yelena fidgeted and squeaked behind her. As Marguerite turned to leave, Yelena ran toward her and knelt on the floor, using her own skirt to mop up a muddy puddle. It had barely been perceptible.

When they reached the room, Zosia stood by the hearth. She put a finger to her lips. Yelena grabbed the books from Marguerite and dropped them on the table by the fire. A pot of tea rested there already, beside a cup with a trace of leaves at the bottom, as if it had just been emptied. Yelena proceeded to strip Marguerite of her garments. Then the girl shoved a linen shift over Marguerite's head, handed her a pair of slippers, and pushed her into the chair by the hearth. Marguerite responded like a puppet, too exhausted to resist. She put her faith in her accomplices.

Yelena rubbed a shawl over Marguerite's damp hair in a fruitless attempt to dry it. The mute was still struggling when a knock came at the door. Marguerite grabbed a book and opened it to the middle, quickly righting it when she saw the volume was upside down. Zosia motioned to Yelena, who picked up the tea tray and shuffled toward the door, head bowed low. Tears welled in the mute girl's eyes. Apparently, she feared for herself; Marguerite could not imagine that the servant felt such empathy for *her*.

"Yes?" Marguerite called. But the door had already opened, and Donskoy now stood upon the threshold, surveying the scene. He held a square bundle under one arm, wrapped in black cloth. Yelena slunk past him, never meeting his gaze.

Donskoy entered the chamber and flung the package onto the bed, then strode to her side.

"So," he said, reaching down to kiss the back of her fingers. "Are you enjoying my library, Marguerite?"

"Yes, thank you," was her only reply. It took all her concentration to keep the hand Donskoy held from shaking.

He let the hand drop and pulled the book from her lap. "*Secrets of Swordplay*," he said. "My dear, are you expecting a contest?"

"I'm a little curious about the subject," she replied.

"Ekhart tells me you wandered out without him this

morning."

"Yes," she said, "I'm sorry, I—"

"I sent her out with Yelena," Zosia interrupted.

Donskoy sneered. "Yelena had other matters to attend to."

"It was for a very short time," said Zosia smoothly. "Ekhart's company is hardly pleasant for a young woman."

"Ekhart told me she has been gone the entire day."

"*Ekhart*," replied Zosia, in a low, gravelly voice, "is mistaken. Apart from her excursion, Marguerite has visited your upstairs library. She spent the remaining time with me in the kitchen, where we discussed how a bride might please her husband."

Donskoy chuckled darkly. "If I catch your drift, old woman, you are not a suitable instructor." He lifted the other two books from the table, and smiled as he read the first title: "*A Good Woman's Primer*. Let's read a bit shall we? 'When you go out in public, shun questionable associates, but surround yourself with companions who are suited to your position. Keep your gaze eight feet in front of you and on the ground without looking at any strange woman and most certainly not at any strange man . . . .' " Donskoy smiled with amusement. "This should be an easy matter for you. Your only suitable companion here is me, and rarely would you meet a stranger."

The second volume, Marguerite saw, was titled *Van Richten's Guide to the Vistani*.

Donskoy did not voice the name. Instead he scowled and flung the book into the fire. "Worthless slop," he muttered. "I must pay more attention to my library. And what are you doing here now, Zosia?"

"I have been reading Marguerite's tea leaves and telling her what a wondrous day she will have tomorrow."

Donskoy was silent, smiling slyly. Marguerite felt

sure he knew the entire scene was a ruse, but for some reason, he chose to accept it—or to ignore it. If he acknowledged that his wife and his servants had deceived him, he would have had to act upon it.

He pointed to the bed. "I have brought you a gown," he said solemnly, "for the wedding."

"Thank you," Marguerite began, "but—" She saw Zosia's admonishing look and Donskoy's own tense reaction. "But you are too kind."

"Until tomorrow, then," he said. He kissed her hand stiffly, squeezing it so tightly that Marguerite winced. Then he turned to leave the room.

Marguerite exhaled slowly. "Zosia—" she said.

The old woman put a finger to her lips, then tipped her head toward the door. "Yelena and I will come to ready you in the morning," she said. Then, Zosia, too, left the room.

As Marguerite slumped in the chair and closed her eyes, she heard the dull click of a key in the lock.

 **FIVE**

Marguerite lay half-awake through most of the night. Time and again, she slipped into the murky pool of dreams only to rise abruptly to the surface, panicked and gasping for air. With each ascension, the demons from which she had fled slithered back into the black depths, patiently awaiting her return. Never did they brave the light and invade her conscious thoughts. When fatigue claimed her at last, morning was near; outside, a pale, cold glimmer lit the horizon. She fell into a dreamless, numbing sleep.

When she awoke, Yelena's hand lay upon her shoulder, gently shaking her awake. The sallow face before her was less troubled than it had been the previous night, but even in her hazy half-lucidity, Marguerite could not miss the new disfigurement; an ugly weal lay across Yelena's cheek. The tongueless girl greeted her with a feeble smile, lips fused as one. Then she went to the window to throw open the shutter.

Marguerite rose and stretched, gazing about the room, struggling to clear the cobwebs from her head. The chamber was dim, but it was as warm and welcoming as she had ever seen it. The bed curtains had been pulled aside and tied with gold ribbon. Flames danced in the hearth, as the logs popped and crackled in contented submission. A tray with tea, bread, and hard cheese sat upon on the table by the fire. A large bouquet of dried flowers lay beside it, faded and mummified, yet still tinted in delicate shades of ivory and lavender.

Marguerite stretched, then shook her head. A round wooden tub had been placed before the hearth and lined with linen sheets. Long, lazy ghosts of steam rose from the water's surface. She could not imagine how Yelena's bony body had managed to haul the tub into her room, much less the heated water. Ljubo perhaps? And all the while she had dozed.

Then it struck her. Today was her wedding day—the day of bonding till death. She had known, and yet she had let this knowledge be blurred by the remnants of sleep. An eddy of conflicting emotion rose within her—hope churned by doubt, longing tainted by fear. It's only wedding jitters, she thought, releasing an unconscious laugh. Every bride succumbs. But she did not feel like "every bride."

The events of the previous day drifted back to her on a wave of guilt. Perhaps she should tell Donskoy about her experience after all. So many questions remained unanswered. The rotting vardo was a curiosity; did Donskoy know of it? Who was Ramus, and why was he in this land? Donskoy probably didn't know, but he might be interested in learning of the gypsy's presence. Of course, by now, Ramus had doubtlessly moved on. Vistani seldom lingered in any place.

Marguerite knew, however, that she would volunteer nothing to Donskoy. While she regretted the subterfuge, her guilty conscience would not control her. The matter had been settled already. Now was a time to look forward. She was grateful to Zosia and Yelena for their assistance. They had risked a great deal with their web of white lies, and she did not wish to betray their kindness. Moreover, if she were honest with herself, she would have admitted that she enjoyed sharing a secret with this pair; together, they had created a fortress of feminine wile. After all, what had Donskoy been doing yesterday? She would never be allowed to question it.

A knock came at the door, and Zosia entered without waiting for a reply. She surveyed the scene, shaking her head. "Zo little progress," she said in her inimitable husky tone. "You haven't eaten, Marguerite, and your bath is growing cold."

"I'm not hungry," Marguerite replied.

"*Tsk*. Then do as Zosia says. Into the tub now."

Marguerite stripped to the skin and dutifully stepped in, immersing her legs to the knees. It was a standing tub; there was not room enough to sit. The water had been scented with rose petals. Zosia reached out and gently turned her backward, then forward again, inspecting her as if buying a bolt of cloth. Then the old woman began to bathe her, humming softly as she stroked Marguerite's limbs. Occasionally Zosia voiced the words to the tune, as if she had suddenly remembered them, but the song was in a language Marguerite did not understand.

Marguerite studied her own body in the mirror opposite, wondering what Donskoy would think of it, if she would please him. Her plump, round curves proved that she had eaten well, though not to excess; her family had never known famine. Her skin was smooth and unblemished, save for the faint marks on her throat. She drew her fingers across the flecks, wondering if they would be apparent enough to draw her husband's notice when the two of them were alone and unclothed. The marks of the snake.

Zosia said softly, "You needn't worry. The vampire only touched you at the neck, did he not? You are still pure enough for Lord Donskoy."

Marguerite's mouth dropped open. "How did you know?"

Zosia cackled. "Your secrets are not so secret after all, eh? Your lord knows of this incident as well, but it doesn't concern him. He is a worldly man, quite capable of overlooking the unpleasantries he deems it best to ignore. What matters to him is that you are strong and pure, the perfect wife, the appropriate vessel for his child. You have worried for naught."

Marguerite was amazed. If Donskoy knew these things, why had he questioned her so over dinner? The answer was obvious. He had wanted to test her. Fortunately, she must have passed, for their wedding was soon to occur.

Yelena stood beside the bed, struggling to unwrap the ominous black bundle Donskoy had delivered the previous night. Marguerite had hesitated to open it herself, fearing the contents might look as grim as the cover. She had once read a tale about a place where brides wore black to signify the death of their youth and innocence. Here in this macabre fairy-tale keep, anything seemed possible.

In her trunk lay the simple but precious dress she and her mother had prepared together: a white shift with a gaily embroidered bodice, and a wide-sweeping overskirt adorned with a profusion of multi-colored ribbons. Her mother had cried with virtually every stitch, half with joy, half with sorrow, in a way that only mothers can. Marguerite wished she could have honored that memory by wearing the gown, but her mother, she knew, would understand. A wedding marked a turning point, after which a bride honored

her husband above all others—after which there was
no turning back.

The black bundle was so well tied that Yelena had to
fetch a knife to cut the string. To Marguerite's relief,
the servant extracted an ivory and blush gown from
within. It was sheer and glistening, and flowed from its
hiding place like liquid silk. The long train trailed
behind as Yelena stepped back from the bed with eyes
wide, as if she were pulling a worm from the earth and
had discovered it was endless. The gown's cut was
narrow and slim through the bodice, flaring slightly at
the hips. The sleeves were wide and flowing. It was a
masterpiece, made of layer upon layer of translucent
fabric, each no thicker than a layer of skin.

The remaining preparations passed in a blur of
nimble hands and muffled compliments. Before she
knew it, Marguerite stood in her gown before the mirror, wondering where her own flesh ended and the
dress began. The fabric was remarkable; soft and velvety to the touch, yet faintly crinkled, and shot
through with tiny glistening threads like capillaries.

Zosia took Yelena and left, saying that Ekhart would
come to escort Marguerite to the chapel. Marguerite
was dismayed, but did not object. As the castle cook,
Zosia would be busy with preparations, as would
Yelena. Besides, the role of escort called for a fatherly
figure, and, aside from Donskoy himself, Ekhart was
the only man appropriate. Certainly, Ljubo would not
have made a gallant figure for the short journey.

Marguerite sank into a chair before the fire, letting
her eyes close, forcing her breaths to become more
even. A log burst, erupting in sparks, and she leaned
forward quickly to check her skirts. Something hissed
and spat beside the grate. Marguerite looked closely.
It was the book Lord Donskoy had thrown onto the fire
the previous night. Amazingly, it had not been

destroyed. The cover seethed and bubbled faintly, but the pages were still visible at the side; they had not been reduced to ash.

Glad for the distraction, Marguerite reached into the fire with a poker and dragged the book forward, allowing it to cool. It seemed a shame to burn any tome, especially a scholarly work. She took the black shroud in which her wedding dress had been wrapped and placed it over the book, lifting it carefully from the floor so as not to soil her hands or gown with soot. Slowly she pushed the cloth into place, until the book was securely wrapped. She looked around the room. The cabinet door hung open. Marguerite laid the charred book inside, near the back.

A knock sounded from the hall. Marguerite barely managed to close the cabinet before Ekhart opened the chamber door and stood at the threshold, saying nothing. Marguerite felt a sudden chill. She went to him quietly, forgetting the dead bouquet of flowers that had been on the table when she awoke.

The pair walked in silence. At the first turn, Ekhart turned and stared deliberately at her—a look full of contempt and condemnation. Marguerite's temper flared. Who was Ekhart to judge her? Who . . . Her unspoken tirade quickly faded. Her mind had slipped easily into this diversion, but she knew this was no time for a battle of wills. She struggled to focus on the upcoming ceremony, and she felt a sudden, peculiar desire to look "fresh." The word echoed in her mind, though she could not determine why.

Ekhart led her through the castle with a slow, stiff gait, never varying his even pace. Once, she stumbled on the hem of her gown and, to her horror, left a ragged piece lying on the floor. The torn fabric seemed to shrink and curl, becoming dark pink at the edge. Ekhart tugged on Marguerite's arm, and she abandoned the piece behind her.

Soon each twist and jog in their winding path was mirrored by a turn of her stomach. Wedding jitters, she repeated silently. Every bride succumbs.

In time she and Ekhart stood at the threshold of a chapel. How they had reached it, Marguerite could not say. Ekhart sank his bony fingers into her elbow and whispered, "Stay here until the priest calls you forth." He looked at her, then sneered and added, "If you can manage."

Ekhart stepped across the threshold and walked toward the front of the dark chapel. His silhouette quickly faded into the shadows.

Marguerite gazed after him. The chapel was small, but the ceiling soared to an impossible height, as if to penetrate the realms of gods. In the inky darkness, she could not discern the apex of the vault; she knew the distance only by the pointed window set high overhead. Light streamed through the crimson glass, creating a pale shaft of color that pooled like blood when it struck the floor near the front of the church. It was the only light of any brightness. The left wall was rent by a row of tall, narrow windows, but the shutters were closed tightly upon them; each dark, heavy panel was illumined by a small candle fixed in a bracket beside it. The tapers struggled in vain to brighten the nearby area, but inches from each flame the darkness won out.

Slowly Marguerite's eyes adjusted to the scene. Pews blackened with age emerged from the shadows. Near the front of the chapel two dark figures sat flanking the aisle—one tall and slim, the other small and stooped. They were mirrored by another unmoving pair seated near the back of the chamber. Marguerite struggled to discern the nearer couple's identity, but failed; they were facing away.

A light flared at the front of the chapel, revealing a dark figure in a hooded robe. His fingers were stroking a line of candles on the altar, coaxing the wicks to life. Marguerite blinked. He held no taper, no burning candle whose fire would be shared with the others. Instead he needed only the long, curving nails of his fingers. A mere touch ignited the flames.

The altar resembled a long platform cloaked in indigo velvet. By the feeble, flickering light, she could see small, dark shapes resting before the candles—a pair of goblets, perhaps, and a collection of objects that refused to let her eyes define them.

The hooded figure lifted a round gold censer and moved slowly about the room, filling the air with a sweet, musky haze. As Marguerite watched, waiting for her cue to enter, she was filled with dread. She closed her eyes and thought of Darkon, recalling dreams of a wedding that never was.

In Malanuv, had she married, Marguerite and her beloved would have knelt outside, before the sacred stones, to exchange their vows. Afterward, jubilant brothers and burly cousins would have borne them through the streets on chairs held aloft, ribbons streaming from the rungs. She had witnessed countless weddings in this tradition, and in her mind's eye, she was there now.

Bards followed behind, singing joyous proclamations. Villagers lined the streets, showering the bride with flower petals. After the procession had passed through this gauntlet, the entire crowd celebrated the event, indulging in food, wine, and song until their very souls had been sated. When at last the sun touched the horizon, the conveyors lifted the couple again and carried them home, straight to the wedding bed. The bearers retreated then, of course, but all through the night, friends and family passed below the bedroom window to tease the lovers with bawdy jokes and songs of procreation. Everyone reveled in the celebration. When the cock crowed, the villagers knew it would be time to resume their simple, quiet routines.

Remembering how she had once anticipated that day, Marguerite felt something precious had been stripped from her. It was not her dead beloved she missed; her grieving for him had ended when she began her journey to Donskoy's land. Rather, she missed the familiar traditions, and she longed to wrap herself in the comfort of ritual. The coming wedding—her real wedding—might be steeped in ritual, but she sensed there would be nothing familiar or comfortable about it.

Marguerite's eyes snapped open as someone coughed at the front of the chapel. The priest stood at the altar once again. He had removed his hood, revealing a hairless head so white that it glowed and pulsed in the flickering light. Donskoy stepped out of the shadows and took his place beside the priest, who beckoned to Marguerite. She began to walk down the aisle, as if stepping into a dream.

When Marguerite passed the first pew, she glanced to see who would witness this union. Ljubo and Yelena sat near the back of the room. She passed ten empty rows beyond, most of them gray with dust. Zosia and Ekhart sat just before the foremost pews, which, of course, would have been reserved for family, had any attended. The onlookers continued to stare ahead, not meeting her gaze. Not even Zosia turned to smile reassuringly upon her. It was if Marguerite were to be wed among the dead. A gentle rasping echoed through the church; it was the sound of her own gown, dragging across the cold stone floor. She longed for music. Donskoy would not have shared this desire, of course; he had said as much to her earlier.

As Marguerite neared her betrothed and the priest, she studied their unwavering eyes. Donskoy's were wide and reddened. The priest's were pale and almost colorless, save for a tinge of pink. White lashes adorned them like a dusting of snow. His brows lacked color as well. An albino, Marguerite thought.

The priest lifted a red sash from the altar and slipped it around his neck so it draped over his chest. As he turned, the light from the candles danced across his smooth skull, creating a cap of writhing tattoos. He began chanting in an ancient tongue.

The albino motioned for her to kneel, and she sank dutifully to the ground. The cold, hard stone stung her knees, but she didn't mind; a numbness had begun to permeate her body. Donskoy took his place at her side. When she looked at him, his eyes were closed, his thoughts seemingly elsewhere. He must have sensed her gaze, however, for he turned and took her hand reassuringly. His soft glove caressed her fingers as he leaned forward to whisper into her ear.

"I will translate," he murmured, "so that you understand the ceremony and its meaning." He squeezed her hand gently. "It is really very quaint, full of tradition and lore. I hope you will enjoy it."

The albino lifted a necklace of white petals from the altar and placed it around Marguerite's neck. Their spicy-sweet scent enveloped her, prickling her nostrils.

"A mark of your chastity," said Donskoy, "and a symbol of your fidelity in the future."

The priest droned on as he placed a wreath of nettles around Donskoy's neck.

Donskoy returned to her ear and said softly, "To ensure my potency, though I shall not need it." He kissed her tenderly upon the cheek, and for the first time, she felt relatively at ease. It was not to last.

The priest drew a shining blade from the folds of his

robe and passed it through the air, making a pattern like a star. Candlelight glinted on the steel as he took Marguerite's hand. She braced herself in anticipation of the sharp pain to come, but felt only the barest caress as he stroked the blade across her palm. The surgeon-priest released her and she stared at her unmarred skin. At first, the cut seemed merely symbolic, a mere brush, not a breaking of her fragile shell. Then, slowly, a thin red line appeared. Marguerite held her hand aloft and watched the blood as it brimmed in the gash, then trickled in streams down her arm until it merged with the sleeve of her gown and disappeared. Presumably, the priest cut Donskoy as well; she was too dazed to watch.

Lord Donskoy turned to face her directly and raised his hand as if to touch an invisible barrier; instinctively Marguerite did the same, mirroring his gesture. He pressed his gloved flesh against her bare skin—palm to palm, finger to finger, wound to wound. He spread her fingers and slipped his own between them, clasping her hand firmly. The priest made a cryptic pronouncement, then began to wind a strip of ivory linen snugly over their touching hands and wrists. The damp cloth smelled of sulphur and smoke. Marguerite's skin grew hot beneath it.

Donskoy's voice was deep and slow. "And so we are bound in flesh," he said.

The albino lifted the pair of silver goblets from the altar and presented one to each of them. Dark red wine filled the vessels, viscous and gleaming. Donskoy spat into Marguerite's goblet, then thrust his own under her lips. She returned the gesture awkwardly. When she had finished, a tiny strand of saliva escaped from her mouth. There was no discreet way to remove it. She had no hands free; one hung at her side, bound to Donskoy; the other held the goblet. To her astonishment, Donskoy leaned in quickly, licking her mouth with a darting tongue. It was so deft, she hardly felt it. His arm snaked itself gracefully around hers and they sipped the warm, bitter liquor while entwined. The wine caressed her throat and descended slowly into her body, pooling in her stomach.

"And so we are bound in spirit," Donskoy murmured, his lips now moist with the red stain.

They drank until the goblets were empty. Marguerite swayed as the priest took the vessels away, and she felt Donskoy's firm grasp holding her in place.

"One final stage, my dear," he whispered hoarsely, "a rite of fertility. Then we will be done."

The priest withdrew a long, slender needle from his sash. Marguerite's eyes grew wide with alarm. She wriggled once in Donskoy's embrace before regaining her self-control.

Zosia stepped forward with a tiny pillow, upon which a small, dark egg was resting. The priest pricked both ends of the shell, then returned the needle to his sash. Marguerite sighed with relief, glad that she was not the one to be pierced. Zosia presented the pillow to the priest, then retreated. Donskoy gingerly picked up the egg.

He smiled knowingly at Marguerite. "Take half into your mouth and hold it gently with your lips," he instructed. "I am to blow the white through. Do not crush the shell or lose your hold, or you will bring bad luck upon us both." Donskoy winked and whispered in her ear. "I do not believe it myself, of course. But it is only proper we appease the priest and his so-called gods."

Marguerite suppressed the urge to laugh at this assertion. Propriety certainly varied with the territory. She took the egg as it was offered, and wondered suddenly whether Donskoy's first wife had undergone the same ceremony. Marguerite pushed the question aside. It would not do to think of the dead while celebrating a marriage.

Donskoy put his lips to the other side of the shell, leaning in gently. It was the most peculiar kiss Marguerite could imagine. There was nothing sensual about the exercise; she had to concentrate fully upon holding the egg and adjust to Donskoy's every change in pressure so as neither to let it drop or be crushed. She felt the contents of the egg slipping into her throat. Donskoy pulled away from her, and the priest retrieved the half-empty shell, crushing it forcefully beneath his foot.

The priest motioned for the couple to rise. They stood facing one another, still bound at the wrist. As the albino slowly unwound the gauze from their skin, Lord Donskoy leaned forward and kissed her intimately. When at last he released her, Marguerite's fingers were stiff and sore. No evidence of her cut palm remained, and the priest was gone.

"Congratulations," announced Donskoy. "You are my bride. Until death do us part, you are mine."

The four onlookers held their palms to the sky and rapidly snapped their fingers. Apparently, this counted as applause.

Her husband turned to the audience as if he were addressing a large crowd. He flung his arms wide to embrace them all, crying, "And now, my friends, we must celebrate!" Then he turned to Marguerite, grinning wildly. "Ah, yes," he said in a low, guttural tone. "And now we must feast!"

Ljubo shambled to the wall and flung open the first shutter. A glorious shaft of light entered through the blue glass and pierced the room. He proceeded to the next window, and then each in turn, until he had flooded the chapel with a riot of colored rays—red,

blue, green, and gold. Marguerite's heart lifted with
each new exposure.

Lord Donskoy put his arm around her waist and
began steering her down the aisle. It was not until they
reached the last pew that she noticed a fifth guest had
entered the chapel.

In the back row, well away from the windows, sat an
elegant young woman in a jet traveling cloak. She
looked like a porcelain doll with dark curls, ghostly
skin, and enormous green eyes. A wide red ribbon
encircled her long, slender neck.

As Donskoy led Marguerite toward the door, the
woman's lips parted in a perfect smile. "Congratulations," she said, mouthing the word so slowly that Marguerite could see her shining white teeth and her tender
pink tongue. The word itself was barely audible.

Donskoy stopped and stared, as if surprised to discover the new guest. Then he nodded curtly to the
woman and swept Marguerite across the threshold.

 **SIX**

After departing the chapel, Marguerite and her new husband entered the keep alone. A single torch flickered far ahead, a feeble beacon shining across a sea of blackness. She found herself nearly blind, but Donskoy seemed unaffected by the murk. He slipped his arm around her waist and led her up a narrow sloping passage, sweeping her along as the wind carries a leaf. When they had walked for several minutes, he paused, drawing her aside.

"How do you feel?" he asked, pressing her back against the cool, damp wall.

"A little strange," she replied. Strange, yes, and somewhat unraveled—still loose from the wine, perhaps. But not so loose that she had forgotten the woman in the chapel.

Donskoy stroked her cheek with his glove, then lifted a handful of her hair to his nose. "In a good way, I trust," he said. He snuffled the hair softly, then drew a lock over his tongue.

The gesture seemed oddly bestial, and Marguerite knew that she should reply, but her own tongue had become heavy and uncooperative. "Yes," she said finally. "In a good way."

Donskoy's fingers slid to her shoulder, drawing her gown aside. The hand slipped to her waist, resting on her hip, as his teeth scraped teasingly across her bare collarbone.

He has announced a feast, Marguerite thought. Perhaps I am to be it. Perhaps, after all, there will be no jubilant celebration, and no one to ferry me to a carefully appointed wedding bed. Lord Donskoy intends to seal our union in the dungeons. She braced herself.

Donskoy pulled away, smirking slyly. He winked, not saying a word, then straightened her gown and patted her shoulder. They continued their winding ascent.

Marguerite smiled. It appeared that her husband had a sense of humor. In a corner of her mind, a great door was slowly closing, locking out the past. Admittedly, Donskoy was mercurial and the apparent product of arcane traditions, but he was not the horror she had fled in Darkon. Isolation and despair had made him rough; he would mellow in time. She would help. And they would succeed as man and wife, if left unimpeded—if no one interfered.

"Who was the woman in the chapel?" Marguerite asked boldly. She already suspected the answer.

"The woman?" Donskoy's voice was casual. "That was Zosia who joined us at the altar."

Marguerite kept her tone equally casual and light. "No, the woman in the back of the chapel. Wearing the black cloak."

"Ah." He paused briefly. "An unexpected guest."

"You did not invite her?"

"Not directly."

Marguerite found this curious. "I hope I am not the cause of some misunderstanding. Certainly I would welcome any friend of yours to the castle."

"How generous," said Donskoy curtly. "And how amusing that you consider such invitations within your purview." His tone remained light, yet it carried a subtle note of warning. She had asserted herself too forcefully.

"I only mean to say that I look forward to meeting any friend of yours, and that you do not have to worry about my reception. I shall entertain any visitor with the same graciousness as you do yourself."

Donskoy gave a throaty chuckle. "That is generous indeed."

"Is our guest Jacqueline Montarri?"

Lord Donskoy halted abruptly, his fingers pressing into her waist. "How do you know that name?" he asked. His tone was soft, yet measured.

"I saw Miss Montarri yesterday morning. I saw her only briefly, and Zosia told me who she was." Marguerite did not reveal that she had seen Donskoy as well.

"Zosia speaks far too freely."

Marguerite answered chattily, as if deaf to any underlying tension. "Actually, Zosia told me very little. Just the name, and that Jacqueline Montarri is an old friend."

"I see . . ."

They walked on, and Marguerite patiently awaited his next response.

"Well, it doesn't matter," Donskoy added resolutely. "Jacqueline's presence comes as something of a surprise, but you would have become acquainted with her soon enough. She visits quite frequently. I must warn you that she may seem rather coarse, despite her elegant exterior."

Marguerite was not at all surprised by this last revelation.

Donskoy continued, "She will join us for the feast

I have planned. My associates are already waiting in the great hall to meet you. We shall celebrate the marriage."

"Your associates?" Marguerite asked. The term was peculiar. Certainly a lord might have henchmen, soldiers, hirelings . . .

"Loyal followers," explained Donskoy, "companions even before I became a lord. But that is the past. And now, we look forward."

Without warning, they had gained the foyer. Donskoy led her to the opposite side, to a pair of wide doors. "Ready?" he asked.

She nodded.

He flung open the doors, exposing the castle's great hall. Marguerite gazed in awe at the immense chamber before her; it was at least four times the size of the room in which they had previously dined. She felt as though she had shrunk. The ceiling vaulted upward through the next two levels of the keep, past a narrow gallery and into the shadows. A row of chandeliers descended from this darkness—spiders of iron and wood, dangling from strands of rusty chain, their legs aflame with myriad candles. An enormous, gaping fireplace glowed in the left wall. Smoke and ash whirled before the open hearth like gray snow stirred by a sudden draft.

At the far end of the hall rose a dais supporting the lord's high table, which was freshly dressed in white linen. Marguerite noted that table seemed small; but perhaps this was intentional, to make the lord seem large. Twin rows of rough-hewn tables and benches created a broad aisle that led directly to the honored position. All of the tables were empty, save the pair just before the platform, which were occupied by about two dozen men, sullen and silent. Marguerite felt a catch her throat.

A man in a black and red doublet rose from his seat, lifting his palms toward the ceiling. He began to snap his fingers. Slowly, the other men followed suit, one by one, until the room was filled with a sound like a hundred pebbles dropping.

Donskoy gripped Marguerite's hand. "Smile," he said. "And show them how lovely you are, how full of life."

He led her forward across the herb-strewn planks, past the empty dust-covered tables, past the grimly nodding men and up the shallow steps to the dais. All the while, Donskoy's followers continued to snap their fingers. The lord took his place in the thronelike chair at the center of the table, before an elegant saltcellar made of silver. He motioned for Marguerite to sit beside him. Then he raised his hand, and the men ceased their strange applause, taking their seats as well. They began to murmur softly among themselves, throwing the occasional glance in Marguerite's direction. One of the men nudged his companion and whispered into the fellow's ear, then both laughed darkly.

From this new vantage point, Marguerite could better view her audience. They formed an incongruous picture of fine clothing and imperfect bodies. One man was missing his right eye and half his face; it had caved in along a terrible scar. Another had only one hand; the left arm ended in a fingerless stump. A third had a hump. Others seemed less tattered, but even the fittest suffered some small deformity, such as a cauliflower ear or a blind white eye, or a profusion of sores and boils.

Smiling stiffly, Marguerite whispered a question to her husband. "Do these people live in the castle?"

Donskoy chortled. "No, my dear," he said, patting her hand. "Rest assured. My associates may lodge here on occasion, but they devote most of their time to . . . ah, watching the borders of my land. They prefer the wild, and I admit I prefer the solitude. You have nothing to fear from them. No doubt they are jealous, but they would never dare harm my pretty wife, if that's your fear. They are not as rough as they seem."

Marguerite breathed a sigh of relief.

Her husband continued, "Of course, they are easily summoned, should I require them. They are always close at hand."

The places had already been set and the wine poured, with full jugs resting on each table. A pewter platter and mug lay before each man, while Donskoy and Marguerite were to dine with fine silver and goblets of precious red glass. The men were already drinking. As soon as Donskoy had taken his seat, they had returned to their libation and chatter. Yelena rustled in through a door behind the dais and added a third setting at the end of the high table. Marguerite raised a brow, recalling the uninvited guest, the woman.

Donskoy did not acknowledge Yelena's actions. He stood, raising a glass toward his associates. "I present to you my bride, Marguerite," he bellowed. The men lifted their mugs and gave a half-hearted hail. Marguerite nodded politely, but few met her gaze. The men's attentions had turned to the rear of the hall, to the sound of large doors opening.

The white-skinned woman from the chapel entered. She swept in as if she herself were the keep's mistress, well acquainted with every nook and shadow. Marguerite frowned. The men rose from their seats and they lifted their mugs again, this time toward the new arrival. The woman's traveling cloak was gone, displaying a sleek gown of dark green silk. It fit snugly to the hips, then flared to allow movement. The wide neckline boldly exposed her neck and shoulders, while the tight bodice thrust her round white breasts up toward her collarbone. Yards of black lace dripped from the gown's snug sleeves and trailed from the waist like a tail. As she crossed the floor, the dress rustled and hissed. Like a snake through autumn leaves, thought Marguerite.

The woman slithered up the aisle, nodding to each associate in turn. Pearls had been woven in the plaits of her raven hair. She stepped onto the dais, and draped her pale white hand across the table to Donskoy, who pecked her fingers stiffly.

"Jacqueline," he said, "may I present my wife, Marguerite Donskoy, née de Boche."

Jacqueline nodded to Marguerite. "Delighted, I'm sure." She darted her pink tongue ever so slightly between her scarlet lips, which echoed the color of a velvet ribbon encircling her neck. "Your bride is quite striking, Milos," she added. "An unusual sort of beauty. Those huge dark eyes against that pale amber hair. I never imagined you could unearth such a specimen from the piddling corners of Darkon."

"I beg your pardon?" Marguerite was incredulous.

"Is Darkon not your home?" Jacqueline asked coyly.

"Yes, but—"

"Oh, I meant no offense. You must tell me all about your roots then, Marguerite. Later."

Donskoy bade them sit. Jacqueline took her place at the end, where she enjoyed a vantage of both her companions. As Donskoy extolled the quaint rituals of the wedding and the lovely quality of his fresh bride, Yelena shuffled in with a tray, presenting a pair of finger bowls to the women. The servant's cheek was still marred by the long weal that looked like a leech sucking her vitality—what little remained to her.

Jacqueline toyed with a curl of her black hair, inspecting it carefully. "It was indeed an entertaining ceremony," she said, not bothering to look up. "I'm so pleased I could attend."

"And I am pleased to see you are feeling better," Donskoy replied, a faint chill in his tone.

"Thank you, my friend. Your kindness warms me."

"Were you ill?" asked Marguerite. "Then surely you should not have traveled."

Jacqueline smiled condescendingly. "How sweet of you to worry. It is nothing serious. I am prone to headaches, which can be maddening, but rarely fatal."

Marguerite noticed a faintly bruised band of flesh that rimmed the woman's neck ribbon, and wondered if perhaps the fabric had been drawn too snugly.

"But I haven't a glimmer of pain now," Jacqueline continued, stroking a pale finger thoughtfully along her jaw. The nail was short but pointed, and stained red with henna. She brightened. "Indeed I feel like a new woman, thanks to Donskoy's generous gift. I couldn't wait to get home before I opened it."

From the dim corners of her memory, Marguerite recalled the black box—the crate that Arturi had unloaded, and that she had last seen lashed to the back of the woman's carriage. Marguerite wondered how this could possibly have effected a cure. She was about to inquire when Donskoy interrupted.

"Yes, the new gown becomes you, Jacqueline. And *home* is where I thought you were destined. What has prompted your return?"

"You did, I thought," she answered sweetly.

"And how might I have done that?" he asked.

"Soon after we parted, the road became impassable, blocked by timber."

Donskoy seemed surprised.

Marguerite found the entire exchange quite curious. "How could that have been Lord Donskoy's arrangement?" she asked. "Are you suggesting he scurried out beforehand and felled the trees himself?"

Donskoy smirked.

Jacqueline smiled knowingly. "The unconscious will," she murmured. Her emerald eyes flashed, reflecting the shimmer of her dark silk gown. "One should never underestimate its power."

"You speak too dramatically," said Donskoy.

"And you underestimate yourself," replied Jacqueline. "There is very little in this domain that does not reflect your will, my friend, or bend to your wishes."

Donskoy gave a low chuckle. "Except women, perhaps." He patted Marguerite's hand. "You see, Marguerite, my land tends toward self-destruction, especially during the spring, when one might expect just the opposite. But I am surprised to hear of it now."

"Well, if you doubt it," Jacqueline replied, "you must see for yourself."

"That won't be necessary," Donskoy said. "I will send Ljubo and Ekhart with a few associates to clear the road for you tomorrow."

"A few fallen trees is hardly self-destruction, Lord Donskoy," Marguerite offered. "It must be a common occurrence when the soil is saturated and the roots are weak. Really, such attributions make things seem grimmer than they truly are."

"Take note, Jacqueline," Donskoy replied. "Already she offers a fresh perspective. She'll bring renewal to this land yet, you shall see."

"Yes, I shall," said Jacqueline, smiling smugly. "And I shall enjoy the spectacle."

An awkward pause ensued. Then Ljubo and Yelena entered bearing the first course: two peacocks, cooked fully feathered. Their brilliant turquoise and emerald tails had been spared from the heat, then reattached with skewers to stand aloft. The necks, too, had been wired erect. Yelena strained under her load, but Ljubo waddled contentedly as usual, bobbing so that the bird's feathers waved before him like an exotic many-eyed fan. Marguerite suppressed a smile. He made a perverse sort of harem girl, she thought. For that matter, he made an equally unsavory eunuch. The peacock's loose head nodded in agreement on its spike. Ljubo had made an effort to formalize his attire, meeting with some success; he wore a clean black woolen tunic over his tattered trousers, and his ragged fingers had been freshly wrapped in crisp white bandages, already soiled by the juices of the bird.

It occurred to Marguerite that she had assumed the castle harbored a few other hands to serve Donskoy—that somewhere, in the keep's foreboding recesses, lurked chandlers, chamber maids, pantlers, footmen—not many, perhaps, but certainly a few. Now she began to wonder if the foursome she had already met maintained the castle in its entirety. Even given the general state of decay, it seemed impossible. She looked around for any sign of Ekhart or Zosia. Neither was present; perhaps they were employed behind the scenes.

Ljubo plunked his platter directly in front of Jacqueline, who sneered at him, then teasingly blew him a kiss. Ljubo chortled as he and Yelena retreated.

"A toast," said Donskoy. "To my bride."

"To new faces," added Jacqueline, lowering her eyes to cast a knowing look at Donskoy. If he reacted, Marguerite did not notice.

As Yelena and Ljubo brought forth other dishes and bread, the feasting began. Donskoy carved a piece of the peacock and placed it on Marguerite's platter. "It is my pleasure to serve you, my dear."

"Take note of that, Marguerite," cooed Jacqueline. "Such words rarely come from his lips. You may never hear them after tonight."

Donskoy ignored the remark, a fact that annoyed Marguerite even more than the comment itself. She fought to keep the heat from rising to her face.

"You mentioned home," said Marguerite, intent on taking the high ground as hostess. "Where is that, Jacqueline?"

"Barovia. My estate lies there."

"Is it a difficult journey?"

"It can seem that way at times, especially for someone who lacks my resourcefulness."

Jacqueline withdrew a dagger from somewhere under the table; Marguerite assumed it had slid from a sheath on her thigh.

"Always carry your own blade," said Jacqueline, relieving the bird of half its flesh. "It's an old rogue's adage. Most hosts fail to supply something suitable, though Milos is, of course, an exception."

"A rogue's adage?" Marguerite asked. "You don't look the type."

"Really . . . And how does the type look?"

"More utilitarian in dress, perhaps. Less fragile."

"I assure you," said Jacqueline, "I am not so fragile. But I will take that as a compliment. It has indeed been many years since I had to struggle amongst savage company to maintain myself. Many years, in fact, since mutual interests led me to Donskoy. Do you still remember that night, Milos?"

"I do," he replied.

"Those times were perhaps rougher," said Jacqueline, "yet in many ways richer. As I recall, Milos, you were flush with the rewards of a successful venture."

"Yes," he replied, smiling. "Highly successful. And,

as I recall, you intended to share in those rewards—without an invitation."

Marguerite intervened, fearing their reverie might soon become a wall that encircled them completely. "What kind of venture?" she asked.

Jacqueline merely smiled, and Donskoy sat chewing, as if to consider his reply before answering.

"Does it surprise you, Marguerite, to learn that I was not born to this so-called grandeur?" He waved his hand at the room.

"No. I suppose I knew it."

"And how is that?"

"No mention of family, perhaps, no coat of arms, no portrait gallery. I'm not certain."

"Perhaps I simply prefer to keep my ancestors well-buried."

Marguerite pondered for a moment. She *had* known that Donskoy was not born to this castle. Then she recalled. "I believe Ekhart told me you were not the keep's original owner, and you yourself said you 'came' to this place."

"Indeed, that is possible. It would seem my lovely bride harbors a deep memory, as well as a clever wit. I shall have to take care what I say."

"I wish you wouldn't," Marguerite replied. "A husband and wife should share all things intimately, and thereby build a fortress, and let no others assault it."

Jacqueline chortled. Donskoy silenced her with a lancing gaze, but a smirk pulled gently at the corners of his lips.

"You've been reading the *Good Woman's Primer*, I imagine," he said with some amusement. "And of course you are correct." He stroked his goblet against Marguerite's cheek, letting it drop to her collarbone. She felt a trickle of spilled wine and quickly dabbed her chest with the edge of the tablecloth. "But do not trouble yourself," he whispered. "Later we shall share things intimately."

Marguerite tensed; clearly her husband's demeanor was getting loose. "So," she said, "you were telling me about a successful venture."

"Was I?"

"Please do. I want to share in all your successes, past and future. What sort of venture was it?"

"How shall I put it . . . ?"

Jacqueline chimed, "May I assist?"

"You may not," Donskoy said firmly. He patted Marguerite's hand. "I have played many roles, my dear, but at the time in question, I was a procurer—no, a kind of savior. I made it my business to fulfill certain special and difficult needs of those who had the means to pay well. Great lords in name, some of them, though of course I was their equal by right. If not their superior."

"Don't you mean by *rite*, Lord Donskoy?" quipped Jacqueline.

Marguerite did not catch the meaning.

"I do not," he growled in disgust. "Such are your own concerns."

"Forgive me, Donskoy," said Jacqueline, in a voice as smooth as melted butter. "I could not resist the pun."

Donskoy sneered. "There is very little you resist."

"*Touché, mon cher.*"

Donskoy added, "Besides, to linger on events long past is a mark of weakness. This is a time for looking forward."

"I agree entirely," replied Jacqueline. "The future is rich with possibilities."

Marguerite wanted very much to hear more about Donskoy's history, but she decided not to press the matter. Staring at Jacqueline's young face, she could not imagine that this woman had seen anything "long past"; Jacqueline was remarkably well preserved, doubtlessly by some dark magic. Donskoy steered the conversation toward more banal topics, such as the quality of the wine, which he described as "a recent import." The feast progressed; eventually the great pig arrived. It offered an obscene amount of meat. When Marguerite commented as much, Donskoy suggested she learn to enjoy such excesses, then informed her that Zosia had a way with old flesh; it would hardly go to waste. The body of the pig went to the associates. Ljubo planted the boar's head on the lord's high table. The mouth was stuffed with the animal's own heart. As Jacqueline and Donskoy smacked their lips noisily, Marguerite sipped at her wine, trying not to meet the boar's shriveled stare.

"So, Marguerite," ventured Jacqueline. "You are from Darkon."

"Yes, from a village near Nartok."

"I've heard an interesting legend about Darkon," said Jacqueline. "Do you know it?"

"How could I," quipped Marguerite, "when you haven't described it." She felt emboldened by the wine.

"They say that Darkonian soil leeches memories from those who tread upon it too long."

"If *they* were correct, we'd all be amnesiacs."

"But how would you know?"

"I beg your pardon?"

"How does a man know what he has forgotten, after he no longer knows he knew it at all?"

"An interesting point." Marguerite paused for a moment. "But an amnesiac understands his plight because he knows what he *should* recall, even though he can't recall it."

"You two are boring me," said Donskoy. "Since when did peasant lore and superstitions become the stuff of polite discourse? I visited Darkon many times, and I remember every moment."

"And are they pleasant memories?" asked Marguerite.

Donskoy drank heavily from his goblet, then let out a sigh. "Some . . ." he murmured.

Both his companions awaited his next comment, but Donskoy had fallen silent, immersed in his own thoughts.

Jacqueline dabbed her lips, then cleaned her dagger and retired it. "Well," she said to Marguerite, "I have not visited Darkon, and I should like very much to go. I've heard that Castle Avernus, Lord Azalin's keep, holds many treasures that could turn one's head."

"No doubt," answered Marguerite dryly, thinking that Jacqueline would fit well with Azalin's reputed decadence. "But Darkon lies quite far from here. One needs the assistance of the Vistani to traverse the terrain with any certainty. And I'm not sure I could recommend the trip. My own passage was not very pleasant."

"It pains me to hear it," said Jacqueline, with only a trace of sincerity. "But then, in the hands of the gypsies, one wonders how you survived at all."

Marguerite laughed. "I understand your attitude. Yet I can't forget that it's the Vistani who brought me to Donskoy's attention. I think a few sinister caravans color the reputation of the entire race."

"You're much too generous. In my experience, the only useful caravans are those who swear fealty to gold. And Donskoy finds even their stench so strong he can barely abide it. Both he and I know just how deep the Vistani treachery can run, and what kind of misery they breed."

Donskoy slammed a fist on the table. Marguerite jumped, then stared at him, agape. The associates, who had been content to enjoy their own conversations, ceased talking as well. The hall fell silent, but for the crackling of the fire and the creaking of wood. It was as if the scene had frozen. When at last Donskoy spoke again, his voice was strained yet even. "Jacqueline," he said deeply. "You must choose your topics more carefully." His pale blue eyes had turned to ice.

Jacqueline arched a brow but said nothing. For a time, no one spoke at all. Then Donskoy excused himself from the table, saying that he would return momentarily. He strode out of the hall, and the associates resumed their rumbling.

Jacqueline smiled sweetly at Marguerite. "Touched a nerve, I guess. But he'll recover. He always does."

"What did you say to set him off?" Marguerite asked. "What treachery did he endure?"

"None but his own," said Jacqueline cryptically. She glanced furtively toward the men at the nearby tables, then leaned in close to her companion. "May I speak freely with you, Marguerite?"

"Of course." Marguerite braced herself for an indelicate comment.

Jacqueline's voice remained honey-sweet. "You think of me as a threat, do you not?"

"Why, no—"

"But you do, I fear. You think of me as some kind of competition. You mustn't, though. Donskoy desires a son. Moreover, he has become obsessed with the notion of sowing his seed on pure ground. It has been many years since I fit that description, and I can assure you, motherhood doesn't interest me in the least, nor does a permanent residence in this grim and primitive palace."

"And precisely what *are* your interests?" asked Marguerite boldly.

Jacqueline laughed. "Yes," she said. "Perhaps a

more direct approach is best. May I share a secret with you, Marguerite?"

"If it pleases you," said Marguerite cautiously. She did not trust this woman any farther than she could sneeze. And certainly any "secret" this snake-woman shared would be some kind of lie, a manipulation.

"Do you not wonder how I came here?" asked Jacqueline.

"I assume you came in a carriage."

"How quaint. Yes, of course, in a carriage. But when the mists are heavy, it's very easy to lose your way. Some time ago I acquired the means to navigate almost as well as the Vistani themselves—the means, yes, but unfortunately not the mastery. I have spent many years trying to understand my treasure, tapping the finest minds in my pursuit. Now I dare to hope my skills are improving."

"How nice for you," said Marguerite. "But I'm not sure I follow your story."

"The point is, it could be nice for you as well," replied Jacqueline.

"I beg your pardon?"

"Business, Marguerite. That is my interest. Your husband hopes to achieve a kind of spiritual renewal through you. I, on the other hand, would like to effect a more tangible renaissance—one that is measured in gold. Lord Donskoy once reveled in his business, but no more. Oh, he still dabbles, but he will never see things reach their full potential again. I, on the other hand, have both the means and the desire. Donskoy once relied on certain Vistani tribes for his mobility. Soon I could fulfill the same role, and more. All I require is his support. And of course, the benefits would flow to him as well as to you."

"Jacqueline," Marguerite protested, "I have no idea what you're talking about. And I truly think—"

"We'll talk more of this in the future," Jacqueline interrupted. She tipped her head toward the door. "When things become clearer, you may find we understand one another better."

Lord Donskoy had returned to the hall. A smile flickered across his face; the stormy mood appeared to have passed. Before returning to the head table, he stopped to talk with some of his associates.

Marguerite looked at the woman beside her, but Jacqueline did not return the glance. She was smiling sweetly in Donskoy's direction. Without turning her gaze, she said, "Are you happy here, Marguerite?"

"Yes, of course."

"And do you sleep well? No bumps in the night to awaken you?"

"I have slept well for the past two nights."

"You have heard no strange creakings, Marguerite?" Jacqueline spoke softly, and she continued to smile in Donskoy's direction. "No unearthly shadows have come to hover about your bed?"

"Nothing has disturbed my sleep," Marguerite said. She did not add that the only unearthly shadow she had seen had been lurking outside the keep, on the day she arrived. "Why do you ask?"

"No reason," Jacqueline said, still not looking at Marguerite. "I find Donskoy's castle somewhat . . . bothersome at night."

Donskoy gave a hearty laugh, then turned away from his associates. As he approached the head table, Jacqueline's smile became coy, and she leaned closer to Marguerite. "I'm glad to hear the castle treats you better than it does me," she whispered. "A good night's rest is what you need to stay fresh."

Sensing that it would not to do to probe further about Miss Montarri's troublesome nights, Marguerite sighed with exasperation. *Fresh*. Why must everyone speak as if she were a item growing stale in the pantry? Why must everyone be so eccentric?

Donskoy took his place behind the high table. "What we need now," he announced loudly, "is the entertainment!" He motioned to Ljubo, who was standing at attention near the men's tables. "Alert Ekhart," he commanded. "And fetch the hounds."

This development took Marguerite by surprise. She tried to imagine what would follow, daring to hope that the strange, somber banquet might give way to a more traditional celebration. In the castles of romantic tales, a feast never ended without the awe-inspiring turns of a juggler and acrobats, and the cheerful songs of a minstrel. Perhaps Donskoy was keeping them in the wings. Marguerite shook her head; it seemed unlikely. But what then? In Darkon's fortress Avernus, she had heard, "noble" guests often debauched themselves in the company of the castle guard, creating an obscene frenzy of pain and pleasure for the amusement of the great lord Azalin.

The door at the rear of the hall opened, and Ljubo reappeared, preceded by a hobbled beast that dragged itself forward on the ground. A leather hood concealed its head, but the rest of the body was exposed. It possessed the features of several animals, mostly bear and boar. A naked gray tail curled over its dark, bristly back. The slender rear legs, small for its immense bulk, ended in tiny hooves that clacked sharply against the smooth stone floor. The forelegs, covered by black shaggy fur, terminated in a pair of great bear paws. Its left front leg had been twisted around and bound against its flank with a barbed tether. Though Marguerite could not see the creature's face, she could hear it breathing heavily inside its hood. The nervous beast was swinging its head back and forth, from side to side.

The associates leaned forward at their tables, their eyes flickering with anticipation.

Marguerite was filled with pity and fear. "What is this abomination?" she whispered to her husband.

"Have you never seen such an animal?" Donskoy asked lightly.

"No."

"You have led such a sheltered life, my angel. This creature was a gift from a Lord Markov, a boon for a favor I once paid him. In fact, it is one of three such creatures he awarded me."

Marguerite wondered what had become of the other two, but she did not voice the question; she had no desire to hear the answer. Doubtless, she would see for herself soon enough.

Ekhart entered the room with a trio of black hounds, securely leashed. He reached forward and cut their tethers.

The hounds scrambled toward the prey. When they came within striking range, they moved slowly into position, circling. The hooded beast swung blindly. Still, it landed the first blow, drawing five red lines across a dog's shoulder. The hound did not flinch, pressing forward to receive another wound. The maneuver gave its companions opportunity; they moved in behind the beast and fixed their jaws on its hind legs. The beast turned wildly, but it was too late; its attackers had already ripped its tendons to bloody shreds.

The creature toppled, then struggled to right itself, its useless legs sliding back and forth and painting the floor with red streaks. The hounds circled, darting in to snap at the pitiful beast until the thing, too exhausted to flail at its attackers any longer, lay still and panting, its neck fully exposed.

Drooling, the dogs began to gather near the head of

their prey. The creature's great barrel of a chest heaved slowly and painfully, and Marguerite imagined she could hear its drumming heart.

Donskoy raised a hand. Ekhart whistled, freezing the hounds. Whimpering and whining, they returned to him.

"Azroth shall have the honor," announced Donskoy.

The man nearest to the high table left his seat and walked over to the beast. With his short sword, he slashed at the back of the creature's head. It was not a killing blow. As the beast writhed, Azroth snatched at the hood, now bloodied but free, and removed it.

Marguerite gasped. The creature had the head of a boar, but the eyes were unnatural—like a man's eyes, she thought. Its gaze, filled with fear and supplication, fell on her, silently pleading for mercy from the one soul who might grant it.

Marguerite winced and turned away.

She heard Azroth's sword strike again. The creature gave a sharp cry.

Marguerite did not look up, but she felt a string of moist droplets strike her face, then she saw the tiny red stains upon her gown, a spray of blood. Azroth had struck an artery.

"Sweet Marguerite." Donskoy gently wiped the blood from her face with a cloth. "So innocent and gentle. Does this sport pain you? You said yourself the creature was an abomination."

Marguerite did not offer an answer, nor, she knew, did her husband really expect one. When she looked up, Ljubo was dragging the bloody carcass from the hall.

Donskoy rose. "The feast has ended," he announced. "All hail my bride."

"Hail," droned the men, voices bare of enthusiasm.

"All hail the renewal."

They raised their palms to the ceiling and snapped their fingers.

"Come, my dear," said Donskoy. "Let us leave them. I have eaten well, but I am still ravenous." He turned to Jacqueline. "Entertain yourself as you wish. Ljubo and Ekhart will assist you in the morning."

"You are too kind," said Jacqueline. "Marguerite, it has been a pleasure to meet you."

Marguerite merely smiled.

The man who had slain the beast spoke up. "And is this all for the entertainment, then, my lord?" His voice sank low with subtle menace. "You promised us more."

Donskoy chuckled. "Yes, of course. And I have kept that promise." He nodded to Ekhart. "Show them to the dungeons." With a gracious wave, he added, "Gentle rogues, faithful friends, your prize awaits."

They filed out slowly, the men's faces twitching in childish anticipation.

Marguerite mustered the courage to ask the question that had formed in her head. "What prize awaits them, my dear husband?"

Donskoy looked at her beneath lowered lids. "That is not your concern, my dearest. You must concentrate on the prize that awaits *you*."

SEVEN

Donskoy led Marguerite to the foyer. Wicked laughter drifted up from the depths of the castle, distant and muffled. His men were enjoying their prize.

The couple crossed into the sitting room where they had first spoken. Now the hearth was cold, the black embers void of life. A small arched door lay in the corner. Donskoy withdrew a key and opened it, and with a bow and a flourish of his hand, he motioned for her to enter.

Marguerite closed her eyes and steeled herself, half-expecting to enter some chamber of horror—a gallery filled with a contorted and unnatural menagerie, stuffed yet animate; a dank closet with a soiled pallet and darkly stained manacles, where "unfresh" wives were left to rot. She swallowed hard to regain her composure; her imagination was running amuck.

As she crossed the threshold, she exhaled sharply, her relief mingled with awe. She had stepped into a strange and lovely dream, a fantasy in red. One by one, the heavy thoughts that played in the back of her mind and weighed on her spirit simply melted away—the crude men, their pox and their disease and their wicked games, her fear that Donskoy's tastes might run in similar veins. Soft opulence enveloped her.

No other room in the castle had coverings upon the stone or wood floors, save for herbs and straw, and the occasional pelt. Here in this small chamber, layers of ornate red tapestries and plush fur rugs cloaked the polished planks, leaving only the outer rim of the floor exposed. Long swaths of crimson velvet hung from the paneled walls, pooling on the dark, gleaming wood. The ceiling was low and divided into gilded squares, each housing a carved rosette, tinted scarlet. A single chandelier dangled in the center of the room. It resembled a large, ornate cage of gold filigree, imprisoning a circle of wax candles carved in the shape of doves. Long strands of red glass beads dripped from the bars of the cage like sparkling droplets of blood. They tinkled softly, stirred by the soft breeze that rushed through the open doorway.

The room was lush, lavish, and decadent, unlike any place Marguerite had ever seen.

"My private salon," murmured Donskoy. "My oasis from decay and despair. I hope it pleases you." He peeled off his jacket and tossed it thoughtlessly onto the floor.

Marguerite nodded.

"I am glad," he continued. "I do not extend the honor of a visit to just anyone."

He watched as she continued to survey the room and its furnishings—the plush red divan, stretched languidly before a pair of low round tables; the throne-like chair and stout square table sitting beside it, each resting proudly on lion's legs; the profusion of red velvet pillows scattered across the floor. A warm fireplace glowed on the left side of the room, with a chimney and a golden hood to keep back the smoke. An exotic water pipe rested on the floor nearby, its glass bowls red and as round as a spider's abdomen, the long hose coiled beside it like a patient black snake with a slim silver head. A row of white marble pedestals stood along the opposite wall—the kind that displayed busts in a gallery, though they were headless at present. On the rear wall loomed a fruitwood cabinet with gleaming inlaid panels and carved rosettes that echoed the pattern in the ceiling. Marguerite realized she had seen similar designs once before, though in a smaller piece—a chest her father had imported from Lamordia, a northern land noted for its craftsmanship.

Donskoy settled himself on the floor beside the water pipe, lighting it with a slender stick from the fire.

"Sit." He motioned toward the divan. "And let yourself relax."

She obeyed, at least the first command. His second wish would be harder met.

Donskoy pressed the tip of the black hose to his lips, inhaling deeply. Marguerite stared. When he exhaled, she noticed that the silver tip was shaped like the head of a cobra; the artisan, too, had envisioned a serpent and conjured its likeness.

"Have you never seen a hookah?" Donskoy asked.

Marguerite shook her head.

"It comes from Sri Raji."

Marguerite had never heard of this place. "It sounds exotic."

"More like a steaming pit. I no longer travel abroad, of course, but it is one place I do not miss. There is a small present on the table before you," said Donskoy. "You may open it."

On the table rested a silver tray with a decanter of plum brandy-wine and two blood-red goblets. Beside the tray lay a small, square black bundle. Marguerite picked up the package and released the gold cord that bound it. The silk wrapping fell away to expose another shimmering cord and another ebony layer. Beneath it lay yet another. Donskoy smiled with amusement as she peeled away the wrapping, venturing ever deeper. At last, she held a small, square wooden box, lacquered and gleaming. It appeared to have no lid.

"How do I get inside?" she asked.

"Try," he responded smoothly, taking another deep draft from the pipe.

She wrestled with the impenetrable block, stroking and prodding, shaking it lightly and pondering its muffled rattle. She searched its surfaces repeatedly for any sign of a hinge or latch.

"It is a puzzle," he added.

"So I gathered," she said, her stomach fluttering like an excited child's. She struggled for several minutes. Then it dawned on her that this might be some kind of test, which she might be failing. Her brow furrowed at the thought.

"Perhaps I am glad you cannot open it," Donskoy said gently. "It marks you as without guile."

He took the box from her hands and fondled it until it slid it apart in two pieces, one cantilevered over the other. Then he returned it to her hand.

Nestled in the bottom half was a brooch—a circle of gold, two arms bound by an entwining ribbon, upon which a message was inscribed.

"What does it mean?" she asked.

"Forever," he said darkly, as if making it so.

"It's beautiful. Shall I put it on?"

"Please do."

She pressed the pin through the bodice of her gown, and as it emerged from the other side, it pierced her fingertip. She gave a little squeak, then lifted the finger to her lips, but Donskoy was faster—moving to her hand and taking it in his own gloved grasp.

"Allow me," he said, gently sucking the blood from her wound. "You taste so sweet."

Despite herself, she blushed, and her jaw tensed.

"But you are too cold," he added. "Your hands are like ice. I can feel it even through my gloves." He reached for the decanter of wine, filling the glass. He settled back into the cushions beside the water pipe and gazed upon her, continuing his smoke.

His stare was unsettling. Marguerite could almost see the busy whirl of thoughts behind his eyes, but she could not read them. They sat quietly. She sipped the wine, then gazed at the small hands wrapped around the glass, her skin smooth and blue-white. What is he waiting for? she thought. Though she felt no desire for him, she did, at least, desire the consummation. The silence was palpable, swelling around her. A log erupted on the fire. The sparks drifted like red falling stars onto the hearth, dying on impact.

"The brooch is beautiful," she offered at last, aware that she had repeated herself. "Thank you."

Donskoy made a little ring with his lips and blew out a slow, long puff of smoke. "As are you," he said from beneath hooded lids. He drew his tongue across the silver tip of the hose. "Drink the wine and let me look at you. It is not necessary to speak."

Marguerite shifted uncomfortably.

"Recline, if you would," he murmured.

She put down the wine glass and pulled her legs up onto the divan, nestling her back against a pillow. Donskoy threw another log onto the fire; the edges of his fine linen shirt reflected the flame, defining his silhouette with a faint red glow.

He kept his back to her, still facing the hearth. "I do not wish you to be anxious," he said. "I cannot tolerate an unwilling wife. I have had my fill of it. Do you understand?" His voice was low and level, yet it carried a desperate, nervous note. Perhaps that was it: he was nervous. She could not read him.

"Yes," she said quietly. She retrieved her glass and sipped at the wine.

"I will not make the same mistake twice," he muttered, slumping onto the pillows. Still, he did not look at her.

In time, he repeated, "I will not make the same mistake twice. To drag a black-haired hellion into my bed only to see her cold and withered, spewing bile at my touch. I dreamed she would yield in time. Beware of your dreams, Marguerite, for they shall lead you into the deepest pits of despair."

He shifted and stared at the ceiling, attached to his pipe as if it were a lifeline. He seemed unaware of her presence entirely.

"It had to be done," he said firmly, eyes red and swollen. "And I was . . . " He laughed sourly, then coughed, choking. ". . . triumphant." His eyes rolled; the whites rose like twin moons. "Perhaps . . . "

He was long silent after that, apparently drifting, asleep, though his eyes remained partly open. Marguerite wondered how much she could trust his delirium. An hour passed, and she too began to flirt with unconsciousness. She shook herself awake and studied Donskoy's still body, then realized she could not make out the rise and fall of his chest. Suddenly it occurred to her that he might be dead. A short marriage, after all. And then what?

She walked to his side, gently nudging him. "My lord?" she said softly.

He gasped and flung an arm across his brow as if to shield it from a blow. His eyes widened, white with terror. "Who goes there?" he rasped. His face had twisted into a hideous mask, contorted beyond recognition.

"Your wife," she whispered with alarm.

"So!" he hissed. "The wretched succubus returns. See what you have wrought!" He snared her wrist in a crushing grip and bared his teeth wildly, as if ready to attack. She winced and struggled to wrench free.

"Lord Donskoy," she pleaded. She knew he did not see her. "It is I, Marguerite."

The white blaze slowly faded from his eyes, and his entire countenance melted into a boyish grin. "Ah, Marguerite," he said lightly, as if they had just encountered one another on some bucolic garden path. "Have I been neglecting you?"

She shook her head, dazed by pity and fear, massaging her tender wrist.

He winked. "Ah, but I think I have." He reached up and took her hand again gently, drawing it to his face and inhaling. Then he tugged playfully at her dress. "Come, Marguerite. Come and lie down beside me."

Reluctantly, she stretched out at his side. He removed her slippers, then smoothed the fabric of her dress over her body and surveyed her slowly with his eyes—following the long rise of her legs, the gentle curve of her stomach, her chest rising and falling in short, rapid breaths. He turned and lifted the tip of his hookah toward her mouth. When she turned away, he took a draught from the pipe himself and leaned over her, sealing her lips with his. Then he slowly exhaled, filling her lungs with warm smoke. Marguerite choked and coughed, her throat burning with the acrid fumes.

He lifted his head. "Are you nervous?" he asked softly, pressing his hand to her chest. "Your heart beats like a rabbit's."

"No," she replied. "I am not."

His hand slid left, fingers working like a blind man reading runes. "Does this please you?"

"Yes." It was not entirely a lie. Her head had begun

to swim out to sea, while her body was taking another trip entirely.

He smiled. "It pleases me as well." His fingers toyed with the brooch on the dress. "And did my present entertain you?"

She hesitated, unsure of his meaning. "The brooch is very beautiful."

"What I mean to ask . . . is whether you enjoyed the unwrapping."

She nodded.

"Then you won't mind if I share in your pleasure. Shall I unwrap *my* gift now?"

"Oh," Marguerite said, feeling stupid, "but I have nothing for you."

Donskoy chortled. "Oh," he mocked, "but you are sorely mistaken."

He freed the brooch from her gown and gently flicked his thumb over the pin's sharp point. She looked down, wide-eyed, to see him plant the point in the valley of her breasts, poised at the edge of the gown's neckline. He gently lifted her chin with his free hand. "Close your eyes, Marguerite," he said, touching his soft black fingertips to her lids. "And trust." He slid his suede fingers to her mouth. "Close your lips and listen."

She heard a faint scratching sound as the edge of her gown bit into the nape of her neck and pressed into her collarbone. Then the fabric popped, releasing its grip, and a sharp point defined a tingling path from her sternum to her navel. When Donskoy lifted his hand from her lips, the dress lay open across her torso as if flayed apart. Her chest looked strangely wrinkled and white in the gap. Then she realized that it was not her own flesh she saw. The final layer of silk—barely perceptible in the dim light—still lay intact against her skin.

Donskoy tossed the brooch carelessly aside and

began to peel away the gown. He worked slowly and methodically, layer by layer. She closed her eyes again, lulled by the hypnotic hiss of his breath. The final layer clung to the hollows of her shape as if it had taken root; his gloved fingers picked gingerly at the edges of the silk, then rolled the fabric away with firm, even strokes. He continued to knead her muscles well after the dress had gone, beginning with her fingers and arms, then turning to her feet and working slowly up her legs until she imagined her own skin would start to peel away willingly. She moaned and stretched like a cat.

He slid his cheek over her body. "So sweet," he murmured. "And so fresh."

She heard a giggle, then realized it was her own. Donskoy removed his clothes—all but the black gloves. Then he proceeded to move over her anew with agonizing slowness, leaving no inch unexplored. He took her hand and gnawed softly on her fingertips, then traced a path up her arm with his tongue. At the tender white crux of her elbow, he lingered, lapping like a kitten at bowl of cream. She shuddered.

"My just desserts," he murmured. He chuckled at his own pun.

Marguerite turned her head toward the hearth and watched the flames licking at the wood, as Donskoy was at her. She grew hot as the coals.

A soft tinkling drifted to her ear like some magical summons. Slowly and of its own accord, her head turned toward the sound. The red beads quivered in the chandelier. One great crystal hung from the bottom; it turned to and fro, flashing rhythmically, pulling Marguerite into its grasp. She looked down and saw her body far below, saw herself and Donskoy, entwined and merging, like angry snakes, writhing before the fire. Without warning, she spiraled downward, plunging into the core of her flesh as if it were a pool and she were a stone. Once there, she found she was not alone. She twisted sensuously under the invader's assault, returning each onslaught in kind.

Her mouth was dry, her throat parched. Donskoy's black hands trampled over her slick skin like furtive animals, like hounds hot for the fox. No longer soft, they seemed hard and sharp, lightly scratching her skin.

"Milos . . ." she moaned.

A dark growl of pleasure echoed through the room. Marguerite could not tell from whose lips it came.

* * * * *

Marguerite awoke to find Donskoy's body cupped around hers.

"A son is made," he murmured against her neck.

She wondered how he could be certain, though of course she did not voice her doubts. She was silent, feigning sleep. The past hours were a blur, recalled like changing weather—cool, then hot, then cool again. Memories scurried forward to be acknowledged, but she brushed them aside. Her head throbbed, still poisoned by the wine and the smoke.

After a moment Donskoy rose and groaned, stretching before the fire. Then he proceeded to dress himself. "Arise, my fair one," he said dramatically. "For methinks you are not sleeping."

Marguerite rolled over and reached for her dress, then saw the pile of fabric, shredded and faintly pink. She sat up, drawing a small fur rug around her shoulders. Donskoy was adjusting his gloves. He went to the cupboard and unlocked it, then opened the doors just a sliver, withdrawing a red gown from the dark slit between them. He tossed the gown over to Marguerite and relocked the cabinet, returning the key to his pocket.

"My gift to a deserving wife," he said simply. He bent to kiss her, pushing away the pelt. "My very deserving wife."

She smiled feebly.

"Raise your hands, and I will dress you."

He slipped the silk gown over her head. When the dress encased her, and the brooch ornamented its neckline, Donskoy led Marguerite to the door and locked it behind them, then escorted her to her chamber. She leaned on his arm for support, wondering if he intended to share her bed. They did not speak until they reached their goal.

"Sleep well," he said, kissing her softly on the cheek. "I shall see you in the morning."

Marguerite's question had been answered. She found herself relieved.

She stepped across the threshold and turned to close the door, but it was already shut. A key rattled in the lock, securing her for the night.

EIGHT

Heavy-headed, Marguerite crossed to the hearth, her red gown rustling as she walked. The dress was a little long and snug through the shoulders, but otherwise splendid—worth a peasant's wages for half a year, an extravagance that should have thrilled any girl of parochial roots. And it did please her. But thrill? No more than trying on a garment that was merely borrowed. She went to the wash basin and splashed her face with cool water, then patted her skin dry.

In Marguerite's absence, Yelena had tended the chamber. The fire was freshly stoked, the wooden tub gone. The desiccated flowers had been planted in a vase, and a steaming pot of tea sat on the table. She lifted the lid and sniffed; the brew smelled of blackberries and honey. As prisons went, hers was not without its comforts.

Marguerite poured herself some of the tea and sank into a chair before the fire. So this is how it ends, she thought—her wedding day, the event she had so long anticipated. She shut her eyes and let a few fragmented images drift across the black field behind her lids: the strange ritual with the dark egg, the brilliant flashes from the stained-glass windows, the fountain of blood from the fallen beast. And, finally, the consummation in the red salon, an event recalled more by her body than her mind. Her chest flushed at the memory, and her thighs tightened. The occasion was hardly the "impersonal rite" that her mother had steeled her to expect; but then, Donskoy's castle held many surprises.

Marguerite wondered if his first wife—the "black-haired hellion" he had murmured about in the salon—had endured a similar wedding day. Obviously, the tragedy of the woman's death still haunted Donskoy—and after twenty or thirty years? Marguerite would not understand her husband until she knew more about his first wife's death, however horrible or incriminating that might be. Only then could they hope to mold a future together; otherwise, Donskoy would forever remain the strange mercurial master, while she played his well-kept prisoner, some kind of prize purchased solely for breeding. In a castle with so few friendly faces, it was a lonely prospect.

Wearily, Marguerite went to the bed to draw back the covers, then stayed her hand. In the hollow at the center of the soft mattress, there was a slight swelling where something lay hidden beneath the embroidered counterpane. The lump shifted. Marguerite stepped back. She drew in her breath, watching as the swollen mass approached the edge of the bed, moving slowly beneath the woolen cover. Then the mass stopped. Marguerite stood beside the bed, immobile. The thing remained frozen as well.

Marguerite had faced this kind of thing before. "All right, you," she breathed, grabbing the poker from beside the fire. "No vermin tonight. No errant cats, no overgrown rats, no—"

She whipped off the counterpane. There sat Griezell,

Zosia's queenly toad, black and shining against the white linens. It gazed at her slyly with its enormous, protruding eyes. Zosia's words in the garden drifted back to her: *Some say a bed filled with toads ensures conception, especially on the wedding night.*

Marguerite cursed. "Tell your mistress her joke isn't funny. Besides, you're late. You should've been waiting in Donskoy's salon, though I'll bet you haven't got the nerve."

Griezell blinked, and Marguerite imagined the creature's wide slit of a mouth lifted subtly to form a smile. She let out a tired laugh.

"Well, as I told your mistress, I do not bed with toads." Grimacing, she poked at the creature's cool, dry hide. The gleaming bumps rippled under the poker's touch. "Off," she commanded. "Off and out. How did you get in here in the first place?"

Griezell did not budge.

"Fine. You're a toad, after all. Perhaps you're too stupid to understand me."

Griezell's throat swelled, forming a huge goiter. With its broad mouth slightly parted, the toad emitted a horrid, reverberant rasp—long, deep, and hoarse. It reminded Marguerite of a death rattle, or of an old man clearing phlegm from his lungs.

"That's enough," she snapped in disgust. "You probably do understand, and I wouldn't be surprised if Zosia understands you in turn. So you can tell her I am not amused."

Marguerite returned the poker to its place, then picked up the toad with arms stiffly outstretched. The spaniel-sized creature hissed and paddled, and if it had wanted to, it could have wriggled from her arms or drawn blood with its claws. But the toad had bowed to her authority, at least for now. She carried Griezell-bub toward the door. Then she remembered the click of the key—Donskoy had locked her in.

Griezell made another goiter and rasped, this time breaking the hoarse sound into short, staccato rattles. Like laughter. Marguerite gasped and dropped the toad at once. Griezell hissed, then shambled toward one of the tapestries flanking the fireplace. With twenty hounds and a frightened fox looking on, the toad disappeared into the wall. Marguerite wondered whether the little black beast had the fabled ability to teleport—moving from one place to another without actually traversing the space between. Either that, or it had become insubstantial, a specter. Unless . . .

Marguerite heard the faint sound of stone scraping against stone. She cautiously stepped toward the tapestry, half-expecting some kind of trap to be sprung. The cloth wavered softly, teasing her, then settled.

She stared at the wall. Every sinew in her suddenly reawakened, tense with excitement. If her guess was correct, the wall had opened to permit Griezell's passage. There was a secret door, just like the one in Zosia's garden. Then she recalled how the old woman had spoken a word to shift that portal, a magical command. If such a thing were required here, Marguerite was lost. But it couldn't be; Griezellbub did not speak, did he? And the toad had gone through.

"Griezell." She shook her head. Did she really think it would answer?

Marguerite picked up a piece of kindling from the stack beside the hearth, then put the end of the stick to the tapestry, poking the belly of a hound. Nothing happened. She poked again, then walked to the side of the heavy fabric, lifting the edge. Behind it lay the wall, firm and stony, seemingly impenetrable. Seemingly, she repeated to herself.

A faint scrabbling and hissing drifted out from the

cover of the tapestry.

"Griezellbub," she repeated. "Show me how."

Her answer came—the scrabbling again, so soft she might have imagined it.

Marguerite went to the edge of the tapestry and slipped into the black sliver of space behind it, sliding flat along the wall until she came to the place where she thought Griezell had disappeared. The heavy cloth pressed against her back. It smelled musty and blocked the light completely, making her nose burn, her eyes blind. She ran her hands over the wall, searching for some kind of latch. There was none. She continued to probe, stretching high, then low, covering every spot she could reach. After several minutes, the weight and the sour stench of the tapestry became unbearable; she imagined herself pressed flat like a flower in an old book, slowly dying between its mildewed pages. Gasping, she slipped out from beneath the shroud and returned to the room. Mold and clotted strands of cobwebs clung to her head like a newborn's caul. She went to the basin and rinsed her face, pulling the worst of the dregs from her hair. Then she returned to the wall and stared at it. The creatures in the scene stared back.

She heard another muffled hiss, impatient and sharp.

To follow a toad, must I be one? she thought. She crouched at the base of the tapestry, which hovered just above the floor. Here, the sound of Griezell's hissing became acute. She lifted the bottom of the rank silk. Blocks of gray stone confronted her.

Something glistened in the candlelight—a tiny pool at the base of a stone. It was as if the rock were weeping, or perhaps drooling. She pressed hard on the surface of this block. It gave way, and an opening appeared, barely an arm's length high, equally

narrow. Beyond lay the black, snakelike throat of a
tunnel. Griezell's insistent little hiss echoed in the
darkness. Marguerite stared in, hesitating. The door
slid shut, narrowly missing her head.

Heart drumming, half with fear and half with
anticipation, she rose and swiftly retrieved a candle
from the table, fitting it with a guard against drafts.
Then she retrieved a second candle, unlit, and
slipped it into her garter. She looked around the
room. Will I need a third? she wondered. After all,
she mustn't be caught in the dark. But if either
candle blew out in a gust, she would have no way to
relight it. No time to hesitate, she told herself. No
time. Griezell might not wait.

Armed with the small fire, she opened the passage
again and crawled inside, pushing the candle ahead of
her as she went. Her progress was slow and discomforting. She yanked the skirt of her gown up toward
the neck and tucked it into the bodice so her knees
were free. Her woolen hose tore on the stones. After
the third bend in the tunnel, she saw a wall looming
ahead. Griezell huddled at the base. The creature
turned to face her, flashing a row of sharp little teeth,
dripping with drool. Then it pushed at a stone, trigger-
ing another door, and went on.

The door closed before Marguerite could reach it. At
the base of the wall lay a little puddle of Griezell's
saliva to mark the spot. She pressed upon the stone's
cool surface, and a door opened in the same fashion
as the last. Marguerite emerged in the space beyond.
She stood slowly, ignoring the complaint of her
cramped limbs. Her skirts escaped from her bodice
and dropped to the floor.

She found herself in a chamber shaped like her
own, but it was smaller and ruined, her room's still-
born twin. The crumbling hearth pitted the opposite

wall like a black, empty wound. Tattered, filthy sheets clung to the modest furnishings. The bed stood completely naked, stripped of the mattress, curtains gone from the spires. The rope supports had been gnawed or rotted and now hung limply to the floor. In the outer wall rose a tall, thin window, bare of glass. The broken shutter hung crazily askew. A sliver of moonlight pushed past it, cutting a white path across the floor. In its glow lay a heap of leaves and dirty rags. Something wiggled inside it. Marguerite thrust her candle forth like a weapon. A mouse squealed on the mound, then scurried away, abandoning a nest of writhing pink babies, hairless and blind.

Griezell sat beside the chamber door, hissing impatiently. The creature was right; this was only part of the journey, not a fitting end. As if to confirm her conclusion, a cold, wet breeze slunk in through the open window. She shivered, then strode to the door and yanked. It gave way noisily, and the toad and the woman went out together.

In the hall outside, Marguerite paused to listen, afraid she might have alerted someone to her escape. But no footsteps came. The castle was quiet. She heard only a few distant creaks, the moaning of old wood.

A wave of excitement washed over her. Moments ago she had been a prisoner, powerless and small. The rest of the castle had loomed all around, taunting her with its forbidden mass. Now she had mastered one of its secret arteries—a passage that Donskoy would never show her, even if he fulfilled his promise of a castle tour. And Yelena or Zosia—would they too have kept her ignorant of this escape? It didn't matter. Soon, she mused, she would discover more of the castle on her own. In this way, she might eventually come to possess it—not by right, of course, but in spirit. While her husband and the others slept, she could stroll the keep as its haughty mistress instead of its simpering captive.

Marguerite took a moment to orient herself. Her own room, she thought, was somewhere to the left. Griezell hissed again and hobbled off to the right, then disappeared around a turn in the passage.

Marguerite hesitated, wary of following a creature most likely Zosia's familiar, and her confidence ebbed. Still, in the wake of her bravado there remained a bit of courage. And, even stronger, her curiosity. Marguerite hurried after her bumpy black guide, one hand lifting her skirt to keep from tripping, the other firmly clutching the candle.

The toad traveled remarkably fast. It moved at the edge of her sight or just beyond, a teasing shape along the wall. They came to a tower stair and descended its winding path. Cold gusts poured through a series of arrow slits in the exterior wall. Marguerite turned her back to them and held the candle low, wishing she had thought to bring a shawl. The red gown left her shoulders and the top of her spine exposed. Further, its layered skirt was awkward and noisy, swishing as she walked. But there had been no time to don anything else.

Marguerite followed Griezell turn after turn down the stairs, descending until she grew dizzy. She stopped suddenly, as a torch, blazing somewhere below, hurled Griezell's silhouette against the wall. The shadow looked immense and looming, a horrible hunchbacked monster. Just as quickly, it shrank and disappeared. Marguerite walked after it. When she passed the torch, she saw that the flame was actually quite weak; soon it would burn out. It stood guard before a door. She wondered where the door led and pressed her ear against it, discerning nothing. Then she hurried after Griezell.

In time they came to a second door, small and arched. With the toad's yellow eyes upon her, Marguerite lifted the stiff latch and put her shoulder against the wood. Reluctantly, it gave way, opening into another passage. This soon led to yet another door, which opened onto another stair in the labyrinth, leading down still farther. Before she descended, Marguerite mentally counted the landmarks they had passed. She hoped no one had heard her progress. It dawned on her that a danger lay in wandering too far, where no one could hear her cries if she were injured and in need of help. Still, she went down. . . .

She felt as if she were descending into the depths of the Abyss itself. From the distance came the sound of water, churning and lapping: the Styx, perhaps, she wondered. The air grew more stale. It seemed to push and pull at her body in long, pestilent drafts, as if the castle were slowly breathing.

At last the stair ended, intersecting a passage with rough-hewn walls that extended both left and right. Marguerite lifted her candle in each direction. The passage was short, ending with an ironbound door at either end. Griezellbub was nowhere in sight. She paused, listening for the toad's familiar hiss, the gruesome rasp. Nothing. Griezell had vanished.

Marguerite considered turning back, then laughed at herself. It was not as if the toad were a comforting companion or a capable bodyguard. What difference did it make if Griezell had gone? No doubt the creature was seeking a meal. And here in the depths, Marguerite could seek something else—something that would offer clues to Donskoy's history, or to that of his dead wife: the castle crypts.

She turned right and ventured through the first door. The chamber beyond smelled of copper and mildew.

She lifted her candle, startling a rat, which squealed
and fled to the shelter of a dark corner. The trappings
of a torture chamber sprang into being around her. To
Marguerite's relief, they seemed in disuse. She
recalled her vision of Donskoy's associates after the
banquet. If torture had been their final bout of "entertainment," it had not occurred here. A large, broken
cage dangled from the ceiling in one corner. Immediately below it lay a blackened fire pit, bare of coals.
An empty rack stretched nearby. Rusty chains and
broken shackles hung from the walls; below them, the
floor was dark. In the far corner she spied a stout
wooden table. An assortment of implements rested
upon it—pocked blades, rusty pliers, bent picks.
Among them were two metal collars, each with
screws for tightening. Sharp spikes lined the inner surface of the bands. Without thinking, Marguerite put a
hand to her throat to protect it.

Beyond the table lay another door. Marguerite
approached it cautiously, then pulled hard. It refused
to open. Something cold seeped into the bottom of
her slipper, and she looked down, discovering a dark
ooze bleeding across the threshold. Hastily she
plucked up her skirt and stepped away. The muck
could be anything—and she had no desire to see it
more clearly. She left the torture chamber and went
down the hall, past the stairs and through the age-
darkened door at the opposite end.

In this room, the walls presented an orderly patch-
work of marble panels stacked one atop the other. In
the center rose a series of rectangular biers, upon
which knights and ladies, carved from stone, lay
sleeping. Marguerite had found the crypt.

She held out her candle and let its flickering light
illuminate the panels of the tombs. Names slid past in
the darkness: Serboinu, Petelengro, Lafuente . . . ,

with dates from centuries long past. In the corner was the tiny stone tomb of an infant. The cover lay on the floor, smashed into a hundred pieces, the small cavity that it had once covered now empty of anything save spiders and dust.

Marguerite moved slowly down the wall, shining her candle upon the name of each occupant. There were many similar surnames, though her husband's was not among them. This did not surprise her greatly; Lord Donskoy had acquired the keep, and his ancestors rested elsewhere. Still, she hoped to come across at least one that bore his surname, one that would list the given name of his first wife—no one in the castle spoke it in Marguerite's hearing, as though merely saying it were enough to earn the lord's wrath. Perhaps, if she were fortunate, the crypt might even have an epitaph that suggested the nature of the woman's tragic death.

Marguerite was nearing the end of the wall when the crypt of "Lord Vladimir Vatrashki" caught her eye.

Cold is this Bed which I Do yet Love,
For 'tis not as Cold as the Ones Above.

She furrowed her brow and moved on.

The next crypt read, "Valeska Donskoy. Home Forever." Marguerite's flesh went chill. In such a dank and dark place, the epitaph read more like a pronouncement of punishment than a lament of grief or love, and she found herself wondering how carefully Donskoy had considered the words before having them struck onto his wife's tomb. There was nothing else, not even the customary dates of birth and death, as though anyone laying eyes on the crypt was expected to know the particulars of Valeska's life.

Marguerite stood before the sepulcher for many

moments, holding her candle close to the cover, as though she might learn more of her predecessor by simply staring at the name. After a time, the darkness of the tomb began to close in around her, a crushing presence—and she realized that the vault was not as silent as it should have been.

As in the torture chamber she had visited earlier, this room had another door in the back wall. From behind this barrier, so muffled and soft that Marguerite could not even hear it if she breathed too loudly, came a gentle purl of water. Curious as to the cause of the sound, she went to the door and pulled it open.

The space beyond seemed a part of the land itself, a cavern with rough walls of basalt. Only the smooth stone steps leading down from the door had been carved by man. Below, a small black stream snaked lazily across the floor, its surface slowly churning at each broad turn. Marguerite descended. From somewhere far above came a soft wind, moaning down from a deep recess in the jagged ceiling. She remembered the pit that Ekhart had warned her about inside the castle's main entrance, and his warning about the demise of "impatient" invaders. Perhaps this was the bottom.

Marguerite reached the foot of the stairs and followed a path of sloping stone along the edge of the dark water. The stream seemed to end at the wall ahead, though she could tell by the swirling currents that it simply sank beneath the rock and continued to flow. She turned to retrace her steps, and saw a shape floating toward her, bobbing in the water. A log, perhaps. She held forth the light.

Then she screamed.

It was a woman's body, lying face down in the water. Marguerite regained her composure, letting a faint hiss escape her lips. She stepped closer to observe the corpse. Stop quivering, she admonished herself. The dead can cause no harm. Unbidden, her vampiric suitor from Azalin's *kargat* came to mind, and she added aloud, "Those who are *truly* dead, at any rate."

The corpse's long black hair swirled around her head like a nest of shining eels. The dark strands contrasted starkly with the woman's thin white blouse, which clung to her swarthy flesh in shreds, held in place by a tight purple corset. The cadaver's arms, cloaked in billowing sleeves, were spread wide like the wings of an angel. A delicate web of chains and coins defined her narrow waist, from which red and green silks swirled about her like scarves. The livid feet were bare, the ankles circled in gold.

A Vistana, thought Marguerite. But how did her body get here?

She looked again at the stream's slow currents. Of course. This was an underground river, or at least its branch. The gypsy must have begun her journey upstream. Perhaps she had even come from another land, eventually drifting to this natural tomb. How ironic that the nomad's final journey had occurred after death.

Marguerite thought briefly about what she could do. Alert someone, and let them know of her own wanderings? Certainly not. Attend to the body alone? Equally distasteful. And even if she had the fortitude to drag a corpse out of the water and bury it herself, the Vistani had their own customs. A "proper" funeral meant something else to them entirely.

The water gurgled, and the body slowly began to roll over. Marguerite watched with lurid fascination. It must be the release of internal gases, she thought. She had read of that once. Still, she took a few steps back.

When the gypsy's body rolled onto its back, Marguerite's mouth dropped open. She had steeled herself for the worst—a bloated face, a bobbing eye loosely tethered to its socket, a long, pale worm wriggling free of an orifice. After all, death held no vanity. But the Vistana remained beautiful, extraordinarily preserved. Indeed, she looked as though she were sleeping upon a black, watery bed. The corpse's soft bosom rose and fell with the swells of water, and her lips seemed full and ripe. The eyes began to move slowly beneath the woman's long-lashed lids, like a dreamer's. Marguerite pressed forward with her candle. It must be a trick of the light. Without warning, the woman's eyes flew open, locking their abyssal gaze on Marguerite.

Marguerite froze, suddenly paralyzed. Her mouth fell open, and she felt a cry welling up inside her—but no scream came. A motion flickered at the edge of her awareness; the woman's hand was rising out of the water, the long fingers uncurling slowly, opening like a flower.

Marguerite jerked back, screaming. She turned and fled, shielding her candle with her hand as she climbed the stair. Too frightened to look back even after she reached the top, she rushed into the crypts and slammed the door shut. She would have barred it, had there been the means.

Instead, she scurried past Valeska's crypt, through the tomb and out into the hall, also closing this door behind her. Only then did she stop to breathe, pressing her back to the wood as if to bar it. Her chest heaved like a bellows. Her candle flickered madly, filling the hallway with spasms of light.

Wait, she told herself. What if the woman is alive? Marguerite could not imagine someone surviving a journey through an underground stream, but neither could she imagine a drowned corpse raising a hand to gesture at her.

Perhaps the Vistana needed help. If that were so, Marguerite couldn't abandon her. Guilt would haunt her forever—if not the woman herself. Marguerite pressed her ear to the door but heard only the silence of crypts beyond.

She had to know. She put her hand to the latch and lifted it, then gingerly pushed the door open—just a crack. Nothing happened. What had she expected? Her mind was playing tricks on her; she had only imagined the open eyes, the fixed stare, the dead woman's subtle, welcoming smile. . . . Maybe, just maybe, Marguerite had imagined the entire body. After all, Donskoy had forced his hookah smoke upon her; who knew what effects it might have had? Perhaps she had experienced a kind of strange waking dream, brought on by the hookah and the foul dungeon air.

Marguerite pinched herself hard and winced. Then she opened the door and slowly retraced her steps through the crypt. She paused by Valeska's tomb to gather her courage. The sound of her own breathing echoed through the vault. She clenched her jaw and opened the next door, then stepped onto the stair, holding her candle out toward the dark stream.

There was no corpse, at least not where Marguerite could see. Grinding her teeth, she descended the stair, then walked along the bank until she had inspected the entire surface of the small stream. The woman was gone.

Perhaps the body had been caught by a current and dragged downstream. Else it had been sucked under the surface and now lingered somewhere below, waiting for its chance to re-emerge. Marguerite didn't like the thought of that. She turned to leave.

When she came to the top of the stair, she saw that

the door had swung shut, though she couldn't recall the sound. No matter; she put her shoulder to the wood and pushed. It held fast. Frantic, she pushed again. Then she laughed. She reached for the latch and pushed a third time. The door swung open with ease. As she stepped past and closed it from the other side, she felt something cold on the back of her hand. It was a sticky black fluid, dripping from the door in a sort of pattern. The pattern looked vaguely familiar— three lines slanting down to the left, running parallel until they intersected a fourth. Like three lines of wind-driven rain, striking the ground. What was it—a devil's mark? And who had left it? Had someone lurked here in this room while she explored beyond? Could Griezell have made such a sign? She raised her candle, scanning the vault around her, but she was alone; only the epitaphs of the dead shone in the light.

Marguerite rubbed the ooze on her skirt. Then she hurried from the tombs, scurrying up out of dungeon and into the keep proper, up the winding stairs, past the low-burning torch now hissing and spitting black smoke. She came to the dismal room with the nest of blind mice and the secret passage to her own locked chamber, then winced at the loud creak as she opened the door and went inside. Crouching beside the stone wall, she searched for the trigger. The passage opened, and she went through, emerging at last in her own room. All the candles still burned in their holders, a dozen warm buds of light. The fire crackled in the hearth. The chamber seemed warm and welcoming. Even safe.

Marguerite caught her reflection in the mirror. The scarlet dress was soiled and torn. Moreover, her hair was slightly singed; she could smell its bitter scent. She must have been careless. She set down the offending candle and peeled off her soiled gown, then remembered the spare candle in her garter. It was gone. No matter; a stray candle was hardly incriminating. She pulled a shawl around her chemise, then put a kettle on the fire and began combing the cobwebs from her hair. She stared at the red silken heap on the floor. Maybe Yelena could save the dress. And if Donskoy asked her to wear it again tomorrow? Well, she couldn't.

Marguerite picked up the rumpled gown and stuffed it into the back of her wardrobe cabinet. Her hand met something square and solid. The book. She had forgotten it completely. In the cabinet lay the fire-scarred manuscript titled *Van Richten's Guide to the Vistani*, still wrapped in its black shroud, where she had hidden it just before Ekhart arrived to take her to the chapel.

She extracted the parcel and carried it to the hearth, laying it on the table beside her favorite chair. Then she took the kettle off the fire, filled her wash basin, and scrubbed the grime from her hands and face. A strange noise, like the flutter of bird wings, sounded behind her. She turned and saw *Van Richten's Guide* lying open, its pages turning as though stirred by a draft.

But the air in her chamber was still.

Marguerite drew in a short gasp, then stepped over to the charred tome. The wash cloth slipped from her trembling hand. On the sooty page before her lay a section marked "tralaks." At the top was a square enclosing a dot: *marked by lord*. Below it was the sigil she had seen in the crypt, three lines intersecting the ground. The caption beside it read: *cursed*.

Her stomach knotted in fear.

It was no coincidence that Griezell had shown her the way to the crypts, then disappeared. Someone had meant her to encounter the body, to see the sigil, to find its meaning in this book. But who? And was she the one cursed? She had done nothing to deserve such a fate. Perhaps Destiny had singled her out with its bony, pointing finger. Perhaps . . .

Cursed.

She crawled into bed and pulled the covers up to her neck. Sleep would not come easily.

NINE

Marguerite slept fitfully, turning in her bed until her body had dug itself a linen grave. She dreamed of a Vistana, a black-haired hellion, who opened her coal-dark eyes and rose from the icy stream deep beneath the castle. Slowly the woman came, a dark goddess ascending, drifting up the stairs and gliding through the halls until at last she stood outside Marguerite's door. Mere wood could not prevent the gypsy's passage; she entered. Her red lips parted, whispering words in soft, even measure: *The seed he has sown.* She raised her white, slender finger toward Marguerite, who lay paralyzed in her bed. *The seed he has sown shall seal his damnation.* And the apparition came nearer, with arms outstretched, slipping over Marguerite's body like a cold, black shadow, sealing her in a tomb.

* * * * *

"Marguerite."

The voice came to her from above, from nowhere, deep and commanding.

"Marguerite, you must rise."

She struggled to lift herself from the depths. Her eyes fluttered open, and she squinted at the light. It was morning. The curtains on the right side of her bed had been parted, and Lord Donskoy loomed in the gap.

"Good morning," he said brightly. He was smiling. "Rise, my fair one. I have summoned Zosia to look after your welfare."

"My welfare?" Marguerite asked groggily, rising to her elbows. The vestiges of her dream flitted at the edge of her awareness, taunting her, but the phantom before her demanded her attention. She puzzled over Donskoy's words. "But I am not ill."

Donskoy gave a feeble laugh. "No. Your stock is too strong for that to happen, after mere days in my company. But you may be with child."

Marguerite pulled herself up from the pit, resting against the pillows. The fragments of her dream disappeared, slipping behind oblivion's curtain. "With child?" she gasped. Then quickly she added, "I pray that is true, for I know how much it would please you—how much it would please me as well." If Donskoy had discerned the slip, or even cared, he didn't show it.

"A son," he said. "A *son* would please me. Last night I was certain my seed took hold. But hope is a vixen, and emotions spawned from passion can deceive even the most potent gods, if one believes in such things. That's why I have asked Zosia to confirm your condition."

"Zosia?"

"Yes. She knows how such things are determined."

Even I know how such things are determined, thought Marguerite, and then mentally added, but not the morning after.

The velvet walls at the foot of the bed parted, as a

stage curtain might be drawn back to reveal the opening scene of a drama. Zosia crouched before the fire, prodding at something beneath the grate. Enshrouded in her coal-black blouse and skirt, with a black kerchief covering her head, she reminded Marguerite more than ever of a Vistani witch.

Yelena's small rough hands pulled aside the remaining bed curtains, anchoring them to the posts. She shyly avoided her mistress's gaze but nodded feebly when Marguerite greeted her with a simple "Good morning." Zosia's dark head bobbed along with the girl's. Donskoy pointed a finger at Yelena and motioned toward the corner. The mute curtsied meekly, then shuffled to her place, head bowed. She stiffened, a sudden victim of taxidermy.

"I am ready to begin now, lord," said Zosia crisply. She withdrew a small iron rod from the hearth and lifted it toward the window, turning it slowly to examine it in the light. A slick green-black mass covered the end of the instrument. She approached the bed, holding the rod before her as if it were an eager divining stick and Marguerite were the hidden water.

Marguerite hoisted herself to the edge of the bed and swung her legs around so they dangled above the floor. "But surely it's too soon for such tests," she said quickly, making an effort to sound bright. "Surely you can't tell in a day." The sudden movement made her head swim.

"It's never too soon," Donskoy replied firmly, regaining the voice of command. "Lie back and keep still." Then he added softly, "You have nothing to fear, Marguerite." He looked over his shoulder. "Does she, Zosia?"

Marguerite lay back and blinked hard. Perhaps she was dreaming. Perhaps this was a farce.

"Oh nay, nay . . ." said the old woman soothingly.

She stepped to Donskoy's side and spread her lips in a genuine smile. "Not from my feeble hands." She blew on the tip of the rod as if to cool the slimy glob clinging to it. The center of the mass glowed vividly from within, like a dying ember teased back to life, except that the heart shone green.

Donskoy pulled Marguerite's nightshift up to her chest. Instinctively she moved her hands in a gesture of modesty, then forced herself to remove them. The blood rose to her cheeks, coloring them scarlet.

Donskoy gave a husky laugh. "Still so shy? I should be affronted, but it becomes you, Marguerite. I will turn away and let Zosia apply the salve to your abdomen. This is women's work, after all. My part is done." He took a seat before the hearth.

Marguerite eyed the rod in Zosia's hand nervously. "Won't that burn?" she asked. If ever there were a rude awakening, surely this was it.

"Of course not," chided Zosia. "What do you think of me, child? I am letting the mixture cool. I shall apply it with my own finger."

"What is it?"

"Hah!" scoffed the old woman, teasing. "Would you have me reveal all my secrets before breakfast?"

Donskoy chuckled darkly.

Marguerite felt the color draining from her face. She had imagined Zosia as her friend, her confidant. But she didn't really know the old woman. She didn't really know anyone here. Suddenly it was just as easy to think of Zosia as Donskoy's faithful executioner, and Yelena the silent witness. Or perhaps Zosia would serve as torturer, applying "justice" whenever he, the great lord, demanded it.

Zosia observed Marguerite's blanched expression. "Don't let your wits scamper off like a mad hare," she scolded. "The salve contains only herbs and a few private ingredients, proffered by your lord." She gathered some of the goop on her finger, then added, "Each is quite ordinary alone, but mingled together they make the test run true."

Zosia gently rubbed the sticky substance over Marguerite's stomach, just below the navel, tracing a pair of warm circles, one inside the other. The salve trailed behind the old woman's white finger like the glistening, slimy wake of a crawling slug. A sour smell pricked Marguerite's nostrils, and she wrinkled her nose in disgust.

Zosia motioned to Yelena, who came forth and wrapped the rod in a linen sheet. The girl took this bundle and retreated to her place in the shadows.

"Do you wish to observe the next step, lord?" Zosia asked. "It is as I described it earlier."

"No," Donskoy replied simply. "But I will observe the outcome."

"Very well." Zosia withdrew a brown egg from the folds of her wide woolen skirts.

Marguerite lifted her brow, half in amusement, half in disbelief. "In these lands, I sense that eggs do more than bind flour." She spoke in a low voice so Donskoy might not overhear. Zosia suddenly reminded her of a great black mother hen.

The old woman clucked her tongue. "Hush, child. Did no one ever teach you of such spells? Did you never read of them?"

Marguerite could not suppress a smile. Her mother's only spell had been turning cream into butter. "No. But I am aware that customs vary."

"*Tsk.* This is no custom, as you say. No quaint little fairy-tale ritual. And no trivial matter to your lord." She shot a glance over her shoulder at Donskoy, who coughed, shifting uncomfortably in the chair.

Marguerite realized her faux pas. "Nor to me," she

said firmly. Then she recalled an old saying, something the old women in the village had sometimes muttered. "Ovum raptum est," she said. "That's about eggs, isn't it?"

Zosia cast her a sharp look. " 'The egg has shattered.' To the ignorant, it warns of a coming disaster." She dropped her voice low. "Or foretells a miscarriage."

"Oh." The talk of disaster made Marguerite think of her dream and the gypsy's curse. It frightened her, but she did not dare speak of it now—not in front of her peevish husband.

"I know another saying," growled Donskoy. "He who wishes eggs must endure the clucking of hens."

Zosia put a finger to her lips and cast another glance over her shoulder. Marguerite could not catch her meaning. Was the old woman asking her to play along? Her mind raced. If a wedding rite of fertility called for her to swallow the egg, what might she do to prove conception? Hatch it? And if Zosia meant to rig the test, proving a pregnancy where none existed, she would refuse. Time had a way of turning that particular ruse to ruin.

"Finish the test now," said Donskoy. The edge in his voice could have cut stone.

Zosia cracked the egg into a clean porcelain pot beside the bed and motioned to Marguerite. "Your own water will tell the tale. Mind you to hold your shift so the salve does not smear."

Marguerite sighed, then reluctantly complied, half curtsying with her nightshift held aloft. Then she stepped aside, her face red with embarrassment. She'd heard of seers who read tea leaves, seers who divined the future from a still pool, but never seers who looked for their answers in a pool like this. Zosia mumbled something while sprinkling an herb into the pot.

Curiosity won over Marguerite. "How does this work?"

The old woman stared intently into the pot. "If the egg floats to the surface with the yolk swirled through the white, you carry a daughter. If it floats intact, with the yolk whole from the white, you carry a son. But if any part of it fails to rise, your belly lies vacant." Her voice dropped as low as the Abyss. "And if it bubbles and seethes," she said slowly, "if it churns and roils, you carry the spawn of a fiend. A monster child, twisted in body and spirit."

Recalling her dream, Marguerite gasped.

Donskoy exploded, "*Faugh!* What nonsense are you babbling now, you old witch?" He strode to the bedside and stared into the pot with red-faced revulsion, then turned away. He did not meet Marguerite's gaze.

Marguerite forced herself to peer into the pot. The egg lay at the bottom, still and intact.

"You are not with child," announced Zosia simply.

Marguerite almost smiled. The dream-curse had been just that, a dream.

"Wretched hag," growled Donskoy. "You have done the test wrong." He raised his hand, then stayed it, waving the black glove contemptuously.

Zosia's eyes darkened. "I have done nothing wrong, my lord," she said evenly. "The pot tells what it will tell; I am only the reader."

"Then there must be some other test. Do another," he commanded.

Zosia clucked. "A few are known to me, but I doubt you would prefer them."

"Such decisions are mine alone. What other tricks can you perform?"

Zosia stroked her plump chin, and her black eyes sparkled in their nest of wrinkles. "I can wrap a severed finger in a lock of her hair, and suspend it over her stomach. If the Powers are willing, the finger points out the truth."

"Do it," he said. "Take Yelena's finger; she can manage without one."

Yelena gasped and dropped the rod to the floor; it landed with a muffled thud. The girl clutched her hands to her chest and sank back against the wall, as if the shadows might keep her safe.

Marguerite was mortified. "Surely," she began, "surely, there's—"

Zosia raised her hand. "Alas, my lord, Yelena's finger would serve no purpose," the old woman said smoothly. "The finger must belong to the one who lay with the mother-to-be." She winked at Marguerite. "Now, I might work the magic with just a fingertip, but the less flesh we take, the more closely the charm holds its secrets. I have seen the appendage of a long-fingered man spin like a maple seed whirling to the ground, while a mere scrap of skin has crumbled into ash before my eyes, too weak to withstand the ordeal of questioning."

"Rubbish," said Donskoy. "A rubbish test. You seek to vex me, old woman. What else can you do?"

Zosia exhaled sharply. "Perhaps you would do better to look toward Marguerite herself, Lord Donskoy. She could stand at a crossroads with a newly sharpened ax, then drench it with her water and bury it. When morning comes, she must dig up the ax and repeat the gesture. Nine times she must water and bury the blade. Then, if the ax shows rust, she is with child."

"Nine days of this?"

"At least," said Zosia impatiently. "And the test is not so sure as the one I have already completed. After nine days of wetting, even an ordinary blade can decay. In your lands, I would consider that a certainty—in half the time."

Donskoy shook his head and began to pace.

Zosia continued, "Moreover, a crossroads harbors danger, Lord Donskoy. Peasants and certain Vistani bury suicides there to hold the restless spirits at bay— even your own lands may not escape such use. And if the dead hear a pregnant woman scrabbling above them—if her scent or her digging disturbs them—then they may rise as ghouls and eat through her belly to reach the tender morsel inside."

Marguerite remained silent, mouth agape.

"Take heart, Lord Donskoy," said Zosia. "And rediscover your patience. Marguerite is young and healthy. She will be with child soon; I have seen it."

"So you have sworn," he grumbled, turning to glare at the old woman. He behaved as if they stood alone; as if Marguerite was of no more consequence than a rug. "Then when?" he demanded.

"It may be never if you continue in this fashion," Zosia replied with a note of warning. "A dry field seldom blooms. You must pay it some attention." She stepped to his side. "And take care what attention you give. Nervous women bear weaklings. The sickly yield worse. If this child is to serve in the manner you hope, you'd do well to heed an old woman's advice."

Donskoy sighed, then returned to the chair by the fire. He drummed his black suede fingers on the armrest, as if to keep pace with his galloping thoughts.

"There is another test I might recommend," Zosia continued soothingly. "The oldest test of all."

Donskoy twisted his face in a wry expression. "What, pray tell? What must we sever or piss upon and bury now?"

"It is the test of time. If the moon passes through its phases and Marguerite does not bleed, then in time she will grow full herself."

Donskoy snorted. "For that bit of wisdom, I hardly needed you, old woman."

"Patience, my lord," Zosia replied. "Marguerite's belly will swell with life soon enough. And I will prepare for you a new smoking potion, to help diminish your internal pain."

Marguerite looked toward the old woman. So it was she who kept Donskoy's pipe burning.

Donskoy growled. "Patience," he muttered. "I should be its master by now." He rose from the chair. "Forgive me, Marguerite, if my eagerness has made you ill at ease."

"I am not so fragile," Marguerite replied evenly.

"Good. For the next month, I shall be the picture of patience. You shall visit me in my salon each day. And after a month, we shall rejoice."

"I am sure you are right, Milos."

"Call me Lord Donskoy," he said, walking toward the door. "Or simply 'lord' will suffice." At the threshold, he paused and turned. "Zosia suggests that I pay you some attention. After you have dressed, join me in the sitting room outside my salon for breakfast. We will discuss how to spend the day most pleasantly." He clasped his gloved hands before him, nervously working the fingers; they resembled two black-furred spiders coupling.

"I'll be there soon, my lord," Marguerite replied.

"See that you are," said Donskoy, stepping across the threshold.

Zosia stood by the hearth, gathering up the components of her strange tests as Yelena hovered nearby. Marguerite gazed at the old woman, studying her dark cronish looks, her unmistakable gypsy looks. Stagnant or not, the old woman had to be Vistani. An outcast, perhaps?

Slowly the pieces of a puzzle began to tumble into

place in Marguerite's head. Donskoy's first wife was a black-haired hellion named Valeska. In the water Marguerite had seen a black-haired gypsy—an apparition, a sign. Could it be that Valeska was a gypsy? Zosia had known her—she had said so. "Soon," she had told Marguerite, "soon you will look upon me as Donskoy's first wife did."

A flurry of questions rushed forward in her mind, each of them angrily demanding attention. Zosia had brushed her queries aside before, but perhaps now she would be more willing. For now, Marguerite was Donskoy's wife.

"Zosia," she said evenly.

The old woman turned. "Yes, my child? You can wipe away the salve; it has served its purpose."

Marguerite struggled to find the words, fearing that Zosia would simply scurry off, avoiding her questions. "I'd like you to tell me about . . . Valeska."

Zosia's eyes flashed, and Yelena's dark mouth gaped. The mute dropped the rags she had gathered and knelt to pick them up. When she had finished, Zosia dismissed her with a flapping wave. Yelena scurried out the door. The old woman turned to Marguerite.

"Valeska," she said, as a jailer might question his prisoner. "How do you know that name?"

Marguerite hesitated, not wanting to give away her visit to the crypt. If Griezell was not Zosia's informant, it would be unwise to reveal her escape. "Lord Donskoy told it to me."

"Hah!" cackled Zosia. "He would never speak her name—especially not to you."

"He was delirious. He did not know what he said."

"Hmmph."

"And I have seen her as well."

Zosia's brow rose.

Marguerite added quickly, "In a dream."

Zosia smiled. "You are very sensitive for a *giorgia*. But then, you and Valeska share a connection in Donskoy."

"Then she *was* Donskoy's wife. His first wife."

Zosia frowned. "He considered her as much. But it was not a marriage sanctioned by her tribe."

"Were you her mother?"

Zosia shook her head. "But I tended her. We suffered here together. She and I, true Vistani no more." Zosia turned, walking toward the door. "You must dress now. Lord Donskoy will be angry if you keep him waiting."

"Before you go, tell me how she died."

"I have told enough," replied Zosia stiffly. "And I warn you, speak of this no more—especially where Donskoy might hear."

With that, she opened the door.

"Wait!" Marguerite's command sounded more like a plea than an order. "I . . . I dreamed of a curse."

To Marguerite's astonishment, Zosia's face showed no surprise or alarm. Without asking any details, she simply nodded.

"You needn't fear the curse, my child." The old woman stepped into the hall. "Valeska means you no harm. She is restless and proud, but she bears you no malice. For you, she knows only sympathy."

The door swung shut.

TEN

Breakfast was a simple affair in the drawing room outside Donskoy's salon—a piece of dry bread; a slice of cold, salty meat of unknown origin; and a sour wine so laden with dross that Marguerite had to strain it through her teeth. After each sip she dabbed her gums surreptitiously, so as not to smile at her husband with clotted teeth.

Donskoy stared off into space while they ate, as if resigned to her company. I have disappointed him, she thought. But if his coolness came from the results of Zosia's test, his expectations seemed patently unfair.

Donskoy dabbed his mustache with a cloth. "Well then," he said suddenly. "I promised you a tour of the castle, did I not?"

Marguerite nodded.

He sighed, and she added quickly, "But we can undertake it another time, if it displeases you."

"No, no," he replied, tossing the napkin on the table. "This is your home now. And one must feel at home, I suppose, to be at home. In truth, you have already seen the only rooms worth occupying. But if it will dispel your curiosity and make you content, then perhaps a quick tour is overdue. At any rate, it will allow me to point out certain dangers of which you should be aware."

At once, Marguerite thought of Valeska floating in the underground river, and of the dripping mark of the curse. She wondered whether Donskoy would take her to the dungeons. And if he did, would the tralak remain? Would he too see Valeska's body rising from the water? Such an event might push him over the edge. Unless he knew, of course; unless he had seen these things himself. And in that case, she could not imagine he would take her below.

Donskoy rose and stretched, assessing her. "This is bound to be a dirty business. Would you like to change your attire?"

She shook her head.

"Then wait here for a moment."

He slipped into his salon, closing the small arched door behind him. When he returned, a ring of large skeleton keys jangled in his left hand. "The tour begins."

Donskoy began by leaving the sitting room and leading Marguerite across the foyer. He gestured to a door beside the main stair. "The guard room, at one time," he announced. "With an armory and sleeping quarters above. Unless you wish to impale someone with a polearm, this room should not interest you."

He made no move to open the door.

"Have you never required guards, then?" Marguerite asked. "If so, this land must be quite peaceful."

Donskoy laughed dryly. "You make it sound like a paradise. I have my associates, of course, but I do not require an army. No one dares to invade. This way, Marguerite."

He strode toward the great hall, and they went in

together. During their feast, the straw and herbs upon the floor had seemed freshly applied. Only a day later, the mixture clung to the stones in moist, dark clumps, completely void of any sweetness. Marguerite brushed a heap aside with the point of her shoe. A shining beetle darted out, careening across the floor in search of new cover.

Donskoy led her to a door at the left side of the hall and inserted a key in the rusty lock, then gave a shove. The door opened just a crack, releasing a sour gust.

"Here lies one of the dangers I mentioned," Donskoy announced. His tone held only the barest interest. "It's the throne room, or once was, I suppose. It seems to me that the castle has undergone many changes through the years. The floor of this chamber is entirely unsafe. Half of it has fallen, plunging to an old storeroom below." He stepped aside and gestured toward the gap. "Do you wish to peer inside, my dear?"

Marguerite shook her head. The stench was unpleasant.

"An intelligent woman," said Donskoy, shutting the door and turning the lock. "Perhaps I chose wisely after all."

Marguerite let the barb pass without response.

"Beyond the throne room lies the solar," Lord Donskoy continued, "a private apartment for the lord of the keep—for myself, I suppose. But it's nearly as ruined as the throne room, so naturally it goes unused. After all, I have my salon."

"How many years have you lived in the keep?" Marguerite inquired.

"Too many," he answered vaguely. "It has been both a boon and a bane."

"Were any of the previous residents kin to you?" she asked.

"You mean, was the keep passed to me by some fluke of relation? Hardly. I acquired all that I possess without benefit of blood—not my own anyway. Moreover, I no longer remember my people in any detail. I was sent away for study at a young age, but I struck out on my own as soon I was able. Now I cannot even recall my family's faces. Like the castle, some of the older recesses of my mind have crumbled."

Fearing a morose turn in his mood, Marguerite pointed to another door, opposite. It stood slightly ajar. "What lies that way?" she asked lightly.

"Ah, the stair to the gallery. The door remains unlocked at most times. Yelena seems to like the perch."

Marguerite peered overhead, gazing at the rail and the long, dark space that stretched behind it. The shadows shifted, as if a figure had moved forward, then retreated. Perhaps it was Yelena, hovering there now like some timid bird bereft of her wing feathers. Or perhaps . . .

"We can go up, if you like," said Donskoy. "You'll find a few empty ladies' chambers off the balcony, reserved for cackling and stitchery, and no doubt for cuckolding in bawdier times."

Marguerite bit her tongue, sure that truth lay in another direction. She stared at the gallery, but saw no further movement above.

Donskoy continued, "On the opposite side from the ladies' rooms lies a portrait hall, though at present the frames hold only dust. One day, when we have children and can fill the castle with life, we will restore the gallery. But for now I see no reason to venture there."

"Then of course we will forgo the climb," said Marguerite.

He nodded.

She noticed a faint smile pulling at the corner of his

mouth, and she knew that her compliance pleased him.

Donskoy said, "If you do go up there alone, perhaps in search of Yelena, be mindful of the rail."

"Is it unsafe?"

He shrugged, then answered simply, "For the incautious." He scanned the wall beside the fireplace in the great hall. "Somewhere there's a secret passage leading to the gallery." He tugged at his mustache, pondering. "No, I believe the passage extends from the throne room, so a lord or vassal might steal to the gallery unobserved and look down at the hall. Or spy upon the ladies, I suppose."

Marguerite struggled to sound light. "How intriguing."

"Not very," he said. "Ekhart tells me this place has many such passages. All lie in disrepair, and none of them leads outside, much less to anywhere new, so they are both useless and redundant."

Marguerite stayed her tongue. Did he know more than he let on? Was he probing to see whether she knew something more of secret doors, pressing her toward confession?

Donskoy continued, "If ever you should discover such a passage—inadvertently, of course—then I suggest you stay clear. It would be so easy for something to crumble or malfunction. You might find yourself entombed in a wall, while I might find myself without a wife, once again."

"I am sufficiently deterred by your description," she said quietly, wondering if he was hinting at the tragedy that cost Valeska her life. "But I'm sure I won't discover such a passage. I'm not that clever."

"You are *too* clever to meet such a fate, or so I would hope," he said. Lord Donskoy pointed to the rear of the hall. "Through there, of course, lie old pantries, a buttery, a stair to the great ovens where our nonexistent serfs might bake their weekly bread. Zosia and Yelena used the ovens to prepare our feast. Otherwise Zosia prefers the smaller kitchen, which gives access to her garden. They are linked by a passage."

Marguerite did not reveal that she already knew of Zosia's kitchen—and of the garden beyond. And she certainly could not comment on the garden's secret door.

Donskoy took her arm and led her out from the hall. They crossed the vestibule and climbed the stairs leading to her own chamber.

"Do you ever wonder who your companions are in this part of the keep?"

Marguerite lifted her brow. "My companions?"

"In the figurative sense, of course. Yelena acts as if the rooms are haunted. I imagine she is only hesitant to add their upkeep to her duties."

"It is so much for one woman."

Donskoy paused as if to counter, then frowned, saying nothing. He opened one room after the other, revealing empty, decaying chambers. Half held only dust and long strands of cobwebs that waved from the ceiling as he pushed forth the door. The others contained a few formless pieces of furniture draped in damp-looking sheets.

"You see?" he said. "Not worth your curiosity. Your own chamber is by far the largest and the best. A sanctuary well worth your appreciation."

Marguerite began to grow tired. "Yes. It's a wonderful room. I am honored to have it." And I should be, she thought. He has obviously taken great pains to make it so comfortable.

"Thanks go in part to Zosia, I suppose," Donskoy added. "She selected the chamber for you, knowing it to be among those least affected by rot." He forged ahead, moving down the hall as if eager to be rid of an unpleasant chore. "Now then," he mumbled. "What else might I show you? Through the first door down in the vestibule, you can reach the east wing and the old workshops. A chandler's room, a joinery, a hermit's cell or two intended for visiting clergy. Naturally we have no need of that wing. I suggest you let it go unexplored."

And what of the dungeons? thought Marguerite. What of the curse? But she did not voice these thoughts.

"Are there many levels underground?" she asked.

He raised a brow. "Indeed. But I must insist that you leave them unexplored as well. They are riddled with tricks and traps, and the air is foul. The combination could prove dangerous, if not fatal."

"I see," she answered quietly, wondering if it had proven fatal in the past.

"You told me you were an accomplished musician, did you not?" asked Donskoy.

Marguerite gave a nervous laugh. "I am not accomplished, I'm afraid. Though I can play the clavier and lute, my skills are not really exceptional."

"I do not ask because I desire a concert," Donskoy replied. "So you needn't fret. However, during our first meeting, I did promise you a glimpse of the music room. I shall take you there now. It is not far."

They headed down the hall, passing the door to her own room. The passage jogged, and they followed it to a tower stair—*the* tower stair, which she had descended in secret.

Donskoy began to climb, but Marguerite hesitated.

"Is something wrong?" he asked.

"No, I—"

Marguerite was about say, I wondered what lies below, but she stopped herself. Two steps down lay the candle she had dropped the previous night. The taper must have fallen from her garter as she raced back to the sanctuary of her room, fleeing Valeska's apparition.

"You must not lag behind," chided Donskoy. "Certainly a woman of your youth can keep stride with me."

She followed his ascent, ignoring the cool blasts from the open arrow slits along the way.

The stair led to a half-rounded chamber. Lord Donskoy held the door open, and Marguerite stepped through. In the center huddled a large instrument beneath a gray blanket: the clavier, presumably. A lopsided stool and a lute with broken strings stood sadly against the wall. Beside them was a harp, threaded with cobwebs.

"What a coincidence," said Donskoy. "I have both your instruments of choice."

Marguerite stepped to the clavier and lifted the sheet, which bore a layer of dust as thick as fur. The keys beneath it were soiled. She pressed one gingerly, and the instrument gave out a sour, muffled cry, as if in pain.

Cursed, thought Marguerite. Suddenly it dawned on her she had been viewing the notion of a curse too directly. It did not portend some great horrendous event. Rather, its effects were immediate and obvious, visible all around her in the castle's steady decay and its melancholia, just as Lord Donskoy had implied. But would she too succumb and slowly rot? Would her mind soon have its own "crumbling recesses," like that of her husband?

"The instrument is worse than I recall," Donskoy said, gesturing toward the clavier. "Perhaps some day we'll repair it, so you can entertain yourself."

Marguerite pressed another key, but this time no

sound came at all. "It may be beyond repair," she said sadly.

"I might procure another, I suppose, though cargo of this size is difficult to transport. Or you might wish to come here for other reasons. This is a good place for reading when you tire of your own room. On warm days, of course, for the firepit is small, and some of the glass panes are missing from the window. Yelena can clean things here, if you'd like."

Why would I wish to visit this sad place? she wondered. As if summoned, she walked toward the tall sliver of a window, aglow with a pale light.

Donskoy prattled on. "Feel free to come here and entertain yourself when you will. At least by day. Contrary to your belief, you are not my prisoner, Marguerite."

She made no response. A breeze wafted in, and she savored its coolness upon her face.

Then she leaned out. The view was breathtaking. The dark green-black sea of pines spread in waves toward the gray horizon. She had not realized how high she had climbed. It was as if the music room were perched as near as possible to the limits of the sky, so that the gods might hear the musicians and smile upon them. It seemed oddly complete. Above, the tower soared straight into the heavens. And below, well . . .

"How far do your lands extend?" she asked.

"As far as you can see," he replied.

The fresh air was bracing, refreshing, and she hated to pull away. The tour had left her drained. She no longer had any wish to revisit the dungeons. Not today.

Donskoy suddenly stood beside her. "You are a picture, standing here with your hair alight. I am glad you do not observe the common style and keep it covered with some silly wimple."

Marguerite felt a blush in her cheeks, unbidden, almost ashamed that she was vulnerable to his flattery.

"You do ride, if I am not mistaken," he said.

She nodded. "Passably."

"Then would you like to explore the terrain? It can much more uplifting than these crumbling walls."

Marguerite turned. "Yes. I'd like that very much." She meant it sincerely. The thought of leaving the castle lifted her spirits greatly.

"Then, by all means, let us depart."

* * * * *

The stable yard was a broad, muddy expanse. In the most remote corner rose the dung heap, its base as solid and ancient as a volcano's. A long, two-story wattle-and-daub building huddled against the castle wall opposite the keep. The wall's crenelated crest loomed twice as high above to meet the cap of leaden sky. Stables and animal pens occupied the lower half of the building. One end housed a smithy's firepit, stone cold. The second floor, ostensibly, held storage rooms and workshops. Time and the elements had treated the structure unkindly; a third of the mossy wood-shingled roof had collapsed.

Marguerite had expected the court to be as empty of life as the castle itself, but she was pleasantly surprised. A flock of black geese wandered at will, honking noisily. A goat bleated, and she spotted it near the gate, tethered on a circle of well-trodden ground. A peacock strutted around the perimeter of the court with a slow, lurching motion, dragging its closed tail behind. In the stables, a row of black, swishing horse tails sprouted from broad gray rumps. The tails swept slowly and rhythmically over the gates of closed stalls, like unnatural pendulums, their effect strangely hypnotic.

An angry growl broke the trance, and Marguerite turned toward the sound. Ekhart was working the hounds near the rear of the court, setting each one in turn to the savaging of a bloody rag. He commanded the activated beast to dive left, then right, then called off the attack to exercise his authority. Marguerite watched with a mixture of disgust and fascination, then turned her head away.

"Shall we?" said Donskoy, gesturing toward the stables and taking Marguerite's hand.

She used the other to lift her skirt. For the occasion, Donskoy had given her a new gown of wool as blue as sapphire, with a matching cape and gloves. The court's flagstones lay half-buried in mud, and the geese had covered them further with an impressive array of slick droppings. She stepped forward cautiously, staring at the ground.

A sound ahead drew her attention. Ljubo appeared, leading a handsome gray gelding and a smaller white mare, dirty, and with a sagging back. Obviously, the mare was meant for her.

"A thousand pardons, Lord Donskoy," said Ljubo, bowing deeply and peering up from beneath his fleshy brow. "I was taking the mounts out front. You never come here to retrieve them—and-and, good day, Lady Donskoy." His eyes slid readily in Marguerite's direction, and he grinned. Something dark and green flecked his broken teeth.

Donskoy replied, "Marguerite is the curious sort. I thought she'd like to see the stables."

"Yes-yes, of course," answered Ljubo, head bobbing. "And I've given her Lightning as you suggested."

"So I see."

Marguerite stared up at the weary-looking horse.

"Pay no heed to the name, my bride," Donskoy added. "The mare is called Lightning because she acts as if she's been struck. She'll never bolt, if you pardon the pun. She's too numb to spook easily."

Ljubo clutched Marguerite's hand, soiling her blue suede glove with his grubby rust-colored fingers, then helped her up into the saddle, doubtlessly leaving a similar stain on her behind. Marguerite ignored the intimacy of the gesture, working to maintain her balance. She shifted uncomfortably and the horse stomped.

"You did say you could ride," said Donskoy flatly.

Marguerite nodded, struggling to adjust her skirts without sliding from her perch. "Yes. Only not recently. And usually a pony."

Donskoy sighed. "We could make adjustments, I suppose."

"I'm fine," she replied. "Just rusty."

He grunted, then swung into his own saddle.

"Take a moment to acclimate yourself," he said. "Have Ljubo lead you by the rein if necessary. I have a matter to discuss with Ekhart."

Donskoy gave the gray a sharp kick and rode toward the back of the yard.

"Are you all right?" asked Ljubo, taking the rein. "Hold onto her neck if you feel unsure."

Marguerite would have preferred her leggings and a tunic to the slippery blue gown, but gradually she felt more comfortable. Ljubo led her in a broad turn.

"You look very lovely today," he prattled, wiping a sleeve across his nose. "Very lovely indeed."

"Thank you, Ljubo."

"It's so nice for Donskoy to have a wife."

"Yes," she muttered, adjusting herself in the saddle as it swayed. "Very nice." Then it occurred to Marguerite that an opportunity lay before her—one she shouldn't pass up. She glanced over her shoulder. Donskoy was still speaking to Ekhart from the saddle, waving a dark hand to punctuate his story.

"Ljubo," she said quietly. "May I take the reins now?"

"Okay," he said simply, handing her the leathers.

"But I want you walk here close beside me, in case I should fall."

Ljubo happily complied. "Like this, milady?"

"That's right. Like that."

They turned, walking away from Lord Donskoy.

"Ljubo," said Marguerite, with calculated smoothness. "Would you like to be my friend?"

Her admirer bared his broken teeth. "Oh, yes, Lady Marguerite. I'd like that very much."

"Good. I haven't many friends to talk to, you know. Yelena is mute."

Ljubo nodded. "No tongue."

"I was wondering if you could tell me about the castle," ventured Marguerite.

Ljubo eyed her over his shoulder, then muttered, "Ekhart doesn't like me to talk."

"But Ekhart isn't with us now," Marguerite replied evenly. "So it's all right."

Ljubo stared at the ground, then shot her a sly glance. "So it's all right," he repeated, lifting one corner of his fleshy mouth.

"Did you know Valeska, Donskoy's first wife?" she asked.

Ljubo stopped suddenly, and the horse halted beside him, not needing any prompting. He looked away, rubbing his hands nervously.

"Vales—" He stopped short of saying the whole name. "Lord Donskoy's first wife, she's dead."

"Yes, I know. I want you to tell me how."

"Can't say," said Ljubo quietly.

Marguerite found this odd. "Why not?"

Ljubo would not meet her gaze. "Ekhart wouldn't like it," he whispered. "It's forbidden—even to say her name is forbidden."

"Forbidden?" Marguerite asked. "Why?"

Ljubo's only response was to shake his head. He cast a nervous look toward the corner where Ekhart was working and said nothing.

"What's wrong? Why are you so afraid?" Marguerite started to reach for his shoulder, then drew back, a terrible prospect taking shape inside her mind. "What happened? Did Lord Donskoy kill her?"

Ljubo's round head snapped around to look at her. "Oh, no. Lord Donskoy *loved* her. But—"

"But what?" Marguerite persisted.

"She didn't like it here. She didn't want to stay, and she got sick."

"Sick? How?"

"Strange sick. Crazy sick. She got weak, and then she got strange."

"And then she died," Marguerite concluded.

Ljubo was quiet. He looked nervously toward Donskoy and Ekhart, who continued their conversation across the yard.

Marguerite said gently, "You can tell me, Ljubo." She touched his cheek with her hand. "After all, we are friends."

Ljubo's eyes darted. He licked his lips.

"Tell me," whispered Marguerite. "How did Valeska die?"

"She did it herself," said Ljubo suddenly. His eyes were wide and frightened. "She jumped into the pit. Zosia said it was the only way she could escape."

"Zosia told her to jump?" Marguerite gasped.

Ljubo frowned. "No—she said it after. When we went down to . . ." He bit his lip, allowing the sentence to trail off.

Marguerite was quiet. An immense relief settled over her. She had not allowed herself to confront it, but the fear had lingered all along—the fear that Lord Donskoy had murdered his first wife. But it wasn't true. What was it Ramus had said? That gypsies fear confinement. Perhaps that was why Valeska had committed suicide. Donskoy had kept her under lock and key, just as he imprisoned Marguerite. For Valeska, perhaps, it had been too much to bear.

"I shouldn't have told you, Lady Marguerite."

"Yes you should have, Ljubo. You did the right thing."

"No," he hissed. "I shouldn't have spoken of her. It's forbidden."

The sound of clattering hooves brought them both to attention. Lord Donskoy was coming across the courtyard.

Marguerite leaned down and placed a hand on Ljubo's shoulder, as if steadying herself. "It will be our secret."

Her husband arrived before Ljubo could respond.

"Ready now?" he asked, frowning at the sight of Marguerite touching the stablehand.

Marguerite pulled herself upright. "Ready."

Donskoy swatted his gray with a crop. The horse lurched forward, starting toward the gate. Marguerite nudged Lightning after him.

Meanwhile Ljubo raced toward the gate in a wild waddle. Purple-faced and damp, he barely had time to lift the crossbar and push the great doors apart before Donskoy passed beneath the lintel, preceding Marguerite by several lengths.

As she emerged behind him, she felt as if a tightness had been eased, as if she had been freed from the dark, tortuous gullet of some bilious beast and cast back into the open air. The deep wall of pines stretched out to her left. She peered into the feathered screen and saw herself, two days earlier, huddled in the protective embrace of the gypsy. Ramus—that was his name. Incredibly, she had almost forgotten. Donskoy paused and allowed her to come alongside. Then they trotted down the road together.

The clearing ended, and the pair slipped into the forest, passing over the little stone bridge. The road was soon joined by the black, glistening stream, which flowed attentively along its flank. Marguerite wondered about the water's source—a spring, perhaps, bubbling up from the depths? Perhaps these same depths gave rise to the stream that ran beneath the castle. Perhaps, in fact, this very water flowed through the dungeon, skulking through the bedrock like a prisoner tunneling an escape route, re-emerging well clear of the walls. Marguerite half-expected to see the gypsy's smiling apparition bobbing down the brook, but the shining water offered up nothing. The road turned sharply, and the stream trailed away into the pines.

They came upon the fetid marshes, with their blood-red brambles and rocky outcroppings, unchanged since Marguerite had passed here in the jostling cart with Ljubo and Ekhart. (After only days, what had she expected?) The slender leaves still clung sparsely to the shrubs, like a bald man's last hairs; and once again, they seemed to shiver at her passage. Then Marguerite noted that one thing had changed: she no longer found the scent of decaying flora quite so nauseating as before. Either the last remnants of the Vistani sleeping potion had left her body completely, or she was becoming acclimated to her new home. Indeed, the bitter, earthy scent seemed faintly pleasing, and she inhaled it deeply.

At the fork, the couple paused. They had been riding for about half an hour. Near this spot, Arturi and his caravan had deposited Marguerite, along with her bridal chest and the strange black box. The place had lost its foreboding edge.

Donskoy reached out and plucked Lightning's reins, drawing the mare closely alongside his own mount. He pecked Marguerite on the cheek. "Still fresh, my dear?"

"Yes," she said. "It's exhilarating."

"I am glad," Donskoy replied. "I used to take this ride often with Ljubo and Ekhart, along with a few associates, but now their company bores me. Unless some extraordinary event dictates otherwise, they go alone." He reached into his jacket and withdrew a silver flask. "A libation to keep you warm. From here, the air may grow colder."

She sipped tentatively at the mouth of the flask, encountering a spiced, thick liqueur that tasted of honey. It delighted her tongue.

Donskoy fixed his eyes on the roadside and scowled suddenly, swinging down from his horse. A small sigil had been carved into one of the trees beside the neck of the fork. Marguerite squinted. It appeared to be an upside-down triangle crossed by a line, but she could not get a good look. Donskoy withdrew a blade and began erasing the symbol, savagely tearing the bark from the tree.

"Wretched Vistani," he grumbled. "They leave their marks as freely as dogs."

"What do they mean?" she asked. She recalled that Arturi had made a sign in the dirt, but he had done nothing to the tree. Of course, she could have failed to notice the mark. Or perhaps another caravan had passed this way in intervening days. Or perhaps, not a caravan, but a single man. Ramus.

"*They*?" Donskoy growled, scraping busily.

"The marks."

"Nothing. Just insults to my honor, and now, I suppose, to yours. They gain power only if we acknowledge them. So don't speak of them again."

Don't speak of this. Don't venture there. Don't . . . Don't what? What next?

Donskoy returned to his saddle, saw her pinched face, and reached over to retrieve the flask from her hands.

"They are nothing. Signposts left by those who would claim every road as their own. Don't let them trouble you." He took a thick swallow of the honeyed brew, then replaced the stopper and returned the flask to his black velvet saddlebag. "Ready?"

Marguerite nodded.

Lord Donskoy backed his gelding in a tight circle, surveying the fork. Then he dug his heels into its flanks, steering it left, the direction in which Arturi and his caravan had gone after ejecting Marguerite. She hesitated, watching her husband, then followed directly behind. His back was as rigid as a sword, as if his spine had been encased in iron. When it appeared to melt and his countenance relaxed, she urged her horse forward until she came alongside him.

"Your lands are beautiful," she said. "Where does this road lead?"

"To the rim. The edge of my domain."

"I thought that was quite far."

"Sometimes it seems that way. And sometimes not," he said. "Like matter over mind. But the views are worth the trip."

The forest hemmed in the road. It was rougher here, with scraggled saplings filling the underforest and pockets of sharp-looking oak. The trail began to rise slowly. Now and then, Marguerite could see a distant red cliff, rocky and bare, jutting out from the face of the low mountains.

As they rode, a fog settled in. Soon, it swirled around them like a soup. Marguerite's hair grew damp with droplets.

"Should we go back?" she asked.

"Why?"

"We cannot see."

"We are not lost," he said simply. "But we may be near the edge."

The horses started to climb out of the fog, and Marguerite was forced to lean forward and grip her mare's neck to keep her balance. Then the road crested a ridge and, on the other side, began to traverse the hillside above a deep, sweeping valley filled with a sea of mist. Here and there a tiny island of green pierced the veil, the tip of a spruce.

Marguerite heard a sound in the distance. Someone was calling. A woman, crying anxiously. Another voice answered. And then a male, calling to the rest. Marguerite could not make out the words—they were muffled. The tones, however, carried a note of distress. The phantom voices echoed across the valley, first near, then far, then near again. It was impossible to tell how distant the people truly were.

Donskoy reined his horse to a halt and listened. He tugged at the corner of his mustache contemplatively. He appeared unconcerned.

"Are they gypsies?" Marguerite asked.

Donskoy barked out a laugh. "What makes you think that?"

"They are travelers."

"Vistani rarely lose their way in the mists."

"If the people are lost, shouldn't we help them?"

"Help them?" He gave a dark laugh. "You don't even know them, who, or what, they are. Besides, I—

we—cannot reach them. They must come to us."

"I don't understand," Marguerite replied.

Donskoy studied her damp face. "No, I suppose you do not. Perhaps I should acquaint you with one of the strange truths of our realm, which only a few seem to have mastered. Do you remember commenting on the legends that the mists can be magical? On the night you first came to me?"

"Yes. But I only half believe it."

"Believe it in full. Those mists hem in my lands, ebbing and flowing like the tide. They are like a strange, great sea, cloaking dangers more horrifying than you can imagine. The Vistani boast the ability navigate this sea, and they seem virtually immune to the dangers within. And, too, there are a few without gypsy blood who manage passage through other means, though never as well. Jacqueline Montarri is one such. But they are all exceptions.

"I believe there are currents in those mists, strange tides or tendencies that are more . . . ethereal than tangible. One of those currents leads near to my land. It often carries the lost, the forsaken, those who attempt to journey through the fog without aid of the gypsies, or who simply find themselves immersed. The people we just heard are undoubtedly adrift on such a current." He sighed. "But such is life. Let us return to the castle." He steered his horse back down the road.

"If there are dangers, as you say, then we should help those travelers," Marguerite insisted. "Is there no way?"

Donskoy looked at her sternly. "Never presume to tell me what I should or should not do, my dear."

"But . . ."

She bit her tongue; his jaw had become rigid.

He smiled, and added, "Though, in this case, you

are quite right, of course. We should not leave them to drift. And we will help them find their way. After we return to the castle, I'll send Ekhart and Ljubo back to attend to them."

"Won't that take hours?"

"They are not as near as you think; it's a trick of the fog."

"We could call out to be sure . . ." she said softly.

"And perhaps lead them into greater danger. Most likely, they will only become more lost, searching for your phantom voice—or fleeing its sound, which the mists might alter to sound like a monstrous roar. No, your attempts would cause more harm than good. Ekhart and Ljubo are quite practiced at such things. Come, let us go. The sooner we reach the castle, the sooner my men will return."

He turned and started down the road at a canter. Reluctantly, she followed.

* * * * *

When they rode into the castle nearly two hours later, Marguerite was exhausted. Donskoy, in contrast, seemed remarkably spry. They stopped their horses before the keep. The lord dismounted and gave a sharp whistle, then helped Marguerite to the ground. Her legs were tired and unsteady. Ljubo emerged from the stables to take the horses.

"You haven't forgotten the travelers in the fog, have you?" Marguerite asked.

"Of course not, my dear," Donskoy replied, taking her hand.

"Travelers?" piped Ljubo behind them. His eyes sparkled, and his tongue darted ever so lightly between his broken teeth.

"Yes, Ljubo," said Donskoy evenly. "Travelers. We

would like you to effect a rescue, if possible."

Ljubo looked puzzled.

Donskoy continued, "You and Ekhart must see to them as usual. Summon the associates, if you'd like."

"Yes-yes, of course," said Ljubo, nodding. He rubbed his fraying fingers together. "At once, Lord Donskoy. Are there many?"

"At least three."

"Three. Three. Yes, well, three is three."

"But maybe more . . ."

"Ah-yes." Ljubo nodded as if he were incapable of stopping the motion. "Yes-yes, Lord Donskoy." Then he turned and waddled hastily back into the stables, tugging the horses behind him.

Marguerite and Donskoy climbed the long stair toward the looming keep.

"Does this happen often?" she asked, legs protesting the ascent.

"I do not understand your meaning."

"A rescue attempt. You used the phrase 'as usual' with Ljubo."

"Often enough, but not every day. It appears tied to the moon. Don't let it trouble you. Ljubo and Ekhart have the situation well in hand."

"Will they go straight away?"

"Straight away, my dear. You can be sure." He gripped her hand firmly. "It is no longer your concern."

And he was correct: Ljubo and Ekhart did depart immediately. As she and Donskoy crested the final stair, the two men burst from the stable doors, riding side by side at the front of the jostling cart. The wagon bed carried a small mass covered by a black tarp. Beside it crouched the three hounds, pressed low against the boards. Ekhart held the reins. He gave a curt nod at Donskoy as the wagon moved swiftly past. Ljubo grinned wildly over his shoulder, one arm clutching a lantern. He lifted the other hand to wave to Marguerite, then quickly returned it to the seat, gripping it for support as the cart careened across the clearing and went out of sight.

"You see?" said Donskoy. "They are making haste. If your travelers are still adrift near the rim, Ljubo and Ekhart will take care of them soon."

Marguerite did not like the sound of that. Somewhere, buried in the back of her mind, was a comment—something relevant, something Ljubo had said to her as they rode together to the castle when she arrived. She struggled to recall it. Something . . . Then Ljubo's voice echoed inside her mind: "We retrieve things, like . . ." followed by Ekhart's curt interruption. Like the lost, thought Marguerite. But surely there was nothing sinister in that . . .

"Come inside, my dear. I am feeling invigorated by our excursion." Indeed, his face, normally pasty, seemed flush with excitement. "We shall retire to my salon."

Suddenly, she did not like sound of that either.

ELEVEN

In the crimson cocoon that was Donskoy's salon, the lord peeled away his outer wear and tugged the bell-pull to summon Yelena. The fire burned brightly beneath its golden cowl, the velvet pillows upon the floor were plumped and neatly arrayed, and the red hookah with its silver-headed snake sat poised before the hearth, ready to serve its master. A sweet, musky scent filled the air. The room had been well tended in their absence.

Yelena appeared at the door to receive Donskoy's command for food and libation, then scuttled away in compliance, scarcely acknowledging Marguerite's wel coming smile. Marguerite felt somewhat abandoned.

Donskoy removed her cloak and gently tugged off her matching blue gloves, then bade her sit on the red velvet divan. His own gloves, of course, remained in place. She noted they were faintly soiled from the day's activity; a streak of something clear and shining had crusted upon the black suede. As her husband leaned close, she smelled the strange perfume of sweat, smoke, and horses that now permeated his hair and clothing.

"Do you think we'll have guests tonight?" she asked, self-consciously smoothing her skirts. "Perhaps we should tell Yelena and Zosia."

"Guests?" Donskoy strode to the fire and looked down at the water pipe.

"Yes," Marguerite replied. "If Ekhart and Ljubo are successful, perhaps they will bring the travelers here."

Donskoy chuckled. He left the hookah unattended and retrieved his long, slender white pipe from a wooden stand on a side table. "Perhaps," he said.

"Have you entertained such travelers before?"

"After a fashion. But one does not often encounter strangers who make good—" Donskoy had reached into the fire with a taper to light the pipe, and he paused now, bringing the bowl to red, glowing life with a few gentle puffs, then finished, "—who make good guests."

"I see," replied Marguerite, though she did not. She stared at the carved stem of Donskoy's ivory pipe, which displayed a strand of interwoven humanoid bodies, writhing and entwined, mouths agape, like a crowded scene from purgatory.

Yelena appeared bearing a tray with two chalices and a jug of wine, along with a finger-bowl of scented water and a cloth, which she carefully laid on the small round table before Marguerite. After a second brief foray, the mute returned with a silver tray laden with meats, cheeses, and pastries. A pair of roasted starlings lay dead at the side, their feathers twice speckled, first by nature, then by the oven's ash. After the mouse-haired mute had decanted the wine, Lord Donskoy dismissed her.

Marguerite dipped her fingers in the bay-scented water to wash. Her husband left his pipe to burn itself out on the stand and busied himself in his cupboard behind her. She peeked over her shoulder and glimpsed his turned back, the cabinet door open just a sliver as before. She looked away, fearful of what would happen if Donskoy caught her spying.

When he returned, he wore a fresh pair of gloves. As he lifted his chalice to his lips, Marguerite stared at the plush, velvety suede covering his hands. Donskoy caught her glance.

"You are curious about the gloves." He uncoiled two fingers from the stem of his chalice and waved them subtly, like antennae.

"No." Then she added, "Well, perhaps a little."

Donskoy's face told her she should have held her tongue; the dismay was obvious in his expression, and his response was menacingly low. "It is none of your business."

"No, of course not," said Marguerite, adding quickly, "my lord." She hoped the pause had not been perceptible. Suddenly, she felt as if she had wandered into a trap, had become tangled like a fly in the middle of a spider's web, and now the spider was approaching.

"Do my gloves disturb you, Marguerite?" asked Donskoy, wriggling his black, furry fingers.

"No, my lord," she replied evenly, regaining her composure. "Your fashions may intrigue me, but, as you say, they are none of my concern."

He studied her.

Marguerite pulled her lips into a smile, intentionally demure, then dropped her gaze. She sipped from her chalice, a wary bird.

To her surprise, Donskoy did not drop the subject. "The matter is somewhat embarrassing, and so I rarely speak of it. But you are my wife, so I shall confess to you that I suffer a certain . . . deformity."

She gave no reply.

"Do you not wish to see it?" Donskoy asked, as if daring her.

Marguerite hesitated, suddenly realizing that she did not wish to look upon his deformity—not really. Once she had seen it, she might be unable to forget it, might think of it hidden beneath the sheath of his gloves each time he probed or caressed her skin. And yet . . .

And yet she was curious. "Only if you wish to show me," she said. "But it is not necessary. I must admit that I am actually quite fond of your gloves."

"Yes," he replied, stroking a finger across her cheek. "They are very soft and fine, are they not?"

She nodded.

"Another time then," he said.

Marguerite nodded again, and wondered whether her head would soon bob unceasingly of its own accord, like Ljubo's. Soon she too might be the affable fool.

Donskoy continued, "Let us not speak of this matter anymore tonight."

"Of course. I won't mention it again, my lord." She stared at her lap as if it suddenly held great interest and thought to herself, Another entry to the list of things not mentioned and things not done. Marguerite wished she had not led him inadvertently toward this topic in the first place. Perhaps something trite and inconsequential would break the tension that remained. He might be appeased by some silly feminine remark; it seemed to fulfill his expectations of her.

"I am amazed," she said, "that Yelena and Zosia can accomplish so much. This food, I mean. And attending to the castle. Granted, we require only a few rooms, but still their efforts are astounding."

"Yes," Donskoy replied. "Somehow they manage. Zosia can be a magician in the kitchen when she wants to. And at times it seems almost as if the castle sustains itself, such as it is." He speared a piece of meat and gobbled it up.

Marguerite ate too, glad to discover that the flavors were pleasing, with heavy notes of mustard, garlic, and onion. She left only the birds untouched. It was a common enough dish, but she disliked picking at the carcasses. The pastries tasted of sweet honey and almonds, and they did not seem stale in the least. For a while, she focused on the food; it kept her from thinking of the liaison to come. Donskoy ate without speaking, licking his lips, eyeing her as if she were edible. When he had finished, he suddenly reached under her skirt and began to remove her stockings. Marguerite held a pastry poised in her fingers, her mouth open with surprise. He moved his hand unexpectedly, and the pastry dropped to the ground.

* * * * *

An hour later, Marguerite found herself back in her room, the door securely locked. Weary from the day's activity, she readied herself for bed, though the sun itself had only just retired, and the sky had not yet gone black. She stripped to her chemise and pulled on a pair of slippers and a dressing gown.

Her first intimate encounter with Donskoy had been strange and surreal, a languid dream, disturbing yet perversely thrilling. It had lasted for hours, or so it seemed, and the details had blurred in her mind. In contrast, the second coupling had been acute, brisk, and rather unpleasant. She had tried hard not to reveal her reaction. Not that he was attuned to such things.

Marguerite noticed that the shutters on her window hung open, and she went to close them against the cold. Something in the darkness beyond caught her eye. Deep in the forest, the phantom fire pulsed again, a heartbeat in the body of wood. *Ramus*. Marguerite did not understand why he stayed, or if he had gone, why he had returned. What does he want here? she wondered. He purposefully avoided Donskoy; the castle itself did not seem to draw him. Maybe he was seeking his own tribe, awaiting some kind of rendezvous. He had told her that Arturi's caravan was not his own. And it did seem that Vistani traveled the roads, at least as far as the fork. The fork—where Vistani left their marks on a tree for other gypsies to discover.

Marguerite recalled the new tralak she had seen during her outing with Donskoy. In her wardrobe cabinet, she knew, lay the half-charred manuscript penned by Van Richten. With these pages, she could probably decipher the tralak's meaning. Marguerite eyed the closed door of her cabinet suspiciously, as if a fiend lurked behind it. Yet what harm could come from consulting the book? It was only a book after all.

Marguerite's hand was poised on the cabinet door when the sound of an approaching wagon drew her away. She went quickly to the window and saw Ljubo and Ekhart returning. Pressing her nose against the glass, she strained, searching for silhouettes in the wagon. She sighed with disappointment. There was only the tall thin Ekhart, the squat form of Ljubo beside him. The back of the wagon appeared fuller, however. A lumpy mound rose in the bed, covered by a tarp. The three black hounds stood upon it proudly, like climbers laying claim to a summit. Their black shapes swayed wildly with the motion of the wagon. It was a wonder the beasts didn't tumble out. One of them threw its head back and heralded their return with a frightful howl. For a moment, Marguerite imagined a red fire burning deep within in its throat, as if she had seen the door to a kiln thrown open. Then the wagon, and the image, passed out of view.

She longed to get a closer look, to rush to the

stables, where she could observe Ljubo and Ekhart unloading the cart. What would she see? An unsettling image came to mind. Perhaps now it was a cart full of corpses—or a cart that mimicked it, whose dead were only sleeping. But then she thought no, not bodies. That was silly. Zosia had planted the suggestion, when describing how some Vistani caravans bore passengers through the mists. But what else might Ekhart and Ljubo have brought? Surely it would be all right if she went to the stables to observe their arrival. Marguerite was halfway to the door before she remembered Lord Donskoy had locked her in for the night.

She gazed at the hounds in the tapestry, and considered the secret passage they guarded. A locked door need not deter her. Yet it could be dangerous to venture away from her room so early. The castle did not sleep. Someone might see her.

Exasperated, Marguerite let out a sigh. She thought of the toad, Griezellbub, who had aided her so deftly in her first escape. He had not visited since that night. She pictured him before her, his mouth wide with a mocking grin. "If you were truly useful," she said aloud, speaking to the air, "you'd be my spy. *My* spy, you ugly little beast." But she knew he answered to Zosia, or to no one at all.

"I will go out," she announced softly, feeling a sudden surge of recklessness. "And I will simply refuse to get caught." Marguerite tossed off her dressing gown and wriggled into a long dark tunic with split sides. Then she kneeled before the tapestry like a supplicant. The wall god answered her prayer, and she crawled into his arms, entering the passage. The decaying chamber at the other end appeared unchanged. Marguerite tiptoed to the door and pressed her ear against the wood. Nothing. She opened it just a crack, grimacing at the familiar protest of its hinges. Turning sideways, she slipped into the hall. She did not carry a light, for it might announce her presence.

To the right lay the stairwell leading to the dungeons. The stables, however, could be reached only by passing through the foyer below—at least as far as she knew. Marguerite turned left, and headed down the hall, as quiet as a mouse. She came to the broad, curving stair and began a careful descent. On the wall, the torches burned in their iron sconces. Below, she could hear a man speaking—Ekhart, perhaps. She dared not venture too close; with her luck, he had the hounds. If he did, the dogs would scent her and scrabble up the stairs to point her out. Fragments of Ekhart's muffled report drifted up to her.

"Five," Ekhart said. ". . . easy . . ."

Marguerite dared to move a step closer.

". . . some silver . . . jewelry . . . wine and sugar."

She took another step.

Ekhart continued, ". . . so we brought . . . "

A second man snapped out a reply. "Idiot!" Marguerite had moved close enough to hear all his words, and to tell that it was Lord Donskoy himself. "When my wife is near, you'll make no procurements for the mere whims of Miss Montarri."

"As you wish, my lord," replied Ekhart. "It was at Ljubo's insistence. Besides, there was some mention of more to follow, so we thought—"

"Well *don't* think, old man," Donskoy intervened. "You've managed it badly." The lord paused, then chuckled. "And since when do you answer to Ljubo? No, I know you, Ekhart. And I suspect you have a few whims of your own concerning the cargo. Eh? Am I right?"

A muffled grunt, half a laugh, came in reply.

Donskoy continued, "Though I suppose I cannot

blame you. Come with me to the drawing room, then, and share a nightcap while we discuss your instructions."

At that moment, Marguerite heard someone coming down the stairs behind her—coming softly and swiftly. She pressed herself to the wall, hoping desperately that whoever—whatever—was coming would not notice her lurking in the shadows.

Directly behind Marguerite, Yelena gasped loudly and dropped her candle. It rolled down the last three steps and into the foyer beyond.

"Ekhart, wait!" Donskoy hissed, his voice close below. "Did you hear that? Between Yelena and that disgusting toad of Zosia's, this castle has far too many ears."

Footsteps approached the base of the stairs. "Show yourself!" Donskoy bellowed.

Marguerite put a finger to her lips. Yelena shook her head frantically and tugged on Marguerite's sleeve, pointing to the top of the stairs. Then the mute girl hastily descended the stairs into the foyer.

Marguerite slunk back around the corner, retreating three steps up. She heard a sudden blow in the foyer below, followed by a soft exclamation of pain.

"Worm!" spat Donskoy. "Were you eavesdropping again?" Another smack punctuated his question. "Too many ears entirely. Well that can be fixed. If I catch you skulking about again, I'll cut off both of yours."

There was pause, then Ekhart said, "I'll handle the cargo. You needn't worry."

Donskoy grunted his assent. Yelena's soft whimpering accented his words.

"Quit whining, wench," he muttered. "Go with Ekhart and assist as he requires. And be sure you clean up after him."

Marguerite crept up the stairs, promising herself that she would find some way to improve Yelena's treatment. Donskoy expected the girl to materialize whenever he required, yet if she happened to be near when he did not want her, she suffered for it.

With that vow, Marguerite hurried through the hall and slipped into the decaying room next to hers as quietly as possible. She stood behind the door a moment, listening. When she was sure no one had followed, she knelt before the wall and opened the secret passage, then crawled inside.

The stones slid into place behind her. She scrabbled quickly through the tunnel, suddenly eager to be safe in her bed. But when she reached out to open the portal into her own chamber, the stones remained motionless.

An involuntary groan rose in her throat. Marguerite pushed with all her might, but nothing happened; the wall refused to shift. She remembered Donskoy's warning: "The passages are crumbling and prone to failure, and you might find yourself entombed in a wall."

Her heart thundered in her ears, the only sound in the otherwise still passage. Slowly, methodically, she began to push every stone that barred her path. Still, nothing happened. Marguerite pounded her fist against the stone she recalled as the trigger. This time, the wall gave way. She lifted the tapestry and scrambled to freedom.

Safely in her chamber, she stood, breathing heavily. "Idiot," she whispered. She had been stupid and clumsy, lacking both stealth and common sense. If Yelena could surprise her so readily, then why not Ljubo or Ekhart, or Donskoy himself? Further, she had not even imagined the secret passage could malfunction, though her husband had warned of the possibility that very day. She would not venture through the tunnel again—not without good reason. Ekhart's activity seemed meaningless compared to the prospect of slow suffocation, or the thought of being discovered and relocated to one of the miasmic chambers that typified the keep.

Marguerite removed her tunic and returned it to the wardrobe. Staring inside the cabinet, she recalled what she had been doing before Ekhart and Ljubo's return distracted her. She donned her dressing gown and withdrew *Van Richten's Guide to the Vistani* from the wardrobe, then took it to her chair by the fire. There she sat and unwrapped the black shroud, spreading it over her lap. The innermost folds of the cloth were coated with ash; she worked slowly, taking care not to soil her garment. The book seemed to weigh no more than a feather upon her thighs. Gingerly she leafed through the pages, those that still allowed themselves to be parted. At length she rediscovered the pictures of tralaks. There again was the symbol that the book had opened to of its own accord, three lines striking a fourth: *cursed*. A shudder ran down her back; she reminded herself of what Zosia had told her, that Valeska's ghost intended her no harm.

What was the symbol on the road? A triangle of some sort, pointing downward. The book showed a triangle and a line, which was titled "recent murder," but the tip pointed up. There was another with a cross through it, entitled "ancient murders." She could find nothing quite like the overturned triangle Donskoy had removed from the tree, but it did not seem a wild guess to think that it had something to do with death. Perhaps it meant "suicide"; that seemed fitting for an inverted version of the murder symbol.

Slowly and carefully, she opened the book to another section, curious what she might find. Most of the tome was illegible, as if the ink had literally ignited and burned away. Whole chapters had been fused

together, the pages having melted and become one. It
was odd, she thought. She had never seen parchment
or ink behave in this way before. Then she laughed at
herself: neither had she ever seen a book that would
not burn, or that opened of its own accord.

A title on a page caught her eye: "Torture and terror." The chapter appeared to contain Van Richten's
theories on curses and the evil eye—the Vistani's
strange ability to cause enchantments with a mere
look. Most often, those enchantments were malevolent. Marguerite remembered Ramus's penetrating
gaze, how it filled her with warmth and threatened to
melt away her caution. It had not seemed harmful, but
had she not looked away. . . . Suddenly another face
came to mind, another set of dark, penetrating eyes.
Valeska's eyes. Zosia had assured her that Valeska
meant her no harm. But what if Zosia was wrong?

Then she admonished herself aloud, borrowing a
phrase from Zosia. "Don't let your imagination run off
like a mad hare, Marguerite." She continued to look
through the book for answers; she had nowhere else
to turn. She could only make out a few words here
and there, describing horrid afflictions that a Vistani
curse might cause: a condition called "the body melt,"
which converted a man into gooey liquid; a passing
mention of gangrene; something about the conversion
of one's skeleton to a baglike form. She shuddered.

Then an intriguing phrase caught her eye: "black
hands." According to Van Richten, they could mark a
man who had wronged the Vistani; the author made
note of a thief who had robbed a caravan and found
his own skin discolored by the act. Marguerite thought
of her husband's black gloves, but there was no connection; they were only gloves, after all. The hands
themselves were not black—not that she knew of. He
suffered from some sort of deformity; that's what he

had told her. She let her mind wander over the possibilities: festering boils, skin like a snake's, a missing
digit or two, or the reverse—a skinny extra finger
tucked alongside its sturdy brother, like a withered
worm. Or a third eye, perhaps, rooted on the tip of his
thumb. Whatever Donskoy's deformity was, it did not
cripple him; his hands remained strong, his grip hard
and firm—like a vise, when he wanted it so.

Marguerite looked down and saw that her own
hands had become black from handling the book. She
shivered. Carefully she rewrapped the tome in its
black cloth and returned it to her cabinet. Then she
washed the ash from her hands, relieved to see her
own clean skin once again.

Her weariness came back to her, now twice as
intense as before. It had been a full day, she mused,
full of exploration and of being explored. She removed
the dressing gown and, with her last bit of strength,
crawled through the bed curtains to curl her body into
the pit of the mattress.

She slept for hours. As a cloud of bats wheeled in
the sky outside the castle, Marguerite dreamed once
more of the dark-haired gypsy, who rose from the
black water and parted the rock and stepped out into
the green-black sea of trees. Marguerite followed
behind her, watching as the Vistana slipped in and out
of view, and then disappeared. In a moonlit clearing,
Marguerite found her again. The gypsy was dancing,
moving slowly, naked but for the myriad snakes that
hung from her arms like black scarves.

And then the dream ended. Marguerite shifted in the
pit of her bed and slept on, slumbering as the sun
climbed from its nightly grave; she slept as it rose
high overhead and merged with the cold gray haze
that covered Donskoy's land.

* * * * *

When Marguerite awoke, Yelena was stoking the hearth. A breakfast tray lay on the table nearby. The mute girl turned and headed for the door.

"Wait." Marguerite slipped out from between the walls of her velvet tent. "I want to speak to you."

Yelena paused and turned her head, gazing at Marguerite wearily from beneath the little brown cap she always wore. The girl's face was a puffy palette of pale gray-and-purple shadows, and her lips had fused in a frown.

"It seems I should thank you again," said Marguerite, "for not giving me away."

Yelena's lips parted slightly, releasing a deep sigh.

"I am very grateful." Marguerite added boldly, "Don't you want to know how I got out?"

The mute rolled her eyes, then shot a glance toward the tapestry.

She knows then, thought Marguerite. "Well, as I said, I am very grateful. And you can rest assured that I won't cause this trouble for you again."

At this, Yelena gave a sharp squeak—a laugh, perhaps, but completely lacking in mirth. The servant curtsied and jerked her head toward the door.

"Of course," said Marguerite. "You may go. I only wanted to thank you."

The mute girl curtsied again and departed. Marguerite slipped out of bed, padding after her. She tried the handle on the door and to her relief, found it unlocked. After washing at the basin, she went to the hearth to inspect the breakfast tray. It held a slab of cold meat, faintly green along one edge; the usual piece of bread; and a ewer of cold wine. She sniffed the wine and wrinkled her nose. Despite the heavy dose of cloves, she could tell it was horribly sour;

some of Donskoy's barrels must be going bad. Or else
Yelena was making a statement. Then Marguerite
noticed something else on the tray: a small piece of
parchment, folded in half. She opened it, and discovered a note from Lord Donskoy.

My wife, it read. *I trust you slept well. You must
content yourself with reading this morning. In the
afternoon, come to my salon. —D.*

Marguerite fed the parchment to the fire and
stretched. At least the rest of the morning was hers.
And the door was open. Given this streak of fortune,
she had no intention of languishing in her room with a
book. Instead, she planned to visit the stables, where
she could examine the cart she had seen returning
last night. It would probably be unloaded by now, but
certainly Ljubo would tell her about the travelers in the
mists. She smiled thinly, recalling her last furtive conversation with the man. Yes, Ljubo would talk. Ljubo,
after all, was her friend.

* * * * *

Dressed in high boots and a simple woolen shift
belted low round her hips, Marguerite emerged in the
court. It had not been easy to find her way alone, and
she had come to several dead ends amid the castle's
jumbled and rotting storerooms; finally she had closed
her eyes and followed her memory like a dream. Now
she stepped out toward the stables, crossing the flagstones that were slick with mud and dung. She looked
for Ljubo or Ekhart but saw only the other animals. The
black gaggle of geese moved through the court like a
raucous cloud. The goat bleated from its tether, and the
peacock continued its walk around the perimeter like a
sullen guard. Five dark horse tails and one that was
dirty white hung over the stable walls, all in a row.

The wagon had been parked in an open stall. Marguerite picked her way across the court and peered inside. The wagon bed itself was bare to the rough boards. On the ground nearby, however, lay the black tarp, draped over a jumbled mound. She lifted the edge, discovering a barrel labeled "sugar" and a few unmarked crates. She probed a little further, unveiling a long black chest. It resembled the crate that had accompanied her from Darkon. Marguerite knelt before it, fingering the clasp.

"Looking for something?"

Marguerite jumped, falling backward onto her seat. It was Ekhart, looming behind her, shovel in hand.

"No, I—," she stammered. "Well, yes, actually."

Marguerite brushed herself off and stood to face him. They stared at one another, her own eyes liquid and challenging, his gray and frozen.

Ekhart said sourly, "And that would be . . . ?"

"It is none of your business," retorted Marguerite huffily. "I am the lady of this castle now, and you shall address me as such."

Ekhart stretched his thin lips into an even wider line, which for him counted as a smile. "All right then, *Lady* Marguerite," he mocked. "Is there some way that I might assist you?"

"No, Ekhart. Thank you," she said stiffly. "I was looking for Ljubo."

"Indeed. And what would you require of my manservant?"

"*Your* man-servant?"

"He answers to me."

"I thought he might tell something about your excursion yesterday."

"Did you? Why don't you ask me instead?"

"All right, Ekhart. I wanted to know what became of the travelers."

"Travelers?"

"Yes. The people lost in the fog. I heard them calling out myself, so spare me any denial."

Ekhart rubbed his chin and chortled. "No. I would not even attempt it. What is it, precisely, that you would know?"

"Just as I said. What happened to the travelers?"

"We were unable to locate them in time."

"You mean they are dead?"

"Yes."

"How?" Marguerite's voice was quiet.

"The mists hold many dangers," Ekhart replied matter-of-factly.

"But what kind of dangers? Surely you must have some idea what occurred."

"Animals. Predators. It's difficult to say. Not much evidence remained, if you can grasp my meaning. Or shall I paint you a more detailed picture?"

"No, thank you," she replied. She waved a hand toward the crates. "And these things," she added. "You took them."

"Of course," said Ekhart. "The dead have no need of such possessions where they are bound. Why should we not benefit? Don't pretend you are shocked, milady. Half the gowns you wear were obtained in this fashion." He tapped the shovel against the dirt floor and stared at her, one white brow raised. "Will that be all then, Marguerite?"

"Yes, Ekhart. Thank you. You may go."

He laughed. "I'm afraid not, *Lady* Marguerite. I take my orders from Lord Donskoy. I am here on his behalf, in fact. And I believe it is you who must go. Are you not expected soon in Lord Donskoy's salon?"

"Not until this afternoon," she replied.

"You have underestimated the hour."

Marguerite looked up at the sunless sky. Was that

possible? Had she slept so long before she arose?

"And of course," continued Ekhart, "you will want to change your attire before you see your lord, and 'freshen up' a bit."

Marguerite flushed with annoyance. His comments were rude and improper, but he was right. When she returned to her room, she exchanged her boots for silk slippers and donned the purple silk gown, the one she had worn on the night she had first met Donskoy. Perhaps the gown would bring her luck.

She found her husband in his salon, sitting beside the hearth, nursing the tip of his water pipe. He greeted her with a red-eyed leer and smiled.

"Do you dance, Marguerite?" he asked abruptly.

Her mouth gaped. "I'm not sure what you mean."

"I mean, do you *dance?* I mean do you strip yourself bare and bend like a willow, and weave your wicked little spells in the moonlight?"

Marguerite paused, her expression blank. He was delirious again.

"No," he said. "I didn't think so." Then he patted the pillow beside him on the floor. "No matter. You can dance for me another way."

* * * * *

The following morning, Marguerite found a new note on her breakfast tray. Donskoy carefully dictated her whereabouts in the castle—her chamber, the music room, the library, and of course, his salon. Ekhart had told him of her visit to the stables, and Donskoy had not been pleased. He said that such forays were "beneath" her. Further, he instructed her to keep contact with "all servants" to a minimum, for to behave otherwise was unbefitting the lady of a castle. When Marguerite sought out Zosia or Ljubo, she could not find them.

A week passed. Marguerite entertained herself by reading a few mundane selections from the library, and, when that grew stale, she collected the makings of a tapestry with Yelena's help and set to work on it in the music room. Her hand was not steady or practiced. She often pricked her fingers and had to stop the work to keep from staining the fabric with blood. It was a wonder, she thought, that she had once helped in preparing her own wedding gown—the white gown she never wore. It saddened her to think of it. Darkon . . . her mother's face softly illumined by the fire . . . the long nights spent stitching and chatting together: these images rose before her. Sometimes, she knew, her mother had torn out Marguerite's own poor stitches and later redone them in secret, in the hours just before dawn. Marguerite had not minded. It all seemed so distant now, so unreal, like stories she had read in a dream.

Soon the days gained their own kind of rhythm. First breakfast in her room, alone. A visit to the music room. Reading and stitching. And, if the weather was passable, a short walk with Ekhart at Donskoy's behest, "to keep her healthy and fresh." Then, as the afternoon waned, the obligatory visit to Donskoy's salon for the ritual coupling. This was followed by dinner with her husband, who clearly preferred that they eat in silence. After a while, Marguerite preferred it too.

TWELVE

One day merged with the next, until more than a fort-night had passed since Marguerite's arrival. A cold gray haze hung over the land, unchanging. The routine in the castle remained the same as well, but with the slow pro-gression of hours, a certain tension began to emerge between Marguerite and her husband. She could do nothing to ease it, despite numerous attempts. Twice she suggested to Donsky that they again ride over his lands. And twice he declined, insisting she walk the grounds with Ekhart instead. In another effort to please her husband, Marguerite spoke of the travels they might one day undertake with their children. Lord Donskoy became venomous and spat at her.

"Do you seek to torment me?" he hissed. "You know I cannot leave." But Marguerite did not know, and she did not really believe him.

The true cause of Donskoy's displeasure was clear. Once, while he lay with Marguerite in his red salon, Donskoy rested his hand upon her bare stomach.

"Do you not share my desire for an heir?" he asked, tracing a circle across her skin. He proceeded to draw another circle within it, mimicking the pattern Zosia

made on the mornings of her frequent pregnancy
tests. After the first divining, Donskoy had remained
patient, as he had promised. But now his patience
was wearing thin, and Marguerite felt its loss acutely.

"My lord," she said, noting that the pressure of his
fingers on her stomach had increased. "You know I
desire a son as much as you do." The scene was so
queer, yet so typical, that Marguerite began to wonder
if she were the one who partook too freely of the
hookah smoke.

"Yet I doubt your sincerity," Donskoy replied, moving his hand, plucking idly at her skin. "I wonder if
perhaps you do something to keep my seed from taking hold." He pressed his sueded finger into the cleft
between her ribs, and Marguerite felt pinned to the
floor like a bug collector's specimen.

She swallowed hard to steady her voice. "Surely
you don't really believe that, Lord Donskoy. Why
would I do such a thing?"

"I could not venture a guess," he replied. "For certainly you must know what happens to wives who
don't conceive."

Marguerite kept silent.

"They are set aside," Donskoy continued, "discarded
for the useless vessels they've become. Sloughed off
like old skin and cast into the mists." He paused,
chortling darkly. "Or they're sold, passed to some
gold-rich party who has no interest in their capacity to
multiply. Sold for pleasure. Sold for parts. . . . " His
fingers trailed across her body, and he kissed her gently
on the thigh. "But I'm sure you wouldn't allow that to
happen to you, my dear."

"No, my lord," she replied quietly. Marguerite
closed her eyes to block out the scene, but what she
saw behind her lids was worse. "No," she repeated, in
a voice too soft for anyone to hear.

* * * * *

Two days later, when her blood came, Donskoy could not contain his rage and struck her. Stunned, Marguerite fled the salon and hurried to her room, where for the first time, she wished the door could be locked from the inside.

Briefly, she thought of leaving. But to go where and do what? She had known only two homes in her life, and despite her idle daydreams, she had never wandered far from either. Life with Donskoy was still preferable to eternal unlife—the fate she surely would have known had she stayed in Darkon. And she had pledged herself to be his wife, giving her sacred promise before a priest—though a priest like no other she had ever seen. If only she could bear her husband an heir, her fortune would turn.

The following morning, her tray contained the usual note from Donskoy. It included a veiled apology and announced that he would not require her companionship that day. For a moment, Marguerite imagined him making arrangements for her sale. Then she managed to dispel the notion. *No*, she thought, he would remain in his salon, savoring the tender bite of his hookah, oblivious to everyone and everything beyond the boundaries of his own mind. Marguerite dressed and went down to the kitchen to seek the only solace possible. To seek the assistance of a Vistani witch. She hoped that Zosia would be there.

The smell of garlic and boiling meat grew stronger in the passage as Marguerite approached the kitchen. She paused at the threshold, staring into the room. On the table lay a pair of rabbits, skinned and readied for the spit, their pink muscles firm and glistening. Nearby was a mortar and pestle, a pile of little skeletons resembling frogs, and a large wooden bowl filled with mash. Small piles of dried herbs rested in a circle upon a wooden platter. At the center of the platter lay a slimy heap of tiny purple-red orbs, presumably roe. It occurred to Marguerite that she had seen comparatively little evidence of Zosia's cooking until this time—usually she saw only the results when Yelena materialized from the shadows bearing a fully laden tray.

Zosia squatted upon a three-legged stool before the fire, her black skirts spreading on either side. Her dark, kerchiefed head was bent toward the sooty maw of the hearth. The embers glowed red, and a thick, churning smoke swirled from beneath the lintel, but Zosia appeared oblivious. She hummed a sort of dirge as she worked, slow and somber. A pair of cauldrons dangled above the fire on metal hooks. As Marguerite looked on like a curious mouse, the old woman swung one of the pots toward the fire and floated her hand above it, sifting a dark powder into the steaming mix.

If Zosia was aware of an audience hovering in the doorway, the witch showed no sign. The longer Marguerite stood watching, the more reluctant she became to announce her presence. She began to wonder if the old woman ignored her expressly; perhaps Zosia knew of Marguerite's failure to conceive, and now disdained her as much as Donskoy.

After a few moments, Zosia ceased her humming and clucked impatiently. "Well, come in, come in, girl. Don't just stand there gaping."

"How did you know I was here?" Marguerite asked, stepping into the room. She sat on the bench beside the table, eyeing the collection of ingredients.

Zosia shrugged, pulling the pot away from the fire. She gazed at its surface intently, as if expecting some response. Then she tossed in a pinch of black powder. A puff of blue smoke rose from the pot, hovering, then fled up the chimney. "You ask a question of very little consequence," Zosia continued. "How do I know you are there? I have ears and a nose, do I not? And I have eyes."

Suddenly Marguerite felt someone else's eyes upon her. She turned and discovered two yellow orbs shining at her from a shadowy corner. Gradually, she discerned Griezellbub's black body squatting in the murk. The toad's meaty tongue shot out toward an unseen target. Marguerite blinked in surprise. When she looked again, Griezell's throat was swollen and lumpy, with a snake's tail wriggling between his lips.

"Ask me something of value," Zosia continued. "For today I am seeing quite clearly again. Like old times, almost. Do you not seek my help?"

Marguerite pulled her eyes away from Griezell. "Yes," she said. "How do you know?"

Zosia shrugged again. "Why else would you visit? I know well what occurred last night. Where else could you turn? Fortunately for you, I can assist."

"How, when even I do not know what I am seeking?"

Zosia chortled. "But you do, Marguerite, you do. You wish to avoid another month like this one."

Marguerite stared at the floor. "Yes. At least the ending."

"Donskoy was most displeased. He accused you of spoiling your own field, did he not?"

"He did," replied Marguerite, her eyes growing moist.

"And he accused me earlier of assisting you. Did you know that, my child?"

"No. I'm sorry for any trouble I've caused."

"*Tsk.* I can handle your lord. Of course I dissuaded him of any notion that I was responsible. I promised him once again that you would become pregnant soon. And you must, Marguerite, before another month is out, or things will become very unpleasant for us all."

"Why did you promise it, Zosia? You have only made things worse. Isn't it possible that I cannot have a child by Donskoy? Such things are not in your control."

Zosia cackled. "If you believe I am powerless, then why are you here?"

"I didn't know what else to do," stammered Marguerite, "who else to see. Even this is a risk. Donskoy prefers I remain alone, that I seek no one's company but his. But of late—"

"Silly girl," said Zosia soothingly. "Have faith. I will help you. The years spent here have diminished my powers, it is true, but I can still lay the course for what must be. I know of a potion that will help you conceive a child."

"And it works?"

Zosia scowled at her. "*Tsk.* Of course it does. Why else would I suggest it?"

"And are there risks?"

Zosia clucked impatiently. "Everything holds a risk. If you do nothing, the risks are greater. Now, do you wish my help or not? I have no time for games."

Marguerite paused. "Yes," she said. "Make me the potion."

"Nothing worthwhile is that simple, my dear. First, you must do something for me. Go out into the forest and find the web of a spider, a white spider. The time is right for this harvest; the moon is waxing. When you have found the web, bring the silken strands to me, and I will make a philter for you to drink."

"You speak in riddles," said Marguerite. "Are you saying I must gather the web by moonlight?"

Zosia eyed her carefully. "Precisely. And it must be tonight. I have seen to it that your lord remains indisposed until tomorrow, but when the dawn comes, he will once again be keen to your whereabouts."

Marguerite said nothing, pondering the dreadful prospect of venturing into the forest after nightfall.

Sensing her fear, Zosia took a tin box from the rough-hewn shelf above the hearth and withdrew a tiny leather pouch on a string. She placed the pouch around Marguerite's neck and whispered, "Something to keep the beasts at bay. But fear not, Marguerite. The time for your death has not come."

* * * * *

Later, as Marguerite pushed past a pine branch in the thick of the forest, she clung to those words. They gave her comfort until another phrase came to mind: "a fate worse than death." Nervously she fondled the little pouch around her neck, pulling it to her nose. It smelled of garlic and mustard and something else she could not identify—something earthy and sour. Whatever lay in the pouch, Marguerite prayed its strength was as potent as its stench.

She had donned leggings, boots, and a heavy tunic, tying a small satchel at her waist. Thinking an early start was prudent, Marguerite had slipped out after lunch. After all, who knew how long it would take her to find a white spider? Zosia had offered little in the way of clues. But if Marguerite could locate the spider by day, she reasoned, then she could gather its web as soon as the sun fell, sparing herself a more difficult search in the dark.

The very notion that a spider web could solve her problems seemed a ridiculous fantasy, but she had no other hope, so she devoted herself to the effort.

Hours passed, and a light rain fell intermittently, dampening Marguerite's clothes. She sought webs in the crevices of rocks, between the rotting limbs of fallen trees, and beneath the low, sagging branches of the forest. She found spiders aplenty—small, large, black, brown, hairy, bald. But none of the eight-eyed creatures that stared back at her or darted for cover had a white body and white legs. Eventually, the sight of so many spiders and other skittering bugs made her flesh crawl. Marguerite began to imagine that someone's eyes were constantly upon her. She never saw them, of course, but she could feel them, like soft claws scrabbling at the base of her neck. She wondered if Griezellbub had followed her into the forest. Later, she thought of Ramus, who had watched her as she wandered before. Certainly by now, he had departed Donskoy's land.

The daylight waned. Marguerite continued her search at the clearing near the waterfall, where she had rested during her previous foray into the woods. As night fell, the mist cleared, and the sky became a dark vault teasingly flecked by low clouds. At least the moon was in Marguerite's favor. Cloud-shadows raced across the ground like hounds on the hunt. Their fleeting images taunted Marguerite; more than once she started and cried out, mistaking the play of light for an animal rushing past, or perhaps a spirit.

Now and again she saw them—the eyes of the forest, frozen in the glow of the moon. The scampering mouse, seized by the owl; the weasel slinking furtively through the brush, with something small and soft in its jaws. Once, as she huddled breathlessly at the base of a tree and clutched at the leather pouch around her neck, a huge black shape shambled past. Marguerite saw its yellow eyes shining in the dark. She thought of the beast from the banquet—the hideous sacrifice that had been part bear, part boar, part . . . else. But the silhouette lumbered on, leaving her unscathed. Marguerite told herself it was an ordinary bear.

Time was running out. She plunged deeper into the wood. She dropped to her hands and knees, willing her eyes to find the webs of spiders. The wind moaned plaintively, achieving a clear, sorrowful note. Then she realized it was not the wind at all; it was an instrument—a violin. She thought at once of Ramus. She crept through the forest toward the sound, which drew her like a siren's song.

Finally she saw him, standing near the old vardo, holding a shiny black fiddle to his chin. He had built a small fire, and its warmth lit his face with yellow-gold light. His black horse stood nearby, nosing the ground.

Marguerite crawled beneath the pungent skirts of a hemlock and hid, amused that the tables had turned. Now she was the watcher. She pressed herself low to the ground, oblivious to the dampness that seeped into her clothing. The music held her spellbound. The gypsy played beautifully, stroking and compressing the strings of his violin until they cried out in elation and agony.

Marguerite thought he must be playing for himself or simply serenading the night. But then she saw white wisps of fog rise from the soil and swirl about Ramus's body. They caressed him, coiling teasingly around his fingers and around the slender bow, streaming between the strings of the violin. As they passed through the instrument, they stretched and bent, assuming the shape of three Vistani women. They were ghosts, ephemeral as smoke, as smooth as white glass. They rose through the air, and the music swelled to echo the rhythm of their whirling dance. Diaphanous white skirts trailed behind them like the tails of comets.

Soon Ramus closed his eyes and slowed his tune.

The women clasped hands, moving three as one. Their features were indistinct, but something about them suggested age and sorrow. They sank toward the ground. The soil steamed beneath them. Ramus continued to play, his notes somber and slow. The women's ghostly white heads began to melt away from their shoulders, dripping down their bodies like candle wax. Then their bodies sagged and slumped, and the shoulders disappeared, and the breasts, and the hips and the legs—melting away until nothing remained but a white cloud upon the ground. Then even that disappeared.

Ramus moved his fiddle from his chin and stared into the forest. Marguerite held her breath, not daring to move. She lay directly in the path of his gaze.

The gypsy walked across the clearing to where his black horse stood waiting. He slipped the violin into an embroidered satchel that hung from the saddle, then retrieved his round-brimmed hat from the pommel. The horse snorted, pawing nervously at the dirt. Ramus stroked the animal's muzzle and whispered something to quiet it. Then he turned once again toward Marguerite's hiding place.

"Lost again, Marguerite?" he asked, flashing a white smile. He tipped his hat.

Marguerite did not answer, hoping that if she remained silent, she might also be invisible.

"Not coming out?" asked Ramus. "Then you must mean for me to clamber in after you. A pleasant invitation indeed."

Marguerite wormed her way out of her hiding place, feeling graceless and chagrined. She took a step forward, then stopped, leaving several paces between them. Still she felt his attraction, and it amazed her. She swayed, unsteady. And she said nothing, for suddenly nothing at all would come to mind.

"So we meet again," Ramus said deeply. "I hope you enjoyed my serenade."

"I did," she replied, almost in a whisper. "It was magical."

Neither of them spoke of the spirits. It occurred to Marguerite that Ramus had summoned them with a powerful spell. If she mentioned his magic, she might somehow fall prey to its power. The dance lay between them like a secret, something intimately shared.

"Do you know the legend of the Vistani violin?" Ramus asked, reaching forward to stir the fire.

Marguerite shook her head.

"The first violin, it is said, was created to lure a lover. A young Vistana longed for the affections of a girl who spurned him. So deep was his desire that he sought the aid of dark powers to win her. The powers consented to help him. In payment, they demanded the spirits of the boy's brothers and sisters. The powers bound them into the strings and bow of the first violin, then gave the instrument to the boy, so that he might serenade his sweetheart. When the boy played, the violin filled the air with his family's pain, as well as their remembered joys, and the girl was spellbound. Unfortunately, she loved the musician only when he played, and eventually the sound of his victims drove the young man mad. He killed himself. But the next Vistana who took up the instrument found he could reproduce the sound with all its beauty. And so the violin was born."

"What a sad story," whispered Marguerite.

"Indeed. But only a legend." Ramus looked up from the fire. "So, what brings you out after nightfall, Marguerite? Was it me you sought? Did I lure you with my violin?"

"No," said Marguerite, struggling to think of some excuse for her wandering. She did not want to share her secrets with Ramus. "I was merely restless."

"Ah. My kind well understands that feeling. But it must take a great deal of restlessness to drive a *giorgia* from her cozy bed and into the forest after dark. Are you finding your home so unpleasant then, Marguerite, that you must escape into the night?"

"Not at all," she lied. "We are very happy at the keep."

Ramus laughed softly. "I am glad," he said. "Though I must say it is surprising."

"And why is that?" she asked, indignant.

Ramus shrugged. "Lord Donskoy's reputation suggests otherwise. But if he treats you well, I am glad to hear it. I must admit that you do not appear entirely abused." He smiled a sly smile. "Of course I myself could treat you better, and please you in ways you cannot imagine."

She had anticipated the advance, but it unnerved her nonetheless. "I'm certain I don't know what you mean."

Ramus's dark eyes flared, and his voice sank low. "And I'm certain that you do."

Marguerite expected him to step toward her, to touch her, but he made no move. "You mistake me," she said, "for another type of woman."

"I think I understand you quite well," he replied. "But I am no fiend. Your answer is no, then?"

"Yes."

He chortled. "Yes?"

"No."

"Such a pity for us both. But if you won't allow me to coax the music from your instrument, perhaps I can help you find what you are seeking."

Marguerite blushed. "I am seeking nothing. I told you I was just restless."

"Indeed. Just as you were not lost the other day?

Your pretense is foolish. I saw you scrabbling about the forest floor, and I watched your face grow dark with the setting of the sun. If you are looking for something, you should let me assist. I know the woods well. Alone you may never succeed."

Marguerite considered this for a moment. The Vistani spent their lives in the wild, and their reputation as trackers and woodsmen knew no equal. Perhaps Ramus could help her after all—if she could trust him. He stood beside his horse, smiling. He had summoned the dead, it was true, and made a few roguish advances, yet Marguerite did not fear him. Strangely, she did not dread him in the least. And she did not wish for him to leave her alone.

"Don't laugh," she said, "but I am seeking the web of a white spider."

Ramus chortled. "Not pregnant yet, is that it? And Lord Donskoy knows no patience."

Marguerite's face grew hot.

"Perhaps I can help there as well," he continued, "and we won't be needing a spider."

"You are too bold," said Marguerite huffily. "I don't want your help after all."

Ramus stepped closer and touched her arm. "Forgive me, Marguerite. I did not mean to offend you—truly. Perhaps I spend so much time alone that rudeness comes easily. Please allow me to assist you. I know where to look, and it is dangerous for you to continue this search alone."

* * * * *

Reluctantly, she accepted his help. Claiming they would do better on foot, Ramus took his satchel from his mount and slapped it on the flank; the horse vanished into the shadows. They wandered together into

the woods. He explained that the spider she sought
could be found only in a cave. Marguerite protested at
first, thinking Zosia would surely have told her as
much, but she followed anyway. She had enjoyed no
success on her own.

The pair walked down into the hollows, and then up
again, until they reached a sharp outcropping of rock,
jutting up toward the sky.

"A cave lies near the top," Ramus said. "Inside, I
believe we'll find the spider you need."

Carefully they picked their way up the slope. As
promised, they came upon the mouth of a cave. Marguerite stooped, following Ramus's lead, then
emerged in an immense chamber. A strange red moss
coated the walls, lighting the cavern with a faint lumi-
nescence. Stalagmites rose up from the floor, reaching out toward their twins above. Between the
pinnacles, great webs hung like lacy sails. Small white
bones were scattered about the floor below.

Marguerite noticed a firepit near the center of the
cave. A stack of kindling and small branches lay
beside it. Someone had been here before—Ramus,
undoubtedly. After all, the cave provided a natural
shelter.

"Sit," said Ramus, "and rest a while. I'll build a fire.
Then we'll wait for the spider to crawl into view. If we
remain quiet, it shouldn't take long."

Marguerite stood gazing about the chamber,
awestruck. The webs were immense, and she could
only wonder about the size of their maker. "But I don't
need the spider itself," she protested gently, "only the
web."

"Until we see the spinner, we cannot be sure of the
product."

Marguerite heard the crackling of a fire behind her.
She turned, and saw that Ramus had already

mounded kindling in the black hollow and summoned a flame. She wondered at his skill. Something nagged at the back of her mind, some inconsistency between the fire and the Vistana's statement, but she was too weary and cold to bring it to the fore.

Ramus took a blanket from his satchel and spread it near the fire. He bowed deeply, then motioned for Marguerite to sit. She smiled and complied. The gypsy added a small log to the fire, reaching across her, brushing her arm. He sniffed, then reached out and lifted the pouch from her neck. "What's this?" he asked, wrinkling his nose.

"Protection," she said. "Zosia gave it to me. Donskoy's cook. She's a Vistani too, or was. She's rather secretive."

Ramus raised a brow, and Marguerite suddenly felt foolish.

"Anyway," she continued, "Zosia told me this would keep the beasts of the forest at bay."

Ramus laughed darkly. "Somehow I doubt it." He sniffed the pouch again and grimaced in disgust. "Though it could deter anything with a sensitive nose. And it might also deter the spider." He tugged at the string circling Marguerite's neck and broke it, throwing the pouch into the fire. The flames reared up, angry and green, then subsided and began lapping at the edges of the leather.

"Thanks a lot," muttered Marguerite.

Ramus looked at her and smiled. "Don't worry. I will see that you return to the keep safely. You should trust me, Marguerite. What other stranger has treated you so kindly?"

Marguerite did not reply. She wished she were home safe in her chamber, carrying the child of the lord she imagined Donskoy could become—surely would become, if she pleased him.

"Are you cold?" asked Ramus, putting his arm around her shoulder.

"No," she said, withdrawing herself. It was like dragging her body through water.

"Then let us sit quietly. The spider will come if we remain still."

Marguerite nodded, staring at the fire. In time, she became hypnotized by the flame.

A tap on her shoulder broke the spell. Ramus pointed toward the corner of the cavern. A creature as large as a dog was dangling overhead, slowly descending. It was white and translucent, glowing like the moon. Ichor dripped from its jaws as its legs touched the cavern floor.

Without bothering to rise, Ramus withdrew a dagger from his belt. With a sharp flick of his wrist, the blade soared toward its mark, planting itself deep in the spider's abdomen. The creature faltered, curling its legs around the dripping wound, mouth working incessantly. And then it was still.

Marguerite scrambled to her feet. Her heart drummed in her chest.

"You see?" said Ramus calmly, slowly rising to stand. "A simple matter. Now am I certain to whom the webs belong." He walked to the spider and withdrew his blade from its body. Two legs wiggled, a final gesture. The Vistana wiped his knife on a rag from his satchel and returned it to its sheath.

Marguerite suddenly recalled her quest. She let out her breath and approached the webs, giving ample berth to the spider's corpse. She extended a hand overhead but found she couldn't reach. Ramus stepped up behind her, standing so close she could feel the brush of his clothing, and he reached up to procure a strand. Marguerite took it from him shyly, tucking it into her pouch. Ramus doused the fire, and they went out of the cave together.

"I suppose I should thank you," said Marguerite.

"It would be appropriate, but I did not assist you to earn your gratitude."

"Nonetheless," said Marguerite, "I am grateful."

Ramus smiled. "Your thanks are accepted."

He whistled for his horse. When they reached the bottom of the slope, the beast was waiting. He returned his satchel to the saddle, then, as the woods were too dense to ride, they walked together. At length, they returned to the old vardo.

Marguerite stared at the firepit. The coals were still glowing, though Ramus had extinguished the flame before they left. She remembered the spirits, and could not resist voicing the question that teased her thoughts.

"While you played . . ."

"Yes?"

"I observed something strange."

"Something strange?" Ramus echoed. His voice was teasing, almost daring Marguerite to continue.

"Yes. Three women. Specters."

Ramus smiled. "Your sight is keen for a *giorgia*."

"Who were they? The spirits, I mean. And how did you summon them?"

Ramus walked to his horse and withdrew his violin from the saddle. "You know how."

Realizing his intent, Marguerite started. "I have to return to the castle," she protested. "Don't summon them now."

"If you don't wish to know the answer, you shouldn't ask the question." Ramus lifted his violin to his chin, drawing the bow across the strings. Marguerite turned, looking at the wall of forest that lay between her and the keep. "I have to go," she said, but her feet did not move.

"Don't be afraid." Ramus continued to play.

The music slid into Marguerite's body, pulling her gently toward the gypsy. She heard Ramus whisper, "You have nothing to fear. And much to learn about your lord, your land. Wouldn't you like to know its secrets?"

Marguerite opened her mouth to reply, but no words came. The spirits were rising before her, three women, returning. They caressed Ramus as before, sliding through the strings of the violin, then rising up to dance sensuously in the sky overhead. One of them beckoned to Marguerite.

Ramus ceased his playing abruptly, and the women vanished.

For a moment, neither spoke. Then Marguerite regained her voice. "Who are they?" she whispered.

Ramus stood across the clearing. His eyes burned into her. "Members of my tribe."

"Dead members?"

Ramus laughed darkly. "Indeed. Thanks to your lord."

Marguerite hesitated. "My husband?"

He laughed darkly. "Donskoy slaughtered them. He is a rogue and a murderer, evil incarnate. And you are his latest prize."

"I don't believe you," she said hoarsely. "You are lying."

"Am I?" Ramus stepped close. He seized Marguerite by the arms. "Then you are a bigger fool than I thought. But not so great a fool as your lord."

She tried to pull away, but he held her fast.

His face loomed near. "It is amusing to me. Amusing that a man who cares nothing for respectability, who knows it as a veneer that cloaks the dark perversions of half the nobles in his acquaintance—that this beast so ardently seeks a pure bride, and seeks thereby a pure get of his own. It's as though he thinks that by immersing himself in your purity he can plunge into the holy waters of heaven itself and make himself clean again—as if he could somehow bury himself in the sanctified soil of your body and be reborn anew. But he is a fool, blinded by his own wickedness. You look heavenly, I'll admit, but you are neither a goddess nor an angel. Like Donskoy, you are just a fool, for you play the game with him."

"And what are you, then, besides horribly cruel?"

"Perhaps a fiend, after all." Ramus kissed her on the mouth, and despite her horror, Marguerite felt the heat swelling within her. She struggled.

"But I am a fiend you cannot resist," Ramus growled, "and a better match for you than he."

Marguerite wrenched herself free.

"You are wrong," she hissed. "I can resist."

She turned away from the vardo, running toward the safety of the keep. He did not follow. Yet even as she raced through the wood, she heard his laugh ringing through the trees.

THIRTEEN

It was nearly dawn when Marguerite emerged from the forest. She followed the path at base of the castle wall, groping for the secret passage that led to Zosia's garden court. She and the old woman had agreed upon this route—agreed that when Marguerite returned she would deliver the sticky white strands of the web directly to the kitchen. To her relief, the secret door lay open to receive her. She turned, giving one more glance to the forest. No one had followed. She parted the curtain of vines and stepped through.

As Marguerite entered, she heard a rustle in the corner—a retreating rodent, perhaps, or the toad Griezell-bub, acting as a sentry to announce her return. She paused to look about. The garden seemed changed since her first visit, though she could not yet tell why. The crimson cabbage still blazed, visible even in the dim light. And the glass domes of the cupping jars still lay nestled against the soil, neatly arrayed, but no longer vacant. A reddish brown fluid had bubbled up from the soil beneath each translucent prison.

Marguerite crouched beside one, studying the contents more closely. The fluid divulged its myriad parts.

Thousands of red ants surged over the corpse of a small frog, scouring away its flesh. The jars were death domes, miniature crematoriums whose contents were kissed and stroked by living flames. In the next jar lay a mouse or rat; only the tiny tufts of gray-brown fur and a wormlike fragment of white tail hinted at the nature of the thing.

Beneath the final dome, the ants had begun their retreat, draining back into the soil. In their wake lay the skeleton of a lizard, as smooth and white as if it had been cleaned with lye. *Perhaps these strange ingredients are meant for Donskoy,* Marguerite hoped. *Or perhaps Zosia needed the components to mix with the white spider web.*

Marguerite pulled her cloak around her, then went to the corner of the garden and opened the small arched door that led to Zosia's kitchen. She entered the twisting passage beyond. At the opposite end, she gently pushed open the second door, and was met by the warm, blazing light of the cooking fire.

Zosia still squatted on the three-legged stool before the hearth, gazing into her pot. It looked as if she had scarcely moved since Marguerite last spoke with her.

"Zo," the old woman said huskily, "you have brought it then." She did not bother to turn toward her visitor. "You have obtained the web."

"Yes," Marguerite replied. "I have it here." She untied the strings of the satchel at her waist and held the parcel out toward Zosia. The old woman remained distracted. Marguerite put the sack upon the table, which was now clear of the bowls and herbs and the skinned carcasses.

"Zosia," began Marguerite. "I'd like to ask you about something." She wanted to query the old woman about Ramus, and his assertion that Donskoy had slain the Vistani tribe. And about so many other things, she realized.

"There will come another time for questions, my child," Zosia said. "But now you'd best return to your room. The castle will soon be waking."

"Another time?" Marguerite asked.

Zosia dismissed her with a wave of her hand. "There is always another time. Go now. But remove your boots first—you'll leave a trail of mud straight from my kitchen to your door."

Marguerite tugged off her boots, then hesitated.

"Go, go!" urged Zosia. "Yelena has seen to it that your chamber is unlocked."

* * * * *

With the door to her room gently pressed shut behind her, Marguerite shed her muddy clothing and gazed at her reflection in the mirror. Her cheeks were streaked with dirt, and her hair was a tangled mess. She pushed out her stomach, making it round, and ran her hands over the skin. Then she pushed out her cheeks to match, imitating the wind-god personified. She deflated with a long hiss. After washing, she climbed naked into the bed, hoping to steal an hour of sleep before Yelena appeared with the breakfast tray, which would hold Lord Donskoy's written instructions for the day.

It seemed as if Marguerite's slumber had only just begun when Yelena's hand poked at her shoulder. Marguerite groaned and lifted her still-heavy lids to squint wearily at the intruder. Then she pulled herself up to her elbows and blinked in surprise.

It was apparent that more than a moment had passed. The bed curtains had been parted and tied to the posts. The shutters on the window hung open, allowing a shaft of white light into the room. The fire blazed, freshly fed. And on the table before the hearth lay the familiar silver tray bearing Marguerite's breakfast, along with Donskoy's parchment note. She cringed at the thought of seeing him again, recalling the sting of their last encounter. But she didn't expect to be summoned back to his salon quite yet. Unless his tastes ran otherwise, he would wait several days before he renewed their liaisons.

The mute held out a steaming stone cup. Marguerite swung her legs to the floor and steadied herself, then took the vessel from Yelena's raw, bony hand. Despite the steam, the surface of the cup was cool.

"What is this?" asked Marguerite, forgetting for the moment that her tongueless maid could not respond. The answer came to mind as she gazed into the vessel and saw the white hairlike swirls moving across the surface of a greenish brown fluid. "Did Zosia send this?"

Yelena nodded.

Marguerite lifted the cup to her nose, prepared to grimace. Then she sniffed hard. Oddly, she could smell nothing at all, except perhaps a trace of smoke. She lifted the vessel toward her mouth, but when the cold rim touched her lower lip, she did not drink. Instead, she pulled the cup away and stared once again at the strange mixture inside.

So this is the potion that will make me the mother of Donskoy's son, Marguerite thought. She didn't really wish to bear his child, she realized; the thought of it held no joy. But it certainly was the next logical step— what had to be. The black stream of fate was slowly turning. The future would come, an unstoppable force. And if Marguerite were not pregnant? If she failed her husband? Surely that would carry her to a fate worse than the swelling of her stomach, worse than a bloody birthing in which her own vitality flowed out with the child, worse than gloomy years of mothering Donskoy's son—a son upon whose shoulders the weight of the entire future would be fantastically placed. But who could say? Maybe Donskoy was right. Maybe their fortunes would magically turn with the birth of an heir. Certainly Lord Donskoy believed it was true. Marguerite herself scarcely dared to hope.

She downed the brew. The icy, tasteless fluid coursed into her stomach, then spread across her loins and limbs. It left her even drowsier than before. Yelena took the chalice, and Marguerite sank back into the bed, descending into the pit, succumbing to a strange, numbing sleep.

* * * * *

A week later, the routine had resumed as if her husband's rage and Marguerite's foray into the woods had never occurred. Donskoy became eager and attentive in the salon, bolstered, perhaps, by Zosia's renewed promise that his efforts would soon be fruitful. Marguerite tried twice to seek out Zosia and query her about Ramus's claim that her husband had murdered members of his tribe, but both times the old woman rudely dismissed her from the kitchen, stating she was too busy with Lord Donskoy's brews and had no time. Zosia admonished her to look toward the future, and soon Marguerite did precisely that.

One morning, she opened the parchment on her tray to discover an unusual message: Donskoy was expecting company. Marguerite was to dress in manner befitting the lady of the keep, and be prepared to greet Miss Jacqueline Montarri in the afternoon.

After breakfast, Marguerite requested a bath. Two hours later, Ljubo and Yelena had finished wrestling

with the tub and heavy pails of hot water. Marguerite
doused her hair and scrubbed herself pink while
Yelena stood in attendance, adding more hot water
from a steaming kettle in a fruitless attempt to keep
the bath from growing chill. When Marguerite had finished, Yelena held out a large linen sheet that had
been warmed by the fire. By the time Marguerite had
dried, arranged herself in a gown, tied the last layer of
blue silk to her waist, and coaxed her shining tresses
into submission, she heard the clatter of wheels in the
distance.

She went to the window and saw a smart black conveyance approaching across the clearing. To Marguerite's astonishment, she saw that it had no driver. It
was pulled by two black horses, but the reins stretched
back to an empty bench where there should have
been a man—or some other creature to hold the
leathers. Instead, the straps simply lay on the seat, as
though Miss Montarri's driver had dropped them there
when he abandoned her.

The carriage drew to a halt before the keep. The
door swung open, and Jacqueline hovered on the step
until Ljubo arrived to help her down. She wore a
sweeping emerald cloak, and her black hair spilled
loosely over her shoulders. She must have sensed
Marguerite's gaze from above, for she looked up
toward the window and flashed a smile as white as
snow. Ljubo looked up as well, grinning broadly.

Marguerite went to the door of her room and hurried
down to the foyer. Ekhart stood at the crest of the
stairs, stiffly at attention. Terse and to the point, he
instructed Marguerite to proceed to the drawing room.
There, she encountered Lord Donskoy, who sat before
the fire, puffing his ivory pipe. The lord's gaze raked
over Marguerite, and he smiled approvingly.

Ekhart appeared in the door. "Miss Montarri has

arrived," he announced dully as Jacqueline stepped past. She dropped her cloak into Ekhart's hands, exposing her bare white shoulders and her signature green sheath. Ekhart grunted and gave a stiff forward bow, then left the room.

As the usual greetings were exchanged, Yelena arrived with a tray, bringing brandy-wine and sweets. Jacqueline peeled off her long black gloves and melted onto a sofa, curving her body into a sensual S. The mute girl decanted the wine, serving Donskoy first, then Jacqueline and Marguerite.

Jacqueline put her glass to her lips and gently licked the edge, smiling over the rim. "Marriage must agree with you, Marguerite," she said, "You're looking only a little worse for wear."

Marguerite ignored the jibe. "What brings you to the keep, Miss Montarri?" she asked sweetly.

"Please, call me Jacqueline. You're not sorry to see me, I hope."

"Not at all. I am pleased to have the company."

Donskoy grunted but said nothing. He puffed on his pipe, staring hungrily at his guest.

Marguerite continued, "Is this a pleasure trip, Jacqueline?"

"After a fashion. It has long been my pleasure to visit Donskoy—didn't you know that? And I always try to mix in a bit of business."

"A little business, you say?" asked Marguerite. Perhaps Donskoy intended to sell her after all. Her eyes slid from Jacqueline, who gazed at her with sparkling green cat-eyes, to Donskoy, who continued to stare at his emerald-sheathed guest.

"Mm-hmm," said Jacqueline. "Nothing extraordinary. It would bore you, I'm sure."

Marguerite found herself studying Jacqueline's face. Something seemed odd about the woman's appear-

ance—but what? She had noticed nothing amiss when
the woman entered the room—there was the same
languid bearing, the same tiny pinched waist, the
same delicate gesturing of finely boned hands.
Jacqueline's face was sly and expressive, just as
before. Her tone was a little lighter perhaps, but the
phrasing and accent seemed familiar—precisely as
Marguerite recalled. Yet something was not quite the
same. Granted, Marguerite had seen the woman only
once before, by candlelight, and a month had passed
since then. But there was something markedly different about her—about her face in particular.

"You seem changed, Jacqueline." At once, Marguerite bit her tongue; certainly she could have been
more deft.

"I seem changed?" echoed Jacqueline coyly. "How
so? All for the better, I hope."

"Actually—yes."

"My goodness, you seem disappointed."

"No, I mean—well, I do believe you look younger.
Yes, younger. If I didn't know better, I'd say I was looking upon the younger sister of the woman I met last
month."

"How utterly sweet of you, Marguerite. And aston-
ishingly keen, I might add. How could you know that I
have enjoyed weeks of pampering and relaxation? I
do indeed feel like a new woman, but it's pleasing to
hear my good fortune is reflected in my appearance.
Now I am thoroughly refreshed and ready for a new
endeavor."

"A new endeavor?"

"A little excitement. A little business, as I said. But . . . "
She looked toward Donskoy. "Such affairs are nothing
for the likes of your pretty little head. Is that not correct, Milos?"

Donskoy shot her a curious glance. "You needn't

concern yourself with Marguerite's pretty head, if that's what you mean."

"Of course not. I have no concerns, really—merely the greatest admiration. What a lovely head she has, indeed . . . You know, I had almost forgotten just how lovely she is, Milos, just how great your catch. Have you ever pondered the aesthetic possibilities, Milos, the combination—"

"Jacqueline!" growled Donskoy. "Remember yourself, my dear."

Marguerite shifted uncomfortably at Donskoy's "My dear." The sound of it left a bitter taste on her tongue. Lords might have their mistresses, but must they flaunt them? Was this insult to be her punishment for failing to conceive? Or something worse? By the gods, she thought. Could it be? Was Jacqueline a merchant who dealt in discarded wives?

"What kind of endeavors are you planning to undertake?" pressed Marguerite. "And does it involve me?"

Donskoy and Jacqueline were consumed with mirth. "Certainly not," said Donskoy.

"Then what kind of endeavors?"

"Oh," Jacqueline replied, "just an excursion with Lord Donskoy's associates, if I can persuade him." She shifted in the chair; the slit of her green gown parted, revealing a length of smooth thigh.

Donskoy chortled. He rose and walked toward the fire, turning his back to them both. Marguerite caught a glimpse of his upturned lips. This gathering amused him somehow. And why not? Here sat two women whose only apparent role was to entertain him. He was indeed lord and master, his harem complete. Only the swelling of his wife's belly might improve the scene. But that did not appear to be troubling him at the moment. He rubbed his gloved hands before the fire—a habit, perhaps, for they could not be cold. Marguerite wondered what kind of thoughts were at play in his mind.

"Perhaps you can persuade him, Marguerite," said Jacqueline. "You see, Milos has largely retired from the life we knew, ever since he came to this castle. But his associates, whose unique talents are utterly wasted of late, they still long for the road. I know it, for I feel the same urge. Until recently, I could offer little to change things myself, but fortune has turned. And now I could indeed lead them, in Lord Donskoy's name, of course."

"Lead them into what?" Marguerite asked.

"Why, greatness, danger, the fields of wealth beyond these lands."

"That's rather vague, don't you think?"

"Perhaps not knowing every detail is part of the thrill," said Jacqueline.

"We can discuss this later, Jacqueline," Donskoy said, turning away from the fire. "Assuming we discuss it at all. At any rate, such things need never concern my wife. Do I make myself clear?"

"Of course," replied Jacqueline demurely, "my lord." She licked her glass and stared directly at Marguerite, taunting. "Whatever you desire."

Marguerite's face burned red.

Donskoy did not even look at Marguerite; instead his eyes were sliding up Jacqueline's long white leg.

"Miss Montarri and I have personal matters to discuss, matters with which I do not wish to burden you, Marguerite. I won't be needing your company anymore today. You may go to your room."

"You don't wish me to come to the salon?" said Marguerite. It astonished her that she wanted it—that she did not relish being replaced. But she feared any rejection might last for more than just one afternoon.

"No," Donskoy replied. "I may not require your

company tomorrow, either."

Marguerite rose reluctantly, catching Jacqueline's sly smile.

"Good day, Marguerite," said Jacqueline.

"Good day, Jacqueline," she replied, struggling not to sound too sour.

Marguerite turned and left. As she crossed the foyer beyond the sitting room, she heard Donskoy turning the key in the door of his red salon.

FOURTEEN

Jacqueline's laughter trailed away behind the salon's closed door. So, I've been dismissed, Marguerite thought, seething with resentment.

As Donskoy had instructed, she started back toward her chamber. Jacqueline brought out the worst in her; with each step, the prickle of anger at the nape of Marguerite's neck grew hotter. When she reached the door to her chamber, she stopped abruptly. Then she hoisted her skirts and spun on her heel, striding back down the hall to the stairs. She descended quickly, then padded across the foyer toward the drawing room. Trying not to be seen, she peered around the edge of the open door frame. The room beyond remained empty, as she had expected. And the door in the corner, which led to Donskoy's red salon, was still closed.

Marguerite entered the drawing room and crept toward the small arched door. When she reached it, she crouched and peered through the keyhole. Only the end of the red divan was visible. A green dress lay upon it, emptied of its bearer. Marguerite pressed her ear to the hole. She felt a cool stream of air—

along with a rush of excitement. She could overhear the conversation almost perfectly. Donskoy was speaking.

"Marguerite will conceive soon," he said. "Mark my words. Zosia has seen it."

"Zosia?" replied Jacqueline contemptuously. "Bah! I've never understood why you trust that crone."

"What does trust have do with anything? I find her useful. But Zosia is really quite harmless, Jacqueline. I do not understand your irrational fear of her."

"It is not fear, Milos. I am wary. I have not lived so long or so well without my share of wit."

"Indeed, my dear. You possess more than your share. After all, you command the intellect of many scores of women, as well as infinite charm."

"Quite true. So you might indulge a clever friend when she tells you to remain on guard, even in the midst of your delirium—a delirium, I might add, that your darling Zosia is all too eager to promote."

"Dear Jacqueline. Fretting makes you, too, an old crone, and all for no cause. Zosia serves me well; that is why I endure her. Her potions merely offer a means to entertain myself between your anxiously awaited visits. I remain fully in control."

"I do not require your idle flattery, Milos. Listen to what I say. You are too dependent upon Zosia and her brews."

"You are mistaken, my dear. I am dependent on no one, not even you."

"No? You live your life wallowing in the throes in some alleged curse, when half of the hex is just a dark fantasy fabricated by a conniving old Vistana."

"Ah, the crux of it surfaces again. Your own abnormal fears, your own hatred toward the dark-eyed dregs of this world. Do not attempt to settle your old scores through me, Jacqueline."

"If the subject weren't so painful to you, I might remind you of your own grudge against their kind. But that shouldn't be necessary—you can never forget, can you, Milos?"

"Enough, Jacqueline!" He paused, but the recovery was smooth. "Why must you pick at every scab till it bleeds? This is an old conversation, and my patience does know a limit. I shall tell you again: Zosia is not a threat. Vistani witches lose their powers when they do not wander. She is like a tiger without teeth and claws, completely tame. We shall end this topic now, Jacqueline, before you sour my temperament completely. I enslave Zosia; the reverse is a fantasy. The old hag serves a useful purpose. Marguerite serves a useful purpose. And you, my dear, might also serve a purpose, if you could remember it. You did not come all this way to quarrel, did you?"

"No, indeed," replied Jacqueline. A little catlike growl rippled up from her throat.

"Then come closer."

"Why?" she purred. "So that you can enslave me too? So that I might know the merciful hand of Lord Donskoy?"

He chortled. "If you desire it. Come closer. You sometimes forget who is Lord, but I *can* be merciful. In fact, I shall allow you to punish me some more with your sharp little tongue."

"Hmmm. So tempting. But not yet," she teased.

"Why delay? You would not have that particular tongue but for me."

"For the game. Only with you can I turn my own condition into such a delicious diversion, and I insist on savoring the chance. How would you like me to look tonight? A redhead, perhaps? A blonde? You appear particularly robust this evening. Perhaps it shall be many."

Still crouched outside the door, Marguerite gasped—
half from jealousy, half from the picture Jacqueline's
words conjured in her mind—then she clamped her
hand to her mouth.

"Hmmm, Donskoy?" Jacqueline continued. "Tell
me your pleasure."

"You present many interesting options, I agree. And
it is so seldom that you grant me first choice."

"I am feeling generous," came Jacqueline's coy
reply. "After all, you have had to endure the company
of your parochial little wife for weeks. It's a wonder
you haven't died of boredom. Shall I open the cabinet
and choose one of your old favorites?"

"I alone open that cabinet," Donskoy said sharply.
His voice carried an unmistakable warning. "I know
you are itching for a glimpse of the old ledger. But
mark my words, it's not to be."

"Donskoy, I am hurt. This is no time for business.
Please, by all means, open the cabinet yourself. If I am
itching, as you put it so vulgarly, it is only with the
urge to entertain you."

"Hah. The woman speaks of vulgarities as if they
offend her."

There was a pause, a brief rustle. Unable to see
what was happening, Marguerite imagined Donskoy
tending the hearth.

Jacqueline continued, "Shall I make the choice
simple, and go without? I shall lose my eyes, but I
shall yet see your fire. And I shall lose my ears, but I
shall yet hear your eager pleas for release. Pity,
though; I shall be unable to speak." She gave a dark
little laugh. "But perhaps you would like that, *mon
cher*?"

Donskoy chortled juicily.

Marguerite grimaced in disgust.

There was a sudden noise behind her. Startled, Marguerite fell over backward, turning her head sharply toward the sound. Griezellbub crouched just inside the drawing room. His throat swelled, and he made the hideous sound of the death rattle. When he had finished, he pulled his mouth wide, as if to grin proudly. Then he shambled out of sight.

Marguerite silently cursed the toad, then quickly returned her ear to the keyhole.

She heard Donskoy asking, "What are you doing, Jacqueline?"

"Didn't you hear that—that rattle? Your little bride might not be so dull after all. Perhaps she is eavesdropping. I'd accuse Ljubo or Ekhart, but they know better than to play the voyeur."

"It was probably Yelena," Donskoy said. "She wriggles about the keep like a worm in a salt barrel."

"Nonetheless, I shall investigate." Jacqueline's voice was playful. "Without the ribbon, hmmm?"

"You would open the door like that? Hah! I thought you too vain for such a spectacle."

"Then you thought wrong. A moment please. Now this could be amusing."

Marguerite stood up so quickly that her vision began to blacken. She raced across the drawing room into the foyer, then pressed herself against the wall beside the entrance. There was no time flee any farther. The door to the salon had creaked open, and she could hear Donskoy calling out from within.

"Why Jacqueline," he cried, between bouts of mirth, "you've literally lost your mind. Come back here and set things right. I choose the one you harvested last month—my expensive imported gift."

Marguerite shivered. She could only guess at the perverse game Jacqueline and Donskoy were playing, but her mind had conjured an unbelievable image— one she could not dispel. Surely she was wrong.

A long pause ensued. Marguerite could hear someone stirring in the drawing room, but no one spoke.
She dared not move.

Then Donskoy called out again. "Jacqueline? Are
you all right?"

"No one," came Jacqueline's disappointed reply.
She was still in the drawing room. "Pity," she said. "I
should have liked to see the reaction." Her voice
began to fade. "So this is the one you choose? The
one I am wearing now?"

The salon door closed again, muffling Donskoy's
reply. Marguerite peered around the corner. The room
was empty. She drew in her breath, then crept back to
her station at the keyhole.

Donskoy and Jacqueline were both laughing.

Jacqueline cooed, "Are you sure? It could be very
interesting without."

"Perhaps," Donskoy replied. "But I would miss your
lips."

"Mmmm. No doubt."

"Without lips you have no voice."

"Why Milos," cooed the temptress, her words dripping with honey. "So often you scold me for excessive
chattering."

"I do not wish you to speak."

"What then?" asked Jacqueline coyly. She paused,
then laughed darkly. "Ah, I believe I understand. Shall
I cry out then, Milos, cry out like some weak wench
desperate to summon the castle guard? No one would
come, of course. Even if your men were here, even if
Ekhart did not think me some recurrent rash, I could
scream and scream, and no one would come."

"Yes," said Donskoy simply, as if ordering a biscuit
for breakfast. "I'd like very much to hear you scream."

Marguerite's face went white. Ashamed and
repulsed, she fled from the chamber and raced up the

stairs, desperate to escape the perversions of her husband's salon.

She found the door to her chamber hanging open, and Zosia sitting in the chair by the fire. Griezellbub squatted upon her bed. Both the old woman and her toad turned to stare at Marguerite, one with eyes that were dark and sparkling, the other with immense yellow orbs.

"Curiosity satisfied?" Zosia chuckled.

Marguerite ignored the question. "Why in the name of the gods are you here?" she asked hoarsely.

"For the test," replied the old woman. She rose, bringing forth a chamber pot.

"The test?" exclaimed Marguerite. "But you always come in the morning."

"Not for this," said the old woman. "This test will be special. And it must be done now."

She handed Marguerite the pot. Marguerite sighed, returning the container when she had finished. By now, this strange event was almost commonplace. More than a week had passed since Marguerite drank the potion, and two tests had occurred since then. Both had confirmed she was not with child.

"Why is this test so special?" Marguerite asked.

Zosia turned and walked toward the door. "Because when I am finished, it will show you carry a son."

Marguerite gasped. "But is it true?"

Zosia shrugged. "Maybe yes, maybe no, but either way it will be true soon enough. And for your sake, Donskoy must believe it is true now."

"But if I don't conceive—"

"You will," said Zosia. "I have seen it. But first, we must calm Lord Donskoy. He grows too anxious, and an anxious man fathers a nervous child."

Marguerite was too bewildered to protest. Then she thought of Donskoy down below with Jacqueline. Perhaps Zosia knew best.

The old woman motioned to Griezell, who leaped from the bed and shambled to the door. Then both the toad and the old woman departed.

Marguerite sat down at the edge of her bed. For a moment, she was quiet. Then she pressed a pillow to her face and screamed. And in the castle below, within the red walls of Donskoy's salon, another scream echoed her own.

 **FIFTEEN**

Marguerite lay in her bed, drifting uneasily toward sleep. She wondered whether Zosia had showed her husband the results of the doctored test. Night had fallen hours ago, but Donskoy might still be preoccupied with Jacqueline Montarri, barring visitors from his salon. Even for such a momentous announcement, Zosia would wait.

From outside came a noise that brought Marguerite upright in an instant. She sat inside her bed curtains, listening. The sound came again: a long, peculiar wail, resembling the eerie moan of a wounded cow. The hairs on the nape of her neck rose like tiny quills.

For a moment, Marguerite hid behind the walls of her velvet tomb. Then came the familiar crunching of wheels on gravel and the anxious, muffled whining of Ekhart's hellish pack. Marguerite climbed out of bed and went to her window. She parted the shutters only slightly, afraid that the light of her hearth would draw the gaze of someone outside—as if it were *her* actions that should be hidden under cover of night.

She needn't have worried. Earlier the clouds had

opened themselves and drenched the land. Now the sky was almost clear, the moon full and bright. Its pale yellow glow readily overpowered the feeble light from her window.

Marguerite squinted, studying the scene below. She failed to see a tortured cow, but she really hadn't expected one; the sound that drew her from bed had not seemed natural. Ekhart stood beside his wagon, holding a lantern aloft. Three black shapes crouched in the back—the hounds, readied for the hunt. Beside them lay a long black crate.

Ljubo stood in the clearing beyond, facing away from the castle. He waved his lantern back and forth, as though signaling. He appeared to be waiting for something—someone. The associates? Jacqueline? The dark-haired woman had mentioned an excursion in the drawing room. But would she and Donskoy's men go out in the dead of night? Marguerite sniffed and shook her head, answering her own question. When else? The night suited this crew quite well.

A slender woman astride a dark horse appeared from the direction of the stables, then turned her high-spirited mount in a sharp circle. Doubtlessly it was Jacqueline. She wore black leggings and tunic, like a man, though her silhouette remained decidedly feminine. Lord Donskoy came next, pulling his mount alongside Montarri's. He raised a black, shining object to his lips, a crescent-shaped horn, and the peculiar wail sounded once more.

After several moments, a rider emerged from the forest that ringed the clearing and approached the castle. One by one, a dozen men followed suit, streaming out of the wood. They were Donskoy's associates, clad in black. Among them, Marguerite spied two guests she recognized from the wedding feast, a man with a humped back and another with only one arm. They each brought a hound or two of their own. Ljubo greeted the newcomers with a nod, then shambled to the wagon and climbed up beside Ekhart.

With the party fully assembled, Donskoy's loyal pair dimmed their lanterns. Ekhart raised a whip. It arched through the air, then cracked sharply over the ponies' backs. The cart jerked forward and rumbled into motion. The riders fell in behind, in pairs. Following the mud-and-gravel track, the procession snaked across the clearing and slipped into the woods beyond.

Marguerite knew where they were headed: to the rim, where lost travelers were brought close by the currents in the mists. And this time, she could hardly convince herself that Donskoy's men were attempting a rescue.

At first, she had no intention of following. Her chamber was locked, and the secret passage in her wall had proved dangerous. Besides, what was it to her how her husband and his men entertained a guest?

Marguerite paced, a caged animal. The hounds in the tapestry watched as she passed back and forth. Without thinking, she made a holy sign in the air, mimicking a gesture she had often seen in Darkon, when the village priest found it necessary to enter a temple defiled by undead.

Moments later, she had donned her leggings and her traveling gear and was crouching before the tapestry. She triggered the moving stone, then followed the dank artery toward the adjacent chamber, silently mouthing a prayer to keep the mechanism working. To her relief, the secret door at the opposite end swung open, allowing her exit. When the door to the hallway groaned and screeched, she did not even flinch.

"Let them hear me," she whispered defiantly. "I am not a prisoner." But her bravado was false; she knew that only Zosia and the mute remained in the castle.

Marguerite went directly to the stables, seeking the horse with the ridiculous misnomer of Lightning. One of the other mounts might have been faster, she knew, but her lack of skill made her choose the familiar beast. She rooted through the tack room for a saddle and bridle, then struggled to prepare the horse. Lightning puffed out her belly to keep the saddle loose, but Marguerite was wary. She waited until the horse exhaled, then drew the cinch tight. With bridle slipped over the mare's flickering ears, she led her mount to the gate and parted the enormous doors. When they were closed behind her, she hoisted herself into the saddle.

Glancing backward only once, Marguerite proceeded down the rutted track that led to the rim. The road was muddy and laced with puddles, but a grassy hump rose in the center above the muck. Marguerite kept Lightning to this ridge, hoping to make better time. She was not sure what she expected to accomplish by following her husband and his associates; certainly, she knew better than to dare interfere with whatever they were doing. But she had to see, to learn for herself if her darkest fears had substance.

As she crossed the stone bridge, a dark shadow swooped low past her ear—an owl perhaps. She gripped the mare's neck and pushed on, riding steadily until she reached the fork in the road. There she allowed herself to pause and regain her breath, wishing she had thought to bring a flask of something warm to drink, or least a skin of water. The wagon's tracks confirmed her suspicions about the group's plans; the mud showed the clear imprint of hooves and wheels, leading to the right, toward the rim.

Marguerite followed. The trees pressed in around her, dark and menacing. Shaken by the wind, a black spruce flailed its arms, freeing a rain of loose cones to assault her. Lightning twitched and whinnied as one struck her flank. Marguerite reached forward to pat the mare's neck, but the gesture was as much to reassure herself as her mount. She tapped her heels against the horse's belly, and Lightning trotted on.

As the road began to climb into the hills, fast, low-flying clouds cast flickering shadows across its surface. Soon, Marguerite knew, she would be approaching the spot from which she and Donskoy had gazed down at the mist-covered valley. She dismounted and led her mare by the reins, picking her way carefully over the sharp boulders that sprouted up from the rough track.

After several minutes, Marguerite heard voices ahead. She tied Lightning to a tree and continued on foot. When the voices grew louder, she left the road and, ignoring her fears, climbed over the top of the ridge. A short distance down the other side, she stopped and crouched on the hill, peering out through the branches of a shrub.

On the moonlit slope below, near the edge of the valley's swirling mists, she could see her husband sitting on his horse beside the wagon. A column of horses, now minus their riders, waited on the road behind the cart. Ekhart and Ljubo stood close by with the pack of hounds—the three from the castle and many more. Donskoy's associates had arrayed themselves on the hillside below the road, spacing themselves several yards apart to form a long line. Each was armed with a mace or flail. Jacqueline paced back and forth behind them, carrying a shortsword, which glinted brightly in the silvery light of the full moon.

Whatever they were waiting for, Marguerite knew it had nothing to do with helping lost travelers. Why would they need weapons to effect a rescue?

Not a soul stirred for several minutes—only the trees, surging and sighing in the wind. Then Marguerite heard voices out in the mist, echoing up the foggy valley. A woman spoke soothingly to a nervous, sobbing child, summoning him close. Men muttered warnings. They sounded very near, but Marguerite knew it for a trick of the mists.

Donskoy lifted the black horn to his lips and blew, repeating the awful wail Marguerite had heard at the keep. The associates hid their weapons behind their backs. Ekhart's hounds began to bay.

"Here!" called Jacqueline. "Here, to safety!"

A figure scrambled up the bank, his face twisted, his clothing torn. It was a young man in robes—a cleric, perhaps. A large medallion hung round his neck. When he saw the line of Donskoy's associates, his expression changed to one of relief. He turned and called something to his companions in a language Marguerite did not understand.

Donskoy blew his horn again, and his associates shouted more encouragement to the wayward travelers. "Come to us, to safety!" Jacqueline cried.

More silhouettes appeared at the swirling edge of the mists, following the cries of encouragement. The young cleric climbed the slope and fell on his knees before the closest associate, clasping his hands around the man's legs and uttering foreign words that sounded to be an exclamation of relief and gratitude.

Then the cleric saw the moonlight glinting on the head of the associate's mace, which was protruding from behind a meaty thigh. The young priest released his grasp and started to rise, clutching at the holy symbol around his neck.

The "rescuer" gave a sharp laugh. He swung his mace, splitting the cleric's head like a red melon. The other travelers, now half-emerged from the mists, heard the awful crack and stopped in their tracks, crying out in confused voices—whether to each other or to the dead priest, Marguerite could not tell.

It mattered little. At that moment, Donskoy's associates raised their weapons and rushed down the hill in a well-practiced charge, falling upon the stunned travelers like a pack of wolves.

Jacqueline squealed with glee and rushed over to the fallen cleric. She ripped the medallion from his corpse, putting it to her teeth to test its metal, then slipped the disk into her pocket. Something on the man's hand caught her attention. As Donskoy's associates slaughtered the other travelers, she severed the dead cleric's wrist. Then she sheathed her sword and pulled a ring from his stubby finger.

The surviving travelers turned, attempting to flee from whence they had come. Ekhart released the hound pack. The dogs sprang into the mists, snapping and snarling, driving the hapless wanderers back to meet their gruesome fates.

Apparently not all the travelers were helpless. A fireball raced up the path and licked at the line of associates, engulfing two, and lashing out toward Jacqueline. In the crimson flash, Marguerite could see one of the associates slitting an old woman's throat.

When Jacqueline felt the kiss of the flames, she leaped back unharmed, then spouted obscenities like a barroom wench who'd just been bilked. She yelled for a counterattack, but it was hardly required. A hound bayed, then came running up the slope after

the offending spellcaster, biting at his heels. The terrified mage, distracted by the growling beast at his
back, did not even see the blade that clove his skull.

Then came the young women, herded like frightened sheep before the dogs. Jacqueline cackled. The
women wore fine garments. Some carried parasols, as
if prepared for a daytime picnic. From their shocked
faces, it was clear they had no idea what had occurred
to change their plans.

One girl shone like gold among the rest, with her
tangled blond locks spilling over her shoulders, obviously a beauty despite the twisted expression her fear
had wrought. Ljubo seized her by the hair and drew
her up the slope.

Jacqueline screeched at him. "Ljubo, remember
yourself! You must leave the head unmarred."

The girl writhed. Ljubo shoved the quivering blonde
toward the road. Blood streamed from her mouth; she
had bit her own tongue in terror.

"Oh, for pity's sake," sneered Jacqueline. "Look
what you've done, you silly twit. I'll have to take care
of you now." She walked over to the girl. "Don't be
afraid, child. There is nothing to fear. Promise me
you'll behave, and I'll make sure that no harm comes
to your pretty head."

The girl nodded feebly.

Jacqueline pushed the blonde to her hands and
knees and, with one swipe of her sword, beheaded
her. The gold tresses poured onto the ground. "No
harm above your neck, that is," laughed Jacqueline.
She sheathed her sword and picked up the head with
great care, examining it in the moonlight. Apparently
satisfied, she carried it to an embroidered satchel resting on the ground nearby. She tucked the head neatly
inside.

Then she motioned to Ljubo. "*Now* you may have

her."

Ljubo grinned and scooped up the headless corpse, cradling it in his arms and scampering off into the woods. The rest of the bodies were soon neatly arranged on the road. Five or six associates worked the row like black vultures, stripping clothing and jewelry, stuffing it into bags. Some of the victims moaned and twitched as their limbs were picked clean; apparently not all the victims were dead.

Donskoy rode along the gruesome line, then stopped and pointed to one of the females. Ekhart called for Ljubo, but seeing him gone, scowled and snapped at an associate to help him. The pair returned to the wagon, then dragged the long black box from the back and carried it over to the woman Lord Donskoy had indicated. They set the crate beside her and poked at her form. When she squirmed feebly, they stuffed a gag into her mouth. Finally the men lifted her into the box, secured the lid, and returned the crate to the back of cart.

Marguerite sat on the ground at her hiding place, her eyes damp, her stomach churning. She had suspected foul play, and yet the scene was even more gruesome than anything she could have envisioned. Before Donskoy and his men finished their ghoulish business, she had to return to her mare and leave. She tried not to think about what she would do then; after what she had seen, it was impossible to imagine returning to the castle to live with Donskoy. But what choice did she have? She knew no other place in this land.

Marguerite forced herself up. No sooner had she risen to her feet than one of the hounds turned toward her and began to bay. Someone raised a lantern and shined it in her direction.

Marguerite started up the hill at sprint, then stumbled, sending a shower of rocks down the slope. A man's voice cried out in astonishment, then barked an alarm.

Marguerite bolted over the top of the ridge and down the other side, into the night, a frightened hare fleeing for her life.

SIXTEEN

Marguerite ripped the reins free of the twisted branch and scrambled onto the back of her mare like a frantic monkey, then assaulted its sides with her heels. The horse jerked its head and kicked savagely, attempting to throw off the demoness that clung to it. But Marguerite stuck fast, so the mare gave in to her demand and sprang down the boulder-strewn road. When the horse stumbled on a jutting stone, Marguerite realized her feet were still flailing. She reached forward and patted the mare's neck, murmuring nervous apologies and reassurances. Lightning took the rein and chose her own pace down the rest of the steep slope.

Over the crest behind them, the hounds continued to bellow. Marguerite could hear their masters shouting, calling the dogs together in some semblance of order. In her mind's eye, she saw Donskoy scanning the ridge with his cold leaden gaze, saw him questioning his associates as to what or who they had seen. She imagined a gray pall spreading over his face as he came to realize it had been his own wife, supposedly snug in her plush prison at the keep, spying on

them in the darkness, observing all that had occurred.
And what would he do then? she wondered. What
would her punishment be? For in Donskoy's domain,
she had learned, the punishments could be harsh
indeed. If Zosia had convinced him she was with child,
she might escape his wrath. But only until he knew
the truth, only until he realized he had been tricked.
Then his anger would flare twice as hot as before.

If only the potion had worked, she thought. It might
work yet—she could sense it—but she was running
out of time. Assuming, of course, she had not run out
already.

Over the crest, the hounds bayed. They were eager
for the hunt, but she could hear the shouts of their
masters, commanding them to wait until everyone
was assembled and the wagon was loaded. Marguerite
thought of the black crate and its cargo. She wondered if this was the way a barren wife might find herself set aside: clubbed into senselessness, stripped
bare of all possessions and securely crated, then
carted away to Jacqueline Montarri's manor, or delivered to another fiendish collector, ferried to some
obscure pit of torment in a long black box.

The road began to level; she had cleared the steepest
part of the ridge. She whipped the reins hard over
Lightning's neck and spurred the horse into a gallop.
The mare could smell her rider's terror; like a sickness
it spread through the beast's flared nostrils and into her
lungs, then through her blood to her quivering flanks.
For the first time the name rang true; Lightning opened
her gait into a thundering gallop, stretching her knobby
white legs as if the hounds of hell were on her tail. The
horse could not long maintain its speed, but Marguerite
clung to Lightning's neck, her hands tangled in the
coarse white mane, whispering hoarsely for the mare to
go faster still, oblivious to all common sense.

Soon the fork lay ahead. Lightning slowed, then began to veer left toward the keep—the most familiar path. Marguerite dragged hard on the bit, struggling to steer the horse to the right. The castle was the only sanctuary she knew, yet it was the last place she wanted to go. To her relief, the mare curved right and sped into the darkness, along the road that had brought Marguerite from Darkon. From home. Some part of her knew this home no longer existed as she remembered it, but she shoved that thought aside. Neither reason nor logic could catch hold among her tumbling, panicked thoughts. She was heading home to Darkon. And if not to Darkon, then away. Anywhere but back to Donskoy's keep.

Clouds of mist drifted across the wagon track like huge, rolling ghosts. She rode into their midst. One of the clouds struck her like an icy wave breaking upon the shore, leaving her shivering and wet. Marguerite heard a scream and realized it was the horse, neighing in protest—or fear. She slowed the pace, but continued on. The clouds multiplied and huddled closer, growing large; soon they loomed all around like great white, buffeting wings. Lightning stopped in her tracks.

Marguerite clucked her tongue and gently squeezed her mount's flanks with her thighs. The horse reared, and Marguerite slid back onto its rump, fully out of the saddle. Her hands gripped the stiff pommel in desperation until the horse dropped back onto its forelegs. Through some miracle she remained seated. She dragged herself back into place and fumbled for the reins, then felt for the stirrups with her clumsy, flailing feet. When she had recovered, the white fog surrounded them completely, blotting out the landscape, concealing the road beneath Lightning's hooves. The horse's white knees seemed to melt directly into the mist. Marguerite became aware that a quiet had settled over the wood. She heard only her own breath, mingled with the heavy breathing of the horse, echoing strangely. The mare's sides heaved under her legs like a bellows.

Marguerite gently urged the horse forward. Lightning stepped backward instead and began to turn, slowly spinning. Marguerite pulled back on the reins to signal a halt, but it was to no avail; the horse continued to whirl through the white mists like a leaf caught in an eddy, until Marguerite became disoriented, losing all sense of direction. A white dream had ensnared her. Something moaned in the distance, muffled and malevolent. Long white shapes stretched and pulled through the air around her. Something brushed against her face. Marguerite laid herself flat on Lightning's neck, clinging desperately, afraid to lose her only anchor to the things she knew. The fog slipped over and around them like liquid—as if it were a milk sea and she and the mount were suspended deep beneath its waves, drowning as they spun helplessly toward the bottom.

And then the fog started to clear. The horse stood rigid, the haze draining away all around, departing with a hushed hissing. The road became visible again, dark and damp below Lightning's hooves. The black feathered walls of Donskoy's forest loomed up on either side. Tendrils of mist swirled through the branches like retreating specters. The horse pawed the dirt nervously, testing for support. Like its rider, the animal sensed that something unnatural had occurred. Marguerite urged her mount forward—hoping that forward was still the direction she desired.

They rounded a bend, and the road slipped out from the forest. By some cruel trick, or an even darker magic of the mists, they now stood miles from the point where Lightning had begun to spin. On either

side of the road spread a fetid marsh dotted with
blood-red brambles—the same marsh that lay halfway
between the keep and the fork. Just a few miles ahead
stood Donskoy's castle. And directly behind her, bel-
lowing in the distance, came the hounds. It seemed as
if space had folded in on itself, creating a slimy chute
that had carried Marguerite and her horse in the opposite direction from that in which they had meant to go.

The mare lurched forward, then stopped and took
three steps back. Confused and panicked, Lightning
seemed oblivious to any command issued by Marguerite's clenching thighs and urgent hands. A dark
shadow, about as tall as a man but much broader,
slithered across the road ahead. Lightning reared,
almost toppling over backward. The mare's head
twisted backward in the air, and for an instant the
horse and Marguerite exchanged panicked glances,
both with mouths agape, Lightning's single visible eye
now wide and rimmed with white. Already half-
unseated, Marguerite found herself flying through the
air. She landed on a wet cushion of grass in the marsh
beside the road. Her mount kicked once, then thundered down the road toward the keep.

Marguerite stood slowly, wincing at the sharp pain
in her right shoulder. She was mired to mid-calf. Her
thoughts raced, and she struggled to quiet them. Perhaps Donskoy will not be angry, she thought. Perhaps
she could still reach the keep before him, and then
Yelena and Zosia would help cover for her as they had
done before, help make excuses, claim she had never
left. . . .

"Perhaps the fall has knocked you senseless," she
muttered derisively. On foot, she could never out-race
Donskoy and his men. It seemed that two choices lay
before her. She could stagger back to the castle, sod-
den and bedraggled, to face her husband and his

associates. The prospect was as humiliating as it was
horrific. Or she could flee into the woods—and then
what? She couldn't hide forever, and escaping her
husband's domain posed a formidable challenge. Lord
Donskoy had told her the mists held him captive on
his land, and it was now painfully clear that she was a
prisoner here as well—how else could she have set
out for Darkon only to find herself nearer to the very
keep she was fleeing?

The Vistani could master the fog. She had to find
Ramus.

Marguerite turned and waded into the marsh. The
hounds might not track her over the water, she reasoned. Later, she could veer into the woods and look
for the gypsy. Ramus would help her; he had helped
her twice before. Mounds of pale grass dotted the
marsh, pushing up from the muck like heads cloaked
in long, stringy hair. After struggling through the water
for what seemed an eternity, Marguerite climbed onto
a mound and leapt from one to the next. It was faster
than wading. Now and again the soft ground pitched
her back into the mire, but she continued on until she
heard the hounds whining on the road behind. She
stopped short, then scrambled behind a clump of bare
brambles and turned to face her pursuers.

On the far side of the marsh, half-a-dozen lanterns
hovered motionless. For a moment, the dogs milled
about the edge of the marsh. But then the lanterns
began to move on, and Marguerite saw the dark
shapes of several riders galloping up the road, back
toward the keep.

She veered left, making toward a black wall of pines
on the bank of the marsh. Brackish water had seeped
through the seams of her leather boots, and her feet
ached with the cold. Her legs felt as if her veins were
filled with mud. Exhaustion sobered her. You're a fool,

she thought. A damned fool, traipsing into a dark wood alone at midnight, half frozen, hoping for the company of a lone gypsy, a Vistana who seemed more phantom than man, and someone whom she knew she should not trust completely.

And yet, as always when she needed him, there he was at the edge of the marsh, a figure in black leaning casually against the silver trunk of a dead, limbless tree. The silhouette was unmistakable, but Marguerite stopped, rubbing her eyes, thinking the vision might be another trick of the mists.

"Ramus?" she whispered.

He signaled her with flash of white teeth.

She trudged forward to meet him. He took her hand and pulled her toward drier ground. When they stood on the forest floor, he turned to her and raised a brow expectantly. Still, he said nothing.

"Aren't you going to speak?" she whispered hoarsely.

He looked at her, dark eyes glinting like black spheres. Marguerite's legs buckled, and he gripped her arm, then suddenly leaned toward her like a hawk swooping for the kill. He pressed his lips against hers. His tongue probed her mouth and seemed to lengthen, slithering toward the back of her throat.

"Stop it," she choked, pulling away. She pushed at him. "What do you think you're doing?"

Ramus laughed. "Pardon me," he replied, a sly smile on his lips. "Surely a married woman knows the answer. I thought it prudent to warm your blood. You look half-frozen."

She stared at him in astonishment, clutching her arms across her chest. Her cheeks *did* grow hot; she felt them redden with anger and embarrassment. Marguerite looked away from him to avoid his gaze, suddenly aware that he might be attempting some kind of magic. She began to wonder if the castle might have been a better choice after all.

"I'm sorry, Marguerite," said Ramus soothingly. "I should not tease you. Obviously you've had a difficult night."

"I have," she stammered. "How did you know?"

He chortled, raking her wet body with his eyes. "Besides the obvious signs? I've been watching. From a distance, of course, but I've been watching. I'm never far from you, Marguerite. Haven't you realized that by now?"

"Then you know. You know about my husband and his associates, and about her, that . . . creature, his paramour."

"I told you the last time we met that your husband is vile. But I suppose, like most *giorgios*, you deny the true eye within in favor of the deceiving eye without."

She kept silent, ashamed.

Ramus continued, "And, like most *giorgias*, you are not made for the elements. Even a firebrand will shiver itself out, if exposed too long. Come with me. I'll take you someplace warm."

Marguerite hesitated.

He shook his head. "Trust me," he said. "Or don't. Who knows? Perhaps you can make it back to the castle before you drop dead from the chill or become the meal of some hungry beast. Follow me or not. As before, it's your choice."

Marguerite kept silent. Hadn't she sought out his help in the first place? Still, she wished she didn't require it at all—wished that she felt certain she could survive a cold night in a haunted forest alone, and could find her own way back to Darkon. But even if she could make a fire from damp wood, even if she could escape the piercing fingers of cold and keep back the forces of the night, she could not navigate the mists. Only the Vistani could manage that—or someone with powerful magic, like Jacqueline. And Jacqueline was not an appealing guide. You could lose your head if you kept company with Jacqueline Montarri.

"Please," said Marguerite softly. "I do trust you. Can you help me leave this place?"

"Leave your husband?"

"Yes. And go back to Darkon, my home."

Ramus laughed darkly. "Tonight is not the time to depart. First, we must seek shelter and get you dry and warm. Then tomorrow we shall see whether you still wish to flee."

He whistled softly. Marguerite heard a rustling in the trees, and Ramus's horse appeared. The Vistana swung up into the saddle and pulled Marguerite up behind him. They passed into the forest together.

There was no path. Marguerite pressed her body behind the gypsy's, trying to shield herself from the clawing of branches. But the branches were soft, stroking her with pungent, feathered arms. The rhythm of the horse was hypnotic; she pressed her face against the damp, musky wool of Ramus's jacket and closed her eyes.

When she reopened them, they had reached the base of a cliff. It looked familiar, and Marguerite realized she had indeed seen it before—the night she had sought out the white spider's web for Zosia's potion. Ramus dismounted, then reached up and helped Marguerite down from the horse, gripping her firmly at the waist. When he released her, Marguerite's knees buckled, weak from the cold. With effort, she straightened them and stood.

"Can you walk?" he asked.

She nodded.

He started up the rocky slope. Marguerite plodded

on behind, stumbling, and he seized her hand to
steady her, drawing her upward.

They entered the cave. A smoky haze filled the air;
a fire already blazed in the center of the cavern.
Ramus's dark satchel lay nearby, beside a log cut to
make a stool.

She looked about curiously.

"My sanctuary," he said. "And it has no other occu-
pants now. You'll be safe here till the dawn."

She was shivering with cold. Ramus retrieved a
black wool blanket from his belongings and tossed it
in her direction.

"Take off your clothes," he commanded. "Or you
will grow weaker still. You can wrap yourself in this
while your garments dry by the fire."

Marguerite looked about for some kind of privacy.
Ramus shook his head and laughed softly, then
stepped out of the cavern. She glanced over her
shoulder. When she was certain he had actually left,
she stripped off her muddy wet clothes and spread
them out over a stalagmite, then settled beside the fire
with the blanket pulled around her like a tent. She sat
as close to the flames as she dared; still, she shivered.
The blood bubbled and burned in her feet and calves;
they ached painfully as they warmed.

Ramus feigned a rough cough, then stepped back
into the cavern. A small kettle lay beside the fire. The
bottom and sides were black, but Marguerite could
still see the ornate designs etched in its sides. The Vistana went to his satchel and withdrew a metal cup and
a small white kerchief, neatly folded. He opened the
cloth carefully, then sifted half the contents into the
cup before folding back the white cloth and returning
it to his satchel. He added the water from the kettle to
the cup, then waved his hand to dissipate the steam.

"Herbs," he said, passing her the cup. "To give you

strength."

Marguerite wrapped her hands around the mug, grateful for anything warm. She sipped at the rim, and a bitter, searing tea warmed a trail from her throat to the pit of her belly. She sighed. It occurred to her that the brew might contain something she did not wish to swallow. She quickly brushed the thought aside; obviously the tea was medicinal. And apart from a few roguish advances and his mysterious ways, Ramus had given her little cause to be so wary.

The warmth of the tea spread to her limbs, melting away the cold ache that had seized them. Marguerite lay beside the fire. Her lids sank of their own accord, then fluttered and sank again. The embers glowed before her like a red-gold haze.

Music began to fill the cavern. Lazily, she rolled her head toward the sound. Ramus stood beside the fire, one black boot planted upon the log he had cut to make a stool, playing his violin. She listened, enrapt and dreamy, saying nothing. Ramus watched her as he played, his dark eyes damp and warm, his lips stretched into the slightest glimmer of a smile. The fire cast a glow upon the polished fiddle, and upon his shining black hair, which seemed shaped from the same gleaming piece of coal. He was playing slowly, methodically, sliding the bow back and forth, then back again, spawning the most bittersweet stream of notes that Marguerite had ever imagined. His fingers on the neck of the instrument fascinated her; she watched them as if nothing else existed, watched them arch and dance, moving like the white spider that once had inhabited the same cave. And then suddenly, as she stared at the fingers on the violin, it seemed to her that those same fingers were stroking her neck, her spine, her thighs, as if she were the instrument being played. Ramus pressed deeply into

a string and shook it teasingly, then moved to another
and pressed again.

A soft moan of pleasure escaped Marguerite's lips.
The music had pierced her heart, then mixed with her
blood and flowed out into her body, flowed through
her, slipping into the deep, dark recesses where things
lie forgotten and denied. She gave in to it, telling herself there could be no harm in listening. The music
coursed into her and sought out her terror, then gently
carried it away. Gone were her thoughts of Donskoy
orchestrating the murder of the lost travelers, gone
were the images of Jacqueline and her lovely embroidered sack, filled with the golden-haired head. Gone
too was the picture of Ljubo, scuttling into the woods
with his beheaded prize flung over his shoulder, like
the carcass of the swine he had brought back for the
wedding banquet. And gone were Marguerite's
thoughts of the keep, her memory of the cold cou-
plings in the red salon, brusque and endless. She
heard only the music of the fiddle, felt only its warmth,
knew only its agony and bliss.

She became aware that Ramus had moved beside
her, had drawn the blanket from her body. Her flesh
shimmered with sweat; she felt aflame. His hands slid
over her, and his skin pressed against hers. The violin
had been set aside, yet the music continued. His fingers played at her thighs. Marguerite did not resist;
she was molten. They melted into one another, merging like two parts of the same melody, and with ever a
quickening tempo, they moved passionately through
the phrases, notes rising and falling, then rising higher
still until at last the music crested in a fierce, climactic
crescendo.

In the quiet that followed, Marguerite felt herself set-
tling back into her body, regaining a sense of its
weight. It was if she had been lifted out of it entirely.

Ramus had wrapped himself around her, warm yet strangely light, like steam. Her mind drifted, and she knew she no longer wanted to return to Darkon. She wanted to stay with Ramus, if he would have her, and travel the mists wherever they might lead, as far away from this domain as possible. Part of her realized it was a fantasy, but it was so sweet, so appealing, that she allowed herself to pursue it.

After a time, Ramus rose and dressed himself, then stepped toward the mouth of the cave. Outside, it was still dark. He cocked his head. Then he stepped back into the cavern, picked up Marguerite's clothes, and tossed them on the ground beside her.

"Get dressed," he said. "It's time to part ways."

"Part?" she said. "I thought you would help me return to Darkon, or at least help me to go elsewhere. I thought—"

"You were mistaken."

"No. You said we would talk of it. You were going to take me back to Darkon. I can't go alone. I need your help to get safely through the mists."

Ramus turned and looked at her strangely. "I could not take you through the mists, Marguerite, even if I desired it. If Donskoy chooses to seal you in, there is nothing I can do to stop him. Now get dressed. I'm taking you back to the keep."

"No, I can't. I don't want to return to the keep." Her words quickened. "How can you suggest such a thing? You have told me that Donskoy murdered your tribe. If you send me back, you'll only be adding my blood to his hands. Surely you can't be so cruel. Surely—"

"You are wrong, Marguerite. I hear his hounds in the wood. Your husband is searching for you even now. It is your fate to return to him."

"But he will kill me!"

"He will not. Lord Donskoy wants one thing more than all else. A son. And now he believes you are pregnant. Zosia showed him the test last night. He will never let you leave, so you must return to him. Unpleasant, I agree, but he will not harm you so long as he believes you are with child."

"How do you know these things?"

"I know all that occurs in the castle. I share a bond with Zosia . . . and with Donskoy as well."

"Bond? What sort of bond?"

Ramus did not answer.

"What bond could you share with Donskoy?" Marguerite demanded, struggling into her clothes. "He is a fiend. I don't—I can't go back to him. If Zosia has deceived him, she has only delayed the inevitable. He will find out soon enough. A month will pass, and then he'll know. He'll see that I have not conceived. And then I'll be dead. Or worse." Her voice ascended to a higher pitch. "Or *worse*. He has warned me. Let me leave here with you. Else I shall certainly depart this domain in a long black box!"

Ramus merely chuckled.

"It is true!" she cried.

"The truth is, a month will pass and you shall grow round with child."

"You can't possibly know that."

"But I do. I have given you a gift, Marguerite. Our paths may part, but I have left something behind."

Marguerite stared at him with a shocked expression. "What do you mean?"

"The web, Marguerite," Ramus said. "Or do you think Zosia's potions as barren as your husband?"

Marguerite's jaw fell, and she said nothing.

"You wanted me to keep you safe," said Ramus. "I have done so in the only way I can. Lord Donskoy is rotting from the inside out. He can no longer spawn a son. So I have done you the courtesy. I have spared you your head, pretty *giorgia*. Now I suggest you use it wisely. Return to the keep and act as though nothing has happened. Play the role you seized upon so eagerly just a short time ago. Donskoy will dote on his burgeoning bride. Play him well, and you will survive to see my son born."

Marguerite sat down hard. Of its own accord, her hand passed over her stomach. "I don't believe you . . . "

Ramus shrugged. "That is nothing to me."

Outside, in the distance, Marguerite could hear the hounds baying. They were growing closer. Her panic rose.

She scrambled back to her feet. "Did you use me only to win your vengeance? Is your heart as black as Donskoy's?"

Ramus threw his satchel over his shoulder, then turned to look at her. "It is not."

"Then take me with you," she whispered. "You must."

Ramus shook his head sadly. "You do not know what you ask. You do not know what I am."

"I know enough," she said. "I know I cannot bear to stay here. I know that only you can help me escape. I know your touch."

Ramus choked on a bitter laugh. "You know nothing. You have no idea what I am."

Outside, the dogs began to howl.

Ramus continued, "Shall I show you then, what you must fear?"

"I am not afraid of you," she said. "Whatever secrets you hold, I do not fear them."

The Vistana shook his head. "You should. This is what I am." He closed his eyes and clenched his fists. "Watch carefully, and then ask yourself whether you want to go with me still."

Slowly, he unbuttoned his shirt and pulled it from his body, and then each garment in turn, until he stood naked before her, adorned only by the play of light and shadow that fell across his smooth, sculpted skin. Each muscle was cleanly defined; compared to Ramus's body, Donskoy's seemed a statue of soft white dough. The Vistana's powerful arms bulged with muscle and vein.

And then it seemed that the veins rose higher and propagated, pressing themselves up against the restraint of his translucent skin, until a pale blue net covered his entire form. The whole of his body rippled beneath the strange mesh, quivering as though his flesh were a separate entity, struggling to break free of the restraining blue web.

Some of the veins darkened, becoming blue-black as they rose higher than the rest. They marked the joining of each appendage to his trunk, of each finger to the palm. Like seams. Like someone had sewn him together.

Ramus raised his index finger high, and the nail lengthened into a long black talon. It was a strange, ugly thing that sprouted from the end of his finger, not like an overgrown fingernail, but like a bone grown too long. He began to cut himself, slicing three deep gashes down his chest, then another across his stomach. Three diagonal lines, raining down to a fourth. The Vistani sign of the curse.

Snakes of red mist poured forth from the wounds. They hissed with blue forked tongues, writhing until their tails slipped from his body; they wriggled away into the night, dissolving into smoke as they left the cavern.

Marguerite sat shaking upon the ground.

"You are flesh and blood." Ramus's voice seemed to rise from the cavern floor. "And what am I? Do you know, Marguerite?" His wounds began to close and disappear.

Marguerite's lips quivered, and she felt tears spilling from her eyes, burning on her cheeks like fire. Her head shook slowly.

"I am blood and mist," Ramus continued, "the thing that steals your breath while you sleep, the thing that pours nightmares into your ears, the thing that makes you grow old and feeble before your time. Do you still want me, Marguerite?"

Horror-struck, she said nothing.

He laughed, then turned toward the mouth of the cave. "I thought not."

Marguerite heard a small voice speaking close to her. It was herself, uttering something softly, a half-choked reply. "Yes," she rasped.

Ramus paused. "Yes, what?"

"Yes . . . I still want you." She tasted the salt of her tears in her mouth. "I still want to go with you."

Ramus laughed again, more darkly than before. "My own race lives in fear of me—those who know what I truly am." The hounds howled again, this time from the base of the slope. "But you, the little *giorgia*. You would have me."

"Yes."

Then he said soberly, "More's the pity then. But, Marguerite, you should understand by now that desire and destiny rarely share the same path."

And then he was gone.

Marguerite sat huddled on the cavern floor, quietly rocking herself, one small hand nervously picking at the other. Outside, she heard the dogs scrabbling up the slope. She started to rise. The dogs. They had tracked her. But how? She had left no trail. Of course, how did not matter.

She had to escape. The woods might conceal her;

she would hide out. She did not need Ramus. Surely, other gypsies traveled across Donskoy's land from time to time. She would wait near the fork, lurking, until at last she spotted them. Or perhaps she could leave Donskoy's domain without a Vistana's aid. If desperate enough, she could stow away beneath Jacqueline Montarri's carriage, and—

"Well, well, well." The voice came from the mouth of the cavern.

Marguerite turned. Ekhart stood just outside, accompanied by two of Donskoy's associates, a half-faced brute and a man with only half a right arm. She shouldn't have been surprised to see them—she had heard the dogs—but somehow she was. Now that Ramus had left her, everything seemed a fog.

Ekhart continued, "The rabbit has legs. But not for long." The associates slipped into the cavern, seizing Marguerite by the arms. She thrashed, but it was useless. Even the one-armed man had an iron grip. He poked at her with his stump, sliding it toward her throat as if it were a knife.

"What now, Ekhart?" Marguerite hissed. "Will you strike me with a flail and pick my body clean?"

Ekhart snorted, but his somber expression scarcely changed. "A pretty prospect. But alas, your lord intends to keep you safe from harm. For a while yet." The associates dragged her to the cavern entrance. Ekhart leaned in close, and she could smell his sour, bilious breath. "For a few months. But when that child is born, *Lady* Marguerite, it might be a different picture then. Then you'll learn what it is to obey. And when Donskoy has done with you, you'll answer to my hand."

Ekhart ran his dry, rough fingers over Marguerite's cheek. She spat in his gray eye, but he hardly blinked. He pulled his thin lips a fraction wider, then lifted his hand to his eye and wiped the spittle from his face. He touched his fingers to his lips and blew Marguerite a kiss.

"Enjoy your insults while you can," he said deeply. "They won't last forever." He turned and started down the slope.

The associates chuckled, shoving Marguerite after him.

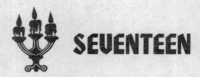 **SEVENTEEN**

At the base of the cliff below the cave, Ljubo stood waiting with the hounds milling about his legs. When the snuffling beasts noticed Marguerite and her escorts, they commenced a chorus of eager baying. Ekhart silenced the pack with a wave of his hand.

Morning was upon them, turning the sky to the color of steel.

"Good day, Lady Marguerite," called Ljubo pleasantly. "We're so pleased to have found you."

Marguerite did not respond. She noticed that her hand had begun to turn blue, so tightly was the half-faced associate squeezing her wrist.

Ljubo began his characteristic nodding, then pulled his fleshy lips apart to reveal his flecked grin. The gesture was as sudden and lewd as a drunkard spreading his cape to expose himself. As Marguerite neared, she saw that a piece of pink, shredded meat jutted out from between the yellow clutches of the fat man's teeth. She recalled the image of him waddling into the forest with the headless corpse slung over his shoulder, and her gorge rose up. She choked it back, swallowing hard.

Seeing her revulsion, Ljubo turned his head shyly, then looked at her askance from beneath the awning of his fleshy brow. "So pleased to see you again," he murmured. "Yes indeed."

"Oh, shut up, Ljubo," snapped Ekhart. "There's no need to keep fawning over this bedraggled little bitch, even if she is whelping. Or will be."

"Yes-yes," said Ljubo, rubbing his raggedy hands together. His smile never faded. "Just trying to make her feel welcome."

"A wasted effort," said Ekhart. He looked at Marguerite contemptuously, sliding his eyes across her body. "She's managed to take, but I have my doubts she'll come to term."

Marguerite's right wrist, still caught in the grasp of the half-faced associate, was growing numb. His companion loomed close behind, touching her hair from time to time, or nudging her with the stump of his forearm. She could feel his fetid breath upon her neck.

"You can release her now," said Ekhart, addressing the associate. He winked at Marguerite—and she thought to herself that this was the greatest display of expression she had witnessed upon his face. He continued, "You won't run, will you Lady Marguerite?" He made the title sound obscene. "Though I'd like it if you did . . ."

Marguerite smoothed her tunic and struggled to stand on her own. Her clothing was still damp, and she was panicked and cold, but she hoped Ekhart couldn't see her trembling. "I have no reason to run," she said evenly. "I am going home, escorted by my husband's faithful servants. I am glad you found me." She thrust out her chin. She had bitten the inside of her lip, and it was bleeding a little, and she hoped this was not too apparent.

Ljubo snorted hard with mirth, then drew his sleeve

across his moist, fleshy nose. Ekhart shot him a glance that could pierce armor. The fat man's eyes rolled meekly away, and he stared off into space.

With the associates flanking her and Ljubo and the hounds at the rear, the five figures walked together through the forest. Ekhart moved just ahead. Marguerite could not help comparing his rigid, brittle form to Ramus's sinewy, catlike body. She tried to thrust the gypsy's image from her mind.

In time the group emerged from the wood and stepped out onto the road. The cart stood waiting, with the pair of weary gray ponies anchored in the rigging before it. The associate's horses were tethered nearby.

The one-armed man and his half-faced companion swung astride their mounts. "Will you be needing us anymore?" asked the former.

Ekhart shook his head. "No indeed. Ljubo and I can handle the likes of this little rabbit. She may bolt, but she won't get far."

"Until next month, then," said the man. "Unless Donskoy summons us sooner." He whistled a long, low note, calling his hounds, which came to stand beside their master's horse.

Ekhart tipped his tall hat to the associates but said nothing. The men rode away, with most of the dog pack trailing behind.

Ljubo bowed deeply and motioned to the wagon. As Marguerite looked back into the forest, Ekhart cupped her elbow. She shook his hand loose, then pulled herself onto the bench. Ekhart slid into place beside her, pressing his side firmly against hers. He pressed a little harder.

"No indeed," he said. "This little rabbit won't be running again. Not unless she likes to be hunted. Do you, Lady Marguerite? Do you like to be hunted like an animal? And what dank hole would you push your proud little head into next?"

Marguerite turned her face sharply away. Ekhart made a gesture to Ljubo, who bounded into the wagon bed, followed by the remaining trio of hounds. Marguerite cast a wary glance over her shoulder. To her relief, the black crate was gone. The wagon lurched forward, jostling along the track, carrying them back to Lord Donskoy's keep.

Presently Marguerite's stomach began to lurch with the motion of the wagon. Her face paled, and she lifted a trembling hand to cover her mouth.

Ekhart smiled. "Not feeling well, milady? Just like the last trip we made together, just a few short weeks ago. But already you look much older. Not very fresh at all. Soon you'll be shriveled and ugly, and who'll want you then?"

Marguerite lowered her hand and gave him an icy stare. "It must be the company I'm keeping," she said dryly. Her stomach twisted painfully, and she was forced to look away.

Ekhart chortled. "Let's see how Lord Donskoy likes his lady when she begins to rot just like the rest of us."

Marguerite's eyes fluttered. She felt a queer, hollow ache rising in the upper reaches of her gut, opening like a wound, slowing expanding with the rocking motion of the cart.

Ekhart continued, "Oh, it takes quite a long time for some, like Donskoy himself, and for me. The strong among us are barely affected by this land, compared to the weaklings. But someone so frail as you? Doubtless you'll be sloughing your own fingers just a few days after you've sloughed the child. You'll run them through your hair one day, thinking you're losing it, and your hand will come up bald instead."

Ljubo gurgled with mirth in the back of the wagon,

but a quick look from Ekhart stilled him instantly.

Ekhart droned on. "Who'll want you then, Lady Marguerite? Maybe even I won't have a use for you . . . "

Marguerite had never heard so many words spilling from the old man's lips. Suddenly, she could contain her nausea no longer. She held her head over the side of the wagon and retched. When she had finished, she pressed her face to her shoulder, embarrassed. But the humiliation was nothing compared to the terror that had taken root inside her, growing with each turn of the cart's wheels, with each turn that brought them closer to the keep.

Ekhart gave the ponies a sharp slap with the reins. They lurched suddenly in surprise, spawning a fresh wave of nausea in Marguerite. She choked it down. Ekhart sneered. "Such a pity you're ill," he said. "Donskoy won't be pleased. Doesn't bode well for the child. Better hang on to that baby, Marguerite. It's the only magic that'll keep his temper at bay."

The cart jostled and creaked. Marguerite struggled to keep her head high, her eyes fixed ahead. She felt unsteady, but she refused to give Ekhart the pleasure of reacting. She would not let him see her swoon, nor would she allow him to goad her into a reply. She set her jaw, hoping her face would become a pale gray mask like his own.

The black stream ran alongside the road, winking reflections of the pale dawn light. Then the wagon traveled over the arched stone bridge. Not long now, she thought. Not long before the keep rises up to swallow me. She closed her eyes to shut out the image, gripping the side of the wagon to keep from falling.

Unbidden, Ramus came to mind. She remembered the horrific display he had made, cutting into his own skin to release the crimson serpents. It must have

been an illusion, she thought. It had to be. He did it to
frighten me away. She remembered his "gift"—the
child he claimed to have left behind. That, too, was
probably a lie, another fiendish trick. And then she
remembered his touch, the sweeping phrases of the
violin's song, and suddenly she wasn't sure anymore
whether truth was any better than a lie.

The Vistana's words haunted her. "Go back to your
husband, and act as if nothing has happened." How
could she possibly manage it? Yet how could she do
anything else . . .

Marguerite felt a tear spilling from one eye, and
she hastily wiped it away. Ekhart must not see her
frailty. She felt sickly and weak, and terrified at what
lay ahead. It took all her strength just to remain
seated on her own, to keep from leaning against his
stiff gray arm for support. But she would not let him
see her yield.

The wagon came to a halt. "Home again, home
again," chimed Ljubo. "Don't you worry, Lady Marguerite. Soon you'll be snug as a thug in your bed.
Lord Donskoy won't be mad for long. He gets angry at
me too sometimes, but he always cools down soon
enough."

Marguerite opened her eyes and saw the keep
looming before them. She was not prepared for the
wave of fear that washed over her at the sight. She felt
weak and flushed; cold runnels of sweat trickled down
her face. With trembling hands, she began to smooth
her tangled hair, trying to make herself presentable, to
make herself fresh.

"Worried?" Ekhart asked, climbing off the wagon.

"Cold," said Marguerite quietly. It was true. Her
teeth chattered together, rattling in her head. "Just c-
c-cold."

"What a pity." He took Marguerite's arm and pulled

her off the bench. "And weak no doubt. I suppose I'll have to help you up the stairs."

He dragged her to the steps. With each footfall, Marguerite grew more weary. It was as before, when she first arrived, only her condition was much worse. When they reached the top of the stairs, she turned her face and retched dryly. Her stomach was empty.

"I'm sorry," she said feebly. "I—"

Ekhart steered her through the door and pulled her up the curving stairs into the foyer. Struggling to regain her composure, Marguerite braced herself against the wall.

"I can make my way alone from here," she said. "I must return to my chamber. Lord Donskoy can visit me there. I must lie—"

Ekhart snorted. "You must come with me." He tugged her forward, leading her into the drawing room. Her husband stood before the fire, pacing. Jacqueline sat in a chair nearby, examining her henna-red nails. They looked up. Donskoy's face was a pale mask of anxiety. Jacqueline smiled with a trace of smug amusement.

"Your wife," announced Ekhart simply, "has been retrieved."

"Zounds," said Jacqueline. "What happened to her hair? Not such a pretty head now. And her skin is positively green. Poor Marguerite. Is it the fever? I hope it isn't catching. Where on earth have you been, dear? We've all been worried absolutely to death."

As Jacqueline prattled on, Donskoy's stare burned into Marguerite. His anxiety quickly gave way to rage, coloring his cheeks a stormy purple. "Well?" he demanded. "What have you to say?"

His anger struck Marguerite like a club. "I must beg your forgiveness," she said meekly, curtsying so deeply that she slumped to her knee with exhaustion.

When no one moved to assist her, she struggled back to her feet. "I have made a mistake. It will not be repeated."

"A mistake?" said Jacqueline coyly. "Which mistake might that be? Where have you been?"

"I followed you," she said.

"So now I suppose you pick locks," boomed Donskoy.

"Well it's not that difficult after all," said Jacqueline, "though it surprises me that she could manage it."

Marguerite continued, "No. I discovered a tunnel attached to my chamber. I was curious as to where it led. And later, seeing you gone, I followed. I did not mean any harm." She regretted having mentioned the passage, but she did not want to suggest that Yelena had forgotten to lock the door.

"No harm?" Donskoy boomed. "No harm?" He strode toward Marguerite and took hold of her arm, forcing her to her knees. "You are carrying my son, you little wretch. It doesn't matter what you do to yourself, but as you are with child, I expect you to behave accordingly." He raised his hand. His open palm hovered like a threat over her head.

Marguerite gasped and struggled for the words with which she might defend herself. "The child," she whispered.

Donskoy's expression softened for an instant, then his mouth twisted in a malevolent sneer. "Then I must aim for your face to teach you a lesson."

"Tut. What a pity," Jacqueline chirped.

Zosia swept into the room, Yelena in tow. "Lord Donskoy!" the old woman snapped.

He turned to face her.

"Think of the child!" Zosia continued. "You should have summoned me as soon as Ekhart returned. Can you not see that the girl is ill? If you value your son, you will leave her to me now."

Donskoy released Marguerite, then turned aside. "Take her," he said sullenly. "Take this mongrel out of my sight."

Jacqueline gasped. "Milos. Are you going to let a servant dictate your behavior?"

Donskoy turned his anger on her. "Hold your tongue, Jacqueline. You forget your own place. The drama with my wife has ended."

Yelena and Zosia pulled Marguerite to her feet, then helped her from the room.

In Marguerite's own chamber, they worked swiftly to remove her clothes and put her into the bed. Zosia placed her hand on Marguerite's forehead, and then on her stomach. She frowned.

"Too hot," Zosia said. "Too hot. You are burning with fever." The old woman turned to Yelena. "Get the herbs—the ones I mixed this afternoon. Bring them to me now."

Yelena scuttled out of the room.

Marguerite turned to Zosia. "Ramus," she murmured. "Ramus said—"

"Shhhh," whispered Zosia. "Do not speak child. And do not mention that name again."

Marguerite allowed her eyes to close.

"Look at me, child." She took Marguerite's chin and shook it. "Look at me and listen. Do not speak of what occurred last night. Do not mention it again, do not think of it again. Do you understand?"

Marguerite nodded feebly. "But how do you know?" she rasped. "You couldn't know it all . . . " Her mouth had become a desiccated hollow with a thick, limp tongue, making it difficult to speak.

Zosia placed two pale, bony fingers on Marguerite's lips, which were now rimmed with white. "Shoosh. Do not mention it again," the crone murmured. "Not again."

Yelena returned with the herbs in a small pewter mug, and doused them with hot water from the fire.

Zosia lifted Marguerite's head and pressed the cup to her lips. "Drink," she commanded. "You are very sick, Marguerite. You must rest."

Marguerite swallowed something bitter and hot, then Zosia's crinkled, dark-eyed face faded from view.

* * * * *

She awoke in a fog of confusion. Donskoy sat before the fire in her chamber, smoking his white pipe as he gazed sullenly into the flames. Immediately, Marguerite let her lids sink low, so that he would not know she was conscious. Sleep, or its illusion, might shelter her a little longer.

A knock came at the door, and Marguerite heard it open. She did not turn her head to look. She heard a soft rustle and muffled footsteps, and then a woman spoke.

"How is the patient?" It was Jacqueline.

"Still unconscious, thanks to you. But Zosia says she will recover in time. She heals as she sleeps."

"Thanks to me? How could this possibly be my doing, Milos?"

"She saw you at the rim. She was babbling about it in her sleep."

Marguerite clenched her fists under the sheet. She hoped she hadn't babbled about anything else. She closed her eyes hard and listened.

"Then she must have seen you as well, my friend," Jacqueline quipped. "And your associates. And Ekhart and Ljubo . . . I hardly acted alone or without your consent."

"True enough. But it was the shock of your actions in particular that drove her into the forest. Ekhart saw her. After you beheaded that girl, Marguerite raced into the woods like a panicked fawn. We could have lost her to the mists forever."

"Oh, don't be ridiculous. She couldn't get far. And if she ran headlong into the fog she would have drifted back soon enough. A little worse for wear, perhaps—"

"I am not amused, Jacqueline. Not in the least."

"Forgive me, Milos. I meant no offense."

"My own child is in her belly."

"So you believe Zosia? That she carries your son?"

"I know it."

"I'm glad for you, my friend. Truly I am."

"Indeed."

"No, I mean it sincerely. This is what you've hoped for, after all. But it doesn't mean that you and I can't share a few dreams, too, does it?"

"You dream only of one thing—finding your own head."

Marguerite let out an involuntary moan. For a moment, her visitors were silent.

After a time, Jacqueline continued, "Well, wouldn't you do the same, if you could track down the one thing that made you vulnerable? But that isn't all I desire, Donskoy. You know it is not. I seek your contentment as well. And I could assist you much more— if only you would allow it, if only you would trust me just a little."

Donskoy grunted.

Marguerite turned her head, ever so slowly, to free her ear from the pillow. But she dared not open her eyes.

"For decades I have proved my unswerving affection and loyalty to you," Jacqueline continued.

"Indeed," replied Donskoy. "You have provided a welcome diversion. I suppose I do owe you a debt of gratitude on that account."

"And you could thank me, Milos, by giving me the ledger, and the services of twenty of your best men."

"No. Gather your own henchmen if you wish; it is within your capacity."

"Ah, but they would not share the unique talents of yours. Ten men, then. And just a page or two from the ledger. Lord Azalin's preferences, for example. And a letter of introduction from yourself."

"No."

"Why not, Milos? With your introduction to his court, I could take up your business where you left off. Please, Donskoy. Tell me what Lord Azalin desires most, and how much he is willing to pay."

"And what makes you think Lord Azalin will receive you at all?"

"Your reputation can scarcely have faded. You were an extraordinary procurer. With a letter of introduction, I could win an audience. And, of course, once he sees me in person, and once he learns what I know about Lord Strahd, and how much I despise Lord Strahd as well he does, then surely Azalin will strike an alliance with me."

"I have no intention of writing you a letter, or of lending you my associates."

"But why not?" Jacqueline's pout was almost audible.

"Because my son will carry on, Jacqueline. My son, when he is of age, will take the name of Donskoy abroad, and rekindle the old business. My son will restore my wealth and rebuild my land. Not you, Jacqueline."

"Your son, you say. After all my years of unswerving devotion."

"Yes."

"And just how do you expect to accomplish this feat? Your own men think you're too far rotted to sire anything."

"Have you forgotten so soon? Marguerite is pregnant. She carries a son."

"So you said. And I have little doubt that she's as fertile as any barnyard bitch. But surely don't imagine that the bastard in her belly is yours?"

Marguerite's eyes fluttered open in horror. Quickly, she let them drop, daring to leave a fringe of lashes through which she could watch her husband and his paramour.

Donskoy's face went white. He took a draft from his pipe, then pressed out his chest and stood erect, suddenly the stout soldier. His eyes flashed with anger, and a vein in his cheek was twitching. "You cannot vex me, Jacqueline," he said evenly, his voice dripping with contempt. "You are a pathetic, jealous woman. You've stooped very low to try to hurt me. But this time, my dear, the ruse does not become you."

"At least I have the courage to face facts. Unlike you—sucking at Zosia's brews, nursing your pathetic fantasies. Are you a man or a mewling lamb? Think on it, Milos. For weeks you've lain with Marguerite, gaining nothing but a little pleasure. And now, she is miraculously with child. Only an idiot would dismiss the coincidence."

"Stay your tongue," hissed Donskoy. "Not a word more. Not one word or you will find you have something in common with my mute."

Even through her half-closed eyes, Marguerite could see the dark woman's anger. Jacqueline's chest was heaving, and her words rushed out in a torrent.

"Could it be," she said, brows arching madly, "that someone else plowed the field while the farmer lay sleeping? Who knows how many times she has snuck into the wood, what degenerate may have crossed her path? Perhaps one of your own men took a fancy to her. Or better yet—ah, yes, better yet . . ." Jacqueline's eyes flared. ". . . A gypsy. Wouldn't that be rich, Milos? You struggle to eradicate the strays, but they leap to your land like fleas upon a rat. Yes—a gypsy lover. That would be rich. Marguerite's bastard could be a half-breed at that."

Donskoy's hands were clenching and unclenching, and his face had turned purple with rage. He raised his fist and swung it across Jacqueline's face. She let out a pathetic, half-choked squeal and sank to her knees.

Marguerite bit the inside of her lip to keep from making a sound.

Jacqueline gripped her head with both hands. Donskoy stood beside her, a faint smile on his lips. Neither turned toward the bed where Marguerite lay quaking. They were oblivious.

Jacqueline rose slowly to her feet, swaying slightly, her fingers working nervously at her neck. Then she pulled them away and stared at Donskoy defiantly.

"Don't ever strike me again," she said, her voice heavy and low. "Not ever. Do you understand?"

Donskoy grabbed the fingers of a suede glove and yanked it off, revealing a withered hand as scaly and black as a rat snake. He flexed his fingers, and five long talons jutted out from his fingertips. The claws resembled those that had appeared at the end of Ramus's finger, round and sharp, like a bone pushing up through the skin.

Marguerite gasped—she could not help it—but neither Donskoy nor Jacqueline noticed. They were occupied with other matters.

Donskoy swung his black hand, dealing another blow to his paramour's cheek. Blood and saliva sprayed from her mouth, but this time she barely slouched. Incredulous, she slowly touched her lips, dabbing at the blood, then held her hand before her eyes and stared aghast at the bright liquid rubies adorning her fingertips.

"Milos," she whined. "I cannot believe it! What have you done?"

"Something long overdue," Donskoy replied, tugging his glove back on. "I only wish I had struck you harder. Lucky for you, the urge is past. Pleasure is fleeting, as usual."

"You—you brute!"

Jacqueline's hands flew to the red velvet ribbon at her throat, then slid swiftly around to the back of her neck, where she fumbled beneath the black curtain of her hair. When she lowered her arms, the crimson ribbon was entwined through the pale fingers of her right hand. And the ribbon was writhing like a living beast.

Jacqueline's head wobbled on her neck, then tilted forward and fell off her shoulders. She cupped her hands and easily caught the head, clutching it upside-down at her waist. The shining hair trailed to the floor like sheets of black rain. She lifted the orb and turned it around to face her empty shoulders. The stump of her neck bent forward, as if Jacqueline were somehow examining her own amputated head, as if she had another set of eyes inside her neck with which to inspect the grisly orb.

The head's red lips gaped in horror, while its wide green eyes darted frantically about the room, panicked and lost.

After a brief inspection, Jacqueline flipped the head around so that it faced away, then shook the black, gleaming tresses into place. With one swift move, she circled the thing over her body until it hovered over her neck, then brought it forward to rest on the stump. Her left hand remained pressed at her temple as if to steady it. She raised her right hand, still holding the red ribbon, and opened her fingers.

The ribbon writhed free, one long end undulating

back and forth in the air, probing eagerly. Jacqueline guided the ribbon to her throat. The scarlet worm slithered into place, circling the seam of her head and neck, then snugged itself down in the subtle groove. Once again, the ribbon appeared to be no more than an ordinary velvet band, worn a fraction too tight.

Marguerite, too stunned to react even had she dared, continued watching through the curtain of her dark lashes, her body rigid with terror.

Jacqueline's face shuddered like a pot at the boil.

"You idiot!" She withdrew a kerchief and dabbed at her ragged lower lip. "You have *marked* me! How could you do such a thing?"

Donskoy glared at her icily. "You should know by now that I brook no insults from anyone." His voice was deep and even. "Not even you, Jacqueline."

"But you have marked my face!" Her anger gave way to a distress that was distinctly feminine.

Donskoy chuckled. "Oh, come now, dear. It's not as if you lack a spare. You possess more heads than a fop owns hats. I know of least six kept here, and hundreds more at your home, and you collect new ones every month."

"But you disfigured me!" Jacqueline repeated. "How could you have done such a thing? Never have you treated me so cruelly, Milos." She sniffed indignantly. "You know every one of my faces is precious to me, and every one must be absolutely perfect. And now you have ruined my favorite."

"They are all your favorites," retorted Donskoy dryly.

"But I don't own many sisterly facades—only two from this set. What would your wife think if I were to show up wearing something from another family?"

"I doubt the charade will fool her much longer," Donskoy said. "Marguerite saw you harvesting a head in the forest. She may be simple, but she is hardly an idiot."

"But you insisted—"

"I thought our habits might disturb her, but that hardly matters now," Donskoy said. "Marguerite is finally pregnant, and Zosia will attend her. And she does carry *my* son, Jacqueline. I will forgive your petty outburst this time—after all, you are a woman and doubtlessly more weak-headed than most—but I forbid you to imply I have been cuckolded. Say it again, and it will be the last peep heard from any one of your perfect mouths."

Jacqueline paced, smoothing her skirts and fingering her neck, pondering. She dabbed at her lip, then turned to Donskoy with a smile.

"Of course, Milos. Let us not mention this little spat again. And I shall forgive you your indiscretion. You were not yourself when you struck me." She stepped to his side and stroked his arm. "We can continue to be good companions, can we not?"

Donskoy did not respond, so she flicked his earlobe with her tongue, then proceeded to suck it.

"We can still entertain one another, can we not?"

Donskoy smiled, but still he said nothing.

Jacqueline continued, "I know you do not wish to forgo our diversions merely because you have a wife and child. That kind of attitude may befit simpletons and peasants, but not us, my dear."

Donskoy grunted and pulled away from her, then went to the table to fill a chalice.

Jacqueline draped herself in a chair beside him, pulling her white thigh free of her gown. "You know, Milos, upon giving it further thought, I applaud your plans for the child. It is only natural, after all. But—"

"But what, my friend? And mind your pretty tongue."

"But . . . it will be many years before your son becomes a man. And in the meantime, I, as you know, am the equal of at least three ordinary men. So why don't you allow me to get things started for your son? Let it be my gift to you both. He will never have the knack of traveling the mists as I do."

Donskoy's expression was as cold as ice. "No."

Jacqueline parted her puffy lips to protest, but she saw that further conversation was fruitless. "Then I am departing," she said. Donskoy did not reply.

She rose from the chair huffily and strode to the door, her skirts rustling as she went. When she reached it, Donskoy said, "Jacqueline."

"Yes?" she answered hopefully.

"Stay away a month or two, until Marguerite has had time to recover. Is that clear?"

"Perfectly," Jacqueline snapped. "Perfectly." And the door swung shut behind her.

EIGHTEEN

Marguerite's sickness continued and grew worse. At times she felt a blush rising in her cheeks, a flicker of her old self returning. But mostly she remained heavy and weak, drifting in and out of a fitful sleep with little distinction between morning and night.

A month passed, bringing a wet winter full upon the land. From her bed, Marguerite could hear tiny arrows of ice pelting the window panes. One morning Zosia announced snow and helped her to the window to look out. But instead of a pristine blanket, Marguerite saw only a gray, slushy sea.

That night, after the castle was quiet, there was a rustling outside. Too weak to drag herself up, she pulled back her bed curtain and, through the window, saw great clouds of wheeling bats silhouetted against a sliver of moonlit sky. Later, she dreamed of Valeska, and of the shattered infant's tomb she had seen in the crypts.

Zosia and Yelena visited continually. They flitted in and out of her chamber, ministering to her like bees. She asked them about the wheeling bats. The mute's eyes remained blank, and Zosia only clucked her tongue. Nightmares were to be expected, she said.

The old woman stung Marguerite's arm with sharp little cuts, and poured potions down her throat. Yelena arrived like clockwork to help her from the bed to the chamber pot. And as night approached, the mute girl rolled her aside to change the grayish sheets. Marguerite surrendered to her keepers, just as she surrendered to her sickness. It was easier that way.

Donskoy came to her as well. Sometimes he would just sit beside the bed and stroke her damp cheek with his glove. Occasionally he would stretch out alongside her and clutch at her belly from behind, whispering his delight at the prospect of a son.

It did not seem to bother him that she was so ill.

Yet in time it worried Marguerite. During a lucid moment, she asked Zosia about the child, if it might be harmed by her fever. The old woman assured her that the next month would be difficult, but the sickness would pass. It was to be expected, Zosia said. Natural. Marguerite was not reassured. She had seen pregnant women in Darkon, and while some became weary or ejected their breakfasts, none suffered a condition as grave as her own. But she was too weak to argue.

One morning, Marguerite awoke to find a dark shape looming on the sill of her window, watching her with a pair of great white eyes. It was so black that it appeared to have no depth, a two-dimensional stain. She cried out and called for Yelena, who was tending the fire, to summon Ljubo to chase the apparition away. The mute girl only looked out the window and shrugged, then returned to her duties.

As the third month progressed, Marguerite at last grew stronger. And it was then, as her mind cleared and she faced her circumstances, that she began to be truly afraid. Her legs were swollen and spotted with blue marks, and they ached at all times. That alone was not unusual. But there was another sign that something was amiss. Although only three months had passed, her stomach had swollen to immense proportions. It hung low on her belly, making it difficult to walk. Something was terribly wrong, she thought; something was unnatural. When she voiced her concerns to Zosia, the old woman clucked her tongue and said Marguerite was imagining things. Everything was as to be expected. The baby was strong, asserting itself.

One day, as she sat by the window while Zosia fed her, Marguerite looked out and saw the courtyard swarming with snakes. The serpents were everywhere, crawling up the walls, even slithering along the sill of her own chamber's casement. Marguerite gasped, and asked Zosia if she saw the creatures. The old woman nodded and replied that of course she did, her calm tone implying that an infestation of thousands of serpents was a common occurrence.

After that, Marguerite kept her window closed and avoided looking outside, but it did her no good. She saw the serpents, and a hundred visions far more frightening, even with her eyes closed. She began to wonder if her fever had driven her mad, but Zosia assured her that she was quite sane. These events were to be expected. Natural.

Marguerite began to dream of her escape. She remembered Ekhart's threats, the scraping of his dry, rough hand against her cheek. When the baby came, she would be expendable. Somehow, if she were strong enough, she might yet steal away to Darkon. She pretended that she was feeling better, but that she still needed Yelena's help to walk, so that no one would know her true abilities.

Her heavy cabinet had been shifted to stand before

the secret passage. One day, while alone, Marguerite padded across the floor and attempted to move it. It stood fast, and the strain of her effort brought such a sharp, piercing pain to her stomach that she doubled over and slumped to her knees. The anguish passed, and she opened the cabinet to search for her hidden copy of *Van Richten's Guide to the Vistani*. The charred tome might help her find the means to travel the mists—or tell her how to call up the gypsies who could ferry her home, if such a thing were possible.

But the book was gone.

Thinking that it might have slid to a different hiding place when the cabinet was moved, Marguerite pawed through the gowns hanging inside. They felt lighter and shifted strangely in her hands. She pulled a sleeve into the light. It was her purple gown, its yards of silk slashed to ribbons. She pushed it aside and examined the next gown. The blue one had been similarly abused. Fully half the garments within had fallen prey to someone's blade—or, more likely, to Donskoy's talons. She only hoped that his rage had long since passed.

Marguerite went back to the bed and sat on the edge. All her secrets had been discovered. The passage. The tome.

But not all.

Lord Donskoy did not know about Ramus. Jacqueline had taunted Donskoy with the suggestion of a bastard, but she did not know about the gypsy either. How could she? She had made a lucky guess, running through a roster of possibilities. If Donskoy believed her—if he even suspected Marguerite's child was not his own—he did not show it.

In truth, Marguerite herself could not say who had fathered the baby that grew within her, pushing her belly to such strange extremes. The gypsy had claimed it was his. But Ramus could have lied.

There was one person who seemed to know the answers. Marguerite chided herself for not seeing it sooner. "It is as expected." During the past months, Zosia had intoned the phrase so often that it had become like a monkish chant.

Marguerite waited impatiently for the next visit. Now that her patient was growing stronger, Zosia appeared less often, sending Yelena in her stead. Still, the old woman came every day, and was due to arrive soon. Marguerite settled into her bed and waited.

At last, the door creaked open. Zosia's black shape swept across the threshold, then shambled to the table beside the fire. She carried a black velvet pouch, and a tray with a pitcher and a chalice. Marguerite watched through slitted eyes as the old woman poured a liquid into the chalice, then pinched some herbs from the purse into the vessel, mumbling something unintelligible. Zosia turned to eye her patient.

"Zo. You're awake," said the crone, though Marguerite's eyes were held purposefully shut.

Marguerite lay still, astonished.

"Why the game, my child?" Zosia clucked. "I know you do not sleep."

Marguerite opened her eyes. "How did you know?"

Zosia shrugged. "I know much. Yet I know little. Now drink your tea."

Marguerite complied, then said, "Yes, I think you do know a great many things. And I'd like to ask you about some of them."

Zosia chortled. "That is not such a good idea, depending on what you wish to ask. I know many things that would make you squeamish."

"No doubt," said Marguerite evenly. "But I'd like to know one thing in particular—how much you can tell me about Ramus."

"Ramus?"

"Yes. A Vistana who visits this land. He spoke of you; you must know him in turn." She paused, remembering. "You *must* know him. You forbade me to speak his name the night I returned."

Zosia cackled. "He is more than a visitor."

"What do you mean?"

"He is as bound to this land as Lord Donskoy. He was born here. These are his roots."

"But he is a Vistana," Marguerite protested. "He is—" She stopped herself, recalling how Ramus had extended a talon from the end of his finger, just as she had seen Donskoy do when he struck Jacqueline.

"Is something wrong, my child?" Zosia asked.

Marguerite shook her head. What she was thinking could not be. "You sent me to him, on the night you told me to search for the white spider's web."

The old woman cackled. "I sent you after something to help you conceive," she replied. "I did not tell you where to find it."

"But you knew I could find the web in only one place, a place that only Ramus could help me find."

Zosia pursed her lips. "Perhaps. Perhaps not. You are growing agitated, my dear. It is not good for the baby. Rest now, and we will talk later."

"Ramus said that he had a bond with you," Marguerite said, refusing to be brushed aside. "And with Donskoy as well. Who is he?"

"I think you know," Zosia responded. "It was not always difficult for Donskoy to sire a child."

Marguerite gasped.

Zosia smirked, then collected her tray and turned to go.

"Wait!"

The old woman sighed. "All right, child. One more question, then I shall go."

"Who is the father of this baby?" Marguerite asked.

Zosia raised a brow. "Not a pretty question for a married woman to ask."

"This is not a pretty place."

"I would have to perform a rite to know that answer."

"Yes," said Marguerite. "And you've already done it, I'm sure."

Zosia smiled at her. "Not so light-headed after all, my child."

"Is Ramus the father?"

Zosia shrugged. "What does it matter? Donskoy believes it is his. And after the child is born, he will require you no more, despite all his sweet promises. Then I will help you return to Darkon. That is what you truly want, is it not? In exchange for the baby, I will send you home."

Marguerite felt the color rising to her face. "A mother should not leave her child."

"In time, you may think otherwise."

"No. I will not make this bargain with you." Marguerite swung her feet to the floor. "I won't abandon—"

As she started to rise, the dull pain of a overstretched muscle shot through her stomach. She hissed, then eased herself back onto her bed. Inside, Marguerite had the faint sensation of gnawing, as if something were scratching at her belly.

Zosia raised a bony finger. "This is enough disturbance for one day. You care for the health of your unborn; that is good. You must rest now." She walked out the door. With her hand on the latch, she paused. "You cannot escape the future, Marguerite. Your mind will turn in time."

The door creaked shut behind her.

Marguerite collapsed back on the bed. "No," she whispered. "I will not barter my child to buy my own future."

* * * * *

Hours later, after the pain had passed, she rose from the bed and went to the cabinet. Taking care not to strain, she pushed at the massive piece of furniture again, this time from the back instead of the side. She could not slide it, she realized, but perhaps she could cause it to tip, toppling forward. Of course the resulting crash would be deafening. She would have only one chance to scramble behind the furniture and open the secret passage—assuming she could reach the trigger at all. So she could not overturn the cabinet now. This would have to be a test, a dry run. If she could budge it at all, she would take it on faith that she would be able to topple it later.

She slipped her fingers behind cabinet and pulled until they ached. It failed to move even the width of a fingernail. She searched the room for any object that might provide leverage. There was a stool in a corner. She carried it to the cabinet and forced a leg between the back and the wall, then jerked. The leg snapped off at the center, leaving the stool with a short, ragged stump.

Then Marguerite saw the poker on the hearth. She picked it up; it was warm, but not searing. With the tip inserted in the slim, dark space behind the cabinet, she tugged. The metal dug into the stone wall, loosening the mortar, yet the neither the cabinet nor its wooden frame yielded an inch.

A soft twinge of complaint rose from Marguerite's belly, but she did was not ready to give up yet. She opened the cabinet doors and pushed her gowns aside, exposing the back. To her dismay, the wood appeared to be a single piece; there were no gaps to dig at. Still, this seemed the best way to get to the passage beyond.

She thrust the poker into the fire until it grew hot. Then she touched it to the back of the cabinet, charring the wood. An acrid smell filled the room.

When the panel became soft and black, she chipped at it with the end of the poker, creating a small, jagged depression. It would be slow going, she realized, but eventually, she could create a hole, then pry and chip at the edges to make it large enough to crawl through. She would burn and burrow her way to freedom.

She only hoped that after all her efforts, the door at the other end would still function.

* * * * *

Three weeks passed, then a month. Donskoy scarcely visited her at all anymore, which came as a relief. Zosia had told him that constant rest was imperative for the health of his son, and that he should no longer join Marguerite in her bed, whatever the purpose. Lord Donskoy readily complied. His only interest was in the child; Marguerite was now just the carrier.

Zosia herself came to Marguerite's room each morning to lay a hand on her stomach and administer a potion. Yelena's visits were more frequent. She accompanied the old woman to help lift Marguerite from the bed and walk her about the room, and the mute girl returned alone three times thereafter each day, like clockwork, to bring broths and assist Marguerite with her personal matters. Each time she left, the dull click of a turning key sounded in the lock.

Between visits, Marguerite toiled at the back of cabinet, praying that no one would discover her work. She tired easily, so it was only possible to labor for a quarter hour at a time, slowly picking and chipping away at the wood. The panel seemed petrified, as hard as rock. Before returning to bed, she tried to

conceal the damage by covering the hole with garments, but she knew her project would be readily discovered if anyone looked closely.

Fortunately, Marguerite had little reason to dress in
finery, and few of her gowns could have covered her
enormous belly anyway. And then, there was the
damage, the slashed silk. Yelena had little reason to
open the cabinet.

As far as her attendants knew, Marguerite still
remained bedridden, moving only occasionally to a
chair by the fire, and then with help. She worried that
Zosia would see through her ruse, but so far, the old
woman had said nothing to suggest she knew of her
patient's true condition. She encouraged the mother-
to-be to rest as much as possible, for the baby's sake;
to all appearances, Marguerite was complying.

After a time, as the hole neared completion, Marguerite told Yelena she was feeling well enough to eat
solid food. She requested hard cheese and bread. Of
these, she ate half, then stowed the rest in her cabinet.
She had no idea how long she would be traveling
when she made her escape. But some preparations
were in order.

Finally, the hole was almost large enough to crawl
through. Just two more days—one if she pushed herself—and Marguerite could make her escape. If she
waited any longer, she might be unable to walk. Her
stomach was larger than that of any pregnant woman
she had ever seen, though by her count she was only
five months into her term.

Her plan was crude and desperate. She would steal
down to the stables and take one of the horses, then
ride out to the fork and turn right. She had never rid-
den past the rim. Perhaps her escape lay that way. It
was not a good plan, she knew, yet it seemed her sole
chance. Once the baby was born, she would be

expendable. She knew it was true. And she did not
wish to leave without her child.

Marguerite was comparing her own wide girth with
the size of the hole in her cabinet when she heard a
carriage approaching. She had heard the same sound
twice before. And both times, it had heralded the
arrival or departure of Jacqueline Montarri. Apparently, with Marguerite bedridden, Lord Donskoy had
forgiven his friend and welcomed her back to the
keep.

Marguerite went to the window and glimpsed
Jacqueline's slender form emerging from her carriage, heading toward the entrance to the keep. Ljubo
stood at the back of the vehicle, examining a frayed
rope. It had come loose from the parcel it entwined—
the long black box.

Ljubo grabbed the crate and tried to wrestle it back
onto the cargo platform. The box shifted suddenly and
slipped to the ground, falling open. Marguerite put her
hand to her mouth, stifling a cry. The crate was
empty. She realized it would probably not remain that
way for long.

The moon was waxing, nearly full. That meant the
currents in the mists would be bringing more "lost
travelers" to the rim. Jacqueline had not come simply
to see Donskoy. As usual, she intended to mix business with pleasure. And, as usual, she would not go
home empty-handed.

A smile spread across Marguerite's lips, one that
was uncharacteristically wicked. Suddenly she knew
how she was going to escape Lord Donskoy's castle.

* * * * *

That night, after the moon had fully risen, Marguerite heard Lord Donskoy sounding his horn outside

on the grounds. His companions gathered as they had done before, preparing for another excursion. Marguerite spied on them from her window. Soon the cart and the riders departed, along with their pack of hounds. It reminded her vaguely of the hunts she had seen in Darkon—her father and his friends, riding out in pursuit of a stag. But in Donskoy's domain, the notion of a hunt was much more distinctive.

Marguerite gathered a few belongings in a make-shift sack: a water skin and food, dagger and flint, a wool cloak and a pair of leather gloves. She also included the brooch Donskoy had given her on their wedding day, the one inscribed "forever." Without funds, she might need something to trade. Then she selected a tunic that would fit over her bulging stomach and placed it in the cabinet beside her high suede boots. After that, all that remained was the waiting. Marguerite settled in a chair before the fire.

Hours later, the cart and horses returned. As the riders dismounted, Marguerite heard Jacqueline's purring voice and Donskoy's warm replies. The party had been successful; her husband was in a good mood. That meant Jacqueline would stay the night, as Marguerite had hoped. And in the morning, after a light breakfast, the dark-haired woman would depart—but this time the black box on her carriage would bear a souvenir from her trip to the rim. Marguerite crawled into her bed, satisfied.

Just after dawn, Yelena and Zosia appeared for the morning regimen, bringing her breakfast. The mute girl assisted with the nurse-maiding, then left the room.

"You have grown much stronger," said Zosia. "Perhaps you would like to step outside today. Some fresh air might do you good."

"Maybe tomorrow," said Marguerite, feigning weariness. "I don't want to take any chances." Her heart drummed and her breathing was swift. She hoped Zosia wouldn't notice.

The old woman grumbled, then lifted Marguerite's nightshift to feel her stomach. She raised her brow, then went to the black purse she always brought with her, extracting a needle attached to a string. Marguerite pushed down her shift and sat up, crossing her arms over her stomach.

"What's the needle for?" she demanded, unwilling to lie passively beneath a sharp metal object.

Zosia snorted. "I think your time is growing near. I want to confirm it."

"That's not possible," Marguerite protested.

Zosia shrugged. "The needle will inform me. I will suspend it above your belly as I ask the question, and it will spin to reveal the time of your delivery. Don't worry. There will be no pricking."

Reluctantly, Marguerite pulled her shift up for the test. Zosia began to hum, watching the needle as it turned one way and then the other, spinning in the air above Marguerite's stomach.

"Not long now," the old woman announced. She returned the needle to her purse. "Not long at all."

"That can't be right," Marguerite protested. "How could the baby be coming this soon?"

"The test tells the truth. But you needn't worry, my dear—this is perfectly natural."

"It is *not* natural!" Marguerite said. "I'm only five months along. If the baby comes now, it will not survive!"

Zosia clucked. "Your sickness has caused you to lose track of time. There's nothing to fear. The baby is very strong, and he wants to be born. Soon he will come."

The old woman left the room. Marguerite climbed out of bed and donned the clothes she had set aside.

Zosia's prediction had unnerved her, but she couldn't believe it was true. And even if it were, it only confirmed that the time to flee was now.

Marguerite retrieved the sack that held her belongings, then reached through the hole in her wardrobe to trigger the secret passage. To her relief, the portal scraped open. She pushed her gowns aside and wriggled through the gaping hole, entering the tunnel beyond. She was so broad that her belly scraped against both walls, but she managed to reach the opposite end without getting stuck.

Marguerite triggered the swinging stone. For what she hoped would be the last time, she crawled into the room beyond, groaning as she struggled to her feet. At the chamber door, she uttered a silent prayer. Donskoy might have locked it, she knew, once he had discovered her use of the secret passage. She held her breath and tugged. To her relief, it gave way. Muttering thanks to the fates, Marguerite slipped into the hall.

Time was not on her side. In three hours, maybe less, Yelena would go to Marguerite's chamber and find her missing. But Jacqueline Montarri might depart much sooner. With one hand supporting her stomach, Marguerite made her way to the circular stair and descended. She kept her back to the wall, eyes darting as she went, vigilant for any sign of company. As she slipped through the foyer, she could hear Lord Donskoy and Jacqueline chatting behind the drawing room's closed door. She did not stop to listen.

After completing the tortuous route through castle's abandoned wing, Marguerite stepped cautiously outside, into the court that held the stables. She ducked behind a barrel for cover. The expanse before her seemed huge and hideously exposed. Jacqueline's sleek black carriage stood across it. To her dismay, Ljubo was already busy at the front, securing the horses in the rigging. Marguerite peered at the rear of the conveyance. The long black crate had not yet been loaded.

Having finished with the horses, Ljubo disappeared into the low building behind him. Marguerite scanned the court for any sign of Ekhart, but neither he nor the hounds were in sight. She saw only the usual menagerie: the flock of black geese, the weary peacock, the tethered goat. She rose from her hiding place. Then she ran—or came as close to it as possible—hurrying across the muddy flagstones. She slipped once, and the black geese honked excitedly, but no one heeded their alarm. Marguerite ducked into one of the empty stalls near the coach. As soon as she was safely behind the gate, she collapsed.

She had arrived just in time. A sharp pain shot through her stomach, as if something had taken hold inside and had begun to twist. Curled on her side, Marguerite cupped her hand over her mouth to muffle her cry. After a long, horrible moment, the pain passed, and she lifted herself to her knees. The exertion of running had been too great; from here on, she knew she would have to be more careful.

Outside in the court, there was a scraping noise, as if something were being dragged. A monstrous grunt followed, then the scraping briefly resumed. After it stopped again, footsteps sounded, trailing away in the distance.

Marguerite found a chink near the top of the gate and looked out to see what had happened. Ljubo was waddling across the court toward a small door that led into the keep.

After he disappeared inside, she took a chance and crept out, moving along the front of the stables until she reached the carriage. Jacqueline's coach required no driver, as Marguerite had observed the first time she saw it approaching the castle. Though Jacqueline had never said as much, Marguerite had concluded that the conveyance's magic both drove itself and guided its passenger through the disorienting mists that surrounded Donskoy's lands.

She checked under the carriage and then peered inside, looking for somewhere to stow away. But the only cargo platform lay on the back, in plain view, and there was no other place to hide. Marguerite sighed. A comfortable place to ride would have been asking too much.

She went to the stable, where Jacqueline's long black box still lay in the back of Ekhart's cart, hanging partway over the back edge. With great effort, Marguerite climbed alongside the crate. It was relatively crude, like the one that had accompanied her from Darkon, with slender gaps between its rough black planks. It seemed unfair to call it a coffin; if placed underground, it would quickly fill with soil and water and worms. But then again, many paupers received less.

Marguerite gritted her teeth and pushed out the latch pin, then lifted the rusty hasp and opened the lid. Inside lay a woman, plump and white, lying on a bed of straw. She was naked, but for a black wool blanket crudely wrapped round her body. She had snowy blonde hair and a wide red mouth, which at the moment was stuffed with a gag. Leather straps bound her hands and feet. Marguerite pushed at the woman's flesh. Though the captive didn't stir, clearly she lived; her skin was soft and warm, and her chest was subtly rising and falling.

Drugged, Marguerite thought. Of course. She herself had made the trip from Darkon in a similarly unconscious state—though she had not been stuffed in a box. Yet that was precisely how she intended to make her escape.

Ideally, Marguerite would have removed the woman from the crate and hidden her away, then taken her place. But the situation was far from ideal. She had neither the time nor the strength to move the heavy captive. And there was still the matter of the latch. If her plan worked, she would need to open it from the inside.

Marguerite closed the crate and studied it. There was a fair amount of play to the lid; the hinges holding it to the box were loose. And the fastening at the side was ordinary: a flat piece of metal with a slot, hinged to drop over a round loop, through which a tapered pin was wedged to secure the flat piece. A chain anchored the pin to the box so it could not be misplaced.

Marguerite removed her sheathed dagger from her traveling sack and climbed alongside the unconscious woman. Carefully she lowered the lid, giving it a little shake until the hasp fell into place. A small gap remained—just enough so she could slide her dagger through the crack and fiddle with the latch; with luck, she could dislodge the pin from the inside, then push the hasp open.

Unfortunately, there was no easy way to secure the pin after she was inside the crate. Left dangling, it might invite investigation, but she had to risk it.

She lay very still in the box. At length, she heard someone coming. A man grumbled sourly. The image of Ekhart sprang to mind. Ljubo spoke in response, whiny and apologetic.

"But it's real heavy," he said. "Wouldn't ask for your help getting her onto the carriage it she weren't so fleshy. And you know Miss Montarri would be mad if I dropped the box and bruised her cargo."

Ekhart groaned. "Let's get on with it. I'll climb in the

wagon and push the crate your way to get it off the end."

The wagon rocked as Ekhart climbed into the bed. He stepped to the back of the coffin, near her head, then growled, "Idiot. You've left the hasp undone. I suppose you opened it to get another look?"

Ljubo did not deny it.

The hasp rattled, then Ekhart commanded Ljubo to lift. The two men heaved and groaned. Inside the box, the sound of wood scraping against wood was magnified, deafening. Marguerite felt herself drop as the crate left the wagon bed. The box swayed like a cradle. Then it was lifted onto another support. She heard ropes being dragged over the top and pulled down into place. We must be on the carriage now, she thought, wondering whether it would be necessary to cut through the ropes at some point. She hoped they hadn't been pulled too snugly to prevent her from pushing the lid up enough for her dagger.

Another pain squeezed her belly, and Marguerite bit into her own shoulder to keep from crying out.

"Told you it was heavy," said Ljubo. "Real heavy."

Ekhart grunted. "Not Montarri's usual taste. Must be passing this one on to Count Strahd. A nice plump virgin to offer along with her taxes. Never hurts to appease the local lord."

"She's a clever one, Miss Montarri."

"She's a bitch," retorted Ekhart. "But what woman isn't? Take the carriage around front and wait."

Marguerite heard Ekhart walking away, then allowed herself to exhale. After a moment, the carriage lurched and began to roll forward. There was a short pause while Ljubo wrestled with the gate, then another lurch forward, another pause, another creak of the doors. Finally the carriage moved along the drive, crunching in the gravel, and came to a rest before the main entrance. Marguerite furrowed her brow, trying to keep her sweat from rolling into her eyes.

It was not long before she heard the lilting tones of Jacqueline Montarri's voice. "Milos," she cooed. "As always, it has been delicious. I'm so pleased we've put aside our differences, at least for the moment. I hope your son will arrive in good health."

"Zosia says it won't be long," Donskoy replied.

"Really? It seems rather soon."

"Not to me, my dear. To me, it has been an eternity."

"Well, I must go. Shall I return to you in another moon?"

"See that you do."

Jacqueline purred. "Splendid. I'll have a surprise for you the next time I come. One of my new heads knows some interesting tricks, and I've been practicing."

Donskoy chortled and bade her farewell.

The coach rocked as Jacqueline stepped inside, muttering something softly. Then the carriage began to move again, proceeding down the drive and turning away from the keep.

In her impossibly tight quarters, Marguerite sighed in satisfaction. Soon, she would reach Barovia. It was an unknown destination, and the challenge of escaping the box still lay ahead, but for the moment she didn't care. The worst was behind her. In a few short hours, she would be free of Donskoy and his accursed domain.

NINETEEN

Inside the moving coffin, Marguerite struggled to find a more comfortable position, shoving at the soft flesh of her unconscious companion. Earlier she had imagined this very picture with horror—she, stretched prone in the darkness, encased in a long black box. But in that scene Marguerite had been riding to her doom. Now she was traveling to freedom; she was escaping Lord Donskoy's domain.

She knew, of course, that trials lay ahead, impossible tests of her luck and wit. The carriage that bore her coffin was heading to the unknown land of Barovia instead of her familiar Darkon. And when they reached their destination, she would have to escape the box. Marguerite pictured herself leaping from the coffin with her dagger fiercely slashing, taking an astonished Jacqueline by surprise. The woman's head would tumble off with one swift strike, then she would flap her arms in confusion like a freshly beheaded chicken.

Marguerite sighed. The picture was false; the bold assassin had not been preposterously pregnant. She felt a sickening twist in her stomach, reminding her of the truth. Her best hope of escape, she decided, was to wait until the box was left unattended; then she could free the hasp with her dagger and climb out unseen. Such an opportunity seemed highly improbable, but she would not have gotten even this far had she let herself worry about likelihoods.

A sudden pain disrupted her thoughts. Marguerite felt as if a crushing weight had suddenly descended upon her abdomen. She bit her tongue to keep from screaming, afraid that Jacqueline's ears might be sharp enough to hear.

The carriage crossed over the arched bridge; Marguerite could hear the change in timbre as the wheels left the soft dirt and began grinding against the gravel-flecked stone. She closed her eyes and envisioned the wheels, making turn after turn, and focused on their image until the pain had subsided.

A horrible thought sprang to mind, and she struggled to deny it. What if the baby were coming after all, coming now, while she rode in a coffin lashed to Jacqueline's carriage? Marguerite thought briefly about calling out to attract her conveyor's attention. But a less suitable midwife could not be found, even if one searched every fiery corner of the infinite Abyss; Jacqueline might help with the delivery, but afterward, she would certainly return both mother and child to Lord Donskoy—perhaps in exchange for the ledger she wanted so badly.

Marguerite had witnessed several births in Darkon, and she struggled to recall the particulars. The first pains could be false, she knew. Sometimes vexing spasms came and went weeks before the birth. Perhaps that was happening to her now.

The fetid air of the marsh began to fill the coffin. Again, the broad band of muscle began to tighten around Marguerite's belly, filling her abdomen with the anguish of labor. She felt as though some giant had taken her in hand and was trying to squeeze the entrails from her body. The agony was worse than before; to hide her screams, she pulled the gag from the blonde woman's mouth and stuffed it into her own.

The unseen band continued to tighten. Marguerite felt the dagger slip from her hand, disappearing somewhere in the dark.

Then at last, the band crushing her belly began to loosen. As the spasm subsided, she felt something warm and damp spreading beneath her. She reached down, hoping she had merely lost control, but fearing she had begun to bleed. Neither had occurred. Her water had broken. The pains were not false after all; the baby was on its way.

"Don't panic," she breathed aloud. Marguerite struggled to remember the births her mother had once described, and how long those labors had lasted. She might yet have a couple of hours before her own baby came, perhaps even as long as a day. And if she were lucky, they might still reach Barovia in time.

The carriage rolled on.

At length, another wave came. Marguerite felt the child slipping lower inside her belly, and then spasms spread to her back and her legs, more like a seizure than a contraction. Something is wrong, she thought. Something is . . .

A scream rose up through her throat and halted behind her gag, momentarily, before gathering enough force to send the rag shooting from her mouth. An ear-splitting screech spilled from Marguerite's lips, as loud as a shrieking banshee. Her body began to writhe and twitch of its own accord. She thought of her lost dagger and hoped she would not cut herself, but she was powerless to stop the thrashing.

The carriage jolted to a halt.

Marguerite tried to clamp her jaw shut, to stifle her

scream, but the pain was too great. She managed only to choke back the sound, hardly enough to keep from being heard.

She fumbled for her dagger, knowing the effort was fruitless. Even if she could recover the blade, she would be unable to wield it. A paroxysm had seized her entire body.

A clatter echoed through the coffin as someone fumbled at the latch, then the lid of the crate flew open. Daylight assaulted Marguerite's eyes. She could see the shape of a woman's head silhouetted against the brightness, but nothing more.

A shriek of surprise sounded overhead. It became a crow of delight, and Marguerite's vision cleared enough to recognize Jacqueline Montarri peering down at her. The face had changed somewhat, but her identity was unmistakable.

"Two for the price of one!" cried the woman, laughing hysterically. "Two for the road!"

Marguerite tried to speak, to ask for help, but she could only manage a strangled croak. Her limbs continued to twitch uncontrollably. Her stomach leaped and jumped, as if the child within were trying to punch its way out.

Jacqueline studied Marguerite with a puzzled expression. "Stop that! Stop it once!" she commanded. "This . . . this demented farce will not save you. I am not so easily fooled."

Marguerite felt her tongue slip between her teeth, then a sharp pain. Her mouth filled with the taste of copper—her blood. She had bitten her tongue. A warm stream spilled from her mouth and began to run down the side of her chin.

Jacqueline's eyes widened in shock. "What is *this*?" she exclaimed. "This isn't right. This is—" She stepped away from the box. "Well, I'll not have this on my shoulders!"

She slammed down the lid and rattled the pin into the hasp. A moment later, the carriage began to turn.

By the gods, no, Marguerite thought. Her body was shuddering less violently now, but she still felt weak—terribly weak, as feeble as an invalid. Please, no, she pleaded silently.

Like a cold black shadow, despair slipped into the box and covered her. They were heading back to the keep, back to Lord Donskoy, who would go mad when he discovered what she had attempted. Perhaps he already knew. Marguerite's hand scrabbled feebly against the wood overhead, pushing at the lid. She searched again for the missing dagger, but it had slipped away and lay lost somewhere in the cramped darkness. She heard her own voice echoing inside the box, moaning more in fear than pain. They were heading back to Lord Donskoy's keep. And she was too weak to do anything about it.

The landmarks passed in her mind slowly like the scenes from a nightmare—the marsh, the trickling stream, the arched stone bridge. Every few minutes the crushing pain returned, like a great fist squeezing her swollen belly, each time worse than the last. She trembled and screamed and convulsed, battering against the coffin walls until her limbs ached with bruising. At length, she began to experience a new sort of agony: something inside, tugging at her entrails like a tiny claw, dragging at her muscles until the small of her back burned with anguish, pulling and pulling until it felt as if her sinews would rip free of their roots.

Finally, the carriage wheels began to rumble more slowly, announcing their arrival at the keep. In moments, the coach drew to a halt. It rocked once, then Jacqueline's muffled voice sounded just outside the coffin.

"Never mind the horses, Ljubo! Fetch your master. Tell him to come at once!"

A soft rasp sounded near the foot of the crate—a rope being loosened. Marguerite's pulse pounded in her ears, filling them with a roar so loud that everything she heard seemed to come from a distance. Her body was in constant agony now, a burning weariness punctuated every few minutes by the cramping aches of labor. She pushed at the lid one more time, making a final, feeble attempt to escape the casket. Then she let her hands drop back over her face, too weak to continue.

Marguerite heard Jacqueline undoing the rope at the head of the coffin, then the crunch of boots on gravel.

"Jacqueline?" It was Donskoy. Marguerite's husband. "What are you—"

"Milos," Jacqueline interrupted. The pin clattered from the hasp. "Have you lost something, perhaps?"

The lid opened.

Marguerite saw Ljubo's face leaning over her, eyeing her quizzically. Then a black glove grabbed him by the shoulder, jerking him aside, and Donskoy's face appeared where the stablehand's had been before.

"What is this?" he gasped.

Marguerite was too weak, too frightened, in too much pain to answer.

Donskoy's skin darkened to the color of a Kartakan beet, then he seized Marguerite's hair and lifted her head.

"Did you think you would run off with my son? Better not to think at all, you little wretch! This will be the last time you disobey me." He began to pull Marguerite out of the coffin. "Get out of there—and quit shaking like an imbecile."

Jacqueline laid a hand on his arm. "Milos—"

Donskoy shook her off. "What?!"

Jacqueline flinched and stepped back, raising both hands in mock surrender. "Far be it from me to come between a man and his wife, but you may wish to take care," she said. "I have never seen a woman shake like that. Something is not going quite right."

"Going?" Donskoy asked. "What do you mean?"

"Just look at her," Jacqueline said evenly. "What do you see? She is not shaking from fright alone. Open your eyes, Milos. Can't you see through your own anger? Her water has broken and her labor has begun."

The color drained from Donskoy's face as rapidly as it had appeared. He released Marguerite's hair, leaving her head to drop limply back into the coffin, and then he leaned in close. He ran his gloved hand over her heaving stomach. Marguerite recoiled at his touch, wishing that she had her dagger in hand, wishing she had the strength to plunge it into her husband's throat. But she did not. She could do nothing but lie beneath his rummaging fingers.

"Is this true?" Donskoy demanded. His breath was heavy with the acrid smell of hookah smoke. "Is the baby coming already?"

Marguerite nodded weakly.

Donskoy turned and grabbed Ljubo by the neck of his tunic, then pushed the plump man toward the keep. "Get Zosia," he growled, "and Ekhart as well. Get them now." He turned back to the coffin and peered over the edge at Marguerite, his sunken eyes burning with anger—no, it was more than anger. Hatred. "So, you chose to depart in a coffin. Well, if the child is harmed because of your stupidity, you'll know this box again soon enough. Soon enough!"

Marguerite struggled to pull herself up out of the crate, but fell back.

"Lie still," Donskoy hissed. "Wait till the old woman comes."

It was only a moment before Zosia's black-ker-chiefed head peered in at Marguerite. Beside her stood Yelena, pale and trembling, her slender fingers pressed to her mouth in horror. The wrinkles in Zosia's brow deepened and her mouth bent downward.

"How long have you been feeling the pains?" she asked.

"I don't know," said Marguerite weakly. "A few hours. Maybe more. Please help me, Zosia. Help the baby."

Zosia's dark eyes narrowed. "Take her upstairs," she commanded.

Ljubo and Ekhart placed the crate on the ground, then reached inside and lifted Marguerite. Their rough handling touched off another convulsion, but so exhausted was Marguerite's body that they had little trouble restraining it. They carried her up the long flight of steps and into the keep. Ljubo looked down at Marguerite, grinning reassuringly even as her back arched up with the unnatural paroxysm and a hoarse scream rose once again from her raw throat. The pain swallowed her, and Marguerite fell into a strange, dreamy state. She was like a boat on a wavering sea of air, floating round and round up the wide circular stairs. The figures and faces around her seemed dis-tant, muffled. Hands carried her, but they did not really touch her.

Ljubo and Ekhart bore Marguerite to her chamber and laid her on a clean sheet that Yelena had hastily spread upon the mattress. Zosia gently rolled Marguerite onto her side, till she lay facing the edge of the bed.

"Bring me rags and a tub of hot water," she boomed at Ljubo. And to Yelena, she said, in a lower intona-tion, "and bring my black bag from below."

Donskoy loomed behind the old woman. "She is quiet now. Is she dead, dead with her eyes open?"

"Of course not," said Zosia. "See how her chest yet

rises and falls."

"And what of my son? Will he live?"

"I have not foreseen his death—but then, I have not seen this either. Who can say, Lord Donskoy?" Her tone was almost taunting. "Not this old woman. Not your tamed Vistana."

"My son must survive," said Donskoy breathlessly. "Do what you must to ensure it."

"Of course," answered Zosia. "And now you must go."

"No." The reply was short, decisive.

"Birthing and midwifery are the province of women. Yelena will go to you when the child is born. You will only add to Marguerite's distress."

"I am staying," Donskoy said firmly. "Marguerite's distress is nothing to me. And you will see to it that the baby is not affected."

Zosia shrugged. "As you wish," she said huskily. "But please, sit by the fire if you would. It may be hours yet. Marguerite may cry out, but you needn't worry. Screams alone are not bad portent."

Donskoy grunted, then settled in by the fire. "Ljubo!"

The fat man poked his head through the door—Marguerite did not even remember him and Ekhart leaving—and asked, "Yes, milord?"

"My white pipe, and quickly!" Donskoy ordered.

Zosia pulled off Marguerite's shift and adjusted her position.

Jacqueline, who had been hovering the whole time near the fireplace, made a sour face, then headed for the door. "If you will excuse me, Milos," she said, "I will take my leave. I have always considered motherhood a messy business—best to be avoided whenever possible."

Without speaking, Donskoy waved her out the door.

Yelena scurried into the room with Zosia's black

satchel. When the mute girl saw Lord Donskoy, she stopped short and curtsied feebly, then hurried to the bed.

Zosia withdrew a small scrap of leather, cut thin, like paper. She unfolded it slowly. Inside was a brown salve. She stroked it over her patient's bulging stomach, cooing. So lost in pain was Marguerite that she barely noticed as the old woman turned her, pulling her feet off the edge of the mattress, until she half-hung and half-squatted beside it. Yelena climbed onto the bed to hold her arms from behind.

It was only a moment before another crushing ache came. Marguerite felt her body splitting, opening like a flower. She grunted and screeched through her teeth.

"Yes," Zosia hissed excitedly. "Come out to us, little one. Come out to us now."

Marguerite felt the child begin to pass out of her. She looked down, and saw a dark head, then a perfect shoulder, and a little fist, clawing and grasping the air.

She cried out in terror. The tiny fingers were black, and talons sprouted from the tips.

"Hush," commanded Zosia. "He is almost here."

Marguerite began to sob. With a sickening twist, the baby slid free of her into Zosia's welcoming hands.

Yelena gasped and shrank away, scurrying from the room.

"What is it?" Donskoy demanded.

Marguerite looked again, and again she saw the dark hands and the tiny claws. And there was something more. Upon the baby's chest lay a hideous purple mark—three lines at an angle, running parallel, slanting down to strike another.

She opened her mouth to scream, but no sound escaped her lips. For a moment, the room went dark, and somewhere in the distance, Marguerite heard her baby crying. Then at last her sight returned. She looked down upon the babe in her arms, a pink-skinned boy, amazing in his perfection. Marguerite put her finger to his pursed little lips, then guided the infant to her breast, and smiled.

* * * * *

Lord Donskoy rushed to the bed. His wife was clutching an empty blood-stained shroud to her breast, rocking it gently. Zosia stood nearby with a swaddling cloth, wrapped around a small form. Its black, clawed hand groped the air.

Donskoy backed away, disbelieving, then spun at once toward the fire and seized a poker.

Zosia cackled, allowing the bundle in her arms to slowly unfold. Inside it, Donskoy no longer saw a child. Instead, he faced a black stain, a shadow, which slipped smoothly onto the floor, then rose up before him like a behemoth. A pair of eyes glowed white in the darkness.

Blindly, he swung, but the shadow disappeared. The poker struck the ground, landing with a peculiar noise, muffled and wet. At the sound, a red wound opened on Donskoy's face, extending along one cheek. The skin puckered and boiled beside the mark. A chasm formed from his temple to his jaw, and his flesh caved inward, disappearing into the fold. Donskoy clutched a hand to his bloody face and screamed, dropping to his knees.

Zosia continued to cackle. "The seeds you have sown," she said huskily. "The seeds you have sown . . ."

Lord Donskoy turned to her in terror. "What are you saying?"

Zosia's voice became taunting and dark. "Have you forgotten Valeska's words, my lord? Have you forgotten your love so soon? *The seeds you have sown shall seal your damnation. The blood of your blood shall bring you to your knees.*"

"It cannot be," he whispered. "It cannot be."

"But it is . . . The son you forced upon Valeska has returned to fulfill her curse. To end it at last." The old woman tossed her head back and laughed wildly. "Though it will not end as you had intended."

Donskoy staggered forward, gazing at Zosia in disbelief.

"I will not fall for your trickery, old witch. With my own hands, I ripped that child from Valeska's womb. With my own hands I laid it to rest."

Zosia spat at him. "And with my own hands, I brought him back."

Donskoy struggled to his feet. Again he raised the poker, this time at the woman before him. Out of nowhere came the shadow, assuming the form of an enormous serpent, coiling swiftly around his neck. He struggled to throw off the beast.

"Strike all you wish," laughed Zosia. "You cannot strike him down."

Donskoy stumbled toward the window. Still armed with the poker, he broke out the glass, creating a maelstrom of sparkling shards. He made one last cry and wrenched the snake from his body, sending it flying from the keep.

When the great serpent thudded to the ground, it was Donskoy's body that crumpled, his leg wrapping backward beneath him, his back twisting sharply. He lay still on the floor, his eyes rolled back in his head.

Zosia spat on his crippled, still body. "The old lord is dead," she rasped. "And the new lord has come."

In her arms she held a tiny bundle. She looked briefly toward Marguerite, still cradling the empty shroud at her breast, rocking gently in the bed. Then Zosia turned and left the room.

EPILOGUE

Marguerite dreamed she was rocking her baby, though somewhere in her mind she knew her arms were empty. The gypsy vardo slid into a rut and jerked sharply, throwing her head back against the planks. She awoke with a start.

In the darkness beside her, the driver called Arturi cleared his throat. The caravan was returning to Darkon.

The hours after the birth had been a blur. Marguerite had babbled incoherently, unable to control herself, terrified and yet ashamed. Her life, her body, her mind—not one had seemed her own.

Zosia had taken care of the arrangements. What Jacqueline had said was true—Darkon was a place for forgetting. Soon after Marguerite returned to its soil, she would cease to recall her former life. A new identity would rise to take its place. Arturi had agreed to take her just across the border. He claimed it was safer there; trouble was brewing at the heart of the domain. Marguerite did not care. One place in Darkon was as good as the other.

The wagon approached the fork and veered left.

As they slipped between the towering pines, Marguerite spied a dark-haired rider just behind the veil of the forest, astride a black horse. He tipped his hat and flashed a smile, then was gone.

Marguerite shut her eyes again.

She was going back to Darkon.

And in Darkon, she would forget.

If you enjoyed reading *To Sleep With Evil*, you may also be interested in the following books, all set in the grim gothic world of the RAVENLOFT® campaign setting.

Lord Azalin makes an appearance in *Tower of Doom*, by Mark Anthony. The book also concerns a hunch-backed bell ringer and a personal agent of Azalin's, as well as a certain monster who occupies the bell tower . . .

Azalin is also featured in *King of the Dead*, by Gene DeWeese. With virtually unlimited powers, Azalin still cannot find peace. Tortured by the death of his son, the unwilling ruler has come to despise the world of darkness and horror over which he reigns. The tale traces the course of his life from a powerful wizard to King of the Dead.

For more about Strahd Von Zarovich, be sure to pick up P.N. Elrod's *I, Strahd*, the autobiography of the vampire lord of Ravenloft. Strahd also plays an important role in *Vampire of the Mists*, by Christie Golden, in which a golden elf lost in Barovia searches for a mysterious woman.

Ask for these and other exciting titles from TSR, Inc. at fine book and hobby stores everywhere.